Ripples
Return to Foggy Point Light

Jeff Burns

DEDICATION

This book is dedicated to Mr. Tim Tutton, one of the best high school teachers that I ever had. His guidance and influence during that period of time left a lasting impression on my life that I'll always be grateful for. When I was considering publishing Foggy Point Light back in 2015, his words of encouragement gave me the determination to make it a reality.

CONTENTS

CHAPTER 1
May 21, 2016
The Storm

A loud boom echoed through the night, rocking the building to its foundation and rattling the windows beside the bed. Dan Nelson awoke with a start. For a minute he wasn't sure exactly what had awakened him, or even exactly where he was. A bright white flash of light illuminated the window across the room, followed quickly by another loud clap of thunder. Torrents of rain crashed against the window, as another bright flash cast eerie shadows on the opposite wall. He sat up in bed and looked around the room, which was completely dark except for when the lightning came in its quick, bright bursts. The flashes seemed to be coming quicker now, and the thunder seemed louder now as well, the deep, low sound shaking the walls and windows so hard that Dan was afraid that a picture might fall off the wall, or some other object might topple off of a shelf onto the floor. He rolled over to one side and felt for the clock radio on the nightstand to try and see the time, but the bright blue LED display was not lit. He realized immediately that the power must be out, which wasn't surprising in this storm. His mind growing clearer now, he recalled the events of the past day and remembered that he was in a room at the Baker Family Bed and Breakfast on Green Island. He looked around the room, and to his surprise Dianne and the kids seemed to still be asleep. "How can anyone sleep through this!?" he thought to himself.

He gently pulled back the covers, trying not to wake Dianne, and quietly sat up on the edge of the bed. Outside, nature was unleashing all of her fury, but in here it was warm and dry. He thought about the previous day, and of the events of that day: The Presidential Reception, the climb to the top of the lighthouse, and the spectacular view of the sunset that had accompanied it. Watching the bright orange and red sunset as the sun slowly slipped below the horizon, there hadn't been even a hint of the storm that was to come later in the night. He stood up and walked over to the window which looked out over Main Street. As the bright flashes came in rapid succession, for a few seconds he thought he saw a man standing under the street lamp, looking up at their window.

"It couldn't be!" he thought, "No one would be out in this kind of weather!"

But even as he continued to stare out the window, and finally determined that there was nobody out there, he still felt an uneasiness that he couldn't quite place. He began to think back to when he first woke up. He remembered the room being completely dark, but there was something else as well. The loud clap of thunder had interrupted a dream. He couldn't remember a lot about it, except for the part right before the thunder woke him up. In that part, he was out at the lighthouse when a thick fog came up. As he walked over to get a better look, a lovely woman with long blonde hair stepped out of the fog and began to walk toward him. He tried to remember if she was anyone that he knew or had seen before, but he drew a complete blank. He was fairly certain that he didn't know her, but still there was something that seemed slightly familiar about her. Just as she walked up to him and was reaching out her arms to him, the clap of thunder interrupted the dream and he was quickly transported back to reality. He probably wouldn't have remembered the dream at all if he'd been allowed to slowly transition out of the dream state and wake up normally, but he had been awakened quickly, and the last few minutes of the dream had been transferred to his conscious memory, at least for a time.

"Who could she be?" he thought to himself, struggling to remember just a little more of the dream. But even as he convinced himself that she was no one that he knew, something in the back of his mind told him that he did in fact know her, and for some reason this made him feel even more uneasy. "It was a perfectly normal dream." he told himself. Nothing at all that should make him feel this strange. Yet it did, and it was a feeling that he really didn't understand. "Strange" didn't fully describe it, and actually "uneasy" didn't quite describe it either. It was more of an apprehensive feeling, but even that wasn't quite accurate. It was almost like the feeling that you get when you suspect that something's wrong, but you can't quite place what it is. It just keeps nagging at you all the same.

"Come on, Dan!" he thought to himself, "It was just a dream! That's all it was."

As the waterfalls of rain continued to crash against the window, he walked back over to the bed and slid back under the covers. Even now, surprisingly, he's still the only one awake. The bright flashes of light through the window had become less frequent now, and the thunder seemed further off as well. The storm was passing, but even as he realized that this storm had passed, he felt that another storm was coming that would totally disrupt his life. For some unknown reason, he couldn't help but think that this dream was more than just a dream, that it was a window into another world. He knew that it was totally irrational to feel this way, but he just couldn't shake the feeling.

As he lay there in the darkness, staring at the ceiling, he still couldn't quite get back to sleep. His mind kept wandering back to yesterday. Thinking that he saw the silhouette of a man standing under the street lamp a few moments ago reminded him of a feeling that he had when he first woke up yesterday morning. While everything seemed normal enough, he recalled a feeling very similar to the one that he was having now, though not nearly as strong. Even as he and his family drove out to the lighthouse dedication ceremony and attended the Presidential Reception afterward, he had the feeling that something was different; something just didn't feel right, even though everything seemed perfectly normal.

He finally drifted off to sleep, but awoke a short time later. He glanced over at the clock radio which now had illuminated numbers which said "1:27 AM". Knowing that the power had been out earlier, he wasn't sure that was the correct time at all; actually it probably wasn't. Most digital clocks reset to twelve midnight when the power finally returns, so all it probably meant was that the power had been back on for an hour and twenty seven minutes. As he continued to lie in bed, he remembered something else about the previous day that he really hadn't thought much of at the time. He remembered a man, whom he had noticed several times during the course of the day. Something about him made him seem as if he didn't quite belong. He was fairly nice looking, with sandy brown hair. He wore tan pants and a dark blue shirt. Dan remembered thinking at the time that he was probably a plain clothed officer there to protect the President.

But for some reason, now he wasn't so sure. He remembered the storm that had awakened him earlier in the night, but that had completely passed now. He also remembered having a dream then as well, but try as hard as he could, he couldn't remember even the slightest detail of that dream now.

He pushed off the covers and sat up on the edge of the bed, listening to the air blowing through the vents in the room. He got up and walked over to the closet in the corner, where he withdrew a pair of khaki pants and a shirt. Purposely being quiet so as not to wake the rest of his family, he got dressed, picked up a room key off of the dresser and quietly unlocked the door to go out into the hallway. As he descended the stairway and turned to walk back to the kitchen, he could see that there was already a light on. He walked through the entryway into the kitchen, where he was greeted by his mother-in-law Jan, who apparently couldn't sleep either.

"That was quite a storm!" she remarked.

"Yes it was!" replied Dan, "Woke me up a few hours ago."

"I've been awake most of the night." said Jan, "I couldn't seem to get to sleep. I guess it was the storm, but I'm not quite sure that was all it was. When I first woke up, I just felt that something was wrong. I'm not sure why I felt that way, but I came out here and looked around. Everything seemed to be in order, so I didn't think much of it. The storm was so strong, that I just figured that was what it was."

"I know what you mean; it was the same with me."

"There was something else." she continued, "I hope you don't think me to be just a crazy old woman, but while the storm was raging at its worst, I walked over to the front window of the parlor and looked out onto Main Street. The lightning was flashing almost constantly at that point, worse than I've ever seen, but what really startled me was that when I looked out there was a man standing under the street lamp directly across the street from the window. He looked straight at me as I pulled the curtain back!"

"What did he look like?" Dan inquired, remembering that earlier in the evening he had thought that he saw a man out front as well.

"I didn't really get a good look." she replied, "The lightning was so bright, and flashing so frequently, that all I could really see was a silhouette, but I'm sure it was a man. When I turned and looked back out, though, he was gone. I really had to wonder if he had been there at all, since the rain was coming down so hard. Who'd possibly be out in that kind of weather?"

"I wouldn't think anyone would, but the funny thing was that I thought I saw a man earlier standing under that same street light!"

"No?!" she remarked, as if his mentioning that he had seen the man as well actually proved that he was there after all. Since that incident, she had convinced herself that he wasn't real, just a trick effect of the lightning. She actually preferred it that way, because there was something about the way that he looked that completely unnerved her.

"I don't think it really was a man," answered Dan, "We were probably both fooled by an optical illusion created by the lightning. He was gone so quickly that he couldn't have really been there."

"You're probably right," she said, "but in the early morning hours, it's still pretty unsettling. Especially with that storm! I've never seen one quite like that one in all the years that we've lived here. There've been storms just as severe, but not quite like that one. Wendell didn't even move! Nothing can wake up that man!"

"Like father, like daughter." said Dan. "Dianne didn't wake up either. I'm sure she'll wake up tomorrow morning and say, 'What storm? Was there a storm?'"

At this, Jan had to laugh. She knew her daughter well, and knew exactly what he was talking about. She had been having a cup of coffee, and now thought to offer Dan one as well. He accepted, and they sat and talked for another hour before both decided to go back and try to get a little more sleep before morning. It was Saturday, which was the last full day of the week long Lighthouse Dedication. Sunday would have some activities, but most of the people that came for the celebration would be leaving then. Life would get back to normal on the island, with normal being the usual summer vacation season.

A few hours later everyone was up and around the breakfast table. As both Dan and her mother had figured, Dianne hadn't heard the storm at all, neither had the kids. Greg came by for breakfast as well. He could only stay just long enough to have breakfast before heading out. President Henderson was scheduled for another campaign stop over in Wilmington this afternoon, and being his Press Secretary, Greg had to arrive ahead of him to be sure that everything was set up and ready for his arrival. At breakfast, he remarked about the storm as well, and told everyone of all of the fallen tree limbs and other damage that he had seen on his way over. He had been staying with the President's entourage out at the Harbor Inn, and the storm had been just as severe out there, maybe more so.

"What did you make of that storm last night?!" he asked everyone. "I grew up on this island, and that was about as strong of a storm as I've ever seen. It almost seemed to be fueled by some unseen energy. At one point, I counted lightning every two or three seconds!"

"It woke me up too." said his mother, "Dan and I sat down in the kitchen and talked about it for awhile."

During breakfast, the storm was the main topic of conversation. Even the guests from the mainland remarked how they were awakened by it. Most said that it was the strongest storm that they had ever seen as well.

Just how bad the storm was, was confirmed when they finally walked outside. They all saw what Greg had been talking about. There were leaves and fallen tree limbs everywhere. Water still stood in the road in several places where the drainage was the worst. Dan didn't fully realize the extent of the damage until they got down the road a little further on their way to the Harbor Inn. Some really large trees had fallen across the road, as well as numerous branches. Mike and his crew, who were the only tree and brush clearing company on the island, were already hard at work trying to get the roads cleared before the traffic really started. At one point, Officer Mark Collins was out detouring traffic around a section of road that was completely blocked by a fallen tree. They saw several trucks from the power company as well. While the power had been restored to the bed and breakfast a little while earlier, apparently a lot of the island was still in the dark.

After a longer than usual drive out to the Harbor Inn, they finally arrived. Since the hotel was hosting an exhibit on the history of the island, particularly the lighthouse, there were more cars than usual in the parking lot, so they had to park a little further away. Danny and Rebekah were excited to see the exhibit. Since their mother had grown up on the island, and their father had spent many vacations here, they were anxious to find out more. The lighthouse had always been one of their father's favorite places to visit, and they both actually liked it too. It was a link to the past that couldn't be found just anywhere. Exactly how much of a link to the past, neither of them could even begin to guess.

The four of them walked across the parking lot and went into the front lobby of the hotel. On the way across the parking lot, Danny had noticed a silver van parked along the side of the hotel that had about a half dozen radio antennas and what looked to be weather instruments on the top. It wasn't the usual TV station van, but had the words, "Coastal Storm Spotters" written along the side. He asked his dad about it and Dan told him that it was probably an amateur storm spotter club.

"They sure came to the right place last night then!" Danny replied. Even though he hadn't personally been awakened by the storm, he had heard everyone talking about it this morning, and had observed the damage that it had caused on the way out here.

As they all entered the lobby of the hotel, they could see numerous exhibits that were set up around the lobby area. Many more had been set up in the various conference rooms located in the Conference Center Wing. They found the Coastal Storm Spotters exhibit set up in the Pelican Room. It was a fairly large exhibit, having a table with various weather literature, pens and pencils with the club logo imprinted on them, refrigerator magnets with the National Weather Service phone number to call if you see severe weather, and numerous other informational flyers. What really caught their attention, though, was a forty inch flat screen LED TV mounted about six feet up on the back wall of the exhibit right under the "Coastal Storm Spotters" banner. Playing on the monitor was a video of one of the most breathtaking storms that any of them had ever seen. Lightning arced across the sky, jumping from cloud to cloud, creating multitudes of unique patterns. The entire atmosphere seemed electrified.

There was constant motion of the lightning, with some going sky to ground, some going cloud to cloud, and some seeming to arc in huge spirals in the clouds, as if they had minds of their own. One of the men at the booth, who was wearing a gray polo shirt with the club logo, said, "That video's from last night. The power was out in the hotel, but we took some of our portable equipment out back and created this 25 minute long film. It was incredible! The energy levels that we measured in the atmosphere were off the charts! I've never seen anything quite like it. By the way, my name's Joe."

"Dan Nelson," replied Dan, "My wife grew up here on the island, and we're down here for the lighthouse celebration."

"Have you ever seen anything like that?" Joe asked.

"No, I can't say that I have. It was quite unique."

Joe looked to be in his twenties with brown hair and a thin, lanky build. He looked the part of your typical weather geek. He talked with Dan some more before another man, also in the club's gray polo shirt, came running up excitedly.

"You've got to see this!" he exclaimed, holding up a color printout that he had just pulled off of the printer. "I just got this from the National Weather Service feed!"

"Man!" said Joe, "That's incredible!"

They both studied the picture for a few more minutes, then, anxious to share their findings with someone else, handed the page to Dan. He stared in disbelief for a few moments, trying to get his bearings on the picture. It was a color satellite photo of the island taken last night by one of the NOAA satellites during the worst of the storm. Lightning covered a large part of the photo, and the island's shape was difficult to make out, since the photo was dark except for the lightning. What had caught Joe's eye, though, and what now drew Dan's attention, was a large lighted circle created by the lightning in the lower right of the picture. Looking at it, it looked to be as much of a perfect circle as any perfect circle could be. Lightning didn't do that, did it? It didn't move that way?

"Where is this circle located?" Dan asked Joe.

Joe replied, "Based on the grid markings, I'd say that circle is right about where the lighthouse is located."

"What could cause something like that?" inquired Dan.

"It had to be some sort of circular motion in the clouds," replied Joe, "but if it were a tornado, the lighthouse would have had to have sustained serious damage."

Dan took out his cell phone and dialed Steve's number. Steve was the director of the Green Island Lighthouse Preservation Society, and his office was in the house connected to the lighthouse tower.

When Steve answered, Dan asked if there had been any signs of a tornado out at the lighthouse last night.

"Not that we can tell," replied Steve, "There are a lot of trees and limbs down, and the power's still out here, but the lighthouse is intact. We went out earlier to look around at the damage. Looking around the area, it doesn't look like the damage that would be caused by a tornado, though. All the buildings are still standing, and it doesn't look like too much serious damage to any of them."

That was good news. If it was a tornado, or any kind of circular winds, they had apparently stayed up in the clouds and not touched down. He hung up the phone and informed Joe that apparently if it was a tornado that it hadn't touched down.

He learned that the man's name that had showed them the satellite picture was Herb. After talking with him and Joe for a little while longer, he went looking for Dianne and the kids, who had gone on around to more of the exhibits while he stayed back at the weather spotter one. After this, they planned on going back out to the lighthouse and doing a few other things for the afternoon. Tomorrow they would be leaving and going back home to Greenville, but today, being Saturday, there was still a lot of activity around the island.

As he rounded the corner, his gaze was immediately drawn to a woman stepping out of the gift shop and walking the other direction down the hall. She had long blonde hair and for an instant brought back a dim memory of the dream from last night.

"Kate!" he whispered to himself, but even as he said it he really didn't know where that name came from. He didn't know anyone named Kate, he was sure of that. Still, just seeing this woman walking down the hall brought back certain emotions that he was sure weren't just from the dream last night. He stood staring at the woman until she disappeared into the elevator at the far end of the hall. He felt that she wasn't anyone that he knew, yet just seeing her had awakened a sense of déjà vu in his mind, but from where, and from when?

As he continued down the hall to find Dianne and the kids, he was so lost in thought that he didn't even notice the man that he had seen yesterday. But the man noticed him, and was watching him. And the man was probably the only one there that actually knew who the woman from Dan's dream was. But he couldn't tell anyone, at least not yet.

CHAPTER 2
September 18, 2018
The Lecture

Two Years Later

Mark was awakened suddenly by the alarm clock beside his bed. He rolled over and hit the snooze button, then grabbed his pillow and put it over his head. After a few more minutes, he suddenly rolled back over and sat straight up in bed. He looked over at the alarm clock which now said "8:42".

"Oh, no!" he thought, "How many times have I hit the snooze? I'll never make it in time now!"

He quickly jumped out of bed and rushed over to his dresser, pulling out a shirt and some pants. He pulled on the pants, then ran into the bathroom and combed through his hair. He raced out the door, buttoning his shirt as he ran down the stairs of his apartment, unlocking his bike from the bike rack beside the entrance as he left. After tying his backpack to the rack behind the seat, he was in such a hurry that it took three tries before finally finding the combination for the lock which fastened the bike cable. Running along beside the bike, he jumped onto the seat with it already moving then quickly began pedaling as fast as he could. Since he lived at the University Apartments on South Campus, and the lecture hall was located on the North Campus, he was still a long way off. It was already eight fifty one, and even pedaling as fast as he could, it was still at least a fifteen minute ride. Luckily, he wouldn't be really late, but he'd still walk in at least five or ten minutes after it started. Most likely Dr. Carson would still be doing introductions, so hopefully he wouldn't miss much.

To Mark, it seemed like he was always running late to everything. Even when he tried to give himself extra time, something would happen and he'd always be rushing around. He couldn't remember the last time that he had actually been early to anything. Life for him was always a constant struggle, hurrying from one thing to the next. Then he remembered Angela! They were supposed to meet for breakfast at the student center at eight fifteen! As he fumbled to get his cell phone out of his pocket, trying to steer the bike with one hand while dialing Angela on the speed dial with the other, he managed to crash into a trash can beside the path, propelling himself and the bike in opposite directions. As he sat up on the ground, his arm and left thigh aching from the fall, he finally was able to dial Angela's number and explain his failure to show up. She had figured as much, since they had been dating for almost six months now. She knew that he tried and had the best of intentions, but somehow keeping a schedule was hard for him. It was lucky for him that she understood him as well as she did. They agreed to meet after the lecture, and then he jumped back on the bike and continued the trek across campus.

It was ten after nine before he finally opened the door to the lecture hall which by this time was packed. He stood at the door, surveying the room for any open seats, and then proceeded to one that he saw about half way toward the front. Dr. Carson had already introduced the speaker, who really needed no introduction. Since Dr. Carson had introduced Mark to the work of Dr. Langtree about a year ago, he had read a lot of his works, subscribing to his internet feeds and regularly reading the blogs on his website. His website featured articles on black holes, interstellar travel, alternate reality theory, and even the theory of time travel. Since Mark was majoring in Theoretical Physics, he was fascinated with the work of Dr. Langtree and was especially interested in this lecture which was titled, "Dynamics of Energy Field Theory". He had read a little about Energy Field Theory on the internet. Most theoretical physicists actually dismissed it as flawed. They felt that the ideas and hypotheses that Dr. Langtree used to support it simply wouldn't work. They felt that his initial assumptions were wrong as well. But to Mark, he was a compelling speaker, and Mark wanted to know more, especially about what he considered the most interesting claim about Energy Field Theory, that it could be used as a window into the past.

He sat down and pulled out his notebook, where he had printed out an article from Dr. Langtree's website on Energy Field Theory. By this time, Dr. Langtree was showing a diagram on the screen, complete with calculations to support the theory. A lab assistant came to the end of his row and passed down an information packet for the lecture, which Mark quickly opened and examined as Dr. Langtree continued to talk about how the "ghosts" that most people see during paranormal investigations are really created by energy fields which remain from all living things. His theory, which he explained as controversial in the scientific community, is that all living things leave an energy imprint at specific intervals of time. The "ghosts" and other "apparitions" that people see and hear are simply generated from residual energy fields created at another time in that exact place, replaying their actions in this time. He emphasized that, according to his theory, it should be possible to use these energy fields to actually see into the past. Using his calculations, he feels that someday it will be possible to see into specific times and actually see events as they unfolded minutes, hours, even years in the past. The universe is filled with these energy fields, which can only be seen when the conditions are right. He surmised that someday, the "right conditions" could be artificially created by using specific scientific instruments.

Mark understood why Dr. Langtree's ideas were controversial. To most people, just the idea of being able to see into the past is pure science fiction. But theoretical physicists propose theories all the time that are "impossible". And that's the part that's so intriguing to Mark. He's fascinated with the impossible. Last semester, he even wrote a term paper for Dr. Carson's Advanced Theoretical Physics class titled, "The Physics of Time Travel". In it he included detailed calculations and probability analysis, including the amount of energy that would be required. Even Dr. Carson, who by his own admission feels that time travel is impossible due to the many paradoxes that would be introduced, was impressed enough by this paper to give it an "A". He planned to further delve into the time travel arena with his final thesis, which he intended to title, "A Theoretical Examination of the Paradoxes of Temporal Physics". He actually had already started it, even though it wouldn't be due until the end of next semester. He planned a detailed analysis of the various paradoxes introduced by time travel and possible solutions to them. He proposed different approaches to time travel which could possibly eliminate most, if not all, of those paradoxes.

As the lecture drew to a close and Mark began packing his bag, he was surprised to be asked by Dr. Carson to come down to the front. He had planned on going down anyway after the lecture finished in order to meet Dr. Langtree, but actually being asked was somewhat of a surprise. He packed his bag and walked down to where Dr. Carson was waiting while Dr. Langtree spoke with some of the other students who had come down to meet him. They waited for a few minutes until most everyone else had left, and then Dr. Langtree came over to where they both were standing.

"So this is the brilliant upcoming scientist that you spoke to me about!" he said to Dr. Carson as he shook Mark's hand. "What did you think of the lecture today?"

"Really fascinating." replied Mark, somewhat taken by surprise. "Until I had read some of the ideas from your website, and actually came to hear you today, I never really thought much about energy fields. And with the supporting evidence, you make it sound like viewing the past really could be possible."

"Maybe I wasn't convincing enough." replied Dr. Langtree, a slight smile on his face. "I was going more for 'will be possible' than 'could be'. Was there a flaw in any of my calculations that would make you doubt the possibility of it?"

"No, not at all. It's just that, well, this is all just theory that we're talking about here. It's hard to imagine any of this actually becoming reality."

"I'm disappointed in you, Mark." replied Dr. Langtree. After reading your term paper, I thought that you were one that shared my enthusiasm for making the impossible possible."

"My term paper?" asked Mark.

Dr. Carson spoke up, "I was so impressed with your term paper from last semester that I showed it to Dr. Langtree. While I do teach a class about temporal physics, he's the real expert. I wanted to get his opinion about your theories and approaches. As it turns out, he was as impressed as I was about your fresh thinking. He was particularly impressed that you didn't seem to be limited by traditional views."

"It's already eleven thirty." said Dr. Langtree, "How would you like to have lunch with me and Dr. Carson?"

Mark didn't know what to say. While he had come to the lecture hoping to meet Dr. Langtree, he would never have even considered that he would be asked to have lunch with him! And apparently no one else was being asked, since most of the other students had already left. Of course, this was an honor that he couldn't turn down. To have lunch and discuss theories and possibilities with Dr. Ryan Langtree, one of the most brilliant theoretical physicists in the world was more than he could have imagined.

"Having lunch sounds great! I just need to call my girlfriend. We were supposed to meet after this lecture."

He called Angela, and then walked out of the building with Dr. Langtree and Dr. Carson. They walked to the side parking lot where a black SUV with the Chandler-Langtree Institute logo was parked. They all got in the SUV and drove off campus to one of Mark's favorite restaurants, Dave's Burger Bar. After they had walked in and sat at a table over near the window, Dr. Langtree began, "Your paper really impressed me, Mark. I've never seen such original thinking. And you have one of the best grasps of temporal dynamics that I've ever seen. There's just one thing that I have to ask, based on our conversation earlier: Do you really believe that what you wrote about in your paper is possible?"

"What do you mean?" asked Mark hesitantly, not really sure where this was leading.

"It's a simple question. You wrote about a lot of theoretical possibilities, but do you really believe that what you wrote about is possible in the real world? Will your theories actually work? Do you believe that time travel really is possible, not just in theory, but in reality?"

This made Mark think, and he really didn't know what to say. While he was interested in the theory that time travel was possible, and he had spent a lot of time researching how it could be possible, in his mind it still was just theory. Theoretical physicists studied a lot of things that were impossible. While time travel definitely interested him, and he had watched numerous movies dealing with that subject, when it came down to really believing that it was possible in the real world, he had to admit that it was a huge stretch.

"That's OK." replied Dr. Langtree, "I realize that it's a little hard for some people to really believe, even those who understand the theory and dynamics of it. What's possible and what's impossible has been reinforced in us from the time that we're just babies, and that can't be changed overnight."

They paused for several minutes while the server came over to take their order. This gave Mark time to ponder what Dr. Langtree had just said. It seemed, at least to Mark, that it was more than just theory to him. It seemed that Dr. Langtree really believed that time travel was possible, not just in theory, but that it was actually possible!

"So," asked Mark, "do you believe that time travel is possible?"

"Of course I do." replied Dr. Langtree in a matter of fact tone, "Why else would I devote my life to studying it?"

The certainty in his tone really struck Mark. He hadn't experienced this with any of the other physicists that he had talked to. This certainty made him start to believe in the real possibility himself.

"But what about the amount of energy needed?" asked Mark, "Let's suppose for a minute that we have all of the calculations, and that they're all correct. You did read about the amount of energy that I'm predicting that it would take, just to open up a doorway in time? We don't have the capability to produce that kind of energy. It would take a fusion reactor of immense proportions to accomplish it."

"You're correct," replied Dr. Langtree, "but think about it this way; we're talking about temporal physics, where we're not limited by a linear time line. Does the reactor have to exist in this moment, or could it exist in the future?"

This gave Mark reason to pause. He hadn't thought of it exactly this way before. It was hard to get away from linear thinking. He thought about this, but still couldn't quite imagine how it would be possible. He thought that given the dimensions of time travel that the power source could exist in the future at any point along the time line, but in their current time period there would be no way to know the future, so there would be no way to know that it exists, and therefore no way to harness it's power.

"I suppose that the power source could exist at any point in the future, but there'd be no way for us to know about it since we can't know the future. So I'm still not sure how that would help us now."

"It's a lot to consider." replied Dr. Langtree, "Just think about it. Use the thinking that I saw in your term paper. Don't limit yourself only to the possible. Remember, theoretical physicists consider the impossible as well."

They continued on with lunch engaged in lighter conversation. Mark wanted to know more about Energy Field Theory, so he asked many more questions that delved into that subject. He wanted to know more about what the Chandler-Langtree Institute really did, but most of those questions were met with vague answers. He knew that it was a government contractor, but from their website he couldn't figure exactly what they did. His best guess was that they were a government "think tank" for theoretical ideas, but exactly what did the government get from these theoretical ideas that they would be willing to pay for? From the talk on Energy Field Theory, he surmised that maybe they were researching being able to actually view the past. That ability, he thought, would certainly be something that the government would be willing to pay for.

As they were finishing up with lunch, Dr. Langtree asked Mark a question that he had definitely not anticipated, nor would he ever have anticipated: "How would you like to work with us at the Institute? You graduate after next semester, so I'd like to offer you a full paid internship starting immediately. It'll certainly pay better than your current job as a lab assistant at the university. If things work out like I think they will, you'll be offered a full time position after graduation."

Mark was speechless. He hadn't expected this at all. He hadn't even thought that his research paper was all that good, even though he was careful in researching the facts. At this moment, he simply had a blank stare.

"Wow! Yes! Thanks!" said Mark. "I've never even considered the possibility of working for the Institute. That would be any theoretical physicists dream job!"

"Great," replied Dr. Langtree, "I'll get everything set up."

They all got up from the table, with Dr. Langtree picking up the check for all three of them, then went back outside to the waiting SUV.

Later that night, Mark was excitedly explaining the events of the day to Angela over a dinner of chicken fingers at the campus student center. She was enthusiastic for the opportunity, but still a little wary as well. She didn't share Mark's enthusiasm for impossibilities. To her it was clear what was possible and what was not. It was also clear in her mind what should be tampered with and what should not. From some of the stories that she had heard about the Institute, they sometimes tampered with grey areas that should be left alone. It was ok for Mark to be interested in time travel and theoretical physics; after all, he was studying to be a theoretical physicist. She had even at times wondered what kind of job he'd be able to get with that degree. But the Institute? It was located about fifteen miles away from the university, and she'd heard stories about what went on there. The stories ranged from top secret weapons, to genetic engineering, to altering reality. There were rumors of monsters roaming the forest around the Institute that were created by the genetic experiments going on inside. She wasn't sure that she really liked the idea of Mark working there.

"You can't believe all those rumors that you hear." Mark explained, "They're all started by people that don't really know anything about it. I'm sure none of them are true."

"Probably not," she replied, "but what really is going on there, and why are they so secretive? People living a few miles from there claim to have seen things that can't be explained. Creatures in the night that didn't look like anything they'd ever seen. Things that couldn't possibly exist."

"All of that's probably explainable," Mark said, "and may not even have anything to do with the Institute."

"Promise me you'll be careful." she said, finally at least going along with the idea a little bit.

"I will. There's really nothing to worry about."

But even as he said this, his excitement at the opportunity which was before him was also tempered with the same wariness that Angela had mentioned. He'd heard the rumors as well; possibly even some that she hadn't. He really didn't have any idea at this point what really did go on there. Most students who were offered internships at least had some idea what they'd be doing. To him, it was a complete mystery. All he did know was that Ryan Langtree had taken an interest in him, and seemed really interested in his report. Exactly why he didn't know, but he was sure that he'd soon find out.

CHAPTER 3
September 25, 2018
The Institute

It had only been a week since Mark had lunch with Dr. Langtree and was offered the internship. He had started at the Chandler-Langtree Institute yesterday, and the entire day had been filled with orientations and getting set up with the right access credentials. He had known that security would be tight around the Institute, but it wasn't until he actually got there and had his first interaction with the gate attendant that he realized exactly how tight. Since he didn't own a car, he'd had his roommate, George, bring him to work. When they arrived at the front gate, the guard wouldn't let them through at all even though he told him that he was there to see Dr. Langtree. In fact, Dr. Langtree himself came out to escort him inside; explaining that since he didn't have an access card yet, that the guard couldn't let him through. Without proper credentials, they were instructed not to let in their own mother. The Institute didn't have many visitors, but what visitors did come had to be accompanied inside by an authorized employee. Nobody outside the company was allowed to simply roam around freely. He was sure that even after he got in the front door that getting through the rest of the building would have been just as difficult if he hadn't had Dr. Langtree to escort him. Dr. Langtree told George that he didn't need to be available to pick Mark up, that he'd take care of getting him back to the campus. As George drove off, Mark got into the black Institute SUV with Dr. Langtree and they drove the half mile to the main campus which consisted of three buildings, unimposingly nestled among the trees, with a quiet stream flowing into a well landscaped pond. It was a picture perfect setting.

They drove up and parked in front of the first building, which was a modern brick and glass structure with four levels. The building closest to it was only two levels, but seemed to be more spread out to form an "L" shape. The third building was apart from the others with a pond separating them. It wasn't like the other two buildings, as it didn't have very many windows and resembled more of a large warehouse. The campus was beautifully landscaped and inviting and Mark could definitely see himself working here.

As they entered the building, the first place that they stopped was the security office to get his access card and get fingerprinted. He was given Level Two Security, which Dr. Langtree explained was one level below his. It would allow him into most of the highest security sections of the Institute in all three buildings, which he felt was odd considering that he was only an intern. He took the card in his hand and looked it over. It wasn't like any access card that he had seen before. It was rectangular metal, a little smaller than a credit card, with a belt clip on one side. A small white light along the top blinked about every five seconds. He clipped it to his belt, and then followed Dr. Langtree into the hallway. The rest of the day was spent mostly in various orientation sessions to acclimate him to the company. Still, even after an entire day of orientation sessions, he didn't have any more of an idea what the company actually did than he had when he first arrived that morning. At the end of the day, he had been met by Dr. Langtree, who escorted him to the company transportation center where he was presented with the keys to a brand new dark blue Honda Accord. It had the license plate, CLI-247, which he assumed stood for Chandler-Langtree Institute Car 247. Glancing around the lot, he noticed that all of the license plates started with CLI. Being given this car puzzled him even more, since he had never known an intern anywhere to have a company car. He didn't want to be suspicious, but given the rumors that he'd heard about this company, he couldn't help it. He could imagine what Angela would say. She was suspicious enough about the Institute already, given the gossip that she'd heard from her friends.

Today, he had at least been able to get through the gatehouse with minimal issues. Apparently the new car was equipped with a transponder that automatically opened the gate as he drove up. As he drove through the gate, a map appeared on the dashboard display which directed him to his assigned parking space. He was further surprised as he walked through the front entrance and was greeted by name by the automatic gate attendant as it opened to allow him access. The building was equipped with the latest in security, with the access card not even needing to be removed from his belt to allow him entry. While he hadn't been told this, he imagined that it also tracked his movements anywhere on the campus as well.

As he paused hesitantly after walking through the gate, wondering where to go from here, he was approached by a tall attractive woman wearing a dark green skirt and white blouse.

"Good morning, Mark!" she said cheerfully, "I'm Melissa Greenwood, Dr. Langtree's personal assistant. Allow me to show you around this morning."

He followed her down the hallway as she showed him around the facility. They toured Lab #4, which contained many electronic instruments and gadgets that he'd never seen before, along with some that he had. She showed him the break room, along with a couple more labs, with technicians busily working on various projects. He imagined that some of the projects might be dealing with Energy Field Theory and attempts to see into the past, but some of the others he couldn't quite figure out. At the end of the tour, they took the elevator to the second floor and after walking down a short hallway, stopped at a spacious office which looked out over the fountain at the front of the building. As they walked into the room, Melissa asked Mark, "Will this be suitable?"

"Suitable for what, exactly?" asked Mark hesitantly, "Who's office is this?"

"It's yours. I hope you like it. I'll leave you alone now to get used to your new surroundings. If you need anything, just hit button three on your phone. It should be labeled, Melissa."

"Thank you." he said, as he settled into the plush leather chair behind the desk, still wondering exactly what was going on here. He was again completely confused. This office looked more like it should belong to the Vice President of the company. Interns usually got cubicles, if even that.

As he looked around the room, there was a bookshelf along the opposite wall, with a sofa and coffee table beside it. A flat screen TV hung from the ceiling opposite the sofa. It was turned to face his desk. A round table with four chairs was along the other wall, with a round conference phone in the center and a lamp suspended on a chain above the table. His spacious desk was mostly empty, except for a lamp on the left, a flat screen computer monitor on the right, and a small box beside the monitor which he discovered had a color touch screen display which lit up with virtual buttons when he touched it. He began looking for the keyboard, since if there's a monitor there must be a computer around somewhere. He clicked a latch on the desk drawer and pulled it out to reveal a tray containing a keyboard and mouse. As he moved the mouse, the monitor, which had been completely dark, showed a login screen. Oddly, there was nowhere to type a user name and password, so he couldn't figure exactly how he was supposed to log in. He turned around in his chair to look out the window overlooking the fountain and the front lot of the building, totally lost in thought. A knock on the door caught his attention as he turned around to see Dr. Langtree at the door.

"May I come in?" he asked. "How do you like your new office?"

"Are you sure I'm just an intern? I feel more like an executive."

"Officially an intern for now, but I'm supposing Lead Scientist before long. This is a new branch of science, so there aren't a lot of older scientists that know anything about it."

"Lead Scientist." Mark thought to himself as he settled back in his chair. He actually liked the sound of that. While things were moving really fast lately, he actually did like the direction that they were going; but he still couldn't understand how all of this was possible just from Dr. Langtree reading his term paper. What exactly had he written in it that so interested him?

Dr. Langtree closed the office door behind him as he settled into the guest chair in front of Mark's desk.

"You know I wasn't joking about Lead Scientist. I think you have potential."

"Thanks, Dr. Langtree." he replied, truly honored that Dr. Langtree had this amount of confidence in him, "I'll do my best."

"First, let's lose the 'Dr. Langtree'. We're family here; call me Ryan.

Second, here's the company handbook. You'll need to be familiar with the company rules, particularly the security part. Since we're a government contractor, there are rules and regulations that have to be followed. Things have to be done a certain way, and you'll need to know what that is. You've been given a security clearance of two. That's higher than most of the employees of this company, but there's a reason for that. The project that you'll be working on requires that level. But with that level is a lot of responsibility. Under no circumstance are you to discuss any of the details of the projects that go on here with anyone outside of the company; not parents, friends, girlfriends; no one. You'll soon understand why. We deal with a lot of things that the general public just wouldn't understand, so we can't take a chance that anything that we do here will be found out. With your security clearance, you'll know more than most of the other employees as well, so also remember not to discuss things that require a Level Two security clearance with anyone below that level. This is of the utmost importance. We just can't afford to have even any 'accidental' leaks of information. "

Mark really was wondering at this point what he was getting into. Maybe Angela was right to have concerns. What exactly did this company do that was so secretive?

"Any questions so far?" asked Dr. Langtree.

Mark actually had a lot of questions, but most of them he decided to just wait and see what played out. The only one that he decided to ask that he really was curious about was, "Will I be working on Energy Field Theory?"

"No, you were hired for something more important than that. While there are several projects which deal with Energy Field Theory that we're working on here, and those projects are the ones that are currently funding the Institute, those projects are still only Level Three Security Clearance. You were hired for another project that we urgently need you on. Here, let me show you how to work your computer and I can show you a few things to get you started."

Mark pulled out the keyboard tray and moved the mouse to bring up the login screen. Logging in, as he found out, wasn't done by typing in a user id and password. A small round indention at the upper corner of the keyboard was a biometric sensor. He knew immediately why he'd had to put his index finger on a sensor yesterday while being processed by security as a new employee. It was to map his fingerprint as a biometric security password. He placed his finger on the sensor, and the screen immediately came to life. The CLI logo was at the top of the screen and it was filled with other icons as well.

"Your computer has been specifically set up with everything that you'll need." said Dr. Langtree. "There's an index card in your top desk drawer that shows the different control sequences for doing things. There's also a booklet which shows how to operate your Digital Control Unit; that's the small black box with the touch screen display. With the DCU, you can control all functions of the TV mounted on the ceiling, as well as set the temperature of the room, adjust the blinds for optimal outside light, and control all of the integrated room lighting."

Dr. Langtree took the DCU, pushed a couple of virtual buttons, and what was shown on Mark's monitor was also displayed on the ceiling TV. He pushed a couple more buttons and adjusted the TV's position. Mark was definitely impressed. He'd never been in another place that was so futuristic. Dr. Langtree instructed Mark to click an icon on the computer monitor labeled "Project Spatial Juncture". He did as instructed and was presented with another screen divided into a series of rectangles with pictures inside them and words along the bottom of each rectangle. He clicked on the "Documentation" section which brought him to another screen which contained a list of all of the available documentation on the project. Dr. Langtree showed him what documents he should start reading first to get an overview, and then instructed him to return back. He went back to the previous screen, and his attention was immediately drawn to a rectangle containing the words "Ripple Theory".

"What's Ripple Theory?" asked Mark.

"That's the core of what you'll be working on, and in my opinion is the most fascinating thing that we're doing here. It's a difficult concept for most people to understand, though. They can't quite understand what they've always known was impossible. I know things are moving fast, but do try to keep an open mind. Think back to your term paper, and the research that you used to come to your conclusions. And use the open-minded thinking that wrote that paper."

"OK", Mark replied hesitantly, not fully understanding exactly what Dr. Langtree was getting at.

"Remember last week when I asked you if you believed that time travel was really possible? You were hesitant to give an answer, and I understand that. But I've developed a new theory, that's substantially different than what most scientists are working on. Instead of having to generate the energy necessary to open a doorway at a given location, we simply find doors that already exist. I've developed a theory that certain areas can contain a naturally occurring temporal field, and that field continually pulsates with what I refer to as "Ripples". Think of them sort of like ripples in a pond. Ripples are doorways to other time periods that we just need to figure out how to open."

"But even if we found a temporal field, wouldn't it still take a massive amount of power to open the door?"

"That's what's so different about Ripple Theory: The ripples don't require EXTERNAL power to open the doorway, they generate their own energy; what I call Temporal Fusion. The energy is already there, we just need to figure out the key to harnessing and controlling it so that we can actually use it to open up those doorways."

"So," answered Mark, "this is still only a theory; nobody has actually travelled to another time period yet, right?"

"Not yet," replied Dr. Langtree, hoping that Mark couldn't tell that he wasn't being completely truthful, "but I feel that we're close, we just haven't figured out the means to harness that energy just yet. And that's where we need you, Mark. With the type of thinking that I read in your paper, you may just be the one to figure out the secret to opening up the ripples."

Even with what Dr. Langtree had just said Mark actually felt a little more comfortable now. He didn't know why, but there was a real difference between watching science fiction movies, and actually participating in that science fiction becoming a reality. Especially science fiction that everyone knows is impossible. He felt comfortable dealing with the theory, but he had to admit that even after almost four years of study at the university, that he was still skeptical if any of what he studied would ever actually be a reality.

"I'll need you to study up and become intimately familiar with the Ripple Theory section." said Dr. Langtree, "And you'll need to get up to speed on it quickly. As you look at all of the data that we've gathered so far, try to think of ways to make it all work together. I need you to think of things that we might be missing."

"Fine." replied Mark, "I'll start looking over this information immediately."

Dr. Langtree then instructed Mark to click on another rectangle labeled "Green Island", which brought up another screen containing other sections documenting all aspects of a part of the project that was currently going on at Green Island. He recognized the name. He had vacationed there with his family several times over the years. He remembered that there was a lighthouse there, the Green Island Light Station. At Dr. Langtree's instruction, he clicked on another button that brought up something that looked a lot like a weather radar display, but had the words "Green Island Light Station Temporal Field Monitor" in the upper left corner.

"What is this?" asked Mark, a little confused.

"Remember earlier when I mentioned finding doors that already exist? Well, we've actually discovered a strong temporal field at the lighthouse on Green Island. We've gotten permission from the Green Island Lighthouse Preservation Society to perform experiments out there. They don't know about the temporal field, though; they think we're doing weather experiments. We've set up remote telemetry devices out at the lighthouse including a remote temporal field monitor, which is what you're looking at now. "

Mark was studying the monitor intently. In his mind, this changed everything; only a few seconds before, this was all "Theory", but now, seeing the image on the monitor changed it from "Theory" to "Reality", even if they hadn't actually travelled through time yet. In his mind, this made the possibility of it all a lot more "Real". There was an "x" in the middle of the monitor that appeared to be the lighthouse, and an irregular donut shape created a circle around it.

"The donut shape around the lighthouse is the temporal field." explained Dr. Langtree. "You'll notice that every few weeks, the field gets stronger then weaker. We call this phenomenon the Ripple Effect, like ripples in a pond. Each time a ripple comes up it takes a few weeks for it to reach maximum strength, then it begins to recede over the next several weeks. Sometimes the cycle can take a month or longer, it's not entirely predictable. What you're seeing now is a ripple getting stronger. We've been watching this one grow since last week. There are also live video cameras around the lighthouse which you can access as well. You can tilt and zoom them pretty much three sixty degrees, so you can look around all you want to. Feel free to look at everything that's available to you including all of the documentation. I know that this is a lot to take in, but I think you'll find Ripple Theory fascinating."

He got up to leave, and then turned back to Mark as he got to the door, "If you need anything, just hit button one on your phone, labeled Ryan, or you can hit button three for Melissa. There's a corporate Smartphone for you to use in the top drawer of your desk as well. Be sure to always keep it with you. It has my number as well as other numbers that you may need already programmed in. When communicating with other company phones, the conversation is automatically encrypted with an advanced encryption algorithm so that we don't have to worry about any of our conversations being accidentally overheard. Be extremely careful not to discuss anything relating to any of our projects over an unsecured line."

"Thanks Dr. Langtr … I mean Ryan. I'll be careful. I think I have plenty to keep me busy for awhile."

Dr. Langtree smiled, "I'm sure you do."

As Dr. Langtree left the room, shutting the door behind him, Mark sat back in his chair, trying to let the events of the day and the conversation that he'd just had with Dr. Langtree really sink in. Just a little more than a week ago, he didn't even know Dr. Langtree, now he was a scientist at the Institute! But he didn't feel like a scientist yet, he still felt like a student. There was still so much that he had to learn. As he was sitting, pondering all of the events of the day, he again heard a knock on his door. It was Dr. Langtree again.

"There's one more thing that I forgot to ask." he said, "Are you available this weekend through next Wednesday? We have a portable field laboratory set up on Green Island and I'd like you to come out there with me. I can show you all of the equipment that we have set up there and what it's used for. We need to take some readings at various points in the temporal field as well."

"The weekend's fine," said Mark, "but I have classes the other days."

"Oh, that's another thing that I forgot to mention." said Dr. Langtree, "I was able to have you dropped from all of your other classes. Don't worry, you'll still graduate on time next summer. This internship will fulfill the remainder of your course requirements for graduation."

"Ok, I guess everything is all set then." replied Mark as Dr. Langtree left. He just sat for a few minutes staring at the closed door to his office. He really didn't know if he liked Dr. Langtree just cancelling all of his classes without asking him. He was actually looking forward to some of them. Still, he knew that it was probably better this way. This internship was sounding like it would be taking up most of his time anyway.

At the end of the day, as he drove the fifteen miles back to campus, he was lost in thought. Things couldn't be moving any faster. And some of the things that he'd read this afternoon after Dr. Langtree had left had been really fascinating. There was a lot that he didn't know yet about Ripple Theory, but from what he had been able to read, he was starting to put together some of the pieces of how it could work. He was sure that he was where he was supposed to be. The Institute was giving him the opportunity to pursue his dream career, and this was more than he had ever hoped for. Still, he wondered where he'd be when the Institute couldn't deliver on all of the wild promises that they had given to the government. At some point, the government officials that have been paying for the projects would want results, not just theories on paper, and he wasn't sure that they'd actually be able to deliver.

He met Angela at the student center for dinner, and she had a lot of questions, but not quite as many as yesterday. He was somewhat relieved about that, since he couldn't really tell her a lot about what happened today, anyway. She'd been surprised when he came driving up in his own company car, and was even more surprised as he described his office. Those things only made her more suspicious about what the company might be doing, since she'd never heard of an intern getting those kinds of perks. Still, they had a nice dinner and took a walk around campus afterward before she had to go back and work on a paper that was due in a few days.

After getting back to campus and having dinner with Angela, he went back to his apartment and called his dad. He'd be really interested to hear all about Mark's day, since his dad knew that he had just started a new job. While he knew that he'd been instructed not to discuss anything that went on at the Institute with anyone outside of the Institute, he didn't think that applied to discussing his office, his security clearance, and even the fact that he now had his own car. While Mark had spent the day getting used to everything, and he'd finally begun to accept how things were, his dad was a little more skeptical. He knew that his son was extremely intelligent, but he still had to wonder about all of the company "perks" that Mark was getting. And for an intern? Like Angela, he'd never heard of an intern getting these kinds of benefits either. He thought that Mark might be getting too caught up in the moment, and in the company benefits, that he wasn't thinking clearly. What did they want from him that would be worth all of the "perks"? There had to be more to it than what Mark was telling him, or more to it than Mark himself even knew.

After getting off the phone with Mark, he went over to his computer and tried to find any information that he could on the Chandler-Langtree Institute, but other than the fact that it's a government contractor, there wasn't a lot of information to be found. He'd hoped to at least find out a little of what his son might be doing there, but instead all of his efforts were met with a brick wall. There was nothing that he was finding anywhere that would even give a hint of what the company might be working on. Next month was Parent's Day at the college, and he and Mark's mother were planning on attending, so he'd have more time then to talk with his son and find out a little more about this internship.

Later that night, Mark woke up from a dream. In the dream, time travel had become a reality, and he was actually able to travel to another time. He remembered the dream, but not all of the details. He knew that he was somewhat uneasy after waking from this particular dream, but he didn't remember enough about it to really understand why. He did remember a man, however, someone that he'd never seen before asking for his help. Why the man needed his help he couldn't remember. He seemed vaguely familiar, like Mark had seen him somewhere before, but the more he thought about it, the further the dream receded from his conscious thought. For the next hour, he lay awake, wondering what tomorrow would have in store for him.

CHAPTER 4
September 29, 2018
Green Island

Mark was awake early on Saturday morning. Since he was going away for several days, he wanted to spend some time with Angela before leaving. They decided to go off campus and get some breakfast at one of their favorite breakfast spots, Waffles and More. Angela had introduced him to it when they had first started dating. She said that it was one of her father's favorite places to eat when he came down to visit. They settled into their favorite booth by the window, and when the server came, they both ordered the stack of pancakes with eggs, which they most often ordered when they went there.

As he had thought when he first took the internship, she wasn't happy that he couldn't discuss anything about his job with her. She had hoped that she'd finally be able to find out at least some of what goes on at the Institute. In a way she understood, but in another way she didn't. The fact that they were so secretive only worked to fuel her imagination of what might be going on there. And if even some of the things that she imagined were true, she definitely didn't like Mark being a part of it. He assured her that the things she had heard and imagined didn't have any basis in fact, but he still couldn't tell her anything about what actually was going on there. Most of it was the Secrecy Agreement which he had signed his first day on the job. That limited discussion of any projects that were being worked on at the Institute, and aside from the two projects that he had found out about, he really didn't know much more. There may be some things that weren't secret, but he didn't feel that any of those would help Angela feel better about him working there. She wanted to know what he was working on, and that unfortunately was one of the things that he couldn't talk about.

After breakfast they came back to the campus and took a walk. It was around eight fifteen and Dr. Langtree was supposed to come by to pick him up at his apartment at nine. They figured that they had time to take a walk as long as they were back at the apartment by that time. He had told Angela that they were going to the lighthouse on Green Island to perform some studies. He really didn't know if he should have told her where he was going or not, but he felt like it was alright since he didn't reveal anything about what they'd actually be doing there. He also thought that she'd be interested that he was going to Green Island because he knew that she had spent a lot of time on the island while growing up, since her grandparents had lived there all their lives. He'd only been to the island a few times himself while on vacation with his family, and he'd only seen the lighthouse a couple of times. During all of the previous times that he had been there, he wasn't able to go up in the lighthouse tower since it had still been operated by the Coast Guard. Now it was a place for tourists to visit and experience the island, and they could get a spectacular view from the top.

"Maybe we can go there together one weekend and I can show you around." she suggested. "We can stay with my grandparents. They'd love to have us, and I'd like you to meet them."

He agreed that he'd like that as well and that they should plan a trip down there some weekend soon after he gets back. Just as they were returning to the apartment, the black van from the Institute pulled up out front. Mark went into the apartment and brought down his suitcase and computer bag. They'd be gone for five days, but since he still didn't need much for his stay, he travelled light. As Dr. Langtree opened up the rear of the van so that he could put his stuff in, he noticed all of the equipment. The van was packed full of electronic equipment and gadgets. He realized then that he had a lot to learn, since he really didn't know what any of it was used for. Angela noticed all of the equipment too, and gave him a look that said, "See, I told you there was something going on there!" He gave her a kiss goodbye, then got into the passenger side of the van and headed off toward Green Island.

Angela was even more curious now. After seeing all of the equipment in the van, she really did want to know exactly what Mark was getting into. As she walked back toward her dorm room, she pulled out her Smartphone and dialed her grandparents' number. Her grandmother answered and was immediately glad to hear her voice. After all of the usual "How have you been" conversation, Angela got to the real reason for the call.

"Grandma, have you noticed any unusual activity on the island lately?"

"Not really," her grandmother replied, "just the usual late summer and early fall vacationers. Wait, I have noticed more black vans and trucks over the past couple of months. I think they're staying out at the Harbor Inn. All of the vehicles were black and had some sort of emblem on the side. I'm trying to remember what it said…"

"Was it CLI, under a green crescent moon?"

"Yes! I think that was it! Do you know what they're doing?"

Angela replied, "CLI stands for Chandler-Langtree Institute, but I don't really know what they're doing there. My boyfriend, Mark, started an internship with them this past week and he's gone to Green Island now. He'll be there until Wednesday."

"Well, he could probably tell you more than I can, then." Grandma replied.

"Not really; they're a very secretive company. He's not allowed to say anything about what they do, but around the campus I hear some really weird stories. And when they left a few minutes ago, I noticed that their van was filled with all sorts of odd electronic equipment."

"I can have your Grandpa go out to the lighthouse and see what he can find out. You know how curious he always is. He's also good friends with Steve, the director of the Lighthouse Preservation Society, so he should know what's going on if anybody does, but I'm sure it's nothing."

"Thanks, Grandma, that'd be great. I know I probably have no reason to worry, but things have just been happening so quickly with Mark's job out here that I can't help but wonder what's really going on. He tells me that he has an office that looks more like a Vice President's office than an intern's. I didn't even think they gave interns offices!"

"You know how things have changed." replied Grandma. "Your

generation has so much more opportunity than we had."

"Yes, I know we do." she said, rolling her eyes. Her grandma did always go on about how much better her generation has it than they did when she was growing up. But she didn't think in this case that was really all that was going on here.

They talked for the rest of the way back to her dorm, then hung up as she walked up the stairs to the second floor. She was glad that her grandpa was going to check it out. Maybe he'd find out something. Still, for now, she couldn't help but worry about Mark and what he might be getting into. He had told her there was nothing to worry about, and she hoped that was true, but some of it just didn't make sense to her. A week ago, Mark had a minimum wage job as a lab assistant on campus, he didn't have a car, and while he had read many of Dr. Langtree's books and articles on his web site, he didn't know him personally. Now, only a week later he had a job that came complete with a spacious office overlooking a fountain and a company car! And according to Mark, the pay was a lot better than he could get anywhere else as well. And if that's not enough, he's travelling to Green Island for five days with the President of the company! How could she not suspect that there was more going on than even Mark realized?

As Angela opened the door to her dorm room and walked inside, she decided to see what she could find out. Now that Mark had left for the island, her curiosity was getting the better of her. She'd actually tried to find anything that she could on the Chandler-Langtree Institute a few nights ago and had come up completely empty, but now she had another thought. She'd heard Mark talk about Dr. Langtree's web site; not the CLI Company site, but Dr. Langtree's own personal site. She turned on her laptop; settled down on her bed, propped herself up by several huge pillows, and did a search for Dr. Langtree. She didn't know his first name, but figured that if he was as famous as Mark said that he was, just typing in 'Dr. Langtree' should be enough, and she was glad to find out that it was.

From the first site that she found, she discovered that his full name was Dr. Ryan Matthew Langtree, and he was one of the founders of the Chandler-Langtree Institute along with his partner Dr. Philip Oliver Chandler. There wasn't much on the site actually about the Institute, and she found that to be the case on every other site that she found as well. What the sites that she found did have were articles written by Dr. Langtree about various things like black holes, interspatial portals, energy fields, and even theories of time travel. These are all things that theoretical physicists think and write about. She had heard about all of these ideas before, but they were all just abstract ideas. Mark had tried to discuss some of these ideas with her, but she just couldn't get into discussing them since they were only theoretical. Why spend a lot of time on things that couldn't actually exist. She had a hard time seeing the point in it all. She was a Business Administration major. Business she could understand. Management was real. Accounting was real. That was all something that could be used in the real world.

For the first time, though, she actually found herself reading an article written by Dr. Langtree on the subject of time travel. A week ago, that was something that she wouldn't have done, but now she wanted to find out more. Not that she honestly believed that the Institute was able to perform time travel, or even that it was something that they were working on, but because it was something that Mark had talked about recently. And it was something that he had mentioned that Dr. Langtree had theories about. They had gone on dates where they went to movies about travelling through time. They were entertaining, but that was all. It was science fiction, which meant that it dealt with something that wasn't true, but only imagined. In science fiction, everything is possible. People can fly, walk on ceilings, and even travel to other planets or other solar systems in the blink of an eye. But that doesn't mean that those things are possible, or even that they ever will be possible for that matter. In reading through Dr. Langtree's articles dealing with time travel, though, he talks about it like it's a very real possibility. She had never read anything by anyone that was so convincing; even though there was no way that any of it could ever actually become a reality. Even Mark really didn't discuss time travel like he really believed it, but more like it was just a fascination. It was something fun to talk about, and watching television shows where it was possible was definitely entertaining. He was a huge science fiction fan. She and Mark had watched a series called Star Journeys on several occasions, and the things that they did on the show were good entertainment, but science fiction nonetheless. But reading Dr. Langtree's article was different. She honestly could tell that he believed what he was writing about; even though she didn't have the slightest idea what a lot of the article was talking about. Things like spatial dispersion, temporal dissipation, energy substitution; she didn't know what any of that meant, but she felt that Mark would understand it completely. In the end, she didn't find out a lot more than she already knew about what Mark might be doing. She did find out more about Dr. Langtree's ideas, and that gave her more of an insight into some of the things that Mark was interested in as well.

As Green Island came into view from the deck of the auto ferry, Mark was lost in thought. He had walked over to the railing and was watching a flock of seagulls off the stern of the boat. He had been lost in thought all afternoon, wondering what the next few days had in store. He was also pondering his conversations with Dr. Langtree and the data that he had been analyzing over the last several days. He was trying to understand the temporal field around the lighthouse. Dr. Langtree had told him that some of the test instruments that they were carrying with them were to take measurements of the field and to analyze its energy and fluctuations. But even to him, someone who had been studying this type of thing for the last three years, it really didn't seem possible that he was here at this moment. He'd been studying the "THEORY". Now, just the fact that it could be measured made the temporal field real, and he looked forward to being able to actually study it up close. Not just running numbers, equations, and simulations, but actually being there and studying an actual temporal field! And even more importantly, to possibly discover how to open it to travel through time! Here he was now, feeling exactly like a character in one of his favorite science fiction novels. He thought of Ron Wyatt and Karen Clark in Amy Davenport Westfall's novel, "Unintentional Journey", and thought now about how the ideas in her book could actually be possible.

The ferry docked at the port and within a few minutes they were on their way through town. Mark remembered coming here with his parents and staying out at the Harbor Inn. There was one time that they'd even stayed at a charming inn called the "Baker Family Bed and Breakfast". It had been nice, but they actually preferred the amenities out at the Harbor Inn. They passed the bed and breakfast as they went through town, and it looked just like it did when they had last stayed there. Most of the island really hadn't changed much, but then it had only been about five or six years since they'd been here. On the drive down here, Dr. Langtree had tried to explain to him some of the things that they'd be doing for the next several days, and while most of it went over his head, he actually was fascinated by it all.

As they turned onto Harbor Inn Lane, it brought back memories for Mark of the vacations that he and his family had taken here. He remembered going out to the lighthouse, even though he had never actually been to the top of it. They passed Lighthouse Road and continued out to the Harbor Inn, which would be their home for the next several days.

"Maybe we can have dinner at the Mariners Cove tonight." said Mark, "The last time that I was here I remember it being really good. They have the best crab cakes I've ever eaten."

"Have you been here often?" asked Dr. Langtree.

"Just a few times; I came here with my family when I was growing up. We stayed at the Harbor Inn then too."

"Let's get checked in, then we can go out to the lighthouse and check out a few things." continued Dr. Langtree. "We can probably eat at the Mariner's Cove when we get back."

After they got checked in and took their bags to their rooms, they continued out to the lighthouse. It looked exactly the way that Mark remembered it, with its tower and the attached two level brick structure that overlooked the water. It seemed that they were pretty busy today, with the parking lot being almost full. The one thing that he did notice that hadn't been here before was a tall, thin steel structure beside the house at the opposite end from where the lighthouse tower was located. It was actually a little taller than the lighthouse tower, but because the structure was thin and narrow, it blended in with the surroundings very well. Atop the tower was a white ball probably about six feet in diameter. It looked almost like a smaller version of a Doppler radar. Dr. Langtree noticed him looking at the tower.

"That's the Temporal Field Monitor that we were looking at in your office." explained Dr. Langtree. "We're using the fact that it looks like a Doppler radar to our advantage. As far as everyone here knows, that's exactly what it is, a Doppler radar. Even the lighthouse administrator believes that we're performing weather experiments out here, so if anyone asks, that's our cover. That tower is really the only visible evidence that we're here, and that's only because we couldn't think of any way possible to disguise it. It needed to be in the center of the temporal field and also at a precise elevation. The rest of the instruments are smaller and also located in the surrounding woods. There are some towers there too, some as tall as this one, but they all blend in with the trees. You're able to receive telemetry from all of them from your office computer, and even from an app on your Smartphone."

Mark was truly impressed. Here they were monitoring a real temporal field and nobody suspected anything. Dr. Langtree walked over to the back of the van, opened the back doors, and began to rummage through the instruments. He pulled out two handheld meters along with what looked like two antennas about 6 feet long. He attached the wires from the antennas to input jacks on the meters, and then pushed the power button on each one which lighted a touch screen on the front. After a few minutes of explaining to Mark how to use the instrument, they walked across the parking lot and into the woods. The further they went into the woods, the image on the monitor began to change color. It started out light blue, and then went to dark blue, and then into orange. A series of numbers began increasing on the display. Dr. Langtree had explained to him the basics of what he was looking at and how to interpret the information on the display. There was a lot of information, so Mark knew that it would take a little while for him to really get comfortable with it. As they walked through the woods, Mark noticed an area of red on the display.

"What's this red area?" he asked Dr. Langtree.

"That's an area where the temporal field is the strongest, but it still hasn't broken through to this time period yet. "

"Are these readings right?" asked Mark. "It seems from what you told me back at the van that these readings are unusually high."

He thought he saw a slightly worried look cross Dr. Langtree's face as he gazed at the display.

"It's fine," he said, "Sometimes the readings will get this high. It's unusual, but lately we've been seeing them this high quite a bit."

As they walked a little further into the woods on this side of the lighthouse, Mark thought he noticed a slight mist forming in the air around them. Dr. Langtree noticed it too and remarked that maybe they should go back out now. The rest of the afternoon was spent travelling a complete circle around the lighthouse, mapping readings as they went. They never noticed the mist again, but several times he did notice that Dr. Langtree seemed concerned about something that he was seeing on the monitor. He didn't know whether to ask him about it or not, and in the end felt that he'd just wait and see what happened. He trusted that Dr. Langtree would tell him what he needed to know when he needed to know it.

In the quietness of his hotel room that night, Mark studied the data that they had gathered that afternoon. They had both downloaded the data gathered from the probes into their laptops before turning in for the night. Mark had been running simulations for the last hour, comparing the data gathered today from data gathered from previous months. He went back as far as a year ago which was when they first started collecting the data, and no matter how many times he ran the simulations, he could only come up with one conclusion: The field was getting stronger. Each ripple was slightly stronger than the one before it. He sat back and reflected on the information that he had just analyzed, and what he was seeing didn't make any sense based on what he knew about temporal dynamics. A naturally occurring temporal field would fluctuate with each ripple, but would remain more or less the same intensity over time unless it was influenced by an external force. The fact that this one was getting exponentially stronger indicated that it was being fueled by some unseen source of energy. He needed to think about this a lot more and think about what it all meant. He knew that he wanted to ask Dr. Langtree more about how they discovered this one. That part was still a mystery to him. How had they known that it was here? With the instruments that he had been introduced to this afternoon, you'd still need to be standing right in the middle of it to see it. He didn't know of any technology that would be able to direct you to a temporal field, even though he really was just getting exposed to all of this new technology himself. The other thing that still bothered him, and that he had been trying to reason out for the past week was the symmetry of the field around the lighthouse. It was almost a perfect circle with the lighthouse in the exact center. How could it happen by chance that the lighthouse was built back in the 1800's right in the exact center of a temporal field? The only logical conclusion that he could come up with was that the field wasn't naturally occurring. The problem was that if it wasn't naturally occurring, then a whole new set of questions came to mind. If it wasn't naturally occurring, then who created it, and how? Where did the energy come from? There was obviously nothing that he had seen around here that would be capable of generating the amount of energy needed to fuel a temporal field. Every time that he thought of this, however, his thoughts came back to what Dr. Langtree had said the first day that they had met, "Does the reactor have to exist in this moment, or could it exist in the future?" He turned that statement over and over in his mind. Was it a clue? He supposed that given the dimensions of time and space that it could theoretically exist in the future, but if that were the case then someone else other than Dr. Langtree could actually be controlling the field. He wondered if Dr. Langtree had considered that possibility.

He found it hard to sleep that night. Even after finally lying down on the bed and closing his eyes, his mind kept wandering through all of the information that he had been exposed to in the last week. He knew that there was an answer to it all somewhere; he just needed to find it. Hopefully, the rest of the week would yield more answers, and not simply more questions.

CHAPTER 5
October 4, 2018
A Quiet Dinner

It was a sunny Thursday afternoon in early fall. One of the first slight chills could be felt in the air. In fact, it was so nice out that Angela and her best friend Janice decided to get some lunch from the student center and eat it outside at one of the tables overlooking the pond. She had spent a lot more time with Janice this past week since Mark had the new job at the Institute. While she knew that it was a good opportunity for him, she couldn't help but worry. And they weren't spending much time together since he started the new job either. A lot of days during the past week, she didn't even get to see him. She actually preferred the days when he had his classes on campus and they could meet several times a day and usually have lunch together. They were only able to have dinner one time last week on the one day that he got home early. The problem was that on the other days he didn't get home until late. It didn't seem quite fair. He'd had a full schedule of classes when the semester started, then suddenly after he got the internship at the Institute all of his classes were cancelled and he spent his entire days there. And his first weekend was spent away from the campus as well. She really did hope that once he got settled into the new job that things would get better. Hopefully, he'd start working regular hours and have more time for their relationship again. She really did enjoy the time that she and Janice could spend together, but she missed the time with Mark as well. She and Janice had decided during lunch to go to a movie when they finished, since they didn't have any more classes this afternoon. The last part of their conversation, therefore, turned to what movie they wanted to see.

As they were finishing up lunch, her Smartphone rang with the familiar arpeggio tone that she had programmed in just for Mark. She hurriedly fumbled it out of her purse and hit the answer button. She hadn't heard from him much this week, so she excitedly answered, "Mark! Hi! I didn't expect to hear from you this afternoon!"

"I know," he replied, "I just thought I'd surprise you. I know we haven't seen each other much this past week and I've really been missing you. There's just been a lot going on here."

"I've been missing you too!" she said.

"So," he continued, "how would you like dinner on the town tonight? At our favorite place, Sandon's Vineyard?"

"Would I!" she exclaimed, "I love you!"

Janice smiled and waved goodbye, so she could give Angela and Mark some time alone together. She'd had to listen to how much Angela missed Mark all week, so she felt she should give them some quality time now. Angela waved back, an excited smile on her face. She sat down on one of the park benches beside the pond, and they talked for another ten minutes before he had to go to a meeting. Those ten minutes were enough, though. After over a week, they'd finally have a proper date! And at their favorite restaurant in Wilmington!

After the phone call, there was definitely a new spring in Angela's step as she made her way back to her dorm. She went through her closet for about thirty minutes trying to pick out just the right dress for the evening. She'd pull one out, and then hold it up in front of herself while looking in the full length mirror that was mounted on the closet door. She finally settled on a dark green short sleeved one that she could wear with a cream colored sweater, both of which looked really elegant with her long brown hair. After that, she had to pick out just the right necklace and shoes, which took another twenty minutes. It had only been two weeks since they'd really spent any time together, but it seemed like a lot longer, so she wanted everything to be just right. After seeing each other every day for the last six months, this last week had been quite a change. After she had everything laid out on her bed, she decided to have her hair done at the salon near the campus. She didn't have a car, so she convinced Janice to take her down there. Since she was going to the salon anyway with Angela, Janice decided to have her hair done as well. Her boyfriend hadn't been noticing her as much as she'd like lately either, so this might just move things up a notch.

After she was finished up at the salon, her Smartphone rang again. This time the caller id indicated that it was her grandma's number. Since Janice was still finishing up, she walked outside to take the call.

"Hi, Grandma!" she chimed in, "Guess what? I have a date with Mark tonight! It's the first time in two weeks!"

"That's great news, dear." Grandma answered, "And I think I might have even more good news for you as well. Remember last Saturday when you asked me if anything unusual was going on with the Chandler-Langtree Institute here on the island? "

"Yes! You found out something?"

"Your Grandpa did. He went down and saw Steve at the lighthouse yesterday and they had lunch. It turns out that they're just performing weather experiments out there. They've even constructed a portable Doppler radar beside the lighthouse. I hope this helps put your suspicious mind at ease that nothing's really going on there." she explained cheerfully.

"Oh…Really?" Angela replied hesitantly. This wasn't exactly the news that she had expected, or even hoped for. But then, she didn't know why she should have expected anything different either. Did she think they'd just tell anyone who asked what they were really doing there? Even though she'd met him once, she actually didn't know Steve all that well. Maybe he was in on whatever was going on out there.

"I thought you'd be a little more excited," remarked Grandma after several seconds of silence, "to find out that there's nothing odd going on there, just weather monitoring."

"I am," Angela replied, "Tell Grandpa thanks for checking on it for me."

As she hung up the phone, she was still a little confused. Mark was studying to become a theoretical physicist, not a meteorologist. Her "suspicious mind", as her grandma called it, thought possibly that the meteorology angle could be a cover for what they were really doing. She was still suspicious about what was happening there, but at the same time she actually did want to find out that nothing really was. Could there really be something that a theoretical physicist would be doing with the weather? After all, there's a lot of physics in weather: wind, clouds, pressure. But theoretical physics is not like standard physics, it's different. Theoretical physics is about things that can't be simulated in the real world. It's all about mathematical models, and simulations. But mathematical models could be applied to weather, she supposed. Now, with this new information, she'd do more research. She felt that she had to find out what was really going on out there.

After getting back to campus, Angela was determined to find out more. Mark was picking her up at six thirty, so she still had another two hours. After spending the first hour getting ready, she turned on her computer, and performed a search on theoretical physics and meteorology together. To her surprise, there really was a branch of theoretical physics called Theoretical Meteorology! Maybe Mark really was performing weather experiments just like her Grandpa had found out! This was great news! It meant that maybe Mark wasn't really involved in anything unusual or dangerous after all! Still, she wasn't completely satisfied that was all it was, but the more that she read about theoretical meteorology, the more that she tried to convince herself that was what he was actually doing.

A knock on her door quickly brought her out of the zone that she was in with her research. She quickly closed her browser and turned off the computer before answering the door. Since she didn't really know what was going on, she preferred at this point that Mark not find out that she'd been researching the company that he worked for. She didn't know how much he really knew about what was going on there, and she thought that it would be better if he didn't discover how paranoid she really was.

As she opened the door, just seeing Mark there took her breath away! He looked more handsome than she had remembered with his sandy blonde hair and blue eyes. With his grey slacks, black shirt, and dark green dinner jacket, she couldn't imagine loving anyone else! By the look on his face, he was just as taken with her as she was with him.

"You look gorgeous!" he remarked.

"So do you!" she replied back.

He gave her a kiss, and then took her hand as they walked out the door. She paused to lock the door, and then got another kiss as she turned back around to leave. He took her hand again and led her down the stairs and outside. As they approached his car, she realized that this was the first time that she had ridden in it. They went around to the passenger side as he opened the door for her, giving her another kiss as she settled into the passenger seat. He walked around the front of the car, giving her a smile as he got in and they drove off.

As they arrived and walked into the restaurant, they were greeted by Sandon himself, as he escorted them to their table. Since they'd been coming here, Sandon had gotten to know them by name and always asked how they were doing. As their server came up, he left them alone to enjoy their dinner and their time with each other. Sandon always worked to make each visit special, especially for his regular customers. He knew their favorite wine and always had a bottle sent over to their table right after they sat down. After they had ordered and their server had popped the cork and poured each of them a glass, they reached across the table and gently held hands, while looking into each other's eyes. It was such a romantic moment that each of them wanted this moment to go on forever, lost in each other's gaze.

"I've missed you." she finally said.

"I have too." he answered, "It's been so crazy out at the Institute. There's just so much going on right now. Things are moving too fast!"

"I hear that you're performing weather experiments out at Green Island." she remarked, hoping that she wouldn't put him too much on the spot with this observation, but really wanting to see his reaction.

"Weather?" he asked, seeming a little confused.

"Yes, weather. I talked to Grandpa and he said that he was told that CLI was working on weather research out there."

Mark just looked at her for a minute, wondering what to say next. He knew that she was curious about what he was doing at the Institute, and he wished that he could tell her everything, but he knew that he couldn't.

He also knew that he couldn't lie to her either. Since they had begun their relationship about six months ago, he had never been untruthful with her, and he wasn't going to start now. He couldn't tell her everything, he knew that, but maybe he could tell her a little just to satisfy her curiosity. He'd have to be careful how much he revealed, however.

"Actually, the project that I'm working on doesn't really have much to do with the weather."

"Oh?" she replied, a worried look coming across her face. Since she had spent the last hour before Mark had picked her up trying to research weather and theoretical physics to convince herself that there actually was something that Mark could be doing with weather research, she had reassured herself that was what he really was doing. That's what she wanted him to be doing. If he was working on tracking weather patterns, then that seemed fairly harmless to her and she wouldn't have to worry about him as much. She had finally convinced herself that's all he was doing, and now here he was telling her that he wasn't working on weather research after all. She was back to the unknown, and back to her concerns. She hoped that she was able to hide her real feelings, but by the look on his face, she knew that she wasn't.

"What's wrong?" he asked, truly concerned about her.

"I just worry about you." she said. "When Grandpa told me that CLI was doing weather experiments, I was suspicious at first since you're not a meteorologist, but then after giving it some thought, I convinced myself that really could be what you were doing there. I wanted to believe that was what it was, since weather experiments seemed harmless enough. But now we're back to me not knowing what you're doing there, and you know the things my mind can come up with."

"You also know that I can't talk about my work," he said gently, "but it's really not dangerous. There's nothing for you to worry about. We're just doing research. I can't say much more than that, and I'm not sure that you'd really believe me if I could tell you what we're doing, but believe me when I say we're not in any danger."

He seemed really sincere as he said this, and that did put her mind at ease a little. If he really believed that he wasn't in any sort of danger, then maybe he actually wasn't. That would have to be good enough for now. She decided to drop the subject and go onto something else, since she really didn't want her mood to ruin a lovely dinner. Their steaks arrived, and they had much lighter conversation for the rest of the evening, just enjoying each other's company. By the end of the evening, when they arrived back at her dorm room and he had walked her to her door and given her a gentle kiss goodnight, she had almost forgotten all about the Chandler-Langtree Institute.

That night, though, she found herself not able to sleep. She'd never been able to just let things go, and this was no exception to that. Their conversation at dinner kept going around in her mind. "I'm not sure that you'd really believe me if I could tell you what we're doing." he had said. What did he mean by that? At the time, she hadn't realized just what he had said, or even what he may have meant by it, but now, after she'd had more time to think about it, that statement really worried her. What could he be doing that she wouldn't believe? She really did wish that he hadn't said that; that he'd left her with something that would actually ease her mind.

She finally did get to sleep, though it wasn't a very restful sleep. She woke up around 4:25 in the morning with an uneasy feeling. She knew that she had been dreaming, but try as hard as she could, she couldn't remember anything about it. From the way that she felt though, it must not have been a particularly pleasant dream. She had a hard time getting back to sleep, but since today was Saturday, at least she didn't have to get up at any particular time.

Mark had trouble getting to sleep as well. He had more on his mind than most college students. He was bothered by Angela's questions at dinner, and he really wished that he could tell her more, not just to ease her mind, but because he really needed someone to talk to about it. Things were moving fast, maybe too fast. And every day that he studied the numbers, ran simulations, and studied the Temporal Field Monitor, only brought with it more questions than answers. And he had noticed something this afternoon that he had previously missed while analyzing a wave form recorded from the temporal field last week. It was a pattern that didn't seem to belong. It had blended so well with the primary wave form that he hadn't noticed it at first, but after discovering it, he went back and analyzed several of the other readings taken several days before. It was there as well, though not quite as strong. Knowing how temporal dynamics worked, he couldn't figure what it could possibly be. He'd show it to Dr. Langtree on Monday. He was a lot more experienced with these things; maybe he'd have an idea what it was.

He finally got back to sleep as well, probably after shifting his thoughts back to Angela. There was no reason that he needed to be at the Institute this weekend, so they'd have the whole weekend together. Since meeting her about eight months ago, he had known almost immediately that she was the one that he wanted to spend the rest of his life with, and he was sure that she felt the same way. Maybe he could tell her a little about what he was doing. He would have to be careful not to reveal too much, though, but if he was careful, maybe he could tell her just enough to satisfy her curiosity. He knew that she wouldn't be ready to hear everything that's going on, and a lot of what he was actually doing wouldn't ease her mind much even if she did know. He'd just have to wait for the right time, and then decide how much to let her know.

CHAPTER 6
October 6, 2018
The Road Trip

It was Saturday morning and the sun was streaming through the window of the Ocean Reef Resort. Angela lay in bed for a few minutes, just enjoying the warm sunlight shining through the window. After a few more minutes, she got out of bed and opened the sliding glass door to walk out onto the balcony and enjoy the morning.

"Good morning beautiful!" came a familiar voice from the balcony next door. Mark was already up, and he rose to lean across the balcony to take her hand. A cool breeze was blowing in from the sea, and it really couldn't be a more wonderful morning.

Mark and Angela had decided to take some time off from work and studying and go on a road trip. It was supposed to be a warm weekend, with temperatures in the low seventies. Mark had been working late almost every day for the last two weeks, and with her class schedule, they just hadn't really been able to catch up with each other very much. Some friends had told them about Thompson Farm, down in South Carolina near Conway, and since it was only a two hour drive, they had decided to start their weekend there.

Mark had taken a day off on Friday, and they had packed their bags and gotten an early enough start to reach the farm a little after five thirty. He had done a corn maze a few years earlier with his best friend Eric during the day, but he'd never been through one at night. He'd mentioned it to Angela, and she wanted to do one as well, so both of them decided on the one at Thompson Farm. They checked the schedule of events and found that it was open on Friday nights from dusk until eleven. This one was an especially good, six acre maze and it took them a little under an hour and a half to find their way out of it. They were both given flashlights so they could find their way, since the maze wasn't lighted at all except at the entrance and exit. It actually was a bit creepy, seeing lights moving in and out of the stalks of corn. Since it was the month of Halloween, a lot of the visitors that were going through the maze, many of them young children, were howling and making other scary sounds. Sometimes, even the adults joined into the sound effects as well. Even Mark joined in the game, and she had to admit, it was a side of him that she'd never seen before. His werewolf impression even sent chills up her spine when he unexpectedly let out a loud howl. It all just added to the experience. Many times, it seemed like they just kept going in circles. Angela swore they had passed one particular scarecrow at least three times. Once, when they had gone into a dead end path, Angela found herself in Mark's arms when she turned around to exit, but of course she wasn't complaining when he wrapped his arms around her and gave her a big kiss. They both were laughing and carefree, just enjoying a lovely evening together, one of the few that they had really gotten to enjoy in a while with their schedules.

After sunset, the temperature had dropped substantially, so they were glad they had worn their warm clothes and jackets. Still, after finally finding their way out of the maze they were quite chilled and decided to get s'mores kits from the general store and roast them in the fire pit while watching the Friday night drive in movie on the lawn. While it was mostly kids roasting their s'mores over the fire pit while their parents just sat in the chairs and watched the movie, they didn't care. They were young and in love, and on this night didn't have a care in the world other than just being together. When the farm closed at eleven, they drove the forty minute drive to their hotel at North Myrtle Beach.

During the evening at the farm, and even on the drive down from Wilmington, they hadn't talked any about Mark's work. Mostly there wasn't much to talk about, since Mark really hadn't decided how much he should actually tell her. Part of it really was that he felt that she wouldn't believe a lot of what he had to say. After all, sometimes he found it hard to believe himself, and he knew how she felt about it. He was still getting used to the fact that everything that he had been studying in theory, might actually be possible. There were still a lot of days when he woke up that he thought it was all a dream himself, until he actually walked into his office and saw the Temporal Field Monitor with its donut shaped ring of glowing color.

As they drove toward North Myrtle Beach at around eleven thirty on a Friday evening, they both were unusually quiet. It had been a really fun, eventful evening and they both were looking forward to nice soft beds at the resort. Since they were very old fashioned, a value that had been instilled in them by both of their parents, they had reserved separate hotel rooms. A lot of their college friends who were dating would choose to both stay in the same room, but for them, even if the room had two beds, it just wouldn't feel right.

Halfway through the drive, Angela spoke up with the question that had been on her mind since their date Thursday night at Sandon's Vineyard, "What is it that I wouldn't believe?"

"What do you mean?"

"Thursday night at the Vineyard, when we were talking about your work, you said that you weren't sure that I'd believe you even if you told me what you were doing."

"Oh, that." he said, looking over at her with a look that told her that he was having a hard time figuring out exactly what to say.

"I actually have been trying to figure out how to tell you. I want to tell you all about what I do, but sometimes I have a hard time believing it myself. How much do you know about Dr. Langtree?"

"I've been to his website and read a few of his articles," she admitted, "but I really didn't understand a lot of what he was talking about. Before dinner last Thursday, I was trying to figure out what you might be doing with the weather, since I had discovered a branch of physics called Theoretical Meteorology."

"So that's what the question about the weather was all about!" he remarked, "I remember that you said that you had talked to your grandpa and he thought we were doing weather experiments?"

"Yes, he said that he had talked with Steve out at the lighthouse and he said that the Chandler-Langtree Institute was performing weather experiments out there."

He was starting to understand now. Dr. Langtree had mentioned to him when they were on Green Island that everyone had been told that they were doing weather experiments.

"I understand why you would think that. That's what the Institute told the folks on the island that they were doing when they got permission to do research out there, but really that's not what it is at all."

"What is it, then?" she asked in a slightly worried tone now.

"Remember that my college major is in Temporal Physics, right?" he asked.

"Yes, I remember."

"Well, apparently to Dr. Langtree and the Institute it's more than just theory. They're studying something called Energy Field Theory, which he thinks will enable them to actually see into the past."

"How can that be?" she asked, a little confused.

"Well, according to Dr. Langtree, he thinks there are different energy fields all around us, that have been left there by people and events that happened there in the past. The energy fields remain even after the people and objects are no longer there. It's his opinion that these energy fields account for all of the ghost sightings that paranormal investigators see. He thinks that once the technology is perfected, we'll actually be able to see into the past and witness events as they happened!"

"What do you think?" she asked, "Do you think that they'll be able to perfect that kind of technology?"

"I'm not sure, but they do have a lot of teams working on it. I think that's what's giving them most of their government funding."

"Is that what you're working on?" she asked.

Mark was thrown off, and also a little disappointed. He had hoped to deflect her questions about what he's working on by telling her a little bit about the Energy Field Theory. He knew that just by telling her about it that he'd probably told her too much already, but since Dr. Langtree had done a college lecture on it, then it couldn't be extremely top secret.

He was silent for a couple of minutes, trying to think of what to say. He knew that he had to be as truthful as he could be. Their relationship had always been built on honesty, but he had never worked in a job with a security clearance before, either. Still, he knew her well enough to know that she could keep a secret, and he also knew that she was concerned about his new job. But if he told her what he was really doing, would that actually stop her from worrying, or would it only make her worry more? He'd have to tell her just enough to satisfy her curiosity, without telling her so much she'd just be all the more concerned, if that were even possible now.

"Dr. Langtree's found a temporal field on Green Island." he began.

"You mean a time portal?" she replied, surprised that he would volunteer that information.

He was thrown off again by her reply. He didn't know that she even knew what a time portal was, yet here she was referring to the temporal field that he had just told her about as a time portal.

"Where did that come from?" he asked.

"We've seen movies about time portals," she replied, "and I have actually read a few of the articles on Dr. Langtree's web site."

He was beginning to think that this conversation wouldn't be as hard as he thought it would be. Prior to this, he hadn't even thought that she really was interested in time portals, temporal fields, and time travel at all. Now here she was, actually speaking the lingo. What more surprises might she have in store?

"Yes, he actually thinks that he's found a time portal at the lighthouse on Green Island."

"Do you know where it came from, and do you think that's really what it is?" she asked, actually a little skeptical.

"That's one thing that I'm still trying to figure out." he admitted.

"Dr. Langtree says that's what he believes it is, but I'll have to ask more questions when I get back next week. While it does seem to have the characteristics of a temporal field, I haven't figured out a lot about it yet to make a determination. And if that's really what it is, I still can't figure where it came from."

They talked more as they approached North Myrtle Beach and finally turned into their hotel. While he felt that she wasn't completely satisfied with all of his answers, she at least appeared to be more at ease now with what he was doing. Maybe time travel wasn't such a far off concept to her after all and she was willing to give it a chance. And, he admitted, just talking about it with someone helped him with it as well. It was a lot for him to get used to, even having studied it for four years, so he knew that it couldn't be easy for her. They were discussing something that both of them had always considered impossible for their entire lives.

Even though it had been late, the check in process had gone well. They were able to get rooms that were side by side on the third floor of the building. Both rooms had balconies that overlooked the ocean, and they both stepped out onto their balconies, holding hands across the space between them as they gazed out toward the ocean, listening to the soothing sound of the surf as it washed up onto the beach. They couldn't see much in the darkness, but tiny specks of light actually could be seen far off into the distance, probably fishing boats at this hour, or even cruise ships on their way to far off destinations. They turned in for the night, both completely tired out from the day's events.

Now as they got dressed and walked down for breakfast, they were ready to start the day. Both of them remembered the conversation that they'd had on the drive in from Thompson Farm, and both actually wanted to continue it today now that they'd had a good night's sleep. They decided to walk two blocks from the hotel to a restaurant called the Southern Pancake House. It was about eight thirty in the morning, and they figured that it must serve good food, given the number of cars parked around it. They went inside and were seated by a window along the front, overlooking North Kings Highway. There was a surprising amount of traffic on the highway considering that it was already October, and the air was getting chillier. They finished up with breakfast, both of them deciding to try the pancakes, since that seemed to be the restaurant's specialty, and then walked three blocks back down 71st Avenue North over to the beach. A walk on the beach in the crisp morning air provided a pleasant start for the day.

As they walked along the beach, hand in hand, they continued the conversation from last night. Last night, when he had gotten to his room and finally turned out the lights, Mark pondered whether he had said too much. He finally decided that he probably had, but was relieved as well that someone other than himself and Dr. Langtree knew at least some of what was going on at the Institute. And he was glad that person was Angela, even though right now he couldn't tell how much she really believed of his story. He didn't think that she fully believed that it was a time portal, but then, sometimes he wondered if he really believed it himself. Of course, he'd never tell anyone at the Institute that he'd revealed any classified information to anyone, and even though it had been to Angela, and he knew that she'd never tell anyone, he still felt a slight twinge of guilt. He always tried to do the right thing, but he had violated company policy, something that usually he would never do.

The rest of the day was spent in various activities. They drove over to Boardwalk on the Beach and went through the shops, even buying a few things to bring home as souvenirs. While they were there, they decided to see a movie, which was a love story having nothing to do with time travel whatsoever. For this day, Mark actually preferred it that way. After the movie, they drove down Ocean Boulevard and purchased tickets to ride the Myrtle Beach Skywheel, which gave a wonderful view of the beach and ocean. With the tickets that they had purchased, they were able to come back for a night ride as well. A romantic walk along the beach was just the thing before turning in for the night, a beautiful way to end a beautiful day.

Sunday, they travelled back to Wilmington. Mark had mentioned taking a detour by Green Island on the way back, but they decided against it since Angela actually had some work to do for a couple of her classes before Monday morning. The weekend getaway had been just what they needed to relax and have an enjoyable time spending quality time with each other. As the preceding weeks had been so hectic, it was nice to just be able to relax. And while Angela knew a lot more than she previously did about what Mark was doing, or at least what he said that he was doing, there were still a lot of questions that she had. She still was worried that maybe he might not realize exactly what he was getting into. Even with the conversations that they'd had over the weekend, she still felt like there was more to the story. It still seemed odd to her that Mark would be given such a prestigious office at the Institute, complete with car and expense account. And she still had to wonder why Dr. Langtree seemed to need Mark so much? After all, wasn't he the expert? How much could an intern really add to their research? She wondered if maybe Mark didn't realize everything that was going on. He obviously was blinded by all of the perks of the job, as well as getting to work on something that he had studied for the past four years. He might not realize that there may be more to what was going on there than Dr. Langtree was willing to let on. And she still hoped that whatever that was, that it wasn't dangerous. Then there was the whole issue of time travel. She knew what Mark had said, and she felt that he really believed it, but she still wasn't completely sure that she was ready to buy into all of that yet. She was still the skeptic, which made her even more concerned about what was really going on. If it wasn't time travel, but Mark was being led to believe that's what it was, then what was it really? Their conversation over the weekend had just made her more determined than ever to find out.

There was also another question that she had asked that made them both stop and think. It was actually a pretty innocent question when she asked it, but the answer had made them both pause to consider it. She had heard a lot about Dr. Langtree, so the logical question to her was, had he met Dr. Chandler yet. When he admitted that he hadn't, they both stopped and looked at each other for a minute, both of them thinking that was at least a little strange. It could simply be because it was Dr. Langtree's project that Mark was working on. That's probably all it was. Still, with the importance that Dr. Langtree seemed to place on Mark, she would have thought that he'd have at least been introduced to the other founder of the company. They decided that he'd ask if he could meet Dr. Chandler on Monday and that question would be answered once and for all.

CHAPTER 7
October 8, 2018
A New Perspective

As Mark drove into work on Monday morning, there was a steady drizzle with some patchy fog, so it took him longer than usual. This gave him more time to think, and the white noise that the rain created as it drummed on the roof of the car actually helped clear his mind so that he could think. He had a lot of questions on his mind. While the weekend had provided some diversion from everything that had been happening for the past couple of weeks, and it had been a much needed diversion, today was back to reality. Now, as he thought of everything that he and Angela had talked about over the weekend, he knew that he wanted to schedule a meeting with Dr. Langtree as soon as he could. He hoped that Dr. Langtree could answer some of his questions to help him make sense of everything. There were still too many things that he just couldn't piece together. He was still wondering how Dr. Langtree had found the temporal field, and why it was almost a perfect circle around the lighthouse. Those questions and others he just couldn't quite figure out. He did have a few ideas, but he couldn't really make those work based only on what he currently knew. He needed to know a lot more. Looking back, even to the trip to Green Island, he felt that Dr. Langtree wasn't telling him everything. Not that he was actually lying, but just that he was omitting some key parts of the truth. And he hoped that it was those key parts that would help all of this start to make sense. And if he were to be of any value to Dr. Langtree at all, he felt that he needed to find these answers.

While he pondered these questions, he also considered Dr. Langtree. He was young, in his late thirties, and likeable enough. He didn't really fit the general stereotype of a person that would be running a multi-million dollar corporation at his age. But then, what the Institute was researching was cutting edge science fiction, not really ideally made for an older CEO. Still, thinking back to the trip out to Green Island, he thought more about Dr. Langtree's general personality. He wasn't someone for whom small talk came easily, but then that could be said about half of the professors at the university as well. There was something else, though; a certain distantness in his demeanor. Mark realized from all of his encounters with Dr. Langtree that he wasn't one that Mark could truly relax and be comfortable around. There was just something that he couldn't quite place, but it was there nonetheless. He knew that Dr. Langtree had to be in control, which had been first evident when he had taken the liberty of cancelling all of Mark's classes without the common courtesy of consulting him first. But he felt that it was actually more than that as well.

Dr. Langtree was in the office early this morning. Now, he sat at his office desk looking out the window at the rain, which was coming down much harder now. The dismal morning gave the scene as he looked out the window a certain foreboding look. He knew that Mark needed to know more, but he just hadn't figured out exactly how much more to tell him yet. Obviously, he wasn't ready to know everything, but time was running out. The amount of temporal energy in the field had almost quadrupled just in the last month, and he had observed several occasions where it had broken through to this time period, even if only for a few seconds. He needed Mark to begin working on the solution to controlling the field and the ripples within the field before it was too late, and to be able to do this, Mark needed to know a lot more about it. Still, Mark couldn't know everything. If he did, he might decide not to help at all. Dr. Langtree knew that he had to be careful about how much he did actually reveal. Like with Dan, everything had to be revealed at just the right time.

He thought back to that night, over two years ago, the same way that he had done many times before, trying to piece together everything that had happened, and more importantly, what that meant now. At first, everything had seemed to be going as planned. Dan had signed the papers, and the world had seemingly reverted back to the way that it was supposed to be if the Vortex Accelerator had never been created. As he and Dr. Chandler had both thought, the ripples had continued even after the Vortex Accelerator was gone. Temporal dynamics are definitely hard for anyone with even the slightest bit of logical thinking to understand. They just don't make sense at all. After all, how could something that never existed create ripples that do exist? It was kind of like saying, "How can a chicken that never existed lay an egg?" Still, they had done a lot of planning, and it seemed at first like everything was going according to his plan; at least until the temporal field collapsed in upon itself, creating the biggest fireworks display the island had ever seen. The energy of millenniums converged upon that single spot that night, almost shattering the time matrix and destroying both past, present, and future. But the field had recovered, and for the past two years, the ripples continued in a fairly regular pattern. That is, until about four months ago, when the energy within the field began increasing at an alarming rate, and even trying everything that he knew, he still was unable to get control of it. Even with all of the careful planning, he had missed something, something vitally important which now threatened to rip apart the very core of the time continuum. And now, with Mark's help, it had to be put back together.

Car lights caught his attention coming down the winding path through the woods to the main parking area. The beams shone like small spotlights through the thin mist. It was Mark's car, and he watched as Mark turned into the lot and drove to his assigned space. He'd give him a few minutes to get in out of the rain and get settled into his office, and then they'd definitely need to talk. He felt that by now, Mark probably knew just enough to keep him fairly confused.

Mark hurried through the rain, splashing through large puddles in the parking lot, the wind ripping at his umbrella. While it was a rainy, dismal morning, it was also a cold morning, and the cold seemed to cut right through his overcoat. Finally, he reached the front entrance and went through the security gate, turned the corner, and caught the elevator to the second floor. As he opened the door to his office and walked inside, the motion sensor turned on the lights and adjusted them to complement the ambient lighting coming in through the windows. He sat his briefcase on his desk, took off his overcoat and hung it on the coat hanger in the corner, then went over and started the coffee maker. He walked over and sat down in his large office chair behind his desk and used the DCU to switch on the overhead television. At once, the temporal field around the lighthouse came into view. He studied it for a few minutes, just staring at it trying to notice subtle differences as it pulsed, first growing slightly larger, and then receding. It did seem a bit like a ripple in a pond, the way that it shimmered and moved. Where could it have come from? More important than that, was it even a temporal field at all as Dr. Langtree claimed? He actually was still having trouble believing that it was real. The tone on the coffee machine rang to indicate that the cup of coffee was finished brewing and was ready to drink, so he got up and walked across the room to retrieve it.

He got back to his desk, turned on his computer, and ran several of the simulations that he had written to analyze the field. He looked for the pattern that he had noticed last Thursday, the one that didn't seem to belong. It was still there, possibly even a little stronger now. While he had missed it at first, now after knowing where to look, it was obvious and stood right out to him as he studied the screen. While it didn't seem to be a part of the field, still it merged with the field perfectly, almost overlaying each wave form with a signature of its own.

A knock at the door caught his attention, and as the door opened just a crack, Dr. Langtree peered inside.

"May I come in?"

"Yes, come on in. I was just going over the field and comparing the readings to last week."

"Any differences?" he inquired of Mark.

"I'm not sure just yet. I did have a few questions, however. Please come in and sit down."

Dr. Langtree walked over and sat in the guest chair in front of Mark's desk.

"So, what can I help you with?" inquired Dr. Langtree.

"Well, there are a few things that I don't quite understand. First, I know that we talked about the temporal field being naturally occurring, but I don't think that it is."

Dr. Langtree arched his eyebrows and looked over the top of his glasses, "What makes you think that?"

"There are several things actually. First, it's just too perfect a circle around the lighthouse. I did some measurements on the screen and the lighthouse is exactly in the center. What's the chance of that occurring naturally? Second, it's definitely increasing in energy. I'm not sure where that energy's coming from just yet, but it's definitely increasing. A naturally occurring field wouldn't be doing that; it would get stronger and weaker, but the relative energy would stay the same if it was averaged over time. And third, I noticed this last week."

He used his cursor to highlight the pattern that he had noticed last Thursday. Dr. Langtree rubbed his chin as if he were thinking intently about something. He actually recognized the pattern immediately. It was the temporal signature of the Vortex Accelerator superimposed on the waves of the ripples in the field. Even he had completely missed that before! But the Vortex Accelerator didn't exist any longer! How could this signature be there? The more that he thought about it, he decided that it must be because the ripples were actually created by the Accelerator in the first place. It would only be logical that they would have the same signature.

"Do you have any ideas about what it could be?" asked Mark.

"Possibly. I'd actually noticed some of those same features, and also started to think that maybe the field wasn't naturally occurring. Those are all compelling arguments that you presented. Let's consider for a moment that it is man-made. Remember what I mentioned the other day about a temporal field possibly having a power source that exists in the future? Maybe that's what's going on here. The pattern might be the signature of the source that created it."

"That does make some sense!" said Mark, "Do you have any ideas about who might have created it?"

"It's the future, so I don't think we can know that information. But that shouldn't stop us from trying to harness its energy and being able to open a door. That energy is here, in this time period, regardless of where it actually came from."

"Maybe, but we have to be careful." said Mark, wondering about what might happen if they inadvertently encountered whoever had created it.

"There is another question that I've been wondering as well." he continued. "How did you find it? Is there something that I don't know about yet that can point you to a temporal field?"

"No, there's nothing like that. You really do have to be right on top of it to even see it, even with our sophisticated instruments. We just happened to luck up on this one because of its location. If it had been in the middle of the woods somewhere, we probably would have never found it. But because it was right at the lighthouse, we noticed some fluctuations one time when we were visiting it. We got permission to do some experiments out there and that's when we found it. I believe that it's the first temporal field of its kind ever discovered!"

Mark actually seemed satisfied with this explanation. He had wanted there to be a believable explanation, so he was ready to accept this one when it was presented to him. He was actually quite a bit relieved. Dr. Langtree, though, still had a serious look on his face, and that puzzled him.

"There's more to it than you realize." Dr. Langtree continued, "Much more. The energy is building within the field. We call that energy Temporal Fusion and that's what actually fuels the ripples. We have to somehow release some of that energy by opening a doorway to another time period. Unfortunately, nothing that we've tried so far has been able to affect the field at all, so we can't open that door. And if that door isn't opened, then the energy will continue building until the field collapses and there's a temporal explosion. We're not entirely sure what that would look like, and quite frankly, I'm not sure I want to know. Everything that we've tried has failed, so we need a fresh perspective. That's where we need you, Mark. We need you to figure a way to harness the energy contained within the ripples to open a doorway. Right now, we're not too concerned with being able to control the exact time that the doorway leads to, we just need it to open to release some of the energy that's building up within it. When Dr. Carson showed me your term paper, I thought that perhaps you were the one that could help us accomplish this."

Mark just stared at Dr. Langtree, trying to let all that was just said sink in. They needed HIM to find a way to open the door!? Dr. Langtree and Dr. Chandler were the experts in the field, maybe the ONLY experts in this particular field. If neither of them could figure it out, how did they expect him to?!

"If you and Dr. Chandler can't figure it out, I'm not sure that I can add much." Mark began.

"Stop right there! Don't limit your thinking by questioning your ability. Dr. Chandler and I have been too close to this. We simply need a fresh perspective. Sometimes when you look at something day and night for so long, you can miss what's right in front of you. Your perspective might be just what we need."

Mark thought about this last statement, turning it over and over in his mind, and then decided that maybe Dr. Langtree was right. Maybe what was needed was a fresh perspective.

"When do I get to meet Dr. Chandler?" Mark asked. Oddly, he noticed a slight change in Dr. Langtree's expression when he mentioned Dr. Chandler. It was a subtle change, but noticeable nonetheless.

"In time." Dr. Langtree said, "You'll get to meet him in time. He's not here at the moment, though; he's on a business trip. He'll be back next month."

So that's why he hasn't met Dr. Chandler yet; he's away on business! That seemed to satisfy him for the moment. A company the size of the Institute, with government funding, must need someone to travel to Washington to lobby for what they need and deliver status reports. They sat and talked for the next three hours, going over different scenarios, trying to find the piece that they had been missing, but it was like trying to find a needle in a really large haystack.

That night, after a full day of both work and classes, Mark and Angela went out to dinner. He had learned so much today, and a lot of this day's events he really didn't feel that she was ready to know just yet. While he had told her about the time portal while away at the beach, he'd begun to rethink that maybe he really had told her too much. How much more should he reveal? He decided to be much more cautious now.

They arrived at one of their favorite Italian restaurants, Mama Rizzoli's, and were seated at a table by the window overlooking the street. He decided that he could tell her about Dr. Chandler, since they'd discussed him the other night.

"I did find out about Dr. Chandler." he said to her. "It turns out that there's not a big mystery there after all. He's simply away on a business trip!"

"Really? Do you know what kind of business trip?" she asked, still suspicious.

Mark hadn't really thought too much about this. He supposed that since the Institute was funded by the government, that Dr. Chandler could be away reporting on the progress of the Energy Field Theory, or getting additional funding like he had first thought this afternoon. After all, he supposed that it did take quite a lot of money to run a business the size of the Institute, especially with their equipment and staffing needs. Still, her question actually made him question something else that he hadn't really thought of this afternoon. If the situation with the increasing energy in the temporal field was as serious as Dr. Langtree seemed to suggest, would Dr. Chandler choose this time to be away? He actually didn't think that would be very likely unless there was no other choice, and it seemed like there would always be another choice. Even if the government were pressing him for a status, he could always tell them that they had an urgent situation that needed his attention. The more that he thought about this, he really didn't think that Dr. Chandler would pick this time to be away. The crisis with the temporal field would be too important. But if he wasn't away on business, then where was he?

Angela thought it strange as well that Dr. Chandler would be gone for this long, and she didn't even know about the energy in the field. Their conversation over the weekend about the temporal field at Green Island, the "weather" experiments there, as well as the absence of Dr. Chandler all made her even more determined to find out more. She needed to know what was going on there, and there weren't too many ways to find out. Mark wasn't telling her much more than the fact that there was a temporal field on Green Island, and she didn't know how much more that he'd actually tell her. Just the fact that there was an energy field that existed there opened up a lot more questions, and she still wondered if that's really what it was. Maybe Mark didn't know the entire truth about what was going on there either. And if he were being led to believe something that wasn't true, for whatever reason, then he might be in danger. She could think of only one way to find out the truth, but it was risky. She'd talk to her friend Janice about it tomorrow.

As they dined on Ravioli and meat sauce with three cheese lasagna, they were completely unaware that they were being watched through the window of the restaurant. A man in a silver sports car had parked across the street and was watching their every move. He needed to know what Mark knew, but he'd have to wait until the time was right. For tonight, he simply watched and waited, trying to find a way to put all of the pieces together.

CHAPTER 8
October 12, 2018
Hackers

Friday was a sunny day, not at all like the week had started out. It was actually fairly warm for this time in October. Angela was sitting outside the student center waiting for her friend Janice and her boyfriend Glen. She had called Janice several nights ago and told her what she wanted. Janice had been slightly surprised at first, but the more that Angela told her, the more she understood why she would want to know more. She wanted to find out exactly what the Chandler-Langtree Institute was doing, and why they were treating Mark like some sort of executive. She needed to know that he was safe, but every time that she asked him, he only said that everything was fine. He said that there was nothing that she should be worried about. But she had a feeling that everything wasn't fine and she didn't know exactly why she felt this way. It didn't seem to be strictly based on the things that she had heard about the Institute, it was more of a feeling that something didn't quite fit.

She stood up as she saw Janice and Glen walk around the side of the student center and she quickly walked over to meet them.

"Is everything set?" she asked hesitantly.

"Everything's set." Janice told her, "Glen talked to his friends and they'll help us."

"Great!" she said, quite a bit relieved.

"There is one thing." Glen told her, "You have to understand that these guys are pretty paranoid. They can't take the chance that anyone will find them out. They'll pick us up over on Hamilton Drive across from the Student Center in their van. They do have one request, though. They insist that we be blindfolded. They don't want us to know where their operation is located, and with some of the things that they've done, I can't blame them. Do you agree to this condition?"

Angela had to think about it for a minute. This was starting to turn into something out of a spy movie, but then what she was asking wasn't ordinary either. Tuesday, she had asked Janice if Glen could break into the computer system at the Chandler-Langtree Institute to find out information about what they're doing. She knew that Glen was a professional security consultant for several corporations in the area and did "ethical hacking" to test their firewalls and other security measures. When Janice had asked Glen about it, he had told her that he really didn't want to be involved in anything that wasn't strictly above board, since he had a reputation to uphold with his company. He did have friends in the business, though, that he felt might be willing to accommodate her request. They were four guys, seemingly an odd bunch of misfits calling themselves "The Protectors", but they were the best in the business when it came to breaking into computer systems. They didn't even work with computers as their main profession, they all had different jobs. Still, they felt like they were providing a service to keep corporations and even the government honest. They did what they did with the highest standards of ethics, not really viewing what they did as wrong at all. And they really were the best in the business. They had exposed around three different companies within the past year and got their CEO's and top board members brought up on conspiracy and embezzlement charges, all without ever exposing who they were. They worked in the shadows, and they liked it that way. Most of the time, their incursions were never even detected by the companies which they hacked, they were that good. On the few occasions that they were discovered, they made the incursions look like they came from Russia, China, or somewhere else equally as hard to trace. Part of it was knowing how to break into the systems, and the other part really was knowing how to cover their tracks to keep from being found out. Both had to work together, or they'd be out of business in no time.

"Yes," she said, "I agree to the condition."

Both girls walked with Glen over to the pickup spot on Hamilton Drive and waited. Within about ten minutes, a dark grey van drove up and stopped beside the curb in front of them. A guy who looked like he was in his late twenties or early thirties with dark brown hair and a moustache and beard got out and walked over to where they were standing. He was carrying a pizza delivery bag and wore a JJ's Pizza Parlor shirt and hat. Angela thought that maybe this wasn't their pickup after all.

"Did anyone here order a Pizza?" asked the man.

As Angela was about to reply "No", Glen replied, "Is it sausage and Canadian bacon?"

"Why yes," the man replied, "that'll be fifteen dollars."

"I only have thirteen." replied Glen.

The man motioned for them to follow him and he led them around to the side of the van and opened the door for them to get inside. After he had closed the door, he introduced himself to them.

"Sorry for all of the cloak and dagger stuff, but we can't be too careful. I'm Benjamin Franklin."

Angela looked over at Janice with a look that said, "Is he for real?"

Benjamin continued, "I trust you were told about our arrangement?"

"Yes, go ahead." replied Angela.

Since this was a cargo van with no windows, they had installed two bench seats along each wall. All of them sat down there now while Benjamin blindfolded them.

"I hope this isn't too uncomfortable." he said, "But we have to be careful. I'm glad that you understand."

Angela wasn't sure that she really did understand just yet, at least not completely. But if she had any possibility of finding out what she wanted to find out, this was the only way that she knew to do it.

After Benjamin had gotten into the driver's seat and they were underway, Glen whispered to the two girls, "That's another thing that I meant to tell you. They don't use their real names. They all go by the names of signers of the Declaration of Independence. They say that it makes a statement about their true mission. You'll get to meet John Hancock, Thomas Jefferson, and Samuel Adams when we get to their office."

It took longer than they had thought it would to get there. They didn't know exactly where they were going, but after a little over two hours, the van pulled into a parking garage and stopped. They were met in the garage by the others who led them inside. Their blindfolds weren't removed until they were inside the office.

After the blindfolds were removed, they looked around to discover that they were in a completely windowless room, possibly in a warehouse. It was fairly spacious, and wasn't at all cramped. Along one wall was a table containing several computers and printers. While all of the men looked to be around the same age, their appearances differed substantially. Thomas Jefferson was clean shaven, thin and tall with short black hair. John Hancock was blonde with just a moustache. Samuel Adams was short and stocky with long brown hair tied into a pony tail. They all introduced themselves and then got quickly to work.

"So you want to find out about the Chandler-Langtree Institute?" John Hancock asked.

"Yes", replied Angela.

"Whoa, that's really heavy!" said Samuel Adams.

"Not sure it can be done." said Thomas Jefferson.

"If it can be done, we're the ones that can do it!" retorted Benjamin Franklin, turning on the computer in front of him along with several banks of routers and other devices.

He began typing, while the others watched. He apparently was querying some information about Chandler-Langtree first, before actually trying to log into their system. After about forty minutes, the Chandler-Langtree login screen came up. Angela noticed at once that there was no place to put a login name or password.

"There's no place for a login name or password because Chandler-

Langtree uses biometric logons." explained Thomas, almost as if he could read her mind. "Still, these systems always have back doors; you just have to know where to look."

Benjamin clicked on a symbol in the lower right corner of the monitor, which sent the cursor to the upper left. He typed in a string of numbers and symbols, but that only beeped and cleared the screen. After about thirty more minutes of trying, he backed his chair away from the table and let out a loud sigh.

"This is not an easy system!" he remarked, "Their system is based on Digital Ventures' Scorpio 7, but they have a custom version of it."

"Does that mean that you can't get in?" asked Angela, a little worried now.

"Don't ever tell Benjamin that he CAN'T do anything!" said Samuel. "He'll go and do it just to prove you wrong!"

Not saying anything, Benjamin got up and walked over to the refrigerator that they kept in the corner of the room and pulled out a Root Beer. He popped the top, then came back over and sat down in front of the computer.

"Whoa, he's got his 'Brain Fuel' now!" said Samuel.

Benjamin took several large gulps of the root beer then set it down on the table beside the keyboard. He then proceeded with his attempts to gain access to the system. "He's definitely determined." Angela thought. Whether he could get in or not, he was certainly giving it his best shot. They all watched and waited, holding their breath, hoping each attempt would meet with success.

This was definitely taking longer than any of them had thought. They had met Benjamin at the student center around eight thirty, and after a two hour drive to wherever they were now, they had gotten started around eleven. It was now around three o'clock and Benjamin was still going at it. They had taken a short break to have some sandwiches that John had fixed for them, but other than that they had been working straight through.

After another thirty five minutes of attempts, Benjamin pushed his chair away from the computer and let out another loud sigh.

"I need to talk to the Squirrel!" he said.

The other three just sat and stared at him like he had antennas coming out of his head.

"Who's the Squirrel?" asked Angela.

"He's an older hacker," replied Glen, "practically put on a pedestal as a god by these guys. None of them have ever actually met him face to face, though; he only communicates by phone. "

Benjamin pulled the speaker phone over and dialed a number. Within a few seconds a man's voice came on the line.

"Hello, who is it?" the voice said. The voice seemed to be one of an older man, possibly in his late sixties or early seventies.

"It's Benjamin. We have a client that needs to get into Chandler-Langtree, and we're having a little trouble. I know the operating system is Scorpio 7, but their custom version doesn't seem to have any of the usual back doors."

"Who wants to get in?" asked the Squirrel.

"Her name's Angela. I'm not sure of her last name; I don't think she ever said."

"Nelson," she replied, "Angela Nelson."

There was a short silence on the line, and then the Squirrel came back on.

"Give her whatever she wants. She might be able to help us."

The three of them exchanged curious glances. Did the Squirrel know Angela? It almost seemed that he did.

The Squirrel continued, "I've just sent you over a new protocol to use, along with some new parameters. Chandler-Langtree has taken out most of the traditional back doors, but the system still has its vulnerabilities. Use the gateway and subnet that I just sent over, as well as the new encryption keys. Change the port to 4444 as well. That should do it."

The Squirrel hung up the phone, and Benjamin retrieved the parameters that he had sent over.

"Whoa dude! We'd have never figured that out!" remarked Samuel looking over Benjamin's shoulder at the computer screen. To Angela and the rest, the data on the screen just looked like a bunch of gibberish. But to Benjamin and the others, they seemed really excited by what they were seeing. Benjamin began typing away at the keyboard again, and while it wasn't easy, within twenty minutes he was into their system. Everyone in the room watched intently as he began to traverse the various menus, looking for anything that might be of interest.

As they all went through the various menus, they found Mark's name under Project Spatial Juncture. They went into Mark's section and discovered that he had actually been hired as Vice President for Temporal Research. Organizationally, he was right under Dr. Langtree! That fact definitely surprised Angela, but it did help to explain the office and car. They went into more of the project material and found that Chandler-Langtree actually was experimenting with using something called ripples to open a doorway in time. Benjamin pressed a button on the keyboard and began downloading the documents from that section. This would provide interesting reading material for later.

"Look," said Angela excitedly, "there's a tab labeled Green Island! Go into that one!"

Benjamin clicked on the Green Island tab and a new screen with various sections containing different pictures appeared. They were immediately drawn to a square containing the words "Green Island Light Station Temporal Field Monitor", which Benjamin proceeded to click on. It appeared to be a map of the section of Green Island around the lighthouse. A colorful donut shape surrounded the lighthouse, pulsing and rippling.

Thomas peered at the screen, moved closer to get a better look and then remarked almost in a whisper, "Could that really be what I think it is?"

"I think it is!" said Samuel.

"Is that the temporal field?" asked Angela. They all looked her way as if to ask how she could possibly know that. As if realizing what they were all thinking, she answered, "Mark actually told me about it last weekend when we went to the beach."

That fact surprised them even more. Nobody at Chandler-Langtree ever told anyone on the outside what was going on there. That would be considered a major breach of protocol.

"He told you?!" asked Thomas.

"Yes." she replied, "I don't think he really wanted to, and I don't think he was supposed to, but he trusts me."

They all continued to stare at the temporal field on the monitor. This was probably the most exciting thing that they had ever hacked! This wasn't just the usual corruption and embezzlement that they usually uncover. This was pure science fiction!

They went into other tabs within Project Spatial Juncture as well and downloaded documents from each one. They wanted to try to stay in the system for as little time as possible, since the longer they were connected the greater the chance of being found out. After downloading all of the documents that looked to be interesting they got out of the Project Spatial Juncture tab.

"We should probably get out now." said Samuel, "I think we've probably been into the system long enough."

"Wait a minute!" remarked Glen, "What's that one?"

He was referring to a button labeled "Project Vortex Elimination".

"Go into that one!"

Benjamin clicked on the button and got an "Access Denied"

message. This made him even more determined. There must be something there if it had extra security over and beyond what was required to get into the main system. The back door that the Squirrel had given him should be one of the higher levels of security. He tabbed out of that screen and went to another screen. On this screen, he started entering different levels of security. He was trying different combinations to grant himself super user credentials! Finally after a few minutes of adjusting the security settings, he tabbed back to the screen and clicked on the "Project Vortex Elimination" button again. This time he met with success and was into the project. Benjamin got into the first folder and they began reading the purpose of the project.

"October 14, 2164 - After careful consideration among members of "The Committee" it has been decided that the Vortex Accelerator must be eliminated. With the security around the Accelerator the chance of success in this time period is deemed to be remote. Our best chance of success is to travel back to the year 2016 and see that the Vortex Accelerator is never built."

"Whoa duuude!" said Samuel, drawing out the word dude and trailing it off, "Does that mean they've actually travelled to the year 2164?!"

"I think it means they've travelled FROM the year 2164!" replied Benjamin.

"I'm confused." said Angela hesitantly.

Benjamin answered her, "I think this may just mean that your Dr. Langtree isn't from this time. If what this says is true, he may just be from the year 2164! Possibly Dr. Chandler as well!"

"Wait!" exclaimed Angela excitedly as she noticed something else on the screen, "What's this tab?"

There was a section of tabs labeled "Major Participants". One of the tabs read "Daniel Allen Nelson".

Benjamin clicked on the tab and several documents came up.

"Who are these people?!" Angela exclaimed, "The one picture is definitely my father, but who are these others? This other picture does say Danny, but that picture is NOT of my brother!"

On the page that she was looking at was a picture labeled, "Daniel Allen Nelson", another one labeled "Katherine Amanda Miller", another labeled "Daniel Allen Nelson, Jr. (Danny)", and the last one labeled "Amy Kathleen Nelson".

"I don't understand! Why is my dad on this page with people that I don't even know? And according to the caption they're supposed to be his family?! What's going on here? What does this mean?"

Thomas had an idea, but he didn't know quite how to explain it.

He whispered to John who was sitting next to him quietly enough so the others couldn't hear, "Do you think they might have already altered the past?"

John thought about what Thomas had just said, stared at the pictures on the screen again, then replied, "Yeah, it looks like that really might be what's happened here."

CHAPTER 9
October 13,2018
Confusing Information

Angela had gotten back to her room fairly late the previous evening. After they had discovered the section on Project Vortex Elimination, Benjamin had downloaded everything that he could reasonably download from that section in the short time that they had that night. He had copied everything that they had downloaded onto mini DVDs, giving one to Angela and keeping another for their group. They had definitely run across something totally unexpected, even for Chandler-Langtree. But deciding what it all meant was a different matter altogether. They had come across a journal entry that was dated October 14, 2164, but what exactly did that mean? Were Dr. Langtree and Dr. Chandler really from the year 2164? And if they were, then exactly why had they come here to 2016? The journal entry had said something about having a better chance of eliminating the Vortex Accelerator in 2016, but what was involved in doing that exactly? Also, what was the Vortex Accelerator and why were they trying to eliminate it? And more importantly to Angela, why did they seem to need Mark so much? How did he fit into their plan?

She woke up and rolled over in bed looking at the clock radio and discovered that it was already 11:18 am. This was definitely longer than she usually slept, even on a Saturday. Mark was working today and in a way she was glad. She wanted time to study what they had found yesterday before talking to him about it. Actually, she wasn't sure exactly how she would talk to him about it. How would she tell him that she had broken into the Chandler-Langtree computer system and found classified information that possibly he didn't even know? He'd think she didn't trust him, but it wasn't really that. She was just worried about him and what he might be getting into. Still, he'd want to know who had helped her do it, since he'd know she couldn't do it alone. And she didn't want to give away anything about The Protectors, even though she actually wasn't sure she even knew enough to give them away. She didn't know where they all had gone the day before, since they were blindfolded and the van obviously didn't take a direct route. The Protectors didn't use their real names and nothing that they had said even gave her any kind of clue as to who they really were. For all she knew, even their appearance may have been disguised.

Getting out of bed, she slowly walked over to her desk by the window and opened the shades. The warm sunlight shone through the window giving the impression that it was warmer out than it really was. She sat down and opened the folder that Benjamin had given her the night before and took out the DVD. Booting up her computer and putting in the DVD, she scanned through several documents, printing out a few, including the one with the picture of her dad and the other three people. She stared at the picture of her dad, along with the other people that were supposed to be his family. She just couldn't figure exactly how that all fit. She continued looking through some of the other pages shown on the screen. They were laid out like a journal with entries on several days, she supposed either written by Dr. Langtree or Dr. Chandler. The first date was March 13, 2016, and she read the entry for that date:

Dan's truck just drove past the lighthouse. I don't think that he saw it, since the trees and brush are so thick at this part of the island. He won't go much further, though, since the road runs out about 100 feet down from here. It's been a few minutes now, and I can hear him coming through the woods. He's walking out to the lighthouse now and going up the steps. I'm going to try to get to a better position to see what he's doing. He's inside the house now. I'm making my way around front, still at the edge of the woods to avoid him seeing me. He's been inside for a few minutes now, and I'm not sure what he's doing. I guess he's looking around examining the interior. He just came out the front door and is overlooking the water. He's walking around the outside now through the tall grass, apparently looking over the lighthouse from all sides. I've moved around the side of the house to avoid him seeing me. Now he appears to be making his way back to the road. He's probably going back to find a place to stay. I'll follow him and see where he goes. I suspect he'll go to the Harbor Inn, since that's the closest place to stay.

She sat for a few minutes, just staring at this paragraph. From the choppiness of it she guessed that it had been transcribed from a voice recording. She was trying to think back to what her dad would have been doing on March 13, 2016. She had been here in Wilmington at school, she was pretty sure of that. And she thought that her dad was probably back at home at work as well. She couldn't think of any reason that he'd be out at the lighthouse then, but since her grandparents did live on Green Island, she supposed that it could have been possible. There were some pictures that accompanied the entry as well, and those pictures brought up even more questions. In one, Dan was standing on the steps of the lighthouse. While the features of the structure did appear to be the Green Island Light Station, in all of the photos the lighthouse was in ruins, practically falling down. There were huge, gaping holes in the side where the bricks had fallen out, and vines had pretty much grown over everything. The roof was missing along most of the exterior as well. It looked like it had been abandoned for decades. The problem was that she never remembered the lighthouse ever being in that state of disrepair. It had always been well cared for, since the light had been lit pretty much consistently for the last hundred and fifty years! She remembered that they had visited the island for Easter that year, which had been on March 27. The lighthouse had been in perfect condition then, because she remembered going out to it that morning and attending a sunrise service organized by Reverend Anderson from the First Baptist Church. They had chairs set up on the front lawn of the lighthouse overlooking the Cape Fear River. There had been a light mist in the air that morning and as the sun's rays shone through the trees, it had made the perfect setting to sing praises and declare the glory of the Lord and of his Resurrection!

So where did these pictures come from? That was also part of the mystery, and the more that she read, and the more pictures that she viewed, the more that nothing seemed to make sense.

As she read on, she came to another journal entry from April 14, 2016. In this one, apparently her dad and his "family" were at a book signing at the Little Book Nook. There were several photos of them together at the signing, along with other photos of the author, Amy Davenport Westfall. How exactly she fit into this story wasn't completely clear yet, but obviously she was important since a portion of this entry read:

Dan and his family are at the Little Book Nook for the book signing tonight. Dan still doesn't have any idea who Amy is … They're all meeting at Amy's table now. I don't think that she'll reveal to him who she is just yet, she needs to wait for the right time.

All of this is cryptic, with an air of mystery, made even more mysterious because of the fact that she has no idea who any of them are except for her dad. How he can possibly be in all of these pictures puzzles her even more. Reading through each of these journal entries really is like reading a fiction novel, since none of this makes any sense to her. But the pictures make it not fiction. They couldn't possibly exist, except that they do.

She continues to read the entries, and the story gets even more fascinating! She discovers that Amy Davenport Westfall is actually her father's daughter who, after getting caught in a fog that frequently came up around the lighthouse, went back to 1986, only to be reunited here on the island thirty years later. She read about the search for Amy and her friend Veronica, who were both thirteen at the time. Then she came to Dr. Chandler's meeting with her dad, which apparently took place out on the boardwalk by the beach. Dr. Chandler had told him everything. Apparently the Vortex Accelerator had been built sometime before the year 2164 and had enabled time travel back to this time period. Dr. Chandler and Dr. Langtree had arrived and had started the Chandler-Langtree Institute. According to what she was reading, they started the Institute to find a way to eliminate the Vortex Accelerator, since apparently it had been greatly misused in their time and had gotten into corrupt hands that had used it for their own benefit at the expense of the greater population. Her father was part of that plan as well, though apparently he didn't know it now.

While she still didn't understand everything, apparently her father ran a company called Perihelion Research Group which actually built the Vortex Accelerator in the future and the lighthouse had been central to that project. They had a plan, which apparently her father had been a part of, willingly at that point, to transfer ownership of the lighthouse from Perihelion to the Lighthouse Preservation Society, and supposedly that would keep the Vortex Accelerator from ever being built.

But all of this didn't make sense at all. How could her dad have bought the lighthouse, since as far as she knew, it had never been for sale? While Dan did grow up in Cincinnati, after marrying her mother, they had moved to Greenville, NC and started Nelson Internet Technology. While it was a large company, one of the largest in North Carolina, it still wasn't the huge government contractor that she was reading about in the Chandler-Langtree notes. The more that she read, the more confused she became, since all of this was like pure fiction. It was like they were referring to an alternate reality, different than the one that she now lived in with her parents and brother and sister.

She finally put everything back in the folder, including the DVD and all of the pages that she had printed, and closed it up. She just sat at the desk for a few minutes staring out the window, completely lost in thought. While it wasn't the same thing, the feelings that she was having right now seemed very similar to just finding out that your father had another family in another state and was living a double life. It was all very unsettling, and she felt that her life had just been turned upside down. But was any of this information that she had just read really true? What gave it more credibility in her mind was the fact that she knew that Mark was working on accomplishing time travel using the temporal field on the island. But still, it all seemed so impossible.

Looking at the clock, she determined that it was already three fifteen in the afternoon. She had been at this for almost four hours! No wonder she was getting a little hungry. She needed to talk with someone as well. She wanted to make sense out of all of this, but she didn't see how she would on her own. But this was something that she couldn't talk to Mark about, at least not yet. She didn't think he'd understand about her breaking into the computer system at Chandler-Langtree, and they had probably gotten in and out undetected. She didn't want to draw attention to The Protectors.

She finally decided to call Janice and see if she wanted to get some lunch. Janice had been with them the night before, so she could talk to Janice about what she'd been reading. She hit Janice's speed dial on her phone.

"Hey, Angela, what's up?"

"Have you had lunch yet?" Angela asked.

"No, I was wondering what I was going to do. Glen has a big project going on, so I probably won't see him until tomorrow."

"Meet me at the student center? I need to talk."

"OK, anything serious?"

"It's the stuff we downloaded last night. I've been reading through it and it's just not making any sense. I need to get another opinion."

"OK, I can be there in about twenty minutes."

"Sounds good, see you then!"

In about twenty minutes, just as Janice had said, they met at the student center for lunch. Janice ordered a hamburger and Angela got her usual chicken fingers. They walked outside and got a table overlooking the lake. Angela had stuffed a few of the pictures into a folder and brought them with her. She now opened the folder and retrieved a couple of them, which she pushed over to Janice.

"Here are some pictures that I found in the file that was accompanying the journal entries. This one's at a book signing on Green Island at the Little Book Nook. This is obviously dad, but I just don't know who these other people are. It's supposed to be his wife, Kate, and their kids Danny and Amy. The date is April 14, 2016. I remember April of 2016, and I don't remember dad going to the Little Book Nook. I don't even remember him going down to the island in April of that year. He usually calls me and we meet, since Green Island's not that far from here. The story actually gets even stranger. According to what I read, dad was part of a project to eliminate something called the Vortex Accelerator which was built around 2164 by dad's company, which apparently was a different company than he owns now. Some men, Dr. Langtree and Dr. Chandler, traveled from 2164 to 2016 to eliminate the Vortex Accelerator by making it so that dad never owned it. This information seems to show that dad had another family prior to May 20, 2016, the family pictured here. After 2:00 pm on that date, everything changed and we were his new family; mom, me, Danny, and Rebekah. But I'm just having a hard time understanding how that can possibly be. I actually have memories of our current family that go back years before that date."

"Of course you do! Those are your memories of what actually happened. Your memories are not suddenly going to start from 2016!"

"But what about what the journal says; and what about Dr. Langtree and Dr. Chandler being from 2164? I know that's what it says, but I'm having a hard time believing that. That can't happen, right?"

"You really have to ask?! Of course that can't happen!"

"But as I'm reading through the pages, there's a lot in there that really can't happen. Those pictures of dad, for example."

"There has to be a logical explanation." replied Janice.

"But what is it? And where did these pictures come from?" asked Angela.

"The pictures have to be fakes." said Janice.

"What?"

"They're fakes. They have to be."

"How can you be sure they're fakes?" asked Angela, slightly perplexed.

"Because that's not your dad's family." she said matter-of-factly. "Do you have a sister named Amy? And while you do have a brother named Danny, I've met him and this picture is definitely not him. I really can't believe that his family just "changed" on May 20! Look at what you know to be true, and the only conclusion is that all of these pictures are fakes. The story has to be made up too, even though I can't quite figure what anyone would have to gain from it."

"I can't figure why either. None of this information has been made public. It was all in a highly secured private file. What could anyone possibly gain by creating a story like this?"

"I don't have all of the answers. All that I know is that when you examine what you know to be true, then anything else has to be false. As convincing as these pictures are, they have to be faked somehow, for some reason."

"Do you think I should show this information to Mark?" Angela inquired.

Janice seemed lost in thought for a few minutes, and then finally said, "No, I don't think I would just yet. Remember, he's part of Chandler-Langtree. He might not understand how you got that information. He might feel the need to let Dr. Langtree know about it, and you don't want that right now. Especially since we don't really know Dr. Langtree's motives, or if he's the one behind faking this information. Next weekend is Parents' Weekend. Are your parents coming?"

"Yes, they're planning to."

"Talk this over with your dad then. Show him the pictures. He's in them, so if they're legitimate then he'll remember when they were taken and the circumstances around them. If he doesn't remember any of them, then they're obviously fakes. In any case, talking to him is what you should do."

"You're right. That's what I'll do! Thanks Janice, you always know the right answer for what should be done."

They finished up their meal with lighter conversation after that. While Angela was still confused about what she had read and the pictures that she had seen, she at least felt better after talking to Janice. And her parents would be arriving on Friday. She could talk to her dad then.

As she walked back toward her dorm room, still lost in thought about the conversation that she'd just had with Janice, her cell phone rang. Pulling it out of her pocket, she immediately saw that it was Mark. Hesitantly, she hit the answer button on the touch screen.

"Hello beautiful!" Mark said cheerfully, "I finished up at the office early. How about dinner and a movie?"

While she had been thinking about him and actually did want to see him, with the information that she had found out, and with how she had obtained it, she found talking to him a little awkward. While she did want to know what was going on, she possibly was feeling a little guilty about what she had done, especially knowing what Mark would think if he found out. A part of her even wished that she could go back to the way things were before she had seen the information, but she knew that she'd do the same thing again if given the chance.

"That sounds wonderful!" she said, trying to sound as casual and normal as possible, but having a slight quiver to her voice nonetheless. She hoped that Mark hadn't picked up on this, but he actually knew her too well.

"Is anything wrong?" he inquired, "You sound like something's bothering you?"

"No, I'm fine. Maybe dinner and a movie is just what I need."

In fact, that did turn out to be just what she needed. He picked her up later that evening and by the time that they had arrived at Luigi's Italian Bistro she had almost put the documents that she had been reading during the morning and the conversation with Janice that afternoon out of her mind, at least for the moment. She was simply letting herself enjoy the time that she was having with Mark, which she truly did enjoy. Mark actually seemed to be in a particularly good mood today. Lately he had been working a lot and seemed somewhat stressed and a little distant, even with her. But today, he was more like the old Mark that she had known before he went to work for Chandler-Langtree. After dinner, he let her pick the movie, which turned out to be a romance. While he pretended to really want an action adventure, secretly he enjoyed the romances, especially when he watched them with her.

Later that night, she was studying in Mark's apartment, while he relaxed with a good book. He made up a batch of his famous spinach dip, and then brought out the chips for them to enjoy a snack. It reminded her of the perfect evenings that she and Mark used to enjoy when they first met. But even in the midst of enjoying such a perfect evening, her thoughts returned back to what they had found out yesterday and also of reading through the notes from Chandler-Langtree this morning.

"How much do you really know about Dr. Langtree?" she asked.

"What? What made you think of Dr. Langtree now?"

"I don't know exactly. Do you know where he's from? What made him and Dr. Chandler start the Institute? Do you know exactly why he hired you?"

"Why all the questions?" he asked, starting to sound a little irritated and bewildered, "You're not thinking there's some sort of conspiracy going on out there again are you? I probably shouldn't have told you about the temporal field. At the time, I thought that it would ease your mind a little, but I really should have known better. I think I know what I'm there for, but I can't really say a lot more than that. As for Dr. Langtree, actually I don't know a lot about him. I'm pretty sure that he and Dr. Chandler started the Institute for temporal research, but beyond that I really don't know a lot more."

She really wanted to ask him about some of the things that she had read from the Chandler-Langtree notes that they had downloaded the night before, especially the part about Dr. Langtree possibly being from 2164, but in the end she thought better of it. Maybe there'll come a time that she can discuss this with him, but not yet. Right now, she knew that it was best that he not know about what they had done.

CHAPTER 10
October 19, 2018
The Journey

Dan and his family started out around eleven in the morning for the two and a half hour drive to Wilmington. They'd be staying in Wilmington for Parents' Weekend, then Sunday night drive down to Green Island and stay the following week with Dianne's parents. It seemed to be a perfectly normal weekend with the morning slightly cool at fifty eight degrees, and the forecast for the day being sunny and clear. It was really one of those picture perfect autumn days in the eastern part of North Carolina.

Still, even though the morning seemed to start out normal enough, Dan felt that there was something not quite right. He really couldn't think of any reason to feel that way; nothing had happened that would cause it, yet he couldn't shake it off. As he thought about it more though, he thought that it might have something to do with his conversation with Angela last night.

Their conversation on the surface had seemed pleasant enough, but there was a hint of apprehension in her voice that left him feeling that something was bothering her. It wasn't even anything that she had said, more the way that her voice had sounded. Thinking back over the last week, he thought that she hadn't sounded completely normal then either, he had just failed to notice. He couldn't even think of what it could possibly be; as far as he knew, things were still going well with her new boyfriend Mark.

He actually liked Mark. They had only met one time a couple of months ago, but he had seemed really nice, and Dan had liked him immediately. His field of study, theoretical physics, was a little strange to him, though. Dan felt that he was fairly intelligent, since he had started his own technology company, but even with that he didn't completely understand what theoretical physics was. Mark had tried to explain it, but Mark's explanation confused him even more. It seemed to him that Mark was majoring in things that couldn't possibly exist; things like wormholes, black hole thermodynamics, dark matter, quantum field theory, even temporal field theory, which stated that even time is not absolute, but can possibly be altered. Mark explained it simply that all of these things really do exist; they just don't lend themselves to traditional experimentation. In the absence of being able to directly experiment on these objects, theoretical physics uses mathematical models and theories to prove the possibility of their existence and predict their behavior.

Even though he was studying abstract theories, Dan was impressed with Mark's intelligence, and felt that he was a genuinely likeable person as well. He certainly seemed to be good for Angela. She hadn't been able to stop talking about him. He really hoped that nothing had happened between them.

As he thought about it some more, though, he felt that her strange tone could possibly be because she was going to meet Mark's parents for the first time this weekend. She had mentioned meeting them during one of the last times that they had talked, and she was a little nervous about it. They lived a lot further away than Dan and Dianne, so they hadn't visited the college since Mark and Angela had been dating. That definitely could be the reason, since meeting your boyfriend's parents for the first time can be stressful. You want everything to go just right, and for them to like you. After all, most parents have high expectations for anyone that their son would be dating, and she definitely wanted to live up to those expectations. Dan convinced himself that this was probably the reason, even though deep down he didn't know if he really believed that or not. And he didn't know if his own feelings were only because of his conversations with Angela, or if there was something else behind them.

They all finished packing up the van and going through the house to make sure that they hadn't forgotten anything, then Danny and Rebekah climbed into the back seats for the ride. They were both looking forward to the trip. Danny was seventeen and liked going down to UNC Wilmington since he'd be starting there next year. It would give him a chance to check out the campus again and experience a little bit of college life. While Rebekah wouldn't be starting college quite as soon, she still enjoyed going down and just hanging out with her older sister. Even though there was five years difference in their ages, they looked almost like twins, with Angela being just a little bit taller, but both having long brown hair, like their mother. Dan locked up the house, then he and Dianne got into the van and they proceeded to exit the circular drive and get on highway 13 to Snow Hill. From there, they'd get on Highway 903 which would take them all the way to Interstate 40, and from there, Interstate 40 would go the rest of the way to Wilmington.

While it had been sunny when they left Greenville, the further they got down Highway 13, the more overcast the day became. About thirty miles the other side of Snow Hill, a light rain started falling which became steadier the further they went. Dianne was reading a book on her Kindle, while Danny was playing a game on his phone and Rebekah was listening to music with her headphones. With the regular clip clip sound of the windshield wipers, and the steady drumming of the rain on the van's roof, Dan's mind began to wander. He thought back to the night in May over two years ago when the big storm came up on Green Island while they were there for the lighthouse dedication. He remembered the image that Joe had showed him at the hotel, of the satellite view of the island with the lighthouse encircled by a bright ring of lightning.

As Dan continued to remember that day, over two years ago, he found himself back there again, at the lighthouse dedication. He was at the top of the lighthouse looking out over the island. Dianne was there along with Danny and Rebekah. President Henderson was there as well, along with his son and the First Lady. They were all together at the top of the lighthouse, all lost in the moment, just enjoying the view. He put his arm around Dianne's shoulder and pulled her close to him. As they stood along the railing surrounding the lantern house, Dan noticed a slight wisp of fog over near the woods. Within minutes, the small wisp became a dense fog which totally encircled the four foot high rock wall surrounding the lighthouse. As clouds moved overhead and covered the sun, he felt the air get a lot cooler. Suddenly everyone that had been with him at the top of the lighthouse was gone, as if the growing fog had reached out and taken them! He looked around frantically calling for Dianne, but nobody answered. He quickly descended the circular stairway, and ran outside.

"Dianne! Danny! Rebekah! Where are you? Is anyone here?!" He ran toward the fog at the edge of the woods, but suddenly stopped in his tracks. Something felt different. He didn't feel the presence of all of the people that had been around him earlier. Everything seemed lonely and desolate, and it seemed to be getting darker as well. Lightning flashed from the clouds above. As he looked up, a bright flash of lightning temporarily blinded him as it arced between a circular cloud and the edge of the fog. He slowly turned around to look back at the lighthouse and was completely horrified at the sight before him. The lighthouse was totally and completely in ruins! The back wall of the structure was almost completely gone and vines and weeds were growing up around what was left. There was no roof on the house any longer, only remains of rotted wood timbers that had once held the roof. The lantern house was leaning as if almost ready to topple off of its foundation. As he stared at the sight before him, his gaze totally transfixed at this scene which couldn't possibly be in front of him, he heard a voice coming from the fog. He spun around wildly, staring into the abyss. The voice, further away at first, but now getting closer was a woman's voice. She was calling his name.

"Dan! Dan! Where are you? Are you here?"

She kept repeating this over and over as she came closer and closer. Suddenly, he saw a shadow seeming to come out of the fog. As he stared at this figure, running toward him now, calling his name, he saw that it was a beautiful blonde haired woman wearing a red blouse and tan pants. Her long flowing hair blew in the wind as she ran toward him and embraced him.

"Dan!" she said, "Where have you been? I thought I had lost you!"

"Kate." he whispered, wondering again where that name came from. He felt that she was someone that he knew, and from their embrace, obviously she knew him, but from where? So far as he could remember, he had never actually known anyone named Kate. As they stood, held in each other's arms, she moved her head back and stared into his eyes.

"I've missed you." she said, "I didn't know where you had gone."

Dan was speechless. What could he say? As they stood motionless, staring into each other's eyes, a cold rain began to fall. As the rain washed over them, and the sound of the rain echoed through the trees and the grass, the sound of the rain began to change.

Suddenly, everything changed. He was back in the van driving down Highway 903, with the sound of the rain on the roof and the familiar clip clip of the windshield wipers. He looked over at Dianne and she was still reading her Kindle, while the kids were still in the back seat with their phones and music. Nothing had changed, yet he had to wonder what had just happened. What he remembered about the last few minutes was not like a dream, but like a vivid memory. The woman that he had just held in his arms was the same one from his dream that he had two years ago, he was sure of that. But as much as he tried, he just couldn't think of who she was. Yet he had called her Kate! Why had he done that? He vaguely remembered whispering "Kate" two years ago as well, but he still couldn't remember where they may have met. Gradually, he began to come out of the daze that he had been in only to feel more and more confused.

By the time that they got to the intersection of 903 and Interstate 40, the rain had almost stopped, and the further that they went on 40 toward Wilmington, the clouds began to become thinner and the sun started to poke through in places as well. As they went even further and pulled into the parking lot of the Davenport Inn, the clouds had almost vanished and it was back to being a beautiful sunny day.

The Davenport Inn was their favorite place to stay when they came to Wilmington. It was a little over a mile from the university, so it was convenient for any of the activities going on there, and it was always kept up well. Dan parked the van under the entranceway and they all got out and stretched their legs. While two and a half hours wasn't an incredibly long drive, still it was nice to finally get out and get some fresh air. They walked into the lobby, and while Dan checked in, the rest of the family found a luggage cart and proceeded to unload the van. He was happy to see Patrick behind the front desk today. Since they were regulars at the hotel, they had gotten to know several of the staff fairly well and Patrick was one of their favorites.

"Good afternoon, Mr. Nelson. I guess you're here for Parents' Weekend." greeted Patrick.

"Yes we are. Good to see you again, Patrick. Do you have our usual suite?"

"Of course, I've kept it just for you!"

As Dan was finishing up the check in process, Danny came through the front door pulling the luggage cart, with his mom and Rebekah following closely behind. As they took the elevator to the fourth floor, and unlocked the door to their favorite suite, it was almost like coming home. Any time that they visited the hotel, they tried to get the same corner suite. The corner suites were the largest, and they all liked to be able to spread out without getting in each other's way. Even with the two queen beds, they all had enough room. Usually Danny had the second bed all to himself, since Rebekah preferred to stay with Angela in her dorm room, and she had talked her sister into doing that this time as well.

After everything was taken to their room, Dianne called Angela to let her know that they had arrived as they headed downstairs. Most of the time, it didn't take more than about ten minutes to get from the hotel to Angela's dorm room, but today, being the start of Parents' Weekend, there was more traffic on the roads around the university, so it took a little longer.

As they pulled into a parking space near the dorm and started down the walkway, Angela ran out to greet them. Dan was glad to see her excitement and see that she seemed more like her old self today. After some of the conversations last week, he honestly hadn't known what to expect.

"We haven't eaten yet." said Dan, "How about let's go down to Rafferty's On The Boardwalk and get something?"

They all agreed that was a good idea, so they piled into the van for the drive down to the ocean. Seeing Angela had almost made Dan forget about the episode earlier on the trip down here, and he was back to his old self as well. Apparently Dianne or the kids hadn't noticed anything at all unusual about his behavior, or if they did, they hadn't said anything.

Even though it was a little cool this afternoon, they chose to eat outside on the deck. Apparently they weren't the only ones with that idea today, since the outdoor deck seemed almost as crowded as it was inside. They chose a table on the deck overlooking the ocean where they could feel the cool salt air blowing in and hear the surf as it crashed into the beach below. Rafferty's was a favorite restaurant and all of them had their favorite dishes there. Dan got the ribs, Dianne usually had the fish and chips dinner, Danny and Rebekah both liked the burgers and fries, while Angela got the fried shrimp. The server came by with their drinks, took their order, then they all just sat and enjoyed the view of the ocean while they talked. After a few minutes, their lunch arrived, and while they were eating it Dan noticed that Angela had gotten quieter than usual, like something was bothering her again. She hadn't seemed that way when they had first met at her dorm, but now she quietly sat and ate her shrimp, while the other kids talked and laughed.

"Is something wrong?" Dan finally asked her.

She looked up and just stared out at the ocean for a minute.

"Do you remember if anything happened two years ago when you, mom, Danny and Rebekah went down to Green Island for the lighthouse dedication?"

The question actually surprised him, and for a moment brought back memories of the lovely blonde woman who came out of the fog. It was funny that he hadn't thought about her at all in the last two years since that night, but just this afternoon had the most vivid and strange vision of her. And now, Angela was asking about that night. He had to wonder why she was bringing that up now, and what even made her bring it up. He didn't remember ever really talking to her about it.

She continued, "Do you remember if anything strange happened?"

When she said this he immediately thought of the storm, and of the satellite picture of the ring of lightning around the lighthouse. And then he remembered the man standing across the street in the pouring rain. He and his mother-in-law had both seen him, which made it too much of a coincidence to just dismiss. And the feeling that he had that something wasn't quite right even though everything had seemed perfectly normal. Yes, the more he thought about it, the whole weekend had been strange.

He had even thought that he saw the blonde woman at the Harbor Inn the day after the storm, but she had disappeared before he had gotten a chance to talk to her.

"What made you think of that now?" he asked, sounding a little puzzled, but also a little concerned.

"There's something that I need to talk to you about later." she continued, "Something that I discovered recently that doesn't make any sense to me."

At this both Danny and Rebekah glanced over her way a bit bewildered. This wasn't like Angela to get all mysterious on them, even though it was close to Halloween. Dianne even looked over at her as well.

"We can talk about it now if you want." offered her mother.

"No, I'd rather wait until later. I actually have something that I need to show dad."

She looked back over at her father, "But really, dad, what do you remember about that night?"

"Well, it was the worst storm that I had seen." he said, "It kept me up pretty much all night. I'm not really sure what could have caused a storm like that."

At this point, Dan paused, remembering the dream that he had that night, and the incident in the van this afternoon. He thought about whether he should mention that now, but decided not to.

"One of the stranger things that happened that night was that both your grandma and I thought we saw a man standing across the street in the pouring rain. It was at the worst part of the storm, so we didn't see how he could really be there, but it did seem so real. He was standing under the street light, so he was illuminated pretty well. The next day, we went over to the Harbor Inn where I met a storm spotter named Joe. They had taken a video outside of the hotel the night before and were showing it on a large screen behind their table. It was of the storm, and it was fascinating with all of the brilliant lightning. But the most unusual thing was a photo that one of their guys printed off from the National Weather Service feed of a satellite view of the island during the storm. There was almost a perfect circle of lightning around the lighthouse.”

At the mention of this, Angela swallowed hard, remembering the circular ring around the lighthouse that she had seen on the Green Island Light Station Temporal Field Monitor. She thought about how the colorful ring had pulsed and rippled almost as if it had a life of its own. The connection between the temporal field and the lightning seemed too coincidental to her.

Dan had noticed her shudder when he mentioned the circle of lightning. “What’s wrong?” he inquired.

“Mentioning the lightning just brought back a memory.” she said, a slight quiver in her voice now, “Can we talk when we get back to the university?”

“Of course.” he said, becoming even more concerned.

They finished up their conversation and, after lunch, they all decided that they’d go for a walk along the beach. They’d have the rest of the day just for their family, since Angela didn’t think that Mark’s parents were flying in until later that night. The walk along the beach in the cool salt air seemed to relax all of them, especially Angela. The serious mood that she had over lunch gave way to a more pleasant, playful demeanor. They were all together now and enjoying just being outside and being a family. They were so lost in the moment though, that none of them even noticed the man who was following them from a distance. He kept enough space between them that they wouldn’t notice him, but he was watching them nonetheless, contemplating what he should do next. Another storm was coming, and he could only hope that it wasn’t too late.

CHAPTER 11

A Day to Remember

When they arrived back at campus, Angela went up to her dorm room to retrieve the papers that she wanted to show her father. Dianne wanted to give Dan and Angela some time alone together, so she decided to take Danny and Rebekah shopping at the mall. While she didn't know exactly what was going on, she did pick up on the fact that Angela seemed to want to talk with her father alone about what was bothering her. She realized that sometimes things did come up in life that just needed father-daughter interaction.

After Dianne had left with the other two kids, Dan and Angela walked over to the student center to talk. Angela always enjoyed the patio surrounding the student center overlooking the fountain. Sometimes she'd even go upstairs to the second level and study at one of the tables outside on the balcony. From the second level, she got an even better view of the fountain and area around the student center. She decided to take her dad up there today, since it was a nice afternoon for being outside and she did enjoy the view.

After they got to the second level and selected a table, neither of them knew exactly how to begin. Since Angela obviously had something on her mind, Dan waited for her to start. She fidgeted for a couple of minutes, her hand resting on top of the folder that she had placed on the table. Finally, she began.

"Dad, how much do you know about the Chandler-Langtree Institute?"

This wasn't exactly how he had expected the conversation to start since he really didn't know anything about the company. He'd heard of them since they had been in the news about a year ago, but that was about as far as his knowledge about them went. From conversations that he'd had recently with Angela, he also knew that her boyfriend, Mark, had gotten an internship there. From just that fact alone, he felt that she probably should know more about the company than he did.

"Nothing really." he replied. "I've heard the name, and I seem to recall that they've been in the news, but that's about everything that I know. I really hadn't thought about them at all until you told me about Mark getting an internship there."

"So you've never worked with them on any projects?"

"No. Why would you think that I have?"

She opened the folder and withdrew one of the pages. She pushed it across the table to him.

He looked down at the paper that Angela had just placed in front of him, and for a moment found it hard to believe what he was seeing. He stared at all of the pictures on the page, but there was one in particular that he couldn't take his eyes off of. Slowly, he was able to look away from the page and meet Angela's gaze, and the look that she now saw on his face was one of startled disbelief. She had never seen this exact look from her father before now. From his reaction, she could tell that he had obviously recognized someone on that page other than himself.

"Dad, are you alright?"

"Where did this come from?" he asked in almost a whisper.

She wasn't sure if she should tell him or not, but the more that she thought about it, she felt that she really had no choice now.

"I've been worried about Mark and his job out at the Institute. I was afraid that he didn't know what he was getting into, and I needed to know that he was safe. My friend Janice put me in touch with some people that were able to break into the Chandler-Langtree computer system, and that's when we found this. Do you know these people?! The caption says that they're your family!"

"No." he replied abruptly, then was silent as he looked back down at the page. "Well … yes, in a way. But I can't really explain it."

"Have you ever worked with Chandler-Langtree?" she asked again.

"No, I've never had any contact with the company. That's what makes it so strange that you would find this in their system."

He became silent, as he looked down at the page again. Finally, he looked back up at her.

"I recognize the woman," he said, "Katherine Amanda Miller, but I can't explain from where. She goes by Kate. I haven't met her exactly, but the night of the big storm when we were on Green Island for the lighthouse dedication, I was awakened by the storm and remembered a dream where I was out at the lighthouse and a woman came out of the fog. She knew my name and I knew hers. We had a connection immediately and Kate was the name that just popped into my mind at that moment. The next day, while we were out at the Harbor Inn, I thought that I saw her again, but this time she disappeared into the elevator and I lost her. In retrospect, I'm not at all sure that was really her that I saw at the Harbor Inn, since I only saw her from behind. It could have just been a woman that reminded me of her. Still, until now I never knew her full name, so that's what makes this so strange."

He purposely left out the part about the vision that he had while they were on the way down here this afternoon. He wasn't sure exactly what had happened there, and he felt really uncomfortable telling anyone, even Angela. A dream at night was one thing, but a daytime vision while driving through a rainstorm was quite another. Especially one as vivid as that one had been.

"So you know her, but you don't remember ever meeting her?" inquired Angela, not fully understanding what was happening here either.

"I know it sounds really bizarre, but that's honestly all I know."

His mind was a total blur now, as he tried to separate reality from fiction. What had started out as a completely normal day had turned into something quite unexpected, and he felt that he needed time just to process this information. Suddenly here was an actual photo of the woman that he had previously only seen for certain in his dreams. He looked at the other people on the page as well. The first picture was definitely him, but the others he really didn't know, and didn't remember them even being in his dreams. He recognized Danny's name, but the photo was definitely not Danny.

"You need to read the complete story." Angela told him. "I'll let you take it with you to read in the hotel tonight. I think something happened on that day in May of 2016 that changed things, and I was hoping that you'd have an idea of what it was. From reading this information, it seems that those people are supposed to be your family, at least until May 20, 2016. After that, apparently mom, Danny, Rebekah and I became your family, but I'm not sure how that could even have happened since I remember our life before then! It talks about time travel, and I think that may have been what's happened here that's changed our reality. All of this has been completely unexpected and confusing. I wake up every morning thinking things are normal, then I remember all of this, and it's just too hard to understand."

Dan listened thoughtfully, then answered, "There has to be another explanation about what's happened here. It's definitely not time travel, I'm sure of that. But I really can't explain anything else either.

"How about these other pictures?" she asked him as she slid the others across the table. As he looked them over, shifting from one to the other, carefully studying the details in each one, he looked more perplexed than ever.

"I just don't remember any of these." he remarked. "And while this one looks like the front steps of the lighthouse, it's never looked this way. It's always been well kept up. And I've never even been to a book signing at the Little Book Nook. I don't remember Amy Davenport Westfall ever doing a book signing there, either. I've seen her picture on the cover of her books as well, and this photo doesn't even look like her. It definitely looks like me in these pictures, but I really never remember being in these places, especially not in these circumstances. I really can't understand how Chandler-Langtree got these, but I still think there's some kind of logical explanation."

"Mark told me that there's a temporal field out at the lighthouse. There's a picture of it back at my dorm room with the rest of the pictures that I printed out. That's why I seemed startled this afternoon out at Rafferty's when you mentioned the picture of the circle of lightning around the lighthouse. It made me think of the circular ring that's the temporal field and I wondered if there was a connection between the two."

"I think Mark might just be having a little fun with you." he replied, though he was starting to wonder. These pictures did come from somewhere, and they had been found in Chandler-Langtree's computer files.

"A time portal out at the lighthouse is not the logical explanation that I was referring to. Still, I have to admit; at this point I'm pretty confused about what the real explanation could possibly be!"

"If you think these pictures are confusing, wait until you actually read the rest of the story! It's like reading a fiction novel! It all takes place out at Green Island, but it's not the same Green Island that we know."

Now he was really wondering what was going on and he was a little concerned as well. He did have to wonder why the Chandler-Langtree Institute had pictures of him, especially pictures that he never remembered taking. The logical Dan reasoned that the pictures must have been altered to place him in them. But, if they had been altered, then why? Why would they go to the trouble to create fake pictures with him in them? And who were those other people that were supposed to be his family? As he reasoned through all of this, a phrase just popped into his mind for which he had no clue from where it came:

"Always consider the impossible."

But Dan had always been a down to earth, logical person. Considering the impossible just wasn't how he was wired. Everything had to have a logical explanation! Things only SEEMED impossible when you didn't know what was REALLY going on. Once you figured that out, then there was a LOGICAL explanation for everything. But why would he even consider that phrase now? It was like it suddenly surfaced from the deep recesses of his mind, almost not even being a conscious thought at all.

Could what Angela was telling him about the temporal field really be possible? Could there really be a doorway to another time period on Green Island? "Of course not!" he told himself, wondering why he was even stopping to consider it. But to his surprise, he really was stopping to consider it!

"Dad? What are you thinking?" asked Angela, "You were just staring into space."

"Oh, I was just pondering what we've been talking about. I know that I haven't been much help; I've got as many questions as you do, but at least we can figure this out together."

"You have been a big help, Dad! Just having someone to talk to about this is a big help. I haven't talked to Mark about any of this, though. He doesn't even know that I broke into the Institute's computer. I think he may be too close to Chandler-Langtree and especially Dr. Langtree. I'm not sure that he could be objective."

"I'm glad that I could be a help then. Don't worry, though. We'll figure this out, somehow."

Dan gathered all of the pictures and put them back into the folder that Angela had given him. He looked forward to reading it later. After seeing the pictures, he was really wondering what the story could possibly be. They went back inside and took the elevator down to the first floor, then walked outside. They'd been talking for quite a while now, so Dan called Dianne to see if she and the kids wanted to meet them at the student center for dinner. Dianne and the kids were actually just getting back from their shopping trip and all of them thought that would be a great idea.

As Dianne and the kids walked up to the student center, they saw Dan and Angela waiting for them right outside.

"Have a good talk?" she inquired of them.

"Yes, we did. It was good just visiting for the afternoon."

It really had been good just spending time together, even if the topic of conversation was a little strange. Since Angela was their oldest child, she had always had a special bond with her father. Even Dianne understood that when something was bothering Angela, she usually wanted her Dad, and that was alright. While Dan and Danny always spent the fun time together, it was his mom that he always went to for life's little emergencies, the same way that Angela went to Dan.

Once they had all gone inside and gotten their food, they sat down at one of the tables over by the large windows overlooking the fountain. While Dan and Angela had just finished a serious conversation, now that it was done they could both relax and enjoy themselves. The conversation was much lighter and more fun now, and they all caught themselves just laughing and having a good time as they ate. It was good just enjoying time together.

After dinner, they took a walk around campus. Since it was Parents' Weekend and the weather was nice, it was apparent that they weren't the only ones who had this idea. They passed numerous families that were having their son or daughter give them the grand tour of the campus. Once they had finished up the tour, Dan, Dianne and Danny decided to go back to the hotel and give Angela and Rebekah some girl time in her dorm. They knew that this time together was one of Rebekah's favorite parts of visiting her sister on campus, and Dan actually wanted to read some of the information that Angela had given him as well.

It was a little after nine when they got back to the hotel. Dianne had noticed the folder that Dan was carrying and asked him about it.

"It's just something that Angela gave me to read." he replied.

That seemed to satisfy her curiosity, at least for the moment. She'd lived with Dan long enough to know that he'd tell her all about it when he was ready.

When they got up to their room, Dianne and Danny decided to watch a movie that they found while channel hopping on TV. The suite was arranged so that they could move the TV so that it could either be watched from the beds or from the living room area. Since neither of them was really ready for bed yet, they decided to open the chips that they had brought with them and sit on the sofa to watch the movie. Normally, Dan would be in for a good movie himself, but after his talk with Angela this afternoon he was too interested in finding out what she had given him to read. He sat down in the chair next to the sofa, but quickly determined that the TV would be too distracting for his reading.

"I think I'll take this down to the lobby to read." he said as he got up out of the chair.

"Ok, see you in a little bit." they both said, not really looking away from the TV, since it was getting to a climactic moment and both of them were completely engrossed in the movie by now.

Dan took his room key, and then walked out into the hallway and down to the elevators. After riding the elevator to the lobby, he stopped by the coffee table to make himself a cup before settling into a corner chair to begin reading. As he opened up the folder and began taking out the pages, his gaze was again drawn to the photos of his "family". He still didn't recognize anyone except for himself and Kate. He was confused at how they had his full name and photo, as well as the other photos of him supposedly out at the lighthouse. It couldn't be him, though, since he never remembered those photos ever being taken or the lighthouse in that state of disrepair. What could the Institute possibly be creating these fake photos for?

Putting these photos aside, he began reading from the log dated March 13, 2016, the date that he supposedly came to Green Island. It began with his arrival out at the lighthouse. It documented how he went out and inspected the lighthouse, detailing all of his movements as he did so. Since this was written as a journal, it was obvious that he was being followed as he did all of these things, with the writer of the journal interjecting his own comments. Being stalked by someone that he didn't know would have been a bit disconcerting if it had actually happened, which it hadn't. It was a fascinating story, however. March of 2016 was only two years ago, and the only time that he remembered going to the island then was to visit Dianne's parents for Easter. He especially didn't remember the events as they were unfolding here. It was all fiction to him, except he had to wonder; was it really? While he honestly couldn't remember any of these events actually happening, he was experiencing an odd sense of deja vu as he read through the pages, as if somewhere in the back of his mind these events really had happened. He couldn't explain it, and he had never felt this way before, but it was the strangest feeling. It actually made him a little uncomfortable, but the more that he read, the more that he wanted to read. And the more that he read, the more interesting the story became. He read about how he had visited the lighthouse several times when he was growing up, and that part at least was true. He did have great memories of the lighthouse and of Green Island, since that's where he and Dianne had met and his family had vacationed there quite a few times. But the lighthouse as described on these pages wasn't the lighthouse that he remembered. In the story that he was reading, the lighthouse was so dilapidated as if almost ready to fall down. A mysterious fog would come up from time to time and things would happen when it did, the most famous happening being the disappearance of two boys, Greg Baker and Tim Henderson. This part was particularly confusing. Greg hadn't disappeared in the fog, he was his brother-in-law! And Tim Henderson was the President of the United States! It just didn't make any sense at all to him.

As he had been reading, several people had caught his attention as they strolled through the hotel lobby or came down to get coffee. He had barely noticed most of them, except just to realize that they were there out of the corner of his eye. He had simply kept on reading, virtually oblivious to anything going on around him. Now, however, after noticing someone come down and walk over to the coffee area, he paused and looked up, not fully believing the scene that he saw in front of him. At first, he thought that he was having another daydream; a vision like he had this afternoon on the trip down here. He almost felt himself sliding into that dream state, except that it wasn't a dream. This was real, however impossible it seemed. It really was Kate! She was standing over at the coffee area getting a cup of coffee. He couldn't take his eyes off of her!

This couldn't be happening! Kate was real?! While he had thought that he saw her at the Harbor Inn during the weekend of the lighthouse dedication, since that day he had mostly convinced himself that it hadn't really been her since he had only seen the woman from a distance and never got a clear look at her. He remembered her picture beside his on the page that Angela had given him, but for some reason even seeing that picture hadn't made him pause to consider that she could be anything other than a part of his dreams. Seeing her here, however, completely changed his perception of reality. In an instant, his dreams had become a part of his real world!

As Kate finished making her cup of coffee and turned to go back upstairs, her gaze met his. Her hand immediately went limp, letting the cup drop to the floor, its contents splattering as it hit the hard surface.

"Is everything alright?" the front desk clerk asked.

"Yes," Kate said hesitantly, "I guess I wasn't holding on to it well enough."

"No problem, I'll call our nighttime security guard to come and clean it up."

"Thank you." Kate replied as she turned back toward Dan.

The look of surprise and disbelief that he now saw on her face seemed to indicate that she recognized him too! Both of them stayed fixed on each other's gaze for more than half a minute, with both trying to make sense out of what was now happening. Slowly she began to walk toward him. He stood up as she reached the place where he had been sitting, still looking into her eyes with total disbelief. His heart was beating faster than he had ever remembered.

"Dan?" she inquired in a low, soft voice. He could detect a slight quiver in her voice as she said his name.

"Kate?" was all he could say.

They stood, still looking into each other's eyes, both feeling a sense of amazement and wonder, and both trying to find the words to say what they were feeling.

"What's happening here?" she asked.

"I'm really not sure." he replied as he stepped over and pulled out the other chair for her. "Please sit down. Let's talk."

As Dan sat back down in the corner, he began, "So you're really here! I can't believe this is actually happening!"

"So are you." she said, still looking into his eyes, "But how did you know my name?"

He thought for a minute, trying to decide what to say. Other than in his dreams, he didn't know her, until now.

"Over two years ago in May, I had a dream during the big storm on Green Island. You were in that dream, walking out of the fog that was surrounding the lighthouse. As I saw you walking toward me in that dream, I immediately knew your name. I can't explain how, but I did."

As he said this, he noticed her expression change. It was as if she suddenly had a realization of something as well.

"Is anything wrong?" he asked.

"When exactly was the dream? Was it on the night of May 20, 2016?" she asked.

"Yes, it was. But how did you know?"

"I had a dream as well on that same night, during a separate storm back home in Ohio. I was also awakened from that dream. There was also a lighthouse in my dream, but I never knew where it was until now. In my dream, I was lost in a thick fog, frantically trying to find my way out. As I finally found a place where the fog was thinning, I saw you looking into the fog, and I instinctively ran toward you. As we embraced, I heard you whisper my name. Usually I wouldn't even have remembered the dream, but there was just something about this one that stirred something inside of me. Over the last two years, I really haven't thought of the dream again, but just today it came back to me, as vivid as on that night over two years ago."

She paused after she said this, seemingly trying to find what to say next.

"I have another question, and you may think this one a little strange." After a short pause, she continued, "Have you ever had a dream during the daytime while you were awake? One that comes on unexpectedly when you least expect it?"

When she said this, Dan felt a lump in his throat. He had an idea what she was going to say next, even before she said it.

"This afternoon, when I was at the airport waiting for our flight, I was sitting in the gate area when I went to sleep; only it wasn't really like going to sleep. I was lost in the fog again, and I found my way out just like the first time, but this time there was a storm going on, and as we embraced, you whispered my name as a cold rain started to wash over us."

"Yes, this afternoon! I had the same dream as well! What time was your dream?" As he asked this question, he knew what she was going to say; both dreams were at the exact same time! Somehow he and Kate were connected, but neither of them could figure out exactly how or even why.

They talked for a few more minutes, and then Kate decided that she probably needed to get back up to her room. She'd only come down for a quick cup of coffee, and her husband would be wondering what was taking her so long. She walked over to the front desk and asked for a paper and pen, where she wrote down her cell phone number and gave it to Dan.

"Call me tomorrow." she said, "I'd like to talk some more. We have some activities planned at the university tomorrow afternoon, but I should have some time tomorrow evening."

"I'll call you." he replied as she turned and walked over to the elevators.

After Kate had left, he sat back down in the corner, still pondering in disbelief what had just happened. This has definitely been a day to remember, and even now he didn't fully realize exactly what a turning point this day would be in his life. As he continued just to sit and think about the day and all of the things that had happened, he noticed an older grey-haired gentleman sitting along the opposite wall. Dan hadn't noticed him before, but the man had noticed him and had been listening intently to the conversation that he'd had with Kate this evening. He'd definitely see the man again, and in time they would meet, but not tonight. It wasn't time yet; but it soon would be.

CHAPTER 12
October 20, 2018
Early Morning Encounter

Dan awoke to the sound of the blower from the heater as it warmed the room. He stared straight up at the ceiling in the dark hotel room. The room was dimly lit through a crack in the bathroom door which they had left open just a bit to allow some light to filter through. He remembered having trouble getting to sleep earlier, his mind going over and over the events of the day. He glanced over at the alarm clock which glowed 2:48 am. It was much earlier than he had thought. Apparently he hadn't been asleep nearly as long as it seemed. He continued to lie in bed just listening to Dianne's breathing as she lay next to him. She and Danny were both still sound asleep, but then, neither of them had nearly as much on their mind as he did.

After another twenty minutes of trying to get back to sleep with no success, he decided to just give in and take a walk downstairs. He pulled on his jeans and fumbled through the suitcase for a shirt. After getting dressed, he grabbed a room key, fumbled through his computer bag for the papers that Angela had given him, and slipped on his jacket, quietly unlocking the door and stepping out into the hallway. As he reached the lobby and stepped off of the elevator, he immediately noticed how quiet it was at this time of the morning. It had been quite some time since he had been awake at this hour. Usually he never had any problems sleeping, but the day before had not been a normal day.

Until yesterday, his life had been mostly routine. For over two years, he hadn't even thought about that night back in 2016 when he had first dreamed about Kate. Now, after the daydream vision of her this afternoon, that first dream came flooding back into his mind. He remembered also thinking that he saw her at the Harbor Inn the day after the dedication as she walked down the hallway and entered the elevator. But was that really her, or just someone that reminded him of the dream that he'd had the night before? He couldn't be sure. As he thought about this, he couldn't even be sure that Kate had been real last night. It still seemed almost like a dream, stirring feelings that he hadn't thought about in years. And not all of them even involved Kate. He remembered waking up the morning of the lighthouse dedication with the uneasy feeling that he felt then, even before having the dream about Kate. That entire day, while perfectly normal on the surface, still harbored subtle feelings of anxiety, as if there was something wrong, yet he never was able to place exactly what it was. Still, as he now realized, those feelings weren't only in the past. He felt them here in the present, almost stronger than they were two years ago, and those feelings of uneasiness definitely worried him. He didn't know where they came from and why they were coming back now. He remembered the storm from over two years ago, and couldn't help feeling that what was happening now was just the prelude to another storm; but after this storm, his life would never be the same again.

He buttoned his jacket and walked out into the cool night air. A slight wind was blowing and a shiver coursed through his body. The early morning was quiet, with only the occasional car driving past. Just standing here taking in the solitude of the morning and breathing the cold night air seemed to calm his nerves and bring back some normalcy to his life. "How quickly life can change!" he thought, as he remembered how completely routine the previous morning had been as they'd packed up the van and began their journey. But things had changed, almost in the twinkling of an eye, as Angela had shared the information that she had found with him yesterday afternoon. Then, last evening, as if his dreams had suddenly become reality, Kate mysteriously walked into his life. And as he stood here in the quietness of the morning, another emotion now stirred within him and gradually surfaced. He realized that he had strong feelings for Kate. Where those feelings came from, he didn't have the slightest idea, but they were there nonetheless. He couldn't help but wonder if maybe she had those same feelings for him, since he had realized last night that they shared some sort of a mutual connection. He felt a twinge of guilt as his conscience told him that he shouldn't be having these thoughts about another woman other than his wife. But how could he even be having these feelings anyway? He didn't really know Kate! They had just met yesterday for the first time, yet he felt that he had known her for a lot longer.

A noise behind him made him turn around. With everything that had happened, he wasn't surprised to see Kate walking slowly toward him.

"I thought I might find you here." she said as he wrapped his arms around her, shielding her from the cool night air.

He realized at this moment that he had secretly hoped that she'd come down to him. He had held her in his arms in his dreams, but as he held her now it was as if she belonged there, together forever. The guilt became even stronger, as he thought about what Dianne would think if she came down and saw them here together. He knew that she wouldn't understand; even he didn't understand!

"I couldn't sleep." he said. "I couldn't stop thinking about you. I'm glad you came down."

"I just don't understand." she replied, "I couldn't sleep either, and somehow I knew that you were awake as well, and that you were thinking about me, too. But where are these feelings coming from? It's like we've known each other for years, yet we've only just met."

"My daughter gave me something today that might explain our connection, but it's really difficult to believe and accept. I was reading it last night when you came down, and I'm not even sure that I believe all of the things in it. Let's go inside, and I'll show you."

They sat down at one of the tables in the lobby and he produced the folder that Angela had given him. He had picked it up on his way downstairs a few minutes ago, possibly to do some more reading. He pulled out the sheet with the pictures of him, Kate, Danny and Amy and placed it on the table in front of her. He followed her expression as she looked down at the page that he'd just given her, and then back up at him.

"Where did you get this?" Kate asked.

"It's part of the journal that my daughter gave me."

"I recognize you and me," she said, "but who are these others?"

He pushed another couple of pages over to her.

"They're supposedly our kids," he remarked, "except that I don't remember them."

"How could they be our kids? We're not even married!" she replied, but even as she said this an image came into her mind of her and Dan's wedding, causing her to pause. She pushed her chair back, stood up, then silently moved toward the window where she stared out into the night.

He slowly went over to her and put his arms around her. He felt her body shaking as he gently held her.

"I know it's a lot to understand, if any of this even can be understood." he said.

"It's not that." she said, in a low voice that had a slight quiver to it, "I saw our wedding, at least an image of it; just now when you showed me the picture of our kids! And it wasn't just an image. In that second, I actually remembered it! How could I remember it? It never happened!"

"You actually remembered our wedding? How? I don't even remember it!"

"I don't know how, but I did. It was as if I was remembering something that actually happened; but it couldn't have!"

They both walked back over and sat down at the table. Dan picked up the folder that had been lying there.

"The pages in this journal describe events and even have pictures that never could have occurred. I don't have any answers for what's going on here. My daughter thinks that something happened on May 20, 2016 that changed things and put us into an alternate reality. To my way of thinking, that explanation is definitely not a possibility. The problem is that I don't really have a better explanation that makes any more sense. Nothing that's happening here could possibly be happening! According to this journal, the reality before that date was one where you and I were together and had our own family; Danny and Amy. It's all mentioned in these pages, if you can believe them."

"What do you believe?" she asked.

"I don't know. I've always thought that there was a logical explanation for everything, but I'll admit, this has me stumped. I just don't know what to believe anymore."

"Something did happen on May 20, 2016." she said. "I felt it then, and I feel it now. I remember that day even before the storm that happened that night. I just had an uneasy feeling all day as well, like something was wrong, but as the day went on, it seemed that nothing was. I had almost put that day out of my mind until yesterday when I had the vision at the airport."

"I still have that feeling too." Dan replied. "After that night two years ago, I hadn't really thought about it anymore either. It was simply in the back of my mind. Those memories resurfaced yesterday about the time that the rain started while we were on our way down here."

"Where did the journal come from?" she asked, "Where did your daughter get it?"

He wondered whether he should actually tell her. After all, he didn't want too many people knowing that Angela had broken into a top secret computer system. He honestly felt that it was better that as few people as possible know about that. But he also felt a connection to Kate. He could trust her, he knew it.

"It came from the Chandler-Langtree Institute." he replied. "My daughter got some friends to help her log into their computer system and they retrieved these documents."

He noticed a look that he hadn't seen before come over Kate as he mentioned Chandler-Langtree. He wondered what she might know about them. Maybe she knew more than he did.

"Are you alright?" he asked after she was silent for close to a minute, a strange, far away expression on her face.

"I'm fine." she said, "This is just a lot to take in right now. Until now, you've only been in my dreams. It was quite a shock to turn around last evening and see you sitting here."

Dan felt like there was more to it than that, but he didn't want to push her too much if she didn't want to talk about it. He had seen her look change when he mentioned Chandler-Langtree, and he felt that she knew more than she was saying.

"I felt the same way. I was shocked when my daughter first showed me the page with your picture on it yesterday, but for some reason even that didn't make me realize that you could be real. I'm not sure why it didn't, since it seems like it should have. I do have another question, though. Since I saw the page with our pictures on it, I've been trying to figure out what it all means. Where did the pictures come from? And how did they get my picture? I haven't been able to come up with anything, though, since I don't remember those pictures ever being taken. Do you know how they might have gotten your picture?"

"No, I don't know either. I've never even been to the Chandler-Langtree Institute, and I don't recall that particular picture ever being taken!"

He took another page out of the folder and slid it over to her. It was the picture of them all at the Little Book Nook.

"Do you remember being here" he asked, "at the Little Book Nook for this book signing?"

She looked carefully at the photo, studying every detail. She studied the people in the photo. It was definitely her and Dan in the picture. But she didn't recognize anyone else. She looked up at him with a puzzled look.

"No. It's been quite a few years since I've been to Green Island. I remember passing the Little Book Nook, and I did go in once to look around. But I've never been there for a book signing by anyone, so I don't know how this picture of us could have possibly been taken!"

"That's the same thing that I've been trying to figure out. I've been to Green Island a lot, but even I don't remember these pictures being taken, and I generally have a logical explanation for everything."

As they sat across the table from each other, lost in each other's gaze, she reached out and gently touched his hand.

"I'd like to see Green Island again." she said. "We've been there several years ago, but now that all this is happening, I want to see the lighthouse again now that I know that our dreams took place there. Maybe it'll bring back some recollection."

"I'd like that too." he said. "We're going there Sunday night after Parents' Weekend. Maybe you could come with us?"

As he said this, he wasn't even thinking of how to explain any of this to Dianne. All he knew was that he wanted her with him, and he had a strong desire for her to come with him to Green Island.

"Yes, possibly," she replied, "I'd like to do that. Call me tomorrow?"

"Yes, I'll call you tomorrow." he answered as they both got up out of their seats.

As they turned to walk toward the elevators, a figure caught both of their attentions standing outside the window looking in at them. He was close to where they had been sitting, but mostly hidden until they had gotten up and moved slightly away from the table. Startled, they stopped and stared in that direction, trying to make out the shape in the shadows of the front of the building. As they stared out into the darkness, the figure began to walk away from the window and cross the parking lot. They both hurriedly walked outside to see if they could get a better look, with Dan putting his arm around her shoulder as the cold air wrapped around them. As the man walked under the street light, they saw that he was an older gentleman, possibly in his seventies, with grey hair and wearing a grey suit. While he appeared harmless, just the fact that he was here at this time of the morning caught them by surprise. Previously, they had thought that they were the only ones awake here, but they now remembered seeing someone else walk through the lobby just a little while ago as they were talking. Right after that, they had heard the front doors open. They had to wonder how long he had been watching them through the window, and if he had heard any of their conversation while he was inside. How long had he been there? As he arrived at a silver sports car, he unlocked the door and got into the driver's seat.

As Dan and Kate walked back into the lobby of the hotel, Dan suddenly stopped and looked over at Kate, his arm still around her shoulders.

"Have you ever seen that man before?" he asked her.

"No, should I have?"

"I think I saw him last night," Dan said uneasily, "after you left to go back up to your room. He had been sitting in the opposite corner of the lobby, but I think he was listening to our conversation. And now he was looking at us through the window, and we didn't even know that he was there!"

"You're starting to scare me now." she replied. "Why do you think he was here? Could it have something to do with the journal your daughter found?"

"I'm not sure," he said, his voice trailing off as he walked back over to the window, "but he's still out there. He hasn't driven away yet. He's just sitting in his car."

"Let's go back upstairs." she said, her voice shaking nervously now. "I don't like this."

"I don't either." he replied, leading her over to the front desk. He had seen that Patrick was working tonight, and he wanted to ask him about the man.

"Hi Mr. Nelson!" Patrick said cheerfully as they walked up to the desk.

"Hello, Patrick!" replied Dan, "I have a question. There was a man outside just now; an older gentleman possibly in his seventies, wearing a grey suit. I saw him in the lobby earlier in the evening as well, and I think he was in the lobby a few minutes ago. When we got up, he was outside staring at us through the window. Did you notice him earlier? Is he a guest at the hotel?"

"No, I don't remember seeing anyone. Did you see where he went?"

"Yes, he's outside sitting in his car in front of the hotel. I just looked out the window and he's still there."

"I can call the police and have them check it out." replied Patrick. "Do you want me to do that?"

"Yes." said Dan. "He's driving a silver sports car."

Patrick got on the phone and dialed 911, describing the situation that Dan had reported to him. He hung up the phone and walked over to the window. The silver sports car was still in the same parking space in front of the hotel. After glancing out the window, he walked back to the front desk so as not to look too suspicious and scare the man away before the police got there.

Within about ten minutes a patrol car from the Wilmington Police Department pulled up out front. Officer Steve Davidson and Officer Janet Reynolds got out of their car and came into the lobby. Patrick was there to greet them along with Dan and Kate. Dan recounted his story to the two officers who listened intently. After listening to Dan explaining how he had seen the man outside just a few minutes ago, and also in the lobby earlier in the evening, both officers walked outside. The three of them watched the officers through the window as they slowly approached the silver sports car. Officer Davidson kept watch while Officer Reynolds walked around to the back of the car and wrote down the license plate number. Officer Reynolds then went back to the patrol car to run the license plate through the computer while Officer Davidson continued to walk around the edge of the parking lot.

After a few minutes, both officers came back into the lobby. Dan and the others approached them inquisitively.

"There's nobody in the car." remarked Officer Davidson. "We looked around the area and didn't find anyone. He must have gotten out of the car when you weren't looking."

"The car's registered to Warren Evans." interjected Officer Reynolds. Turning to Patrick, she asked him to check to see if he was registered at the hotel.

"Warren Evans, the millionaire CEO of Evans Microsystems?" inquired Patrick, surprised.

"Yes," answered Officer Reynolds, "that Warren Evans."

"What would the CEO of Evans Microsystems be doing here looking through the window at us at four thirty in the morning?" inquired Dan with a puzzled look as Patrick went to check the hotel reservations.

"Who knows," answered Officer Davidson, "it might not have even been him. All we know is that the car is registered to him. We never found anyone outside. I don't think there's anything to worry about here, but we'll come by several more times tonight just to be sure."

As everyone continued to stand around discussing the situation, Patrick came back from the front desk.

"There's no Warren Evans registered here," he said, "but he could have been visiting one of our guests, or even be registered under another name."

"Give us a call if anything else happens." says Officer Davidson. "If it was Warren Evans, I'm sure he had a good reason for being here. He's seventy six years old, and the CEO of one of the largest corporations in North Carolina, so I can't see him posing any threat. Have a good night."

As the two officers left and got back into their patrol car, the three of them watched them leave from the front window. They weren't the only ones watching as the officers left, however. From a dimly lit corner of the hotel, a single man watched intently. He was an older gentleman in a grey suit. He had a serious look on his face. He had been seen, and that was unexpected. He'd have to be more careful from this point on. Dan and Kate had both seen him, which meant that they could probably recognize him again. He'd definitely have to be more cautious.

Dan was surprised at how late it had gotten, since it was already around four thirty in the morning. He pulled up a picture of Warren Evans on his phone and showed it to Kate.

"Yes, I think that is who we saw!" she remarked.

"I think so too, but I still can't figure why. I don't know Warren Evans, and I can't imagine that he'd know me!"

It was all starting to turn into one big puzzle which didn't seem to have an answer. Dan wondered if there was really a connection between Evans Microsystems and what was going on here. Were they also connected somehow with the Chandler-Langtree Institute?

Since he had a busy day planned for tomorrow, he decided to go back upstairs and see if he could get some sleep now. He wanted to know more, but it would have to wait. It was early, and he did need at least a little more sleep before the activities at the university tomorrow, but after all that had happened this evening, he didn't know whether he'd be able to sleep or not. He and Kate both said goodnight to Patrick, then walked over to the elevators to go back to their rooms. Patrick stood at the front desk staring after them. He knew Dan well, since he and Dianne had been coming here for the last three years, and he thought that he may have seen the woman that was with Dan before as well. He had to wonder about them, though, since they had been holding hands while walking to the elevator.

As they stopped on Dan's floor, he paused and gave her a smile as he was getting out.

"I'll call you tomorrow." he said.

"Goodnight, Dan." she replied as she returned his smile before he walked away and the doors closed behind him.

CHAPTER 13

The Meeting

Saturday morning was the start of a beautiful fall day in Wilmington. The temperature had dropped significantly overnight, and the day was forecast to be slightly cooler than it had been the day before.

Dan had finally gotten back to sleep around five thirty. After the events of the past evening as well as the early morning hours, it did make it difficult to sleep. He kept going over and over the events in his mind, not really able to make sense of any of it. He awoke around nine thirty after getting only four hours of sleep, but he was actually wide awake and didn't see any reason not to go ahead and get up. Dianne was awake as well as Danny, and they were both ready to start the day. Danny was looking forward to the soccer game later, and Dianne was just looking forward to spending time with Angela. Since she had decided to go to school in Wilmington instead of East Carolina, they hadn't seen as much of her as they'd have liked and if things worked out with Mark, she might not be moving back home after graduation.

They all got dressed and went down to breakfast, which they always enjoyed at the Davenport. It was more than just a standard Continental Breakfast; they served a hot breakfast with eggs, sausage, bacon, biscuits and gravy, as well as some fruit and muffins. On weekends they even had a chef preparing made to order omelets. As they got off of the elevator and walked into the lobby, Dan looked around for Kate. Since he knew that she was staying here at the hotel, he halfway expected to see her, and was actually hoping that he would.

"Looking for someone, Dad?" asked Danny.

Being caught off guard, Dan replied, "No, who would I be looking for?"

"I don't know, but it sure looked to me like you were looking around for someone. You seemed lost in another world."

"I'm still a little tired. I didn't sleep well last night."

They all went through the serving line, and then sat down at one of the tables near the front window, actually near where he had seen Warren Evans the night before. All he saw looking out the window today, however, was a bright sunny day. He looked for the silver sports car, but it seemed to be gone this morning. Where it had been parked the previous evening was now a green Toyota. Apparently Dianne hadn't noticed Dan's odd behavior this morning, or if she did, she hadn't said anything. They all just sat and talked as they ate their breakfast, with Dan occasionally looking around the lobby, trying not to be too obvious about it this time.

As they got up from breakfast, Dan gave another glance around the lobby, and then went back upstairs with the rest of his family. They were supposed to meet Angela and Rebekah at the student center at eleven thirty, and then attend the parent/student luncheon in Warwick Center at one. They were meeting Mark's parents for the luncheon so that the two families could become acquainted, since this would be the first time that they had met. After lunch, they all planned to walk over to the stadium for the soccer game against NC State.

Angela and Rebekah had gotten up around eight thirty, which was really early considering what time they went to bed. They had actually stayed up most of the night catching up on everything that had been happening in each other's lives, popping popcorn, and watching movies on the DVD player. It's what they usually did when Rebekah came to visit, and it was one of the things that they both looked forward to. Of course, Angela left out most of the events surrounding Mark and his job at the Institute, since she knew that Rebekah would have a lot of questions, and she really didn't have any answers. That didn't stop them from discussing all of the other things about Mark, however. He was actually the main topic of their conversation for most of the night, and this served to get Angela's mind off of the mysteries that had been happening, at least for a little while.

Deciding that they were both a little hungry, they took a walk over to the dining hall to get breakfast, not even bothering to get dressed, just putting their coats on over their t-shirts and pajama pants. It was a nice day, a little cool, but still sunny and inviting. After they walked into the dining hall, Angela looked around for Mark, not really expecting to see him though, since his parents had gotten into town last night. She actually hoped that she wouldn't run into them, however, since she wanted everything to be perfect for their first meeting. Rebekah noticed her looking around, and thought that it was probably Mark that she was looking for. Angela had gone into quite a bit of detail about her and Mark's weekend getaway to the beach two weeks ago, and Rebekah had thought that was just the most romantic thing.

After returning to Angela's dorm room, Rebekah wanted to style her sister's hair. She pulled the sides back with a hair clip, then let the rest drape over her shoulders and down her back, falling almost to her waist. After that, they both got busy trying to pick out just the right outfit for Angela to wear to meet Mark's parents. It wasn't easy, since she wanted to make just the right impression, not too casual, but not too formal either. It was a lot of fun as the two sisters looked through Angela's closet and dresser and produced various pieces of clothing of all styles. They lay some possible choices out on the bed and both of them looked them over, with Angela trying on some, then looking in the full length mirror on her door. Most of the outfits that she tried on, while they did look good on her, just weren't quite the look she wanted for today. After a little more than an hour, Angela finally decided on a purple tunic top with her best dark blue jeans and brown boots. Pearl earrings and a pearl necklace completed the ensemble. Looking in the mirror now, Angela liked what she saw, and felt that Mark would approve as well.

As Angela and Rebekah approached the student center, they saw their parents and brother already out front waiting on them.

"How was your night?" asked Dianne.

"Wonderful!" said Rebekah, "I hope one day I can find somebody just like Mark!"

"I bet Mark's ears were burning all night!" joked Dan.

"What?!" asked Rebekah, not really understanding what her father had just meant.

"That's what you say when someone's being talked about a lot!" laughed Dan.

"His ears were definitely burning then!" replied Rebekah.

Everyone got a good laugh out of that one.

After discussing what to do next, they decided to go into the school bookstore, which was in the student center on the lower level and look around before walking over to Warwick Center for the luncheon. While the rest of them were looking around the store, Dan pulled Angela off to the side.

"Let's walk back outside for a minute." he suggested.

As they both walked out onto the porch outside the bookstore, Angela wondered what this was all about, especially remembering their conversation from yesterday, and knowing that she had given her dad the Chandler-Langtree information to read.

"What is it, dad?" she asked, with a concerned tone, "You read the journal that I gave you?"

"Yes, I read most of it, but that's not why I brought you out here. I met Kate last night."

"Kate?! The woman whose picture is in the Chandler-Langtree journal?! You mean she's real?!"

"Yes, she's real; and she's staying at our hotel!"

"So you talked to her?" inquired Angela.

"Yes, I talked to her! And we seem to have a connection somehow. Do you remember when I told you that I had a dream the night of the storm when we were staying on the island during the lighthouse dedication?"

"Yes, I remember that."

"Well it turns out that she had the exact same dream at the same time, hundreds of miles away! She told me her dream, and it was identical to mine, only from her viewpoint!"

"How did you meet her?" asked Angela, extremely curious at this point.

"Your mom and Danny were in the room watching a movie. I had gone downstairs to the lobby to read the journal information that you gave me. While I was sitting in the corner reading, Kate came downstairs to get a cup of coffee. When she turned and saw me, I could tell that she instantly recognized me too! She came over and we talked, and that's when I found out about her dream as well."

"Where's she from? Do you know why she's staying at the hotel? Since she's in the Chandler-Langtree journal, she must have been to Green Island at some point."

"She says that she's only been to Green Island a few times, but like me she never remembers being in the pictures. She doesn't remember who anyone else in the pictures are either, so that's still another mystery. Come to think of it, I don't think that I ever asked her where she was from, or why she's here. I think I remember her mentioning that she's from Ohio, though. I'm supposed to call her later today and maybe we can meet again."

"Does mom know about her?"

"No, I haven't quite figured out a good way to tell her. Your mom doesn't even know about the dream. You're actually the only one that I've told, so I'm not exactly sure how to explain Kate to her in a way that she'd understand, especially since I can't fully explain Kate to myself."

"I know what you mean. But if you're going to meet her later, won't mom get suspicious?"

"She let you and I talk yesterday. Maybe we could tell her that we want to talk some more? "

"Won't Mom start to wonder if we begin having too many private conversations?"

As it turns out, Dianne was already wondering. She wondered what had happened to Dan and Angela right now, and went over to the window of the bookstore to look for them. She saw them outside in front of the bookstore talking. She knew that Angela had been preoccupied with something since they had arrived, and now she was really starting to wonder what was going on.

She walked out the front door and came up behind them.

"OK, guys; let somebody else join in the fun!" she remarked.

Both Dan and Angela were startled as they quickly turned to face her, looking like they had just gotten caught with their hands in the cookie jar.

"Oh, did I really interrupt something?" remarked Dianne.

"No, we're fine." both Dan and Angela said in unison.

"Come on guys, when I walked up you both looked like you had just gotten caught. Doing what I can only guess right now, but I suppose that you'll tell me when you're ready."

"No, really; Angela and I were just talking about Mark and his new job and meeting his parents today. It's the first time that she's met them, so she's a little nervous."

"Right; like I said, you'll tell me when you're ready. Rebekah and Danny are finishing up inside. Ready to go on over to the event hall when they come out?"

"Yes, I guess we'd better be heading on over there." said Angela.

After Danny and Rebekah came out of the store, the five of them walked over to the van to put their purchases in the back before heading over to Warwick Hall. On the way over, Dan and Angela both exchanged knowing glances at each other. They'd just gotten caught and they knew it. If Dan was to be able to meet with Kate now, they both knew they'd have to come up with a different plan other than just needing to talk some more. What that could possibly be neither of them could figure out right now, but they'd keep thinking.

They were supposed to meet Mark and his parents right inside the main entrance of Warwick Hall just off to the right side as you come in the door. When they got there, there was no sign of Mark, so they figured that he must be running a little late. It was actually about ten after one when Angela saw Mark walking up from beside the area around the fountain. She smiled as she saw him, moving closer to the door now as he and his parents approached. Suddenly, however, she stopped walking, a confused look coming across her face as she looked up at her father. He had seen what she had seen and they were both as confused as ever at this point.

As Mark entered the foyer, he spotted Angela immediately and began walking ahead of his parents. He came up to her to give her a big hug and kiss, but noticed immediately that she seemed to be preoccupied with something; not herself at all.

"What's wrong?" he remarked, trying to keep a pleasant mood, "Aren't you glad to see me?"

"Yes, it's not that. I am glad to see you." she said, but her tone seemed suddenly distant, as she turned back to her father and gave him her "What's going on here?" look.

"Hello Mark." said Dan as he shook his hand, "Good to see you again."

By this time Marks parents had arrived where everyone was standing and he began the introductions.

"Mom; Dad; I'd like you to meet Angela. Angela, these are my parents, Scotty and Kate Duncan. And these are Angela's parents, Dan and Dianne Nelson, and her sister Rebekah and brother Danny."

"Nice to meet you both." said Angela as she approached them for a hug, first from his mom, then his dad. Scotty shook Dan's hand with a huge smile. He was a tall man like Mark, also with sandy blonde hair, but while Mark was clean shaven, his dad sported a full beard and mustache.

"Glad to finally meet you." he said, "Mark's told us a lot about you.

And Angela, you're even prettier than Mark described. Ready to go in and find a table?"

As Mark's parents had walked through the door earlier, Dan and Kate had exchanged surprised looks. They hoped that nobody else had noticed, though. Dan knew that Angela had, but hopefully she was the only one. And she had reason to, since it was her that had given her father the pictures. As they now began walking into the event hall to find a table, everybody seemed to act normal enough as they carried on a pleasant conversation. It appeared that none of them had noticed anything odd about either of their behaviors when they had met, though this was definitely unexpected.

Dan realized that when he had met Kate the previous evening that he had never asked her why she was here. He had just been so surprised to see her actually walk into the lobby that it never occurred to him. Now it was clear that she was here for Parents' Weekend the same as they were. Kate and Dan kept exchanging quick glances, but were purposely more discreet now so as not to be noticed. Dianne, however, had noticed a change in Dan's mood when Scotty and Kate walked in, though she wasn't sure exactly what had caused it. He actually acted surprised by something. Now he just seemed more distant and preoccupied. While he had been laughing and carrying on a pleasant conversation only minutes before, now he was quieter and a lot more reserved, as if he was suddenly lost in thought. So was Angela. She couldn't help but wonder if it might have something to do with all of the personal talks that Angela and Dan seemed to be having lately, though from the timing, she couldn't imagine how they would be connected. As they sat down at the table and waited for their server to come, Dianne actually did see Dan give Kate a quick glance, and she returned that glance, quickly looking away. She didn't think either of them knew that she had noticed. To her, it seemed like they might know each other, but she couldn't imagine how or from where. Mark's parents lived in Ohio, and they were all just meeting for the first time today.

The menu for the luncheon was already preplanned, so they didn't need to view a menu or place an order. That had already been done weeks ago when they had first sent in their confirmation that they would be attending. All that was required today was for them to just wait on their server to arrive with their meals and drinks. They didn't have to wait long; after about ten minutes their food and drinks arrived and they began eating.

During the luncheon, Dan and Scotty talked quite a bit, finding out more about each other. After the usual, "What do you do for a living?" conversation, Dan told them about how he had met Dianne while vacationing down on Green Island. Scotty had his own story as well about how he and Kate had met at college, and were married right after graduation. They found out that they were both in the computer business, with Dan owning an internet hosting company in Greenville, NC and Scotty owning a computer server and networking company in Strongsville, OH. And they also found that they both were really into the television show "Star Journeys". If they hadn't lived so far apart, they may have actually run into each other prior to this at one of the "Star Journeys" conventions that they both went to a couple of times a year.

The rest of the dinner was pleasant, with the usual dinner conversation among families that had just met. Kate and Dianne chatted as well, and got to know each other better. Dianne wasn't sure just why, but Kate also appeared like she had something on her mind other than the conversation that they were having. Several times she had asked Dianne to repeat something, as if she really wasn't fully engaged in the current conversation. Angela, however, was so preoccupied with everything that had just happened that even though she tried to join into the conversation, it seemed that she just couldn't get into it and kept stumbling over her words. While Mark did wonder what might be bothering her, he could tell that both of his parents genuinely liked her. Of course, he had never even considered that they wouldn't. Since she seemed quieter than usual, though, he put his arm around her and pulled her close.

"Are you sure you're ok?" he asked, a little concerned.

"Yes, I'm fine. Just a little tired from my all-nighter with Rebekah!"

That may have been part of it, but he actually could sense that there was more to it than that. But obviously she wasn't ready to talk about it just yet.

As they got up to leave, and walked out into the cool afternoon air,

Dan had an uneasy feeling that they were being watched. Where that came from, he didn't know, since there actually was a crowd of people outside the event hall. He looked around and that's when he spotted the man! It was Warren Evans watching him again, this time as he was here walking with his family! This had to be more than coincidence, and he needed to get this taken care of once and for all.

"I'll be back in a minute." he told everyone, as he began to walk briskly in Warren's direction. But Warren was fast for a seventy six year old man, even faster than Dan. Dan unfortunately lost him in no time, with everyone left staring off in the direction that he had just ran. Dan walked fast around the pond, looking around as he went for any sign of where Warren might have gone. He was walking faster now, not wanting to lose him this time. After about five minutes, however, with no luck in finding him, he returned back to his group, who all were definitely wondering by now why he had left so quickly.

"Did you see someone that you recognized?" asked Dianne, curious at this point since Dan was definitely not acting like himself at all.

"It's nothing. I just thought that I saw someone that looked familiar. I don't think that it was who I thought it was, though."

But Kate had seen him too, and knew that it was exactly who Dan had thought that it was. It was Warren Evans again. He gave her an uncomfortable feeling as well, mostly because she, like Dan, couldn't figure why he'd be following them. Just the feeling of being stalked by someone that she didn't know, even if he was a wealthy CEO, gave her the feeling of being violated. Was she really safe? Why was he following them? She really didn't like the feeling of having to look over her shoulder all the time, wondering if she was being watched. And she didn't feel like she could talk with Scotty about it just yet either. He'd have too many questions; questions to which she had no answers. She knew that the only one that she could really talk to, and who would actually understand, was Dan.

The group continued on to the soccer stadium. When they got there it was already crowded, even though the game wasn't scheduled to start for another thirty minutes. They walked about half way up the stands and found seats where they had a good view of the field. Dan sat next to

Scotty and Dianne sat with Kate so they could continue their conversations. Mark sat with Angela. He was concerned about her. He knew that there was something bothering her, and he wished that she would tell him what it was so that he could help. But she apparently wasn't ready to talk just yet.

It turned out to be a really good game. NC State and UNC Wilmington held one of the chief rivalries in the state, and they were a good match to make for a lot of excitement. Everyone could tell that they wouldn't be able to tell how it would end until it was over. It was what was called a "real nail-biter" down here in North Carolina. Still, even with the excitement of the game, Dan, Kate, and Angela just couldn't get into it at all. And this was a real change for Dan, who would usually be standing up cheering with the rest of them. But today he had too much on his mind. At half time, Dan got up to get hotdogs for Dianne, Danny, and Rebekah. Angela had said that she wasn't hungry, which was definitely not like her at all either. After Dan left, Kate decided to fake a trip to the restroom so that she could catch up to him. Ever since they all had met this morning, Kate had been wanting to talk to Dan alone, but with the two families constantly together since then, there had just been no way for that to happen. She knew that they didn't have long now, since everyone would start to wonder if they weren't back soon, so she caught up with Dan in the hotdog line. While it wasn't exactly private, everyone around them was so caught up in the game that they really didn't pay any attention to Dan and Kate's conversation.

"You didn't tell me that Angela was your daughter!" she said.

"It just never came up. When we met last night, I didn't make any connection at all between you and Angela and Mark."

"I know. I didn't either. I was just so surprised to see you actually sitting there in the hotel lobby, that to find out any background about your life never occurred to me either. It was all happening so quickly."

"So what do we do now?" Dan asked.

"While this is unexpected, I don't think it really changes anything." she said. "We both have some kind of connection to each other's lives. I don't know what that is, but we have to find out. After all, we both had the same dream twice, and at the exact same times! And when we were talking earlier, I actually did have a flashback of our wedding! Don't ask me how, because I don't know, but we still have to find out."

"Remember last night, when I invited you to come out to Green Island with us on Sunday?"

"Yes." she said hesitantly.

"Why don't you and Scotty both come. Bring Mark too if he's available. I'll see if Angela can miss some of her classes and come with us as well. We can see the island together."

"I'd like that," she said, "but Scotty and I have a flight scheduled to fly back home tomorrow afternoon!"

"Can you see if it can be rescheduled? I think we really need to go to the island together."

"I'll talk to Scotty. I think he may actually like spending a week on the island."

By now, Dan had reached the concession stand and ordered the hotdogs and drinks. He gathered straws and napkins, and then he and Kate walked back to where the rest of the group was still enjoying the half time band celebration. Angela gave him a look when she saw him return with Kate, but apparently the rest of the group hardly gave them a second glance. He'd discuss the new plan with Angela tonight. Hopefully Kate would be able to convince Scotty to stay for the week on Green Island, and maybe they'd finally find some answers.

A loud roar went up from the crowd as UNC Wilmington pulled off a 3-2 win. They all got up to leave and slowly made their way down to ground level and then followed the rest of the crowd out of the stadium. In all of the excitement, neither Dan nor Kate noticed that they were still being followed, this time close enough for him to almost touch them. It was Warren Evans again. He was following them now, and he had been following them earlier. He had been close enough to hear their conversation in the concession line, and now he knew that they planned to go to Green Island together. Everything seemed to be falling into place. Maybe now he could finally put his plan into motion. He knew what that would mean for both families, but he also had an idea of what might happen if he did nothing. It was a chance that he would have to take.

CHAPTER 14
October 21, 2018
Arrival

As it turned out, Scotty didn't need too much convincing to spend a week on Green Island at the invitation of Dan. He felt like it really would give the two families a good chance to get to know each other as they spent more time together. Besides that, an island vacation sounded like it would be a lot of fun. It had actually been several years since they had been there. He called the airline and moved his and Kate's flight to a week from Monday. That would give them the entire week plus next weekend. Things were working out with Mark as well since Dr. Langtree had requested that he go down to Green Island that same week to work on getting the Mobile Command Center operational. Since his mom and dad were staying with Dan and Dianne at the Baker Family Bed and Breakfast, he requested to stay there too so that he could spend more time with them. That was fine with Dr. Langtree, since they'd be working out at the lighthouse for the better part of each day anyway. He could work at the lighthouse during the day, and visit with Angela and his family during the evenings. He hadn't really been to the island yet, other than several weeks ago when he went with Dr. Langtree, but that was entirely for work. This time would be partly for relaxation as well.

Angela also decided to miss her classes for the week to go down to the island with them. Most of her professors had given a list of assignments at the beginning of the term, so she did know what she needed to keep up with already. The way everything was happening, she felt like she needed to be on Green Island more than she needed to be in class this week. She definitely didn't want to miss anything, and Mark would be on the island as well, so she actually hoped to get to spend more time with him than they had been able to recently. And from what she had found out from the Chandler-Langtree journal, having both families out on the island together at the same time might actually help her find out more, since both her dad and Mark's mom were in the journal.

Since all of the weekend's activities at the college were finishing up right after lunch on Sunday, they decided to head on down to Green Island. They checked out of their rooms at the Davenport and loaded up their vans in preparation for the drive down to the island. After driving down the street to gas up both vehicles, they finally got underway, with Scotty following Dan in the rental van. Exiting onto Highway 133, they continued the trip down to Southport to catch the ferry out to Green Island. Kate remembered this trip, since when they had vacationed on Green Island the times before, they would always fly into Wilmington first. This time though, the trip seemed somehow different. Things were happening that she just couldn't understand, and somehow they seemed to be connected to the lighthouse on Green Island.

It took about forty minutes for them to reach the ferry port at Southport. As they were arriving, they saw the ferry just coming in to dock. "What perfect timing!" Dan thought, "We should be there in no time at this rate!" He had talked to his mother-in-law, Jan, last night after Kate had discussed the trip with Scotty and they had agreed to come down to the island for the week. She had been excited that they were coming, and got to work immediately getting their best room ready for Scotty, Kate, and Mark. She had been trying to get Angela to bring Mark down for a weekend visit for several months, and now she'd finally get to meet him along with his parents. And having Dan, Dianne, and the kids down for the week was a bonus as well, since she always enjoyed having them come and spend time at the bed and breakfast. Luckily, as it turned out, they weren't full for this week, so she had rooms available for them.

Angela wished that Mark could be with them now, but he had to stay back in Wilmington to get the Mobile Command Center ready to move down to the island. He had gone over to the Institute right after lunch to finish working on the command center, which was basically a converted Airstream travel trailer. Most all of the equipment had already been installed and tested; he just needed to run a few more tests to make sure that it was ready for the trip down to the island tomorrow as well as coordinate with Chandler-Langtree's transportation department on the plan for transporting it. Mark had been excited about this phase of the experiments. While he couldn't tell her exactly what they were doing, he had said that this part would "Finally put everything together". With the temporal field on the island, she could only guess that they were planning on attempting time travel. Remembering some of the movies that she and Mark had seen, for a moment she wondered if maybe Dr. Langtree had somehow gotten stranded in this time period and needed Mark's help to get home. Especially since the journal implied that he might be from 2164. She quickly dismissed this idea, however. This part still seemed too unreal to her. A part of her actually felt that time travel couldn't be what they were doing, since she still felt like that was impossible. Especially on a bright, sunny, autumn day like this; time travel seemed a very distant impossibility. At least Mark would be coming down tomorrow, even if he would have to work most of the day. She could still look forward to spending time with him tomorrow evening and hopefully most of the other nights of the week as well.

As the ferry got underway for the trip over to Green Island, Dan got out of the van and walked over to the railing to get a better view of the trip. From that vantage point, he should be able to glimpse Green Island when it first comes into view off the starboard side. Danny and Rebekah had gone over to the back of the ferry to throw some bread crumbs to some seagulls that they saw flying around there. Dianne and Angela had found a stairway to the upper deck which had seating for the passengers to enjoy the trip. Thinking that Kate might have gone up there as well, Scotty followed them up the stairs. As Dan leaned over the railing, totally lost in thought, he felt a light touch on his shoulder. Turning around, he saw Kate as she leaned over the railing beside him, her long blonde hair blowing in the wind.

"What do you think we'll find on the island?" she asked.

"I don't know that we'll find anything, or if we do, I can't imagine what it would be now. Has Mark told you anything about the experiments that they're doing out there?"

"No, he mostly talks with Scotty about that. But I don't think that he's mentioned much to him either."

"They're a pretty secretive company. He probably can't say a lot about what they're doing. Still, our dreams started over two years ago, a long time before Mark went to work there. I'm actually starting to agree with Angela; I believe that something did happen on May 20, 2016 that changed our reality. And I'm thinking that it does have something to do with Chandler-Langtree. I was actually wondering last night if some of the dreams that we're having could be flashbacks into our old reality."

"I'm really having a hard time with that, Dan. While I can't explain what's happening, I still can't quite bring myself to really believe that we had totally different lives in an alternate reality. I know what I read in the journal, but that just can't happen!"

"What about our wedding? You said that you actually remembered it."

"Yes, I still do remember it. And I can't explain how I remember it and that scares me!"

"There you are!" came a voice from behind them.

They both turned to see Scotty walking up.

"Hi, Scotty," remarked Dan, "we were just getting acquainted. Have you seen Dianne?"

"Dianne and Angela are on the upper deck. There's quite a view from up there!"

The three of them decided to join Dianne and Angela so they walked over to the stairs and up to the observation area on the upper deck. Scotty was right, there was quite a view! From there, they actually could see the outline of the island off in the distance. They all continued their conversation as the ferry slowly made it's way toit's destination.

They were completely engaged in their conversation, when they were interrupted by three long blasts from the ship's horn. Turning and gazing toward the front of the ferry, they saw that they were almost ready to dock. They had been so lost in their conversation that they had completely lost track of time. The captain's voice came over the speakers instructing everyone to return to their vehicles, since they would be docking shortly. Kate went with Scotty while Dan, Dianne and Angela walked back over to their van, meeting Danny and Rebekah there.

After the ferry docked and they were back on their way to the bed and breakfast, Angela asked her father if they could go out to the lighthouse this afternoon. She had remembered the picture from the temporal field monitor and actually wanted to go out there to see if anything looked any different now that she knew that it was there.

"Sure, let's get settled in at the bed and breakfast, then we can drive out there. Maybe Scotty and Kate might want to go out there with us."

They turned left onto Main Street and within a couple of minutes were turning into the alley beside the bed and breakfast. They pulled into two parking spaces near the front, got out of the vans, and spent a few seconds just stretching their legs and breathing in the clean island air. As they walked around to the front of the building and started up the stairs, the sign hanging from the roof of the porch caught Dan's attention. It read, "Island Charm Bed and Breakfast".

"That's odd." he thought to himself, before continuing inside.

As they entered the front parlor, Wendell and Jan were there to greet them.

"Did you have a nice trip?" asked Jan.

"Yes." replied Dianne, "It was very pleasant."

As Scotty and Kate walked in, Angela handled the introductions, "Grandma, Grandpa, these are Mark's parents, Scotty and Kate Duncan."

Wendell stepped forward to shake Scotty's hand, while Jan gave Kate a hug.

"Where's Mark?" asked Jan, "We're looking forward to meeting him as well."

"He's not coming until tomorrow." replied Angela, "He had some work to do back in Wilmington before coming down."

"When did you change the name of the bed and breakfast?" inquired Dan.

"Change the name?!" remarked Wendell, "We didn't change the name."

"Yes you did. When we just walked up, the sign said, "Island Charm Bed and Breakfast".

"Who did that?!" inquired Wendell as they all walked out onto the porch and down the steps. Everyone was looking up at the painted wooden sign which now said "Baker Family Bed and Breakfast".

"Looks like it always has." said Wendell in a matter of fact tone. But Dan had a puzzled look on his face as he stared up at the sign. He knew that it had just said "Island Charm Bed and Breakfast", or at least he thought that it had. And as he looked now, even the color of paint on the siding looked slightly different than it had just a few minutes ago. Still, there was no denying now that it was back to normal. They all walked back into the front parlor and chatted for a few minutes before heading back down the steps to bring their bags in out of the vans.

After they had gotten settled into their rooms, they all got into Dan's van, since it was the bigger one, with 2 captain's chairs in the middle and a bench seat in the back. Scotty sat up front with Dan, while Kate and Dianne took the captain's chairs, and all three kids settled into the bench seat in the very back. Since it was a little after four on a Sunday afternoon, the lighthouse would be closing in less than an hour. Still, the island wasn't that big, so it wouldn't take long to get out there. They turned onto Harbor Inn Lane, and then made the left turn onto Lighthouse Road. Within about three minutes, they were turning into the parking lot of the Green Island Light Station. Even though it was less than an hour until closing, the parking lot was still crowded. They found two spaces over near the woods on the back side. It was a little further to walk, but it was a nice autumn day, so none of them really minded.

One of the first things that Angela noticed after getting out of the van was the steel tower with the white ball on top that had been erected next to the house.

"Could that be the temporal field monitor?" she thought to herself as she stared at it. The rest of them really didn't pay too much attention to it, but she had seen the monitor page on the Chandler-Langtree computer, so that made her slightly more observant. She did see how it could be mistaken for a Doppler radar.

As they walked inside, Steve's wife Arlene was there to greet them. Steve and Arlene were the directors of the Green Island Lighthouse Preservation Society, and they ran the lighthouse museum. Dan introduced her to Scotty and Kate. Hearing Dan, Steve came out from the back and offered to give Scotty and Kate the full lighthouse tour. He informed them that the lighthouse would be closing in about thirty minutes, and after that, he'd give them a private tour. While they were waiting, they looked around the museum, which had various artifacts from the lighthouse over the years. The central feature of the display was the original lighthouse lens, which had been fully restored and was now proudly displayed in the center of the room and was the first thing that visitors saw as they walked through the front door. LED spotlights mounted on the ceiling around it made the hundreds of prisms that made up the lens glisten and sparkle with a multitude of color as a person walked around it. There were other displays as well which highlighted the history of Green Island and the light station. A diorama of the island was featured in one room. It had buttons on a panel that when pressed would light up a bulb on the diorama showing where that structure was located. Another room held a small theatre where they all went to view a short fifteen minute movie about the history of the light station. Dan was surprised during the middle of the movie, when he saw that they had incorporated the video from the Coastal Storm Spotter group of the storm from two years ago. As Dan stared at the screen with its flashes of lightning, suddenly he was standing in the yard looking into a thick fog surrounding the lighthouse. "Not again!" he thought to himself, as he turned to see the lighthouse completely in ruins, with the roof missing, and most of the front wall collapsed. He remembered Kate, and called her name as he walked over to the edge of the woods where the fog had completely surrounded the lighthouse. When he didn't get a reply, he walked around to another section and called her name. A loud clap of thunder and flash of lightning startled him as a cold rain began to fall. It seemed to be getting darker as well as thick clouds closed in overhead. "Where had everyone gone?" he wondered. The rain was coming down harder now, as he heard a voice coming out of the fog.

"Dan! Where are you?" Kate called to him.

"Over here!" he called, "I'm over here!"

She called to him again, her voice getting closer this time, until he could see her shadow appearing through the fog.

"Over here!" he called again as she ran out of the fog and raced into his arms. She was wet and shivering as he held her close.

As she looked into his eyes, the rain running down her face, he could see that she was frightened.

"Where is everyone?" she asked in a voice that could barely be heard over the steadily increasing rain. Another flash of light and clap of thunder startled them both.

"Where are we?" she continued.

Just as he was about to answer, another bright flash of lightning temporarily blinded him and as his eyes adjusted he could see that he was back in the lighthouse theatre listening to the rain and seeing the lightning on the movie screen.

"Wow, that seemed so real!" he thought to himself. He looked around the room and apparently nobody else had noticed anything odd about his actions. Everyone was still sitting watching the movie as if nothing had happened, which for them apparently nothing had. But as he looked over at Kate, her wide eyes and startled look told him all he needed to know. She had been in the same dream with him this time as well! But was it really a dream? They were awake and hadn't really felt like they had gone to sleep. They had their families with them; Dan was sitting beside Dianne and Kate was sitting beside Scotty, yet neither of them seemed to have noticed anything.

As the movie was ending, Steve came in to see if they were ready for the tour. As they all were leaving the room, Kate walked over beside Dan.

"Did you ...?" she whispered a little shaken.

"Yes," he replied, "I just had the same dream."

"But it didn't feel like a dream at all! It felt real!"

"I know." he whispered as they began to walk up the circular staircase to the top of the lighthouse, "We'll talk about it later."

As they reached the top and looked out over the island, the orange sun sparkled on the shimmering water. It reminded Dan of the evening over two years ago when they climbed the tower with the President during the lighthouse dedication. There couldn't be a more beautiful sight.

As they were looking out over the island, just taken in by the view, Kate walked up beside him and whispered, "Look!" as she pointed to a small car parked in the corner of the parking lot. Dan looked over toward the direction that she was pointing and saw a small silver sports car. Both of them gave each other a look that said, "Could he really be here? Now?" Both of them scanned the parking lot for any sign of Warren Evans. Dan walked completely around the lantern house, focusing on the parking lot as well as the shadows around the buildings, even the edges of the woods surrounding the area. Still, there was no sign of the grey haired man. He even strained to see if Warren could still be sitting in his car, but the way that the light reflected off of the car's windshield made it impossible to tell.

As they walked down the circular staircase and into the lobby of the main house, Steve continued the tour while Dan walked outside. As he stood on the porch looking across the parking lot toward the direction of the silver sports car, he noticed that the car appeared to be gone! He walked across the parking lot, looking around for the sports car, but as hard as he looked, it was nowhere to be found. Slowly, he walked back across the parking lot and into the main house to rejoin the others on the tour.

Kate whispered to him as he came in, "Did you find him?"

"No, the car was gone when I got out there."

"I know that was the same car!" she whispered.

"Yes, I know. We'll need to be careful."

He could tell that she wasn't happy that Warren Evans was apparently here on the island. Both of them wondered what he could possibly want. And why was he following them? There was no doubt that he was, especially since he was here on the island now. They'll need to be careful, and they'll need to keep a watch out for him.

Later the same night, back at the Baker Family Bed and Breakfast, everyone was in the sitting room, having a pleasant time watching a movie on the DVD player. It was a movie that Scotty had picked out, about a soldier who was missing in action for 10 years, only to come home and find that his girlfriend has gotten married and has two children. He makes the painful decision to not let her know that he's alive so that she can continue on with her life. When her husband dies in a car accident six years later, however, he gradually tries to rekindle the romance and both of them end up living happily ever after.

As Dan went into the kitchen to pop some more popcorn, Kate followed him to get another drink.

"What happened today out at the lighthouse?" she asked.

"I don't know, but this one was more real than any of the others, and it lasted longer too. I can't explain it, but I think it's the island. I know that the name on the bed and breakfast sign was different today when we walked in as well, but I can't explain that either."

"It was different." she said. "It did say Island Charm Bed and Breakfast" but I was too surprised to say anything when we walked back outside and it was back to normal. But you were right, it was different."

"I'm glad someone else saw it too. I just wish I knew what caused it. "

She looked deep into his eyes, pondering what possibly could be the cause. Finally she replied, "I think you may be right. I think it may be the island."

CHAPTER 15
October 23, 2018
Albert

Jan had cooked up a good country breakfast for all of the guests on Tuesday morning. While they had started out on Sunday with plenty of vacancy; with Dan and his family, along with Scotty, Kate and Mark, all but two rooms had been taken. Those two were quickly reserved later Sunday evening with a couple of walk-in families who were staying for the week, so there was quite a crowd around the table this morning.

Mark had arrived yesterday as planned, so he was here with them this morning. After breakfast, he and Angela had planned to go on a bike ride along the beach before he had to go to work. Last night hadn't gone as well as Angela had hoped. While she had looked forward to him being able to join her around five, it was actually ten thirty before he got back to the bed and breakfast. The set up of the Mobile Command Center had taken a little longer than anticipated. Dr. Langtree had to stay behind in Wilmington for a couple of days, so Mark had to set everything up by himself. Angela had actually offered to help, and while he really would have liked that, he thought that she probably shouldn't due to security reasons. He didn't think that Dr. Langtree would like it if anyone else actually saw the inside of the command center. Of course, Mark didn't realize how much she suspected already about what they were doing.

This morning, though, Mark didn't have to go out to the command center until later. Dr. Langtree wasn't coming to the island until tomorrow, and Mark had gotten everything pretty much functional yesterday. Today he just needed to run some more calibrations on the equipment and do some more low level tests. He was actually happy with how the equipment all checked out yesterday.

They both got up from the breakfast table, and went around to the storage shed to get their bikes. It was a cool morning, since it was getting near the end of October, so they both grabbed their coats before heading out. All of the family's bikes were stored in the shed around at the back of the house, and Danny had said that Mark could use his. They got on the bikes and turned left onto Main Street, then made the slight right onto Henderson Road. It was exhilarating as the cool air blew in their faces as they pedaled down the road. It was nice just being alone out here together. It was around eight thirty in the morning, and not a lot of traffic was on the roads yet. They were just enjoying the peacefulness of the autumn morning here on the island. It seemed like no time at all for them to travel the three and a half miles to Ocean View Lane where they turned left and crossed over Sea Spray Drive to get to the boardwalk that leads to the beach. They had to walk their bikes up the stairs, but once they got back onto the beach they headed north where most of the private residences were located. Nearer to the boardwalk, the houses were smaller and closer to the beach, but the further that they rode, the larger the homes became. There were a few people out walking this morning, but not too many along this section of the beach. Most of the beachcombers would be down south where the beachfront hotels were located. Angela knew that Steve and Arlene, the directors of the Lighthouse Preservation Society had a home up this way somewhere, but she never had figured out exactly which one it was. There were also a few homes owned by several wealthy millionaires. As they rode up a little further, they seemed to run out of the populated area and it seemed that there were no more houses. Upon riding for another three minutes, however, they spotted an extremely large mansion sitting a little ways back from the beach. It was surrounded on both sides by trees and had a large deck on the second floor that wrapped around the entire house.

"Wonder who lives there?" asked Mark.

"I'm not sure. My grandparents don't really know anybody up this far."

Mark had stopped his bike and was looking up toward the direction of the mansion. There was an older man standing out on the deck holding a pair of binoculars. He appeared to be watching them.

"Don't look now, but I think we're being watched." said Angela as she spotted the man on the deck as well.

"Is he watching us?" inquired Mark.

"I don't think so. He's probably watching something a little further out to sea."

But as both of them turned to find what he could be viewing, all they saw was ocean and waves as they broke on the beach. Looking back toward the house, the man was still appearing to watch them through the binoculars.

"Let's go." Angela said, "That guy's starting to creep me out!"

"I wouldn't worry about him too much. He's probably just some old rich guy with nothing better to do than watch people as they stroll and ride along the beach."

Still, they decided to continue their ride up the beach, and pretty soon had left the house and the man on the porch far behind. They rode up almost as far as they could go before the beach ended and it was just woods and scrub brush the rest of the way to the ferry dock. At the end of the beach was another boardwalk that led back up onto Sea Spray Drive. They decided, however, to turn around and ride back along the beach, passing the beach mansion with the man with binoculars again as they went. This time, there was nobody on the deck as they rode past.

"He must have gotten tired of watching whatever he was watching." said Mark.

Back at the bed and breakfast, everyone had finished up their breakfast, and was getting ready to start their day. Dan suggested that they walk into town and maybe do some shopping. It was always fun to look in the little shops along Main Street and maybe have lunch at the Sand Crab Diner a little later. They even invited one of the other couples, Richard and Bernice Sorensen, whom they had met last night, to join them. They were also vacationing here for the week and had checked in late Sunday night. They were both in their early fifties, and were from Cary, which was just a little ways out of Raleigh, so they were fairly local too. Richard remembered a few vacations to Green Island that he had taken with his family when he was younger, but this was Bernice's first time to visit. Everyone that they had met here so far had been friendly, and Richard had definitely found a friend in Dan. They had been inquiring about some of the things to do on the island, and that's when Dan had invited them to go into town with them. Richard had also been asking Dan some questions about the lighthouse, so he had obviously remembered it from his visits while growing up. Dan told him that the museum was open now, and they could go out there and actually take a tour and climb to the top.

Since it was a nice day, and he was already this far down, Mark decided to ride his bike the rest of the way out to the lighthouse. He had his keys to the Mobile Command Center, and everything that he needed was either in there or in the cargo trailer that they had set up next to it. He had a few more things to get set up, but he told Angela that he'd still probably be able to leave around five or six. Angela couldn't get the events of the past several weeks and the Chandler-Langtree journal off of her mind, so she decided to sit along the boardwalk and just think for awhile. The beach along Sea Spray Drive had always been one of her favorite spots just to relax and clear her mind when she needed some alone time, and she felt like that was exactly what she needed now.

After Mark had left to go out to the lighthouse, she just sat and stared out toward the ocean. There wasn't anything more relaxing than just sitting along the boardwalk listening to the sound of the surf as the waves crashed in upon the beach. To her it was nature's symphony, and just sitting here enjoying it with the warm sunlight shining down upon her made the events of the past few weeks seem much more distant. Whatever Mark was working on, it had to be something logical. Science fiction seemed a long way off this morning. She watched as about three other couples strolled along the beach. Watching them made her think of her and Mark. They'd only been together for about six months, but already neither of them could imagine being with anyone else. She wished that she could stop worrying about him so much, and again tried to tell herself that there was nothing at all to worry about. But try as she did, she couldn't quite convince herself of that. Deep down, she knew that something wasn't exactly right with this whole situation, though at this point she didn't know exactly what it was. What she was certain of, though, was that it had something to do with Chandler-Langtree.

As she sat, staring out at the deep blue ocean, totally lost in thought, she heard footsteps come up behind her on the boardwalk.

Turning, she saw an elderly man probably in his seventies. He reminded her a lot of her Grandpa Wendell.

"Nice morning to just sit and think isn't it." he said.

"Yes it is." she replied, "I always like to come out here to just enjoy the peacefulness of it."

"The island can be a peaceful place," he replied, "away from all of the problems of the city. May I sit down?"

"Please do." she replied. There was something about his mannerism that immediately put her mind at ease.

"Do you live around here?" he asked.

"No, we live in Greenville. My grandparents live here on the island, though. They've lived here all their lives and my mom grew up here. We're visiting for the week."

"This would be a nice place to grow up. I just moved here a few years ago. I bought a beachfront house up the beach a little ways."

When he said this, she remembered the man on the deck a little while ago.

"Were you the one watching us from the big house a few minutes ago when we were riding along the beach?"

"Yes, I'm guilty." he replied, a slight smile on his face, "That's one of the things that I enjoy doing; just watching people as they go up and down the beach. Most of the time they don't even notice me. I hope I didn't make you uncomfortable."

While she had to admit that when she first saw him watching through the binoculars, he had made her a little nervous, talking with him here now eased her mind completely.

"Maybe a little, but I'm fine now."

"You and your boyfriend seem really in love."

"We are." she said as a huge smile lit up her face. "He's wonderful, and charming, and I love him more than anything. How about you? Is there someone in your life?"

"No, I never married. There was someone, a long time ago, but it just wasn't meant to be. I had obligations, and settling down with a family just wasn't possible. How about your boyfriend; does he work here on the island?"

"His name's Mark, and no, he doesn't work here full time. He actually works for a company called Chandler-Langtree up near Wilmington. They're doing some experiments out at the lighthouse, so that's why he's here for the week."

The more that they talked, the more that Angela felt that there was something familiar about the man, like they had met somewhere before, but she couldn't quite place where.

"My name's Angela." she told him, realizing that she hadn't introduced herself earlier.

"I'm Albert." he replied, "My friends call me Al. Nice to make your acquaintance. Do you know what kind of experiments that Mark's doing here on the island?"

"No, he doesn't really talk about them much."

That's all that she really wanted to say. While she did suspect that it had to do with time travel, she didn't feel comfortable talking about that with a complete stranger. After all, how would that sound? Al would think that she was crazy for sure!

"Is the tower out by the lighthouse something that he's working on?" Al asked.

"Yes, I think it is." she said remembering the temporal field monitor.

"Do you know what it's for?" Al asked.

While Al was pleasant to talk to, it was starting to concern her just a little that he was asking so many questions about Mark and the things that Mark was working on. She had to wonder if maybe he knew more than he was letting on. While she knew that the tower was supposedly a temporal field monitor, she wasn't about to tell him that.

"Why are you asking so many questions about what Mark's doing?" she inquired.

"I'm just curious. When you mentioned that he worked for Chandler-Langtree, I remembered seeing a lot more cars and trucks with their logo on them over the past several weeks. I imagine that there may be a lot of people around here that are curious about what's going on."

That explanation did seem to satisfy her. After all, even her Grandma had noticed all of the Chandler-Langtree cars and trucks on the island, and she had to admit that even she wondered about all of the activity.

"That's fine," she said, becoming less suspicious now, "even I'm curious about what they're doing. I've been told weather experiments, but I'm not sure that's all it is."

"What do you think it is?" he inquired, a curious look on his face now.

Again, she definitely didn't want to mention time travel, so she simply replied, "I'm really not sure. I just don't think that it's weather."

"I doubt that it is either." he responded, "From what I know about Chandler-Langtree, they're really not into weather experiments."

"Do you have any ideas?" she asked, slightly intrigued by his last statement. It made her start to think that maybe he did know more than he was letting on.

"Not really. I don't really know much about them, but I do think that it's curious that they've had so much activity going on here on the island for the past several weeks, especially out at an old one hundred fifty year old lighthouse. It just makes me wonder what they might be doing. I've actually grown to like it here. I'd hate for anything to spoil that."

"I would too! My grandparents have lived here all their lives, and I enjoy coming here as well."

As she looked at Al now, he had a more serious expression on his face. She had to wonder why. Was it something that she had said?

"Are you worried about Mark?" Al asked.

"What do you mean?" she asked hesitantly. At this point she really was starting to not like the direction that this conversation was going.

"With him working for Chandler-Langtree. You've heard the stories about things that go on there, right?"

"Yes, but Mark's assured me that they're not true."

"Maybe ... But maybe he doesn't know everything that goes on there yet. Maybe they're just telling him what he needs to know."

Now he was starting to scare her. She actually had these same thoughts, but Mark had convinced her that they were just irrational fears. Now here's a total stranger implying that she may actually have reason to be concerned after all.

"Do you think I should be worried?" she asked.

"Let's just say that I've been watching the company since they came here to the island. I've heard all of the rumors as well. I think that they could be working on some dangerous projects; projects that cross the boundaries of what man should even try to tamper with."

NOW she was really worried. If she hadn't had reason to be before, now she surely did.

"What kind of projects? she asked, her voice shaking now.

"I'm sorry; I didn't mean to frighten you. I just felt like I should warn you to be cautious. Especially around Chandler-Langtree."

"What kind of projects?!" she said, more forcefully this time.

He knew at this point that she wouldn't be dissuaded. He'd have to tell her something.

"Have you read some of the articles on Ryan Langtree's website?" he asked her.

"Yes, some of them."

"So you know that Ryan Langtree is obsessed with time travel."

"Yes." she replied, hesitantly again. She had read some of his articles on the website, but actually didn't really know enough about him to know if he could really be called OBSESSED or not.

"I think that's what they're doing here. They're working on the ability to travel through time."

While she had half way expected that was what they were doing, it did totally catch her off guard when Al actually said it. It was a confirmation of what she was suspecting all along, and just served to validate what she'd been reading in the Chandler-Langtree journal. She hoped that she had been able to hide her startled look, but the expression on Al's face told her that she hadn't.

"Surprised about that?" he asked.

"A little. I've sort of suspected that might be what they're attempting, too, but I'm not sure that I really believe that it's possible."

"Why not?"

"Well, because ... because it just isn't."

"What's that in your pocket?" he asked. She thought that he was trying to change the subject.

"My Smartphone."

"What does it do?"

"You know what a Smartphone does. I can talk to my family and friends."

"Can you talk to someone on the other side of the world?"

"Yes, if I knew someone on the other side of the world!"

"What do you think that people back in the eighteen hundreds would think about your Smartphone? Do you think they would think it was possible to talk to someone on the other side of the world?"

"No, but that's different!" she protested.

"How is it different? They would have thought the Smartphone was just as impossible as you're thinking that time travel is now because radio waves hadn't been discovered yet. Until radio waves were discovered, it actually was impossible for them to talk around the world."

She was nodding her head as he said this as if she was actually starting to understand.

"I think I'm starting to see what you're saying. Before temporal fields were discovered, time travel was impossible. But now ..."

"Exactly!"

"So why do you think that's what they're doing?" she asked him, "They could be doing any number of things."

"Because I've been studying Chandler-Langtree. And I've studied Ryan Langtree. I feel that's definitely what they're doing."

She was wondering at this point if she should show him the journal that she had downloaded from the Chandler-Langtree computers. Maybe next time she met him she'd think about showing it to him. She didn't have it with her now anyway.

"Well, Al, it's been nice talking to you, but I probably need to run."

"Nice talking to you, too, Angela."

He took out a piece of paper and wrote down his phone number.

"Call me if you need anything." he said as he passed her the piece of paper. "And one more thing; it might be better if you don't tell anyone about our meeting here today."

"Why? I think my dad would like to meet you."

"I think he would too, but I'm not ready to meet him just yet. And Mark would be suspicious. He'd want to know more about me. I think we could find out more together if we just keep it between the two of us for now."

"Ok. I won't tell anyone. You're probably right. And I haven't told Mark about any of my thoughts on this, anyway; at least not yet."

As she walked away, putting the piece of paper in her pocket, she waved goodbye to him. He smiled and waved back, then he headed across the boardwalk and began to walk back up the beach.

As Angela rode back down Henderson Road, she kept going over and over the meeting with Al. While it was unexpected, in a way she was glad to have an ally here on the island. Still, a part of her didn't know whether to trust him or not. As she reflected on the conversation, she began to wonder how he knew so much about Chandler-Langtree. And the way that he was practically making a case for why time travel could be possible. He almost sounded like the articles on Ryan Langtree's website! But he did seem so nice, and for some reason, she actually did trust him.

On the way back to the bed and breakfast her Smartphone rang, and after a challenging task of fishing it out of the back pocket of her jeans while still maintaining her balance on the bike, she saw that it was her father. She hit the answer button with her thumb, and then put it to her ear.

"Hi, Dad, what's up?"

"Have you and Mark finished up yet?"

"Yes, we finished our ride along the beach a little while ago. I'm on my way back to the bed and breakfast now."

"We're heading to the Sand Crab Diner for lunch. Do you want to join us?"

"Sounds great! I'll be there in about ten minutes."

"See you then!" Dan said as he hung up the phone. Being here on the island with Mark had definitely been good for her. Even with everything that had been happening lately, she still seemed to be handling it well, but she still wasn't sure how much she really believed. While Al had made a compelling argument of why time travel could really be possible, she had to wonder; was it really?

CHAPTER 16

The Doorway Opens

When Angela arrived at the Sand Crab Diner, everyone was already there waiting on her. Since there was quite a crowd, with her mom, dad, Danny and Rebekah, along with Mr. and Mrs. Duncan, and Mr. and Mrs. Sorensen, the server had pulled a couple of tables together near the side of the diner. Her dad had saved her a seat next to him, so she sat down and picked up a menu. Picking up the menu was mostly just habit, since she always got one of two entrees there; either the pastrami sandwich with potato salad, or the chicken fingers.

"How was the ride?" asked her mother.

"It was nice, just a little cool, but still pleasant."

Then pausing she inquired, "Do you know who lives in the large mansion on North Sea Spray Drive?"

"Which house are you talking about?" asked Dianne.

"It's the biggest one along the beach. It kind of sits back a little farther than most of the others and has a deck that goes all the way around the back side of the house facing the ocean. It's the one at the far north part of the beach, pretty much set apart by itself."

"No, I don't know anyone that far up the beach. Steve and Arlene live up that way in the tan house with the green shutters, and the Johnson's live just north of the boardwalk, but they're the only ones that I know personally that live out that way. Why do you ask?"

"No particular reason. There was a man out on the deck as we went by that waved to us. I was just wondering if it was anyone that you knew."

"No, sorry, I can't help you there." replied her mother.

"So you're Mark's girlfriend?" asks Richard.

"Yes, I'm Angela."

"I'm Richard Sorensen, and this is my wife Bernice. It's nice to meet you."

Richard went on, "We actually have something for Mark. Will he be back at the bed and breakfast this evening?"

"Yes, he should be back around five or six." Angela replied, starting to wonder what all the interest in Mark has been today, "What do you have for him?"

"It's a box" replied Richard, "that our father, Blake, gave to us to give to him."

"Oh, how did your father know Mark?" Angela asked.

"That's the part that we're not exactly sure about." answered Richard. "My father was always a little eccentric. He was a professor at NC State in Raleigh. He was all the time engrossed in odd theories, most of which I never fully understood. When he died three years ago he specified in his will to give the box to Mark Duncan, here on Green Island, specifically this week. He actually specified that we stay here at the Baker Family Bed and Breakfast."

"Do you know what's in the box?" Dan asked.

"No, it's locked."

"Then how is Mark supposed to get into it?"

"Dad said that the letter taped to the top of the box would tell him how to open it. He talked to me several times about the box, though. He said to be sure that Mark gets it this week. But we still have no idea how he even knew Mark. We're both hoping that maybe Mark can give us some idea about that."

Angela looked even more puzzled. Could this day get any stranger? First, the meeting with Albert out on the boardwalk, and now meeting two complete strangers that have something for Mark. Since Mark had gotten the job with Chandler-Langtree her life had definitely taken a turn toward the bizarre. Her thoughts were interrupted by their server coming to take their order. They all took turns giving their orders, and then got back to the conversation.

"What did your father teach at the university?" asked Angela.

"Theoretical physics." answered Richard. "I never understood a lot of what he taught, but for the last ten years he was the chairman of the department. He was good at what he did."

As he said this Angela thought that she should have expected this. It was another piece to a puzzle that still had more questions than answers. She did have the answer to her previous question, however; the day definitely could get stranger. Here was a theoretical physicist who died three years ago, but left a box containing who knows what to Mark. And how he even knew Mark was a big question. She supposed that since he was a professor in the same field as Mark that they could have talked on several occasions. Maybe Mark had contacted him about some research. That's probably what it was; he was leaving Mark some of his research to continue his work.

As their food was served and they all started eating, the conversation shifted to other topics. Still Angela had to wonder what was in the box, and how Richard's father knew Mark. Maybe Mark would be able to shed some light on why Richard's dad was giving him a box. Maybe he was someone that Mark had met even before he met her.

The rest of the afternoon was relatively uneventful for Dan and Kate as well. After lunch, Dan accompanied the Sorensens out to the lighthouse while Dianne and the kids along with the Duncans continued down to the Shoppes on the Boardwalk at the end of Main Street on the opposite side of town. Richard and Bernice were definitely intrigued by the lighthouse. They took the complete tour to the top, and as they looked out over the island to the waves crashing in on the shore, they couldn't help but feel that what they had was no ordinary box. Richard's father had been insistent about it being given to Mark this week, so what was in it must be important, but as they thought about it now, even they didn't know exactly how important and how many lives would be changed by its contents, including their own.

That night at the bed and breakfast, Angela kept going to the window and pulling back the curtains, waiting for Mark to arrive. He was supposed to come home around five, but it was already fifteen after seven. She pulled out her Smartphone and dialed his number. As she figured, he was still out at the lighthouse, but he was getting ready to start home. Since it was already dark and he didn't have his car, since he had ridden his bike out there today, he asked her to take the spare key and come to pick him up. She agreed, and after a few minutes, he saw car lights coming up Lighthouse Road, their beams shining through a thickening fog. He shut down the equipment in the Mobile Command Center, and then walked out the door to meet her, locking it behind him as he stepped outside into the cool evening air and got into the waiting car. The fog had come up suddenly, and was noticeably thicker now than it had been earlier as she came up the road. As she turned the car around and the headlights shone on the lighthouse, she stopped the car and intently studied the scene in front of her.

"What's the matter?" asked Mark.

"I don't know, something looks different."

"What do you mean?" he asked.

"Look at the lighthouse. Something's different."

"It looks the same to me."

"No," she replied, "there's something definitely different."

She shut off the car and opened the door to get out. As she started walking through the fog toward the lighthouse, Mark got out and followed her.

"Where are you going?" he shouted after her.

"Out to the lighthouse."

"Why?"

"To see what's different."

"I don't know what you mean." he said, "It looks the same to me."

As they got closer, she realized what it was.

"Where's the tower?" she asked.

"What tower?"

"The one with the white ball on top; where is it?"

"Right over there …" but as he said it, he realized that it actually wasn't there.

"Where did it go?" he asked, a slight hesitation to his voice now.

"I don't know, but it's definitely not there."

They both walked around the side of the house, looking for the tower, but somehow it just wasn't there. At least everything else looked pretty much as it should be. As they looked out toward the car, however, with its headlights shining in on the lighthouse, they noticed something else peculiar that they hadn't realized before as they walked out here. They had been concentrating so much on the lighthouse that they had failed to notice that the fog was only outside of the circular wall surrounding it. There was not a trace of the fog inside the wall where they were standing. It was also completely clear around the lighthouse as well. Looking up, it appeared that they were inside of a large tube created on all sides by the fog. They both looked at each other inquisitively, wondering what was going on here. It was at this point that they also realized how much colder it had seemed once they walked inside the wall.

Not being able to make any sense out of what was going on here, they both walked back into the fog and got into the car. As Mark began to drive out onto Lighthouse Road, he suddenly stopped. After pausing for a few seconds, he put the car in reverse and did a three point turn to head back to the command center. After pulling up beside the command center and getting out, he went to the door and pulled out his keys to unlock it. Angela had gotten out of the car and was standing beside the passenger door watching him. As he opened the door to the command center he looked back over toward her direction.

"Come on!" he said, "I need to check something inside."

"I didn't know if I was supposed to go in there."

"I don't think it matters any more. Close the car door and come inside."

As they both entered the command center, all of the lights were out, but a dim glow from the various panels along the wall illuminated things enough for them to be able to see where they were going. Instead of switching on the main lights, which would have hampered their ability to see outside, Mark switched on some panel lights which illuminated several dials, a couple of computer monitors that were built into the wall, and a couple of keyboards. As the monitors lit up, Mark typed some commands on one of the keyboards. On the one monitor, the words "System Offline" appeared.

"What system is offline?" Angela asked.

"The monitor on the missing tower!

Mark typed a few more commands into the keyboard while Angela looked over his shoulder, but nothing changed on the monitor. He tried to access the video cameras out at the lighthouse on the other terminal, but came up with "Video Feed Offline". He went to another keyboard and typed in a few more commands. This time, columns of data appeared on another monitor and Mark began to closely examine the numbers.

"What video feed were you trying to access?" she asked him.

"The cameras out at the lighthouse. But the system couldn't reach any of them."

"Why not? What's wrong with them?"

"Nothing's wrong with them, they're just not here anymore."

"Where did they go?" she asked, more bewildered than ever at this point. She just wasn't putting the pieces together the same way that Mark was.

"They're in another time!" he answered excitedly.

She looked back out at the lighthouse. While nothing had really changed, it somehow looked different.

Mark continued, "I think the lighthouse and everything inside the wall is in another time period. When we were out at the lighthouse several minutes ago, I don't think we were in 2018 anymore. That's why the tower is gone. Whatever time period the lighthouse is in, the tower hasn't been built yet. That's why we can't access it with the computers here in the command center, because in this time period it isn't here!"

"So we actually travelled back in time?" she asked.

"Yes, I think so."

"But what caused it? All of the equipment here in the command center was turned off at the time, right? Nothing here should have triggered it."

"I'm not sure, but when we were out here a few weeks ago we were getting some strange readings from the portable field monitors. I think it just opened up by itself."

"Can it do that?"

"It must be able to. I'm trying to run temporal traces now to see if I can find out the time period that the lighthouse is in right now, but that part of the matrix hasn't been loaded yet. I didn't expect it to do this tonight! My best guess based on these numbers is that it's somewhere between 1990 and 2010. The Coast Guard emblem is still on the door, so it's probably still operated by the Coast Guard at this point."

As she looked through the window of the command center at the lighthouse, she couldn't take her eyes off of it. She suddenly realized that she was looking back in time! It really was possible!

As she stood staring out at the lighthouse while Mark frantically tried to narrow down the time period that they were looking at, she noticed slight variations in the scene. The outline of a tree appeared in the foreground that previously hadn't been there before, then a hedge around the side of the house, and finally the light outline of the tower with the white ball on top began to reappear. Suddenly the display on the monitor on the right changed. Where it previously had displayed "System Offline", now the temporal field monitor was booting up and reconnecting! Within minutes, the donut shaped temporal field monitor display was back online. Looking out the window of the command center, everything was as it should be. The tower could be seen beside the house, and thin wisps of fog were quickly dissipating outside the window.

"Did you get the year?" she asked.

"No, I couldn't narrow it down any more, but it was definitely before 2010!"

They both sat silently, alternating stares out the window and then back at the monitors inside the command center. They were both trying to process exactly what had just happened. It seemed so impossible, yet neither of them could deny the events of the past several minutes and what they had just witnessed.

Dianne walked into the sitting room where the rest of them were gathered. She walked over to where Dan was sitting talking with Scotty.

"Shouldn't Angela have been back by now? She left to get Mark around seven thirty and it's after ten now."

"I've been thinking the same thing." replied Dan. "Scotty, why don't we take a ride out to the lighthouse and make sure everything's alright?"

"Let's go!" said Scotty as he got up off of the sofa and headed over toward the door leading to the foyer. Dan grabbed his jacket and followed him out the door.

"Be careful!" called Dianne after them.

Walking out onto the porch of the bed and breakfast, then down the stairs to the sidewalk they could see that the night was completely clear. Dan was always amazed at how clear the night sky looked here on the island away from all of the city lights. They got into the front seats of the rental van, cranked it up and then turned left onto Main Street.

"Keep a lookout for them coming back this way." advised Dan.

"I will. So far there doesn't look like too much traffic out tonight."

They took a slight right onto Henderson Road where they continued the three and a half miles down to Ocean View Lane where they would turn left to get onto Sea Spray Drive. Dan was quiet for most of the trip. While he tried not to worry Dianne, he had actually been a little concerned for the last hour. He was glad that he and Scotty were on their way to check on the kids now. After making the turn onto Lighthouse Road, they suddenly found themselves driving through a moderately thick fog. They slowed to about twenty miles per hour since the visibility was greatly reduced.

"Where'd this fog come from?" asked Scotty. "It was perfectly clear when we started out!"

"Looks like it's not now, though. Fog can come up fairly quickly here on the island."

The closer that they got to the lighthouse, the fog began to thin. As the visibility improved they felt that they could safely go thirty five. By the time that they pulled into the lighthouse parking lot, the fog was down to thin wisps. They could still see the headlight beams shining through what was left of the fog, but they were not as pronounced as they had been earlier. Dan spotted Mark's car parked over beside the Mobile Command Center.

"There's their car!" he said, pointing in the direction of the command center, "At least she made it here!" Scotty pulled the van up beside Mark's car and both he and Dan got out into the cool night air. They could see dim lights inside the command center. Dan walked over and knocked on the door. After a few seconds, the door opened.

"Mr. Nelson; Dad; What are you doing here?" asked Mark.

"We were starting to worry," replied Dan, "Angela left over two and a half hours ago."

"Oh, has it been that long? Let me go and turn everything off and get her."

He closed the door and walked over to where Angela was still sitting, looking out at the lighthouse which looked perfectly normal now. As he was shutting down all of the equipment, he said to Angela, "Maybe we shouldn't say anything about this to anyone."

"Why?"

"Who'd believe it for one thing? And for another, I'm not supposed to say anything about what we're actually doing here. Remember, everyone thinks that we're doing weather experiments!"

She did remember that, but she also remembered the conversations that she'd had with her dad. He already knew more than he was supposed to as well, even though Mark didn't know about his and Angela's conversations and of the Chandler-Langtree journal that she had. She wasn't ready to tell him about breaking into the computer system either, so for now she agreed not to say anything to anyone.

As they exited the command center and Mark turned to lock the door, Angela approached her dad.

"You had us worried." Dan said, "We thought you were coming right back."

"Sorry, I thought we'd be right back too, but when I got here Mark was just finishing up some things. I guess we sort of lost track of time."

"That's OK, no harm done. Why don't we head on back now?

Your mother's probably still worried."

As they pulled up in front of the bed and breakfast, she saw that Dan had been right. Her mother was looking out the front window wondering when they'd be home. Dianne ran out the front door when she saw them pull up and gave Angela a huge hug as she got out of the car.

"We're OK, Mom! Mark just had to finish up some things before we could come back. I'm sorry I worried you."

"I'm just glad that you're safe! Come on, let's go inside and get some hot cocoa!"

As they walked up the steps to the bed and breakfast, Angela and Mark exchanged knowing glances. Tonight they'd been somewhere where nobody had ever been before, or so they thought. They'd actually travelled through time, simply by walking into the past and back out again!

As they walked into the kitchen to get the cocoa Angela remembered the conversation from earlier in the day.

"Mark, do you know anyone named Blake Sorensen? He was a professor at NC State University in the Theoretical Physics Department."

"I don't think so, why?"

"Because his son, Richard, has a box to give to you that his dad gave him before he died. He says that his dad specifically instructed him to give it to you this week."

"What's in it?"

"He doesn't know, since it's locked. There are instructions in an envelope that supposedly explain how to get into it."

The hot cocoa was ready now, so they both poured themselves a cup then walked into the parlor.

"Where are the Sorensens?" asked Angela.

"They went back to their room about a half hour ago. Mark can talk to them tomorrow." Dianne answered.

As they were driving back from the lighthouse tonight, Angela had hoped that the Sorensens would still be up and they could find out what was in the box. Now they'd have to wait until tomorrow, and since Mark was going in early to meet with Dr. Langtree, it would probably have to be tomorrow evening.

That night, Angela had a hard time getting to sleep. She lay awake for hours, just staring into the darkness. As usual, Rebekah and Danny had gone to sleep almost immediately, but her and Mark had done the equivalent of walking on another world! They had travelled back in time, and she felt that nothing would be the same again.

CHAPTER 17
October 24, 2018
Pondering the Impossible

Angela had finally gotten to sleep last night. It had taken a while, but sleep finally came. This morning, since she had slept until almost nine thirty, Mark had already left to go out to the lighthouse to meet Dr. Langtree. She had decided last night that she'd talk to her dad today about what had happened. She'd ask him not to tell anyone else, since she didn't want to get Mark in trouble. She'd promised Mark that she wouldn't say anything to anyone, but she needed to talk with her dad about these new developments. She wasn't even sure that he'd believe her, but if anyone would, he would. Their time travel excursion last night proved that since time travel was really possible then it could have been what changed their reality on May 20, 2016. Events around the temporal field could have affected the time line so that her father had a different family. This part sort of bothered her, since she wasn't part of her father's original family. Was she not actually supposed to be here? If the time line hadn't been altered, then she wouldn't even be alive today. Or would she? Her father might not have married her mother, but her mother could have married someone else. But if her mother had married someone else, then would any children that she had actually be her? After all, she was a part of both her mother and father's DNA. She was a part of both of them. Thinking about this actually made her brain hurt! It was so impossible, yet here she was forced to deal with it.

By the time that she got downstairs, breakfast was over, but then it wouldn't be long until lunch time either.

"Good morning, sleepyhead!" her father said as she walked into the parlor. He and Scotty were the only ones in the room, and they had been sitting in two of the large chairs having a conversation over a cup of coffee.

It was taking her longer to wake up this morning than it usually did.

"Good morning, dad."

"We talked to Mark this morning before he left," said her father, "and he said that he'd try to get home earlier tonight. He wants to see what's in the box that Richard has for him."

"I wouldn't count on it!" said Angela, somewhat sarcastically, "Dr. Langtree's coming today."

"We'll see." replied Dan. "I think there might still be some eggs and sausage left over from breakfast if you're hungry."

"I'm starving! I think all that I had yesterday was what we had at the Sand Crab Diner. I was worried about Mark later in the evening, so I didn't eat dinner."

Dan accompanied her into the kitchen where he opened the refrigerator and pulled out the leftover eggs and sausage. Fortunately, there was still some gravy as well. He put some in a plate and put it in the microwave as Angela sat down at the table.

"How much does Mr. Duncan know about what's going on?" asked Angela quietly so that Scotty wouldn't hear.

"I don't think much; At least not nearly as much as we know. From what I can tell Mark hasn't told him a lot."

"That figures. Mark's really secretive about what goes on there. But then I guess he has a reason to be. Where are mom and Mrs. Duncan, and Danny and Rebekah?"

"Your mom and Mrs. Duncan are in town. It seems like they didn't get all of their shopping done yesterday. Danny and Rebekah took a boat trip around the island with the Sorensens. They should be back around one."

Dan noticed that Angela suddenly got a more serious look on her face.

"Is anything wrong?" he asked her.

"Dad, can we talk … privately? "

"Sure, we can go for a walk after you finish eating."

At this point Scotty came into the kitchen to join them.

"I think I'm going to take a drive out to the beach." he said. "Anyone want to join me?"

"You go ahead." said Dan. "I think we'll just stay around here for a little while."

Scotty realized from Dan's expression that he and Angela probably wanted some time together, so he decided to go on out to the beach anyway. After Scotty had left and they heard his van drive away, Angela finished up her breakfast and both she and Dan grabbed their jackets and walked out the front door and down the stairs to the sidewalk. They turned right and began walking toward town. Since today was a lot colder than yesterday, they both buttoned their jackets as a light cold wind blew in their faces.

"Dad, something happened last night that I don't fully understand."

Now it was Dan's turn to be concerned, as a worried look came over his face.

"Alright, go on."

She paused for a minute trying to find just the right words to explain what happened.

"Please don't share what I'm going to tell you with anyone else. I promised Mark that I wouldn't say anything to anyone, but he doesn't know that I've already been talking to you. I think Mark and I may have travelled back in time." She studied his face as she said this, trying to tell if he actually believed her or not. The look that she saw indicated interest, but not total disbelief. She knew that he had been skeptical of time travel from the start, after all who wouldn't be. Even she had been having trouble believing it.

"When? Where?" Dan asked.

"It happened last night at the lighthouse. After I picked Mark up from the Mobile Command Center and I was turning the car around, the lights illuminated the lighthouse. I noticed that it looked different, but didn't know exactly what was out of place. I stopped the car and Mark and I walked out to the lighthouse. It wasn't until we got closer that we saw what was different. The tower that had been erected earlier this year beside the house was missing. We walked right up to the house and it just wasn't there. There were no signs that it had ever been there either. While we were out at the lighthouse is when Mark thinks that we were in a different time period. Before we walked out to the lighthouse, it had been really foggy. But after we got out to it, when we looked toward the car with its lights shining through the fog toward us, we noticed that there was no fog actually inside the circular wall, only outside of it. Looking up, it looked like we were inside a huge grey tube."

This last statement caught Dan's interest as he remembered the visions that he'd had of being at the lighthouse and hearing Kate in the fog. He had been standing in the middle of that same grey tube. When she mentioned the grey tube, Angela noticed a change in her dad's expression.

"Dad, what is it?" she asked him.

"When you mentioned the fog and the grey tube, it reminded me of the dream where Kate and I were out at the lighthouse. I was inside that same grey tube when she came out of the fog. But I've never actually seen the fog from inside the wall; just in my dreams. I've read about it in the journal that you gave me, it just never occurred to me that it could still be happening."

"Yes, apparently it's still happening," she went on. "After that, we walked back into the fog and went back over to the Mobile Command Center to try and determine what was happening. We went inside and Mark tried to bring up pictures from the cameras out at the lighthouse. All of them seemed to be down. He couldn't get a picture on any of them. He kept trying to figure out exactly what year the lighthouse was in, but he never could narrow it down any more that just 'sometime before 2010'. After about fifteen more minutes, we started seeing various features around the lighthouse start to reappear, including the tower and a few trees. Once the tower reappeared, then he was able to get pictures from all of the cameras again! It was all very fascinating."

"Did it feel any different inside the wall than in the fog?" Dan asked.

"Yes, it was colder. It was quite a bit colder actually."

"Had Mark been doing anything to open the doorway to another time before all of this started?" he asked her.

"No, we were in the process of leaving actually. He thinks that it opened up all by itself."

"Can it do that?"

"That's the same question that I asked him. He wasn't sure, but he thought that it might be possible."

"Does he have any idea what caused it to do that?"

"I'm not sure. If he did, he didn't tell me."

Dan was silent for a few minutes, just pondering what Angela had just told him and trying to figure exactly how it applied to him and Kate. THEY hadn't walked into another time, but yet here they were having these visions together at the same time anyway. What could be causing those to happen? The only thing that he could figure was that it had something to do with the temporal field that Angela told him Mark said was there. Somehow, it must be recalling the alternate reality, the life that he had before May 20, 2016, but he still wasn't exactly sure how that could happen.

"This is unbelievable!" Dan remarked. "I'm still trying to figure out how all of this could apply to the dreams that Kate and I had. Somehow I know it's all connected."

"It probably is." Angela replied, "It seems that a lot has changed for our family based on what it says in the Chandler-Langtree journal. I'll admit, I was fairly skeptical at first as well, but after actually being there last night, and walking into another time, that made me a believer!"

"You really seem sure that's what happened."

"Yes, you would too if you'd been there. It was unlike anything that I've ever experienced!"

"I think it may extend beyond just opening a doorway to another time. I think there's more that we don't understand."

"What do you mean?" she asked with an inquisitive look.

"Last Sunday, when we arrived on the island and were walking up the steps of the bed and breakfast, remember when I thought the name on the sign was different?"

"Yes, but it wasn't. We all went outside to look."

"Actually, it was. I talked to Kate and she saw the same thing that I did; the sign actually said "Island Charm Bed and Breakfast".

"But if it did, what does that mean?"

"I don't know, but whatever caused that to happen might be the same thing that caused the dream that Kate and I had. We just don't understand it yet."

"Do you want me to ask Mark about what might have caused the sign to be different? He might have an idea of what could cause that."

Dan thought about this for a minute, and then finally replied, "Yes, ask him about the sign. You were there, so you remember what happened. He might have an idea. I'd rather not mention the dream that Kate and I had to him just yet though."

"Alright, I won't mention the dream to him; just the sign. It'll be interesting to see what he might have to say about it."

Angela seemed to be staring off into space again as they walked as if again trying to think of exactly what to say next. Finally, she continued, "Dad, there's something that's been bothering me lately that I read in the

Chandler-Langtree journal."

"What is it?" he asked.

"You've read the journal. Do you remember the year of the first entry?"

"Twenty one something, I think. I know it was sometime in the future."

"It was 2164. Do you think that Dr. Langtree and Dr. Chandler could really be from 2164?"

He had to admit, it would be a stretch. And prior to the events that had been happening lately he would have said with certainty that it couldn't be possible. But now, after the visions that he'd been having, and Angela and Mark stepping into another time last night, and all of the things that he had read in the journal; he honestly couldn't say for sure.

"I don't know. A week ago, I'd have said that it definitely wouldn't have been possible. But now I'm not so sure."

"If he is from 2164, then maybe he really did alter the future on May 20, 2016 by getting you to sell the lighthouse just like the journal says. Maybe the reality that we're in now really isn't the same one that you were in prior to that."

Dan interjected, "I'm still not sure how that could be, though. I don't remember any of it."

"Maybe you wouldn't remember any of it if it took place before May 20, 2016. Maybe your past would be altered too, so that your memories are only memories of your current life and your current family, even going back before May 20. And if you believe what the journal says, the purpose was to eliminate something called the Vortex Accelerator, whatever that is. The events that happened in our lives may have just been a side effect of the real purpose. Remember that movie, The Ripple Effect? Remember where the main character went back in time and changed things, only to come back and find that other things had been altered as well?"

Dan pondered this for a minute, "Yes, I remember that. But that was just a movie."

"Yes, but don't you think that if it really were possible to alter the past, that there would be other repercussions that weren't planned that could occur? We don't understand it yet, but maybe the Vortex Accelerator being eliminated is what caused our reality to change."

"I'm actually a little surprised to hear you talking this way. Out of all of the kids, you were always the practical one, but I do see your point."

Angela continued, "The part of the journal that I haven't been quite able to figure out, though, is if the purpose was to eliminate the Vortex Accelerator and it actually was eliminated, then what happened? Why is all of this still going on? Why is there still a temporal field? If there had been no Vortex Accelerator to create it in the first place, then how is it there now?"

Dan thought about this for a minute, "Maybe something went wrong. Maybe everything didn't happen the way that it was supposed to, or things didn't work the way that Dr. Langtree and Dr. Chandler thought that they would."

"I think you're right dad; something didn't go the way that they thought that it would. And they're trying to correct it now, but they don't know how! Maybe that's why they need Mark!"

"Hold it now! Even if any of this is true, what makes you think that experienced time travelers from the future would need Mark to figure out anything? Between now and 2164, wouldn't the technology be so advanced that it would be hard for even Mark to comprehend?"

"Maybe, but I still think that may be part of the story." replied Angela.

As they got into town, they ran into Dianne and Kate. When Dan saw them from a distance coming out of one of the shops, he asked Angela to ask her mother to take her shopping so that he and Kate could have some time to talk. She agreed, since she felt like she would like to find out more as well.

"Where're all of your shopping bags?" Dan asked.

"Mostly window shopping today." remarked Dianne.

"Mom, can we go shopping together, just the two of us? Maybe have some lunch?" asked Angela.

"I don't know; what would Kate do? You could join us if you'd like to, but I wouldn't feel right just abandoning her."

"I can walk her back to the bed and breakfast." offered Dan. "You and Angela haven't been able to spend a lot of quality time together so far during this trip. Shopping and lunch might be just what you need."

"Well, if it's alright with Kate."

"Yes, that's fine. You go ahead and spend some time with your daughter." said Kate, "I'll be fine."

As Dianne and Angela walked down the street and disappeared into one of the shops, Dan and Kate headed back up toward the bed and breakfast. This was actually what they both had wanted. Since they got here, they hadn't been able to spend as much time together as they'd hoped, and they had wanted to go out to the lighthouse together while they were here on the island.

"Where's Scotty?" Kate asked, "I thought you two would be doing something together today."

"He drove out to the beach. He asked if we wanted to go, but Angela and I had something that we needed to talk about. We took a walk to talk and ended up here."

"Was your talk about the Chandler-Langtree document that your daughter found?"

"Yes, in a roundabout way."

"Remember the other night back at the hotel when you said that

Angela believes that our realities had been altered on May 20, 2016? Do you think that both of our realities could have been altered by time travel? I know it's a lot to believe, but I've actually been reading some of the articles on Ryan Langtree's website. I hoped to find out a little bit about the man that my son is working for. After reading some of his ideas, I'm not even sure that I like the fact that Mark is working for him."

This last statement surprised him. He was trying to figure out how to tell her what he believed without getting into the time travel angle, now here she was coming right out and asking about it.

"I don't know, but Angela believes that it could be."

He really didn't want to tell her everything about what he and Angela talked about this morning. Since Mark didn't want Angela to tell anyone about last night, if he told Kate, she might be just too close to Mark. What would happen if he told her that Angela and Mark believed that they had travelled to a different time period? She'd probably ask Mark about it. He knew that if he were in her place, that's exactly what he would do. And Mark would think that Angela hadn't kept the secret.

"Dan, do you ever wonder what things could be possible that we just don't know about yet?"

"Sometimes."

"And what's happening here could be something that we just don't understand, at least not yet."

"Yes, I suppose I have thought about that."

"So," she continued, "maybe somebody altered our realities on May 20, 2016. I'm still having a hard time believing any of this, but I'm trying to at least consider it since there doesn't appear to be another explanation that makes any more sense. If Ryan Langtree is experimenting with time travel here on Green Island, and eventually he's successful, then maybe he could be the one that changed things. I've been thinking about Danny and Amy too. I had a dream about them last night."

"You're talking about our kids, right?"

"Yes. I don't remember a lot about the dream except that I was arriving out at the lighthouse with Danny, Amy, and another girl. I think the other girl was a friend of Amy's, but I can't remember her name. I remember that it had been a while since we'd seen you and we were surprising you by coming for a visit. I'm also not sure what you were doing here, but the lighthouse was surrounded by a lot of scaffolding like it was being repaired, so maybe that was it. I also remember that something happened to Amy. I'm not sure what it was, but I remember being very upset. That's about all that I do remember. Have you had any similar dreams?"

"No, I haven't had any dreams about Danny and Amy. I've just read about them in the journal."

"Let's drive out to the lighthouse." she suggested.

"Now?!"

"Yes, now! Everyone's occupied doing something else right now. This might be our best chance to go out there alone together."

"You're probably right. I'm not sure that we'll find anything out there, but we can go and see."

They were both so lost in conversation that they never even noticed the grey haired man, lurking in the shadows of the buildings, following them. They also never noticed the silver sports car parked across the street from the Little Book Nook. But the man had heard their conversation and he knew that they were going out to the lighthouse, and he planned to follow them.

CHAPTER 18

Altered Reality

When Dan and Kate got back to the bed and breakfast, Kate went upstairs to change clothes while Dan waited downstairs for her. For their shopping trip downtown, she had been wearing dress pants and a nice blouse, probably not the best outfit to go wandering around in the woods around the lighthouse. She decided on a pair of jeans and a turquoise long sleeve pullover, along with her brown boots with the silver buckles. As she left the room, she grabbed her jacket as well then headed down the stairs.

On the drive out to the lighthouse, they talked about what they might find. While she had read some of Dr. Langtree's articles on his website, those still didn't fully prepare her for what to expect. What exactly are you looking for while exploring the unknown?

"What are we going to do when we get out there?" she inquired of Dan.

"I'm not sure exactly. Explore the woods around the lighthouse I suppose. Maybe whatever we're supposed to find will find us."

She wasn't sure that she liked that last statement. It reminded her of Warren Evans stalking them at the hotel. It also reminded her that they had thought that they saw his car in the lighthouse parking lot last Sunday while they were at the top of the lighthouse. Now she'd be looking over her shoulder the entire time that they were out there, since he could be out there as well.

"I really don't like the idea of something 'finding us'." she replied.

"I'm not sure that I do either, but with the visions that we've been having at some of the oddest times, and all of the other events that have been going on, you never know what to expect."

He was actually thinking about Warren Evans, too, but he didn't want to mention him so as not to worry her. He had no way of knowing that she had already had the same thought.

He continued, "When we get there, I'll park around to the side, out of view of the Mobile Command Center. I'm not sure that I want Dr. Langtree knowing that we're snooping around out there, since he might know more about what's happening to us than we do. There'll still be a short distance that he'll be able to see us if he's looking, but if we hurry maybe we can get past undetected."

As they continued the journey, Dan turned onto Lighthouse Road for the mile long drive. It wasn't the same road that he remembered when his family used to come here for vacations. It used to be much narrower then. When he had first visited the lighthouse when he was younger, it was just a gravel road. The only folks really going out there were members of the Coast Guard who operated the light and they only needed a smaller one lane road and it wasn't even paved. Later, soon after he married Dianne, they did pave the road, though they didn't make it any wider. Now, since the lighthouse belonged to the Preservation Society, they had both widened the road to two lanes and repaved it. They had cut a lot of the trees back from the road as well so that they wouldn't scrape against the cars as they drove past.

As they approached the lighthouse, they could see the Airstream travel trailer that had been converted to the Mobile Command Center sitting at the edge of the woods in the far corner of the parking lot. Mark's car, along with a black Chandler-Langtree van, was parked next to it. Dan turned right at the first entrance to the main parking lot so that he could get into the lot and park over to the side out of view of the command center. That would also give them better access to the woods running alongside the lighthouse without being seen. The spot that they finally selected was bordering the woods at the far end of the side parking lot, with the lighthouse completely blocking the view of them from the Mobile Command Center. When they got out of the van, Dan went around to the back, opened the lift gate and retrieved two flashlights from the small toolbox which he kept under the back seat.

"We're not planning on being out here long enough for it to get dark are we?" asked Kate.

"No, probably not, but some of the areas in these woods can be fairly dark even in the middle of the day. And who knows if we'll stumble across something that we might need to get a closer look at."

He gave one of the lights to Kate and slipped the other one in his right pants pocket.

"Let's start out over there." he said.

They walked across the grass over toward the woods. Kate immediately saw what he meant about the woods being dark even during the daytime. Even though it was one thirty in the afternoon and there was a hazy sun shining through a light cloud cover, there were still some places where she found herself shining her light into the woods to be able to see well as they walked along at the edge. They were walking outside of the circular wall since probably all of the scientific instruments that Chandler-Langtree had placed there would be concealed in the woods. They walked at the edge of the woods all the way down to the water's edge, then walked back up another fifty or so feet and found a small clearing where they could enter the woods. It got surprisingly dark the further that they went, and there were several areas that were wet and boggy as well. They both had their flashlights on now, their beams moving back and forth in front of them as they walked deeper into the woods. About a hundred feet into the woods, Kate's beam shone on a silver box about six feet wide by four feet high.

"I've found something." she announced, as the beam from her light illuminated the silver box.

"Looks like an electrical box of some kind." Dan said, as they walked over closer to where it was. There was also a tower next to it extending maybe fifty or seventy five feet into the air. Mounted at the top of the tower was what looked like some kind of antenna consisting of a horizontal bar with five hexagonal elements mounted along the length of it.

Inside the Mobile Command Center, Dr. Langtree and Mark were busily running calculations and calibrations on the equipment. Right now, they had all of the equipment running in simulation mode, which meant that they could enter the parameters and simulate an actual temporal incursion without actually firing up the emitters located at various places in the woods around the lighthouse.

Suddenly, a perimeter alarm broke the silence inside the trailer. Startled, Dr. Langtree came over to the main console which displayed a map of the area around the lighthouse. A red dot was blinking on an area not too far from the water's edge around toward the back side of the lighthouse.

"Probably just a deer." said Dr. Langtree as he punched up the camera for Sector Seven and moved the joystick to pan the camera around. Since the area of the woods where they placed most of the cameras was fairly dark, the cameras all had an infrared mode as well. He'd switch that on if needed, but for right now the high resolution mode was working fairly well. As the camera picked up movement as he was panning around, he stopped and used the zoom to go in closer.

"Is that my mom?!" asked Mark in a surprised tone.

"And Dan Nelson as well." said Dr. Langtree.

Both Mark and Dr. Langtree watched them intently as they came closer to the silver box.

"What are they doing out there?!" inquired Mark.

"I think they're trying to find out what we're doing out here." remarked Dr. Langtree.

"Why would Mr. Nelson and my mom be wondering what we're doing out here?"

"I'm not entirely sure." replied Dr. Langtree as he continued to watch them on the monitor, a curious tone to his voice. He was also curious that Dan and Kate were together. While he knew about their connection in their previous reality, he was puzzled at why they were together here in this reality. It didn't make any sense to him. He watched as they studied the box, taking pictures with their phones, and then taking more pictures of the emitter at the top of the tower.

As they were walking away, he brought the camera in closer and detected another strange behavior; they were holding hands! They couldn't know that they had been married in their past reality! But how else could he explain this behavior? This entire scenario was completely confusing to him.

As Mark and Dr. Langtree were watching Dan and Kate as they moved further from the camera as they walked through the woods, movement in the lower left corner caught their attention. At first, they both wondered if they had really seen it, then the movement started again. It was another man; an older man with grey hair! He came into a better view of the camera as he began walking in the same direction as Dan and Kate, though they still could only see him from behind.

"Who's that?!" asked Mark, "Is he following them?"

"I don't know. I don't recall seeing him before, but it looks like he is following them!"

They both continued to watch him until he finally disappeared into the thickness of the woods as well. Dr. Langtree punched up another camera, this one at the edge of the woods near where he had seen them go. He panned the camera around, but didn't detect any movement at all.

"Where did they go?" he quietly said under his breath, not really talking to anyone in particular.

He punched up another camera further up toward the parking lot, panned it around, but still came up with nothing.

"They couldn't have just disappeared! Bring up the emitters, five percent power, .00587 phase variance. Temporal angle at twenty six degrees."

"But we haven't calibrated the emitters fully yet. And it's still daylight; the lighthouse museum still has visitors! I thought all of our experiments were going to be attempted after hours to affect the fewest number of people!"

"Don't worry," said Dr. Langtree, "five percent power won't be enough to open a doorway."

"What are we even bringing the emitters up for, then?" inquired Mark.

"I just want to bring the field into alignment. Monitor the variance in the field when you do it, though. If we need more power, we can turn it up some." replied Dr. Langtree.

Mark was fairly confused. He really didn't know what any of this would accomplish. He agreed with Dr. Langtree that five percent power wouldn't be enough to open a door, but he didn't quite understand what bringing the field into alignment would accomplish either, especially if you weren't planning on actually firing it to open a doorway. They'd already tested it earlier and proven that the emitters would bring the field into alignment, so he really didn't see what any of this would accomplish now. Dr. Langtree was still bringing up various cameras around the perimeter trying to find Dan and Kate. He really wanted to know what they were doing here, but he just couldn't quite figure it out. Mark entered in the parameters, and then brought up the emitters to five percent power as requested. On the temporal field monitor, he could see the donut shape become more of a perfect circle as the field was energized by the emitters.

Out in the woods, Dan and Kate were walking back up toward the lighthouse. They had decided to stay about fifty feet into the woods both to avoid detection and to see if there were any more devices. Dan speculated that they probably surrounded the lighthouse. Suddenly, they both heard a twig snap behind them. They came to a sudden stop, their senses on alert, listening for the slightest sound.

"What was that?!" Kate whispered to Dan as she looked around behind them in the direction that the sound had come from.

"I'm not sure." Dan whispered back, "It could have been an animal."

"I suppose." she replied, not sounding totally convinced.

"Let's go back out of the woods." Dan suggested, as they began to walk out toward the clearing.

As they continued to walk, thin wisps of fog began to appear around them.

"Is it getting foggy?" Kate asked.

"Looks like it is. Let's move a little faster." Dan answered.

He had no more gotten this statement out than they found themselves in the clearing, facing the lighthouse.

"How did we get here?!" asked Kate, a surprised look on her face as she stared wide-eyed at Dan.

"Something's happening." he replied, "Things feel different."

As they both turned around to look over the scene before them, suddenly Kate was gone! It seemed to have gotten colder as well. He could tell that he was inside the circular wall now, and the fog outside the wall which had only been thin wisps before was beginning to get a lot thicker. He ran over to the edge of the fog and called for Kate, but didn't get an answer. This seemed to be one of the visions that he and Kate had been having lately, but somehow this one was different. Thick clouds moved overhead, and darkness completely overtook him. It seemed like it must be around midnight. He pulled out his flashlight and shined it around, turning back toward the woods. The beam shone through the fog outside the wall, but there was still no fog inside the wall. He could see the streetlights which were around the lighthouse and in the parking lot, so he walked over toward that direction. He honestly couldn't tell if what was happening here was real or not. As he approached the edge of the parking lot, he noticed that the van was gone! He was sure where he had parked it, but it was nowhere to be seen now. The rest of the parking lot seemed fairly empty as well, with only a handful of cars. He walked over to the lighthouse and gazed up at the tower. Something didn't seem quite right here either. He shined his light around and discovered that the Doppler radar tower that had been erected beside the house was gone! He walked over to the side of the house, shining his light around where it had been, but there was no evidence that it had ever been there! He stood still, listening to the sounds of the night. Crickets were chirping and cicadas were singing their song, so it must really be nighttime. He thought that he heard a voice in the distance, but he couldn't be sure. Even though it had only been a short time, the fog had gotten remarkably thicker now; so thick in fact that now his light barely penetrated it. He began running in the direction that he had heard the voice.

"Kate! Are you here?!" he yelled back.

As he got closer to the edge of the wall where the fog was, he could hear that the voice was definitely closer and it did sound like Kate.

"Kate! I'm over here!"

"Dan, I can't see very far through the fog! Where are you?!"

"Over here! Just follow my voice!"

After about five minutes, he could see a shape coming through the fog holding a flashlight, its beam barely penetrating through the mist. She ran toward him and was quickly in his arms.

"It's happening again." she said nervously, "I don't understand."

"I don't either." he admitted as he looked around. At least this time the lighthouse still seemed intact, except for the Doppler tower missing. He thought that maybe there were other things different as well, but he couldn't quite put his finger on anything in particular.

"Where did this fog come from?" asked Mark surprised, "We're not giving it enough power to actually open a door! Should I back it off?"

"No, leave it where it is," replied Dr. Langtree, "it won't open a doorway."

"How can you be sure?"

"Look at the readings, especially the temporal velocity. It's way too low to fully energize the field."

Mark looked at the screen in front of him. Dr. Langtree was right; the temporal velocity was only at twenty one percent. It would have to be above eighty to even begin to energize the ripples enough to open a doorway.

"So what's happening then?" he inquired.

"The field's just ionizing the air as we're forcing it into alignment. Nothing to worry about."

Dan and Kate were still both wondering what was happening. They were at the lighthouse, but at what time exactly, both time of day and year? Somehow Dan knew that they were no longer in 2018. He could feel it, though he didn't know exactly what it all meant.

As they stood at the edge of the circular wall looking over at the lighthouse, a sound caught their attention over to the right. A car was coming! Since neither of them had any clue as to what was going on and they really didn't want to encounter anyone, they both stepped over the wall and hid just inside the fog at the edge of the woods, turning off their flashlights as they did. As the car lights slowly made their way into the parking lot and parked over in one of the parking spaces nearest to the lighthouse, they could see that it was actually an SUV. As they watched, two men got out and walked over to open the rear hatch. They were too far away and it was too dark for them to be able to tell who either of the men were. One of the men got something out of the back of the SUV and walked with it to the front of the vehicle while the other man shut the hatch then went back to the front to join him. At this point both men were standing in front of the SUV slightly under a streetlight, but the streetlight was behind them, so all that Dan could see was their silhouette. He could hear the men talking, but unfortunately he was too far away to be able to tell what they were saying. The object that the one man was carrying was fairly large. He thought that it was probably about five feet long based on the height of the men, but not very wide. After about five minutes, the men began carrying the object toward the lighthouse.

"What's that they're carrying?" asked Kate.

"I can't tell. Let's move a little closer to get a better look."

"Not too close," answered Kate nervously, "They'll see us."

"We won't go too close, but we need to get a better look at what they're doing."

As they walked across the parking lot, they lost sight of the men as they walked around behind a storage shed, and they couldn't hear them talking anymore either. This worried Dan somewhat. As long as they could at least hear them he could tell where they were and approximately how far away they were as well. He definitely didn't want them sneaking up behind him and Kate.

After listening for a few more minutes, they heard the men again, this time louder but not necessarily closer. They appeared to be arguing about something, their voices still coming from behind the storage building. Suddenly they saw one of the men run quickly out from behind the storage building and head toward the parked SUV. Both Dan and Kate, not wanting to be noticed, stood completely still as they watched him. About a minute later, the other man came running out from behind the storage building. They had no sooner spotted him than a brilliant white flash of light blinded them as it penetrated the darkness, followed immediately by a loud whooshing sound accompanied by a low rumble. They instinctively looked away, but it was too late. Neither of them could see anything as they groped around in the darkness, finally finding each other's hand to hold. As their eyes slowly adjusted from the effects of the flash, another flash not quite as bright as the first one caught their attention. This one was followed by a loud clap of thunder as a cold rain began to fall. As their eyes slowly adjusted, Kate noticed that the SUV that the men had been driving was gone.

"Let's take cover at the lighthouse." said Dan as the rain began falling harder and the lightning and thunder increased in intensity. They both were running as hard as they could toward the lighthouse. Suddenly, they both stopped in their tracks, staring in disbelief at the scene in front of them. The lighthouse was in ruins again, the roof mostly gone and the tower leaning.

"Why is it like that?! cried Kate, "What's happening here?!"

"Let's keep going." Dan instructed as he pulled her toward the lighthouse with him.

The storm was growing in intensity now, with lightning flashes and thunder almost continuous. The rain was coming down so hard that they could barely see the lighthouse in front of them, but they continued running in the direction where they knew that it was. Finally they reached the lighthouse and went up the front steps. The door easily swung open as they pushed it to go inside. They found a corner of the room where the roof was still intact enough to block most of the rain, but in other areas the rain was pouring in like waterfalls. They were both shivering as they looked around the room to see ghostly shadows projected on the walls by the lightning flashes through the rotting ceiling timbers. They were startled as a particularly strong clap of thunder shook the ground and caused something in the house over to their right to fall, making a loud crash. Kate moved closer to Dan as he put his arm around her to comfort her. She was shaking harder now, partly from the cold, but partly from fear. This dream was completely different than any of the others. Dan didn't know exactly how long they had been here, but he figured it must be at least two hours by now. Neither of them said anything as they huddled in the corner of the room as the storm grew in intensity outside. Dan didn't know what was happening. Previously the visions had been short, probably five or ten minutes at the most. This one had been longer, probably at least thirty or forty minutes just since the darkness came. In his mind, he was trying to think of a way out, to think of what to do next, but not knowing exactly what was happening made that immensely harder. Where would they go? Their van was gone!

The wind was picking up in strength as well, as several of the roof timbers came crashing down.

"Are we safe in here?" Kate asked, startled.

"At least as safe as we'd be out there." Dan replied.

Just as he said this, the wall to their left came crashing down. As the whole house seemed to come down on top of them, suddenly the sound of the wind and the rain stopped. They opened their eyes and looked at each other, almost in disbelief. They were sitting in the van facing the lighthouse, which looked completely normal again! Both of them were still shivering, but at least they were dry now.

"What just happened?" Kate asked, apprehensively.

"I don't really know." said Dan. "It must have been one of our visions. But this one was different."

"Let's go back." Kate said, "Our families will probably be missing us by now."

"Maybe not." replied Dan, "Look at the clock. It's only one forty five."

"That's only twenty minutes after we arrived here! It seems like we've been here at least three hours or more!"

Dr. Langtree looked over at Mark. "I think that was a successful test, don't you?"

"A successful test of what exactly?!"

The temporal field of course! We're one step closer to our goal, don't you think?"

Mark really didn't know what to think. All he really saw it do was create a little fog. He wasn't sure how that was a successful test, but apparently Dr. Langtree saw something that he didn't.

As Dan and Kate pulled out of the parking lot onto Lighthouse Road, they were both too stressed to really notice the silver sports car that pulled out behind them, following at a safe distance. He had been out there the entire time, but had he seen what they had seen? Only time would tell.

CHAPTER 19

More Questions Than Answers

As Dan and Kate arrived at Harbor Inn Lane and made a right turn toward the beach, they were still both visibly shaken by the events of the past half hour. The brightness of the afternoon, however, with the hazy sun shining through a light cloud cover helped them to slowly regain their composure. It was a stark contrast to the dark, stormy night that they had just encountered.

"I'll never get used to these visions!" Kate remarked, "This one seemed even more real than the others! And this is the first time that other people have been there with us as well. Do you have any idea who those men were, or what they were doing?"

"It was too dark to get a good look, but my best guess would be Dr. Langtree and Dr. Chandler. And from the intensity of that storm, I'd also guess that it was the same storm from May 2016! I think we may have just witnessed what happened that night, but I still can't really explain exactly how it happened, or even exactly what happened for that matter."

"So ... you think we went back to 2016?"

"Possibly, or it could have just been another flashback. Either way I think it could be a clue to the puzzle."

"Do you think whatever it was that they were carrying is what caused the storm?"

"I don't know exactly, since I couldn't tell what the object was. I wish that they hadn't gone behind that storage building. We didn't see the last five or six minutes of what they were doing."

"It sounded like they were arguing about something, though." Kate interjected.

"Yes, I think so too. I just wish that I'd been able to hear what they were saying enough to tell what they might have been arguing about."

"I know. We still don't know any more than we did about what might be happening."

"Don't we?" Dan asked. "We know that two men were out at the lighthouse and were carrying some sort of device that seemed to explode into a bright white light. At least we can guess that it was the device that caused the bright light. After that came the storm. I've thought all along after seeing the satellite image of the storm that there was something just not natural about it. The way that the lightning seemed to be in a perfect circle seemed to indicate that there was something else causing it other than just nature. If what we witnessed tonight was the storm from two years ago, then just the fact that the men were there means that they might have caused it. And if they were Dr. Langtree and Dr. Chandler, then that links what happened directly to Chandler-Langtree. This along with the journal entries that Angela found definitely implicates them with what is happening."

"You're right! We have an idea where to look now!"

"Yes, and maybe the box that Richard Sorensen has for Mark might even be another piece to this puzzle."

"I hadn't thought of that. I'd almost forgotten about the box."

"I haven't. I've been thinking about it ever since Richard mentioned it. There's just something odd about the whole thing."

"What do you mean?" Kate asked.

"Well, think about it for a minute. According to Richard, Blake Sorensen died three years ago. Mark would have been a college freshman then. And the contents of the box would have had to have been gathered even before that. But the part that really interests me is that he left instructions for the box to be delivered here on Green Island specifically this week. How could he possibly know that Mark would be here this week? We didn't even know until last weekend. And Mark couldn't have known before he was hired by Chandler-Langtree."

"I see what you mean ... but what could be happening then? It doesn't make sense."

"You're right, it doesn't make sense. There would be only two ways for Richard to know that Mark would be here this week. Either Richard's not telling the truth, and he actually followed Mark here, or Blake Sorensen was a time traveler."

"You think Blake Sorensen was a time traveler?!" Kate exclaimed.

He looked over at her wide-eyed look of surprised disbelief.

"Actually, I was leaning more toward the first explanation. Something about Richard showing up here this week with a box for Mark and a story about his late father just doesn't add up. I'm curious to see what's in that box."

"I am too." she answered, "Maybe Mark really will get home early tonight and we can finally find out."

Warren Evans continued to follow them, though he was keeping his distance so as not to be spotted. After the incident at the hotel, he was purposely more careful now. He could barely see the van up ahead, and when they turned off of Sea Spray Drive onto Ocean View Lane he lost them for a moment. It was a small island, though, so they couldn't get too far away. And he couldn't risk getting any closer and possibly being seen; at least not yet.

Warren was a little confused as well about what he had seen out at the lighthouse, though he did have some ideas of what might have caused it. He had been watching Dan and Kate from the edge of the woods, when suddenly a fog came up quickly. From the suddenness of it, he figured that Mark and Dr. Langtree must have turned on the emitters. He just couldn't figure out exactly why. It must have been at a low power, but for a fog to form as quickly as it did it still would have to be at a high enough level to force the field into alignment. Just after the fog formed he watched Dan and Kate walk out of the woods and over to their van. When they got to it,

Dan unlocked their doors and opened Kate's door for her to get in before walking around the front of the van and climbing into his seat. After they got into the van, they just sat there for a little over five minutes until the fog began to dissipate. When he saw them get into their van, he walked over to his car and watched them from there. He wanted to be ready when they finally started to leave. Finally, Dan did crank up the van and pull out of the parking spot. Warren let them get through the parking lot and turn onto Lighthouse Road before he began following them.

Back out on Henderson Road, Dan slowed the van down slightly.

"Why are we slowing down?" inquired Kate.

Dan was looking in the rear view mirror now.

"I thought I saw movement behind us."

Kate turned around to look behind the van but didn't see anything. They had just turned a corner, so if there was another car behind them, it might not have caught up to them yet. Dan continued driving slower, hoping that if the car behind them was following them that whoever was driving might not realize that they had slowed after going around the curve. He would come up behind them quickly and be closer than he wanted to be before he realized it. Then they'd be able to get a closer look at who it was. The plan worked! The silver sports car came around the corner, close enough for them to definitely make out the driver before he slowed suddenly before coming to a complete stop. Dan stopped as well, as the silver sports car did a quick three point turn and sped off in the direction from where it had come. Unfortunately, Dan's van didn't turn around quite as quickly as the sports car, so it had gained some distance before he finally was able to give chase.

"Was that Warren Evans?" Kate asked.

"I'm pretty sure that it was." said Dan as he sped up, trying not to lose him. The silver sports car was quite a ways ahead of them now. He was definitely faster than they were. When they got to Ocean View Lane, Dan turned onto it and sped down to Sea Spray Drive. As they arrived at Sea Spray Drive, they both looked left then right to try and see what direction he had turned. They didn't see the car in either direction. He was obviously fast.

"Which way should we go?" asked Kate. "Do you think he would be going back out to the lighthouse?"

"Maybe, but if he's staying here on the island, he might be staying at the Harbor Inn. He could be going back there."

Dan turned right onto Sea Spray drive and drove the mile down to Harbor Inn Lane where he turned right. They still had not caught up to the silver sports car yet. As they drove down the lane they only passed two other cars coming away from the Harbor Inn.

"Do you think he could have gone the other way up Sea Spray Drive?" asked Kate.

"Maybe, but I'm not sure where he'd be going, unless he was just trying to lose us. There aren't any hotels up that way, only private residences."

They drove past the rock columns with the sailboat emblems and the sculpted seagulls on top as they entered the parking lot area of the Harbor Inn. Dan immediately turned right and drove slowly down a row of cars, while he and Kate surveying each space as they drove by. They drove through the entire parking lot then went around to the back of the hotel to see if he may be hiding back there. They still found no sign of him.

"He's obviously not here." remarked Dan, a little disappointed.

"Maybe he did go back out to the lighthouse." said Kate.

"He could have. Let's drive out there and check it out."

They drove slowly as they continued down Harbor Inn Lane, both Dan and Kate scanning the bushes and drives along the side of the road for any sign of the silver car. They reached Lighthouse Road, where they turned right and still continued slowly. If he had pulled off the road, they wanted to be driving slowly enough to spot him. Finally, the lighthouse came into view as they rounded the corner. They turned into the parking lot and drove slowly around.

"I don't see him." said Kate.

"I think we lost him." replied Dan with a hint of disappointment in his voice. Warren Evans was certainly elusive. On every occasion that Dan had spotted him, he had managed to slip away. How could a seventy six year old man be so fast?!

As they drove back to the Baker Family Bed and Breakfast, they both were quiet, pondering the events of the day. Dan still couldn't quite figure exactly how Warren Evans fit into the picture, and why he was following them. And was he also following them when they were in the woods out at the lighthouse, and when the fog came up? And what exactly was happening when the fog came up? Why did it get so dark and the storm come up so suddenly? This had been the first time that had happened, and it only showed them that there was still a lot about this situation that they didn't know.

As they turned into the alley beside the bed and breakfast where the parking spaces were, they spotted Richard and Bernice's car, so they figured that Danny and Rebekah were back as well. When they walked through the front door, however, no one was around except for Jan.

"Danny and Rebekah walked into town with the Sorensen's." she told them. "I think they wanted to get something to eat after the boat ride."

"Is Scotty back yet?" inquired Dan.

"No, I haven't seen him since he went out to the beach. I imagine he'll be back any time now."

"That's fine. Tell him we've walked into town as well when he gets back. He can call me on my phone and we can let him know where we are."

"I'll tell him." replied Jan, an odd tone to her voice. While she didn't say anything, she actually was wondering why Dan and Kate were alone together, and why Scotty wasn't with them. Still, she told herself there must be a good reason, so she decided not to let it bother her much.

Dan and Kate were both actually glad that Jan was the only one home. They still felt somewhat conspicuous when they were together and wondered what the rest would think. While the others may not think anything of it, they knew how they felt when they were together, and that only worked to make them more self conscious when they were around everyone else, including their kids.

Jan stepped out onto the porch and watched as Dan and Kate walked down the street until they disappeared around the row of houses and shops. While she couldn't quite put her finger on it, there was just something odd about how those two were acting when they were together. She didn't know if any of the others saw it or not, but she did. She saw it in silent looks that they gave to each other. Also in the way that Dan always acted when Kate came into the room. What she was noticing was so subtle that everyone else could easily miss it, but it was there nonetheless. While she really couldn't imagine that Dan would ever be unfaithful to Dianne, she also couldn't imagine what else could be going on. She'd just have to continue watching them closely.

If Jan really knew what was going on, she'd know that she had nothing to worry about there. Dan would never think of being unfaithful to Dianne. He loved Dianne more than anyone that he'd ever known, and wouldn't dream of doing anything that would ever drive them apart. They'd built a life together along with the kids and he would never do anything that would destroy what they had. Still, what was happening now was much bigger than any of them could possibly know. That's what confused Dan so much. He and Kate had somehow been brought together by an impossible series of events. They had a connection that neither of them could understand. What pieces of the puzzle they knew now just didn't seem to fit together in any way that made sense. Still, for their own sanity, they needed to make sense of them. Yet somehow they felt alone in this search. Dianne, Scotty, even Danny and Rebekah just thought this was a simple vacation; a chance for the two families to get to know each other. But for Dan, Kate, and Angela it was different. Because of the events of the past several days, their worlds were different now. They couldn't even talk about it with any of the others. How could anyone else really understand?

As they continued to walk down the hill toward town, this time it was Kate who sensed that they were being watched. But were they really, or was she just paranoid because of everything that had been happening? She stopped and looked over at Dan, intently listening for even the slightest sound. She had thought that she heard something, possibly someone watching from the shadows of the buildings that they were passing.

"What is it?" asked Dan.

"I don't know; I think I heard something. I think someone's watching us. I can't really tell if it's something that I heard exactly or just a feeling, but whatever it is, I still feel it."

At this suggestion, Dan's senses were also on alert. He silently looked around, his eyes scanning the shadows of the buildings; his ears listening for any sound that would give away the watcher's position. They actually felt a little silly about feeling this way. After all, it wasn't the middle of the night. It wasn't even dark. It was only a little after four in the afternoon. The sun was out now, shining even brighter than it had been when they were out at the lighthouse. There were other people out walking around enjoying the amenities of the island. It wasn't like they were in a dark alley alone; this was the busy part of the day in a quaint tourist town.

"I don't hear anything unusual. Besides, we're not exactly alone here. The sound could have come from anywhere." Dan said after several minutes of listening intently.

"You're probably right. My nerves are just on edge from everything that's been happening. Let's go on into town and see if we can find the others."

They continued their walk into town. What they didn't know was that Kate's initial fear wasn't simply the paranoia of the day's events. They actually were being watched as they made their way down the sidewalk into town. As they entered the main downtown area, Dan called Danny on his cell phone to find out where they were.

"Hi Dad! We're at the Island Mist Cafe. It's over beside the Little Book Nook. We ran into mom and Angela a few minutes ago and they decided to join us."

"Sounds good. We'll be there in about five minutes." Dan replied.

As they walked through the front door of the Island Mist Cafe, they spotted Dianne and the others over along the left wall. Dianne waved her arm to get their attention, but Dan had already spotted her and began walking over to the table. Their server had pushed a couple of tables together, so there was plenty of room. There was even a place for Scotty if he got back in time, so Kate decided to give him a call to see where he was. As it turned out, he was almost back to the bed and breakfast, so he decided to drive on into town and join them there instead. Within ten minutes he was walking through the front door as well. As he sat down, he told everyone that he had run into an older gentleman, Bud, who has lived on the island all his life.

"He owns the general store at the intersection of Main Street as you come into town from the ferry port. These days, he's mostly retired, though, and only works at the store when he wants to. His son, Bud Jr. is the store manager now. He runs the store with his wife Marla and her brother Carl."

Bud had been walking along the beach at the same time as Scotty, and they had started a conversation. After a refreshing walk down the beach, Bud had invited him back to his house to see his ham shack.

"Bud is an amateur radio operator, also called a 'Ham'. He's been in this hobby for quite a number of years and has made contacts in every state and most foreign countries using his beams mounted atop a one hundred fifty foot tower. Within the past couple of months though, he's been picking up strange transmissions, mostly around the 1900 MHz band. The transmissions are always garbled, like they're encrypted, so he's never been able to make out what they're saying. He did find it odd, that after living on the island all of his life that this was the first time that he had picked up these transmissions. They seemed to start about the time that Chandler-Langtree came to the island to do their weather experiments, though he can't quite figure exactly why they'd need encrypted transmissions for a weather study. When he first started hearing the transmissions, he had asked his friend Steve, who ran the Lighthouse Preservation Society, about what Chandler-Langtree was doing out at the lighthouse. That's when Steve had told him about the weather experiments. He has another friend who also lives here on the island just a little ways up the beach from him, and he had mentioned the transmissions to him. Apparently his friend knows a lot about phone encryption, so he's coming over tomorrow to listen and see if he can figure out how to decrypt them."

After the events of the afternoon, Dan and Kate found it refreshing to be in the company of friends and family. They had wondered if anyone would think anything of them walking in together, but nobody seemed to really notice. That was definitely a relief. Danny and Rebekah had enjoyed the boat trip with the Sorensens. It had been a three hour charter that took them around the tip of the island, then back up to where they could get a good view of the lighthouse. They then turned slightly inland to pass Southport as they made their way up the Cape Fear River toward Carolina Beach. It had been a relaxing trip, as the boat gently rocked back and forth as it travelled up the river. They had gone slightly north of Carolina Beach before turning around to head back to Green Island.

After their conversation in the van earlier, both Dan and Kate watched Richard Sorensen a little more closely than they had before, but they were also trying not to be too conspicuous. To Dan, Richard now seemed to be hiding something, though it might just be his suspicions that made him see things that weren't really there; he couldn't be sure. But the story that he'd told of the box earlier kept going around in his mind. It just didn't make any sense. Soon Mark would be home, though, and they'd find out what was in the mysterious box. Though the box wasn't brought up during the dinner conversation, Dan was sure that everyone there was curious. What could the enigmatic Blake Sorensen possibly have left for Mark before he died, if it even was Blake Sorensen that left it? Dan was still suspicious of Richard, even though he genuinely liked him and had developed somewhat of a friendship since he'd come to the island. There was just something about this whole situation that didn't make logical sense. But then lately what did make sense. With more puzzles than answers coming up, they'd just have to wait and see which one the box would be.

After a nice dinner, they all got up and headed back toward the bed and breakfast. Scotty had driven the van into town so he needed to drive it back and Kate decided to ride with him. The rest wanted to walk back since it was a pleasant day. The slight chill to the air made the events of the past few days seem even more distant and also served to help clear their minds. They waved to Scotty and Kate as they passed them in the van, then within a few more minutes, joined them on the front porch of the bed and breakfast where they both were standing by the railing enjoying the fresh island air. Dan joined them while the rest went inside. As they stood by the railing looking out across the street, Dan thought that he saw movement in the shadows of one of the buildings. He nudged Kate, then nodded in the direction that he'd seen the movement. As Kate also looked in that direction, she also saw that there really was movement in the shadows. It was slight, but still perceptible.

"Wait here." Dan said softly as he started down the steps toward the building across the street.

"Be careful." Kate replied, watching him as he crossed the street and disappeared into the shadows around the side of the building.

"Where's he going?" asked Scotty.

"He thought he saw something across the street. He's walking over to check it out."

"Saw something? Like what?"

"Like someone watching us." she replied, as she looked into his face to see his expression, since he didn't know about all of the strange things that had been happening lately. Maybe it was time to bring him into the mystery; at least part of it.

"Why would someone be watching us?" Scotty asked, somewhat confused.

"Dan's not sure exactly why; that's what he's been trying to find out. But he's seen him on several occasions, the first time being back in Wilmington. Remember when Dan spotted someone and went looking for him as we were headed over to the stadium after the luncheon?"

"Yes, I do remember that!"

She continued, "And the first day that we were here on the island, I saw him from the top of the lighthouse when we went out there, so apparently he followed us here."

"Does Dan know who he is?" asked Scotty, becoming concerned now.

"He thinks the man is Warren Evans. He's seventy six years old and the CEO of Evans Microsystems."

"Why would the CEO of Evans Microsystems be following Dan?"

"It may have something to do with some information that Angela found out. There are things happening here on the island that are beyond logical explanation. Dan's actually not sure how Warren fits into everything, but he's sure there's a connection."

She purposely left out her and Dan's visions of the fog at the lighthouse, and the dreams they had been having. She didn't think he was ready for that yet.

"Does he think that it has something to do with the Chandler-Langtree Institute?" Scotty asked.

"Why would you think that?" she asked with a surprised hesitation.

"Remember when I told you that I was out at Bud's beachfront house this afternoon, and he had picked up the encrypted radio transmissions? He said that they started about the time that Chandler-Langtree came to the island. Since his friend is coming over tomorrow to see what he can make of the transmissions, I might call him and see if I can go over and meet with them as well. You've got me curious now that there may really be something going on here, and if it's Chandler-Langtree then Mark might be involved, even if he doesn't realize it. I know that he can't tell us much, since he works for the company, but we might be able to find out something if the transmissions can be decrypted."

"That might be a good idea. He is suspicious that Chandler-Langtree might be involved somehow, he's just not sure how Warren Evans might be connected." she said.

"I also don't like the fact that we're being watched, especially since I don't know the reason."

"I'm not thrilled about that fact myself." Kate answered with a worried look.

After leaving Scotty and Kate standing on the porch, instead of walking directly toward where he had seen the motion, Dan walked around the opposite side of the building and around to the back. He tried to move as silently as possible as he moved stealthily through the overgrown grass and brush behind the building. When he reached the side of the building, he slowly peered around the corner looking toward the front where they had seen the motion. There appeared to be nobody there.

"Where did he go?" thought Dan as he began walking in the direction of the front. He moved cautiously, because there were still some corners and crevices where someone could possibly hide. When he got to the front of the building, however, he discovered that the man had apparently vanished. He looked up and down the street but all he saw were some late afternoon tourists out for a walk. He decided to give up the search and began walking back across the street.

Seeing movement, Scotty and Kate both looked up to see Dan walking toward them.

"Did you find him?" Kate asked as he climbed the porch stairs.

"No, he slipped away again." Dan answered.

"Kate tells me that you think this man's been following you?" Scotty asked.

Surprised, Dan replied, "Yes, we've seen him on several occasions. I don't know why, but I think that he is watching us."

"I'm going to call Bud" Scotty said, "and see if I can go over to his house tomorrow when his friend comes over to see about decrypting those radio transmissions that I told you about earlier. If he agrees, do you want to come with me?"

"Yes, I'd like to do that." answered Dan. "Maybe if he can decrypt the transmissions, it'll help clear up some of the mysteries of what's been happening here. Right now there are more pieces of this puzzle that don't fit than do. Anything that we can find out that could provide some answers will definitely be welcome."

The three of them turned around and walked in the front door to wait on Mark. He should be home any time now. When they walked into the parlor where everyone had gathered, they noticed that Richard had the box on the table in the center of the room. Dan and Kate exchanged knowing glances about what they had discussed this afternoon.

Outside, a stranger lurked in the shadows just outside of the bed and breakfast. When Dan had spotted him and walked across the street to find him, he had slipped away between the buildings and came out about a block down the street. After he crossed the street, he made his way back up to the bed and breakfast undetected. He had been crouching in the bushes near where they were standing and had heard their entire conversation. They knew about the radio transmissions that Bud had picked up! That was unexpected. He'd have to decide if he was ready to meet Dan yet. This was definitely sooner than he had planned, but then things were moving much faster than he had thought they would as well. He had several decisions that he had to make, and he'd have to make them soon.

CHAPTER 20

The Time Box

When Mark arrived back at the bed and breakfast, it was a little after six o'clock, not as early as he had been planning, but at least not too late either. As he walked into the parlor where everyone was gathered, Angela jumped up from the sofa where she had been sitting with her dad and ran over to give him a big hug and kiss.

"I'm glad you're home." she said.

"Me too." he said with a grin, glancing around at everyone in the room.

Dan got up off of the sofa so that Mark would have room to sit with Angela. He walked over to the table and pulled a chair over beside Kate. As he did this, Mark glanced in his direction with a puzzled look. He remembered this afternoon out at the lighthouse when he had seen Mr. Nelson and his mom in the woods together.

"Hello, Mark; Nice to finally meet you." said Richard as he rose to shake Mark's hand.

"It's a pleasure to meet you, too." answered Mark, "I hear that you have something for me."

"Yes, it's a box that my dad wants you to have." replied Richard as he walked over to retrieve the box off of the table as Mark sat down beside Angela. He walked over to where Mark had just sat down and handed him the box. It was a beige metal box about eighteen inches wide by twelve inches long by eight inches high. The hinged lid, which had a handle in the middle, opened from the top. There was a combination lock with three tumblers on the front below the latch. All of the tumblers were set to zero. There was a manila envelope with his name written on it taped to the top.

The box was reasonably heavy, but he thought that most of the weight might be the box itself, especially if the contents were mostly papers. He pushed down on the latch to see if it would pop open, but it was obviously locked.

"Dad said that the instructions for opening the box are in the envelope." offered Richard. He had already gone over and sat back down next to Bernice.

Mark pulled the envelope from the top of the box and opened the clasp. He pulled out a handwritten page and began reading it. As he read it, his face displayed more and more of a puzzled look. Obviously, whatever he was reading was not what he had expected. He laid the note down beside him and moved the tumblers on the lock. He set the first one to a three, the second one to a one, and the third one to four. After moving all of the tumblers to their appropriate positions, he pressed down on the latch again and this time it popped open. He looked over at Angela with a confused look. He actually seemed surprised that the box had opened! He picked up the letter and gave it to her to read. After reading for about a minute, she looked back at him with a confused look of her own.

"How could he have known that number?" she asked. "There would have been no way that he could have known that number!"

"What was the number?" Dan asked.

Angela looked up at him with a look of total bewilderment on her face.

"The number is 314 … my hotel room number from when Mark and I took the trip to Myrtle Beach … two and half weeks ago! But the letter doesn't actually give the number! It simply says, 'The combination is Angela's hotel room number from North Myrtle beach'."

When Angela said this, Dan looked over at Kate with a look that said, "See, I told you! There's something suspicious going on here." Dan then looked over at Richard, who seemed as surprised as the rest of them. There would have been no way for Blake Sorensen to know the number of Angela's hotel room three years after he died! It just wasn't possible! Unless

… the thought was just too crazy to consider, yet he had actually said it to Kate earlier in the day, albeit in somewhat of a joking manner: Unless Blake Sorensen really was a time traveler! The more that he thought about it, though, he quickly dismissed that idea. It had to be Richard! He must have been following them! That thought alone caused him some level of apprehension. He didn't like the thought that someone had been following his daughter, especially since he didn't know why!

"Something's going on here!" said Scotty as he looked over at Richard accusingly. "You expect us to believe that your father just guessed what Angela's room number was going to be three years before she checked in? How did you know that number?" He actually said "you" when he asked, implying that at this point he was thinking as well that it was really Richard that was orchestrating this mystery.

Richard really was as confused as the rest of them looked. "I don't know." he said hesitantly. "I can't explain how he knew that number, but I didn't have anything to do with it! That note really was written over three years ago! It's been on the top shelf of our bedroom closet since dad passed away!"

"That's not possible. Nobody could have known that was going to be Angela's room number until two and a half weeks ago. That note couldn't have been in your closet for the last three years!" repeated Scotty.

Richard hesitated, slightly on the defensive now and becoming increasingly uncomfortable, "But it was! We put it there after we cleaned out Dad's house and found it where he told us that it would be! I didn't write the note!"

Seeing that he was getting nowhere with this line of questioning, he let it drop for now, but he knew that the note had to have been written sometime since Mark and Angela had gone to the beach. Everyone in the room was contemplating how the combination could possibly be Angela's hotel room number. Some, including Scotty and Dianne, thought that Richard had to have something to do with it. Logically, the note had to have been written after she checked in, not three years ago as Richard claimed. Others, however, including Dan, Angela, and Kate were open to more extraordinary explanations. After what they had seen and read, their minds were more open to the impossible.

Thinking more about it, Kate leaned over and whispered to Dan, "Do you think Warren Evans could really be Blake Sorensen? Could he really have been a time traveler after all? That would explain his interest in us."

He looked at her as if he himself was having trouble considering what she had just said. He leaned back over and whispered, "I don't know. I guess it's possible. We can talk about it later."

He had seen Mark looking over toward their direction. He didn't know if Mark suspected that there was anything going on between him and Kate, but Mark had been watching them more than usual since he had come home this evening. He didn't really want to arouse any more suspicion than he had to.

Scotty looked back over at Mark, "What's actually in the box?"

They had all been focusing so much on how the note could have contained the hotel room number, that the contents of the box had almost been forgotten. Mark looked back down at the contents inside the box and withdrew a stack of papers fastened together with a rubber band. As he pulled off the rubber band and began separating the papers to look them over, his face took on more of a perplexed look than it had earlier.

"What is it?" asked Scotty, "What are those papers?"

"I think I'm going to have to take these and study them some more. This top stack looks like it has some calculations on it. It could be what he was working on before he died. Since he was a theoretical physicist, he might have thought that some of what he was working on could help me in my research."

As he had been going through the papers in the box, he had spotted a small envelope at the bottom with the words, "Mark … Personal" written on it. He didn't mention it because he really wanted to take the box and read that particular letter in private. Who knows what it might contain, and he knew that the rest of them would want him to read it out loud. He fastened the rubber band around the papers and put them back in the box, closing the lid as he did. He was thinking that if these papers really were the key parts of Blake Sorensen's research, then they really might help him in his work as well. The possibilities definitely intrigued him.

While everyone in the room was trying to figure out how Blake Sorensen would have known the room number three years ago, only three of them were actually considering time travel, since they all developed their ideas based on their background and what they already knew. Angela's mind was going in a different direction than Kate and her father's however. Since she didn't know about Warren Evans, she was considering the possibility that Al might really be Blake Sorensen! It would make sense, with him trying to convince her that time travel really could be possible. Maybe some of the pieces to the puzzle really were starting to fit together, she just didn't know it yet. He had given her his number after they had parted company yesterday. She had put it in her purse, which was up in her room. She'd definitely give him a call tomorrow.

Kate got out of her chair and walked into the kitchen to get a drink. She halfway expected Dan to follow her, since she felt that they really needed to talk, especially now. It was Mark that followed her into the room, however, and as she looked into his eyes, she could sense that there was something bothering him.

"Mark ... What is it?" she asked.

He was silent, not exactly sure how to begin. He wanted to know the answer, but somehow he wasn't sure that he really was ready to hear it. He decided that the direct approach would be best.

"What were you and Mr. Nelson doing out at the lighthouse today?"

This caught her totally and completely off guard. She had expected that whatever he had on his mind had something to do with what he had seen in the box a few minutes ago. She really wasn't prepared to answer this particular question.

"Who told you that Dan and I were out at the lighthouse?" she asked hesitantly, hoping to deflect the question.

"Nobody told me … I actually saw you there. In the woods in sector seven. You and Mr. Nelson were taking pictures of the monitoring tower. We have cameras mounted on every tower that we can view from the Mobile Command Center."

Now she really didn't know what to say. Even though they had tried their best not to be, they had been caught in the act! Now she'd have to think of something to tell Mark, and there wasn't time to get her story straight with Dan. Mark was staring at her inquisitively, anxiously awaiting her answer. She didn't want to tell him about her dreams, or visions, or whatever they were. Not just yet, even though they were the real reason that her and Dan had gone out to the lighthouse and were looking around in the woods. They had hoped to find some clues, but instead they were pulled into another dream. She supposed that in itself was a piece of the puzzle, even though she couldn't figure where that particular piece fit yet.

"We just wanted to visit the lighthouse again, that's all." she replied to his question, knowing that the excuse sounded pretty lame, but feeling that it was the best that she could come up with right now.

"Why were you in the woods, though? What were you looking for?"

"Nothing in particular, we just felt like taking a walk."

She knew that this statement sounded even more inadequate than the last one, but she just couldn't come up with anything better, at least not instantly. Some people were good at coming up with answers on the fly; she wasn't.

He kept staring at her, and his gaze made her feel uneasy. She felt guilty for not telling him the truth, but in a way she wasn't even sure that she knew what the truth was. There were things going on that none of them could understand yet. His next question, however, made her feel more uncomfortable than the ones before it, and she was sure that she was completely ineffective at hiding her surprise.

"I've seen you and Mr. Nelson exchanging glances. Is there something going on between the two of you?"

"No!" she remarked quickly, realizing only too late that the quickness of her answer only made her appear guilty, like she had just been caught with someone that she wasn't supposed to be with.

"What I mean is; there's nothing beyond me just wanting to get to know your girlfriend's father better. That's all. There's no real mystery."

The look on his face told her that he believed there was more to it than that.

"I haven't noticed the same thing between dad and Angela's mom. Dr. Langtree even seemed surprised when he saw both of you together today, though I didn't understand that either."

This was definitely getting out of hand and she wished that she was back in the parlor with the group. These questions were making her really uncomfortable, mostly because she knew that she didn't have good answers for any of them.

"One other question, though;" Mark continued, "There was another man out in the woods with you and Mr. Nelson today. I didn't see his face, since he was walking away from the camera, but he looked like an older man with grey hair, and he appeared to be following you. Do you know who he might be?"

Whatever she answered at this point, he knew that she knew the man, or at least had seen him before. Her surprised look had definitely given her away this time. She was at least glad to see that his questions were moving away from her and Dan. She felt that she could talk to him about Warren Evans. Maybe he might even have some ideas of why Warren might be following them.

"I've seen him." she said. "His name's Warren Evans. I suspected that he might have been out there with us today, because we saw him following us after we left to come back here."

"Why would he be following you?" asked Mark, still a little

confused.

"We don't know. Every time that Dan tries to approach him, he disappears."

"Do you have any ideas, though?"

"No, we can't figure why." she said. Actually they did have a few ideas, but she didn't want to discuss any of them with Mark quite yet.

"When I know more, I'll let you know. Let's go back in with the others now."

She picked up her drink and walked back into the parlor. Mark had fixed one for himself while they had been talking so he walked back in with her. He noticed Dan glance up at his mom as she walked back into the room. There was definitely more to her and Dan than she had admitted, but it looked like he'd have to wait to find out exactly what.

Angela, still wondering if Al could really be Blake Sorensen was asking Richard several questions about his dad.

"What did your dad look like?" she asked.

"Mostly like any other seventy four year old man. Grey hair, slightly balding. Not particularly tall, with a medium build."

She thought that did sound a lot like Al. Even though that description really could be almost anyone that age, just since hearing the story, she had convinced herself that Al really was Blake Sorensen. Still, if it did turn out that he was Blake Sorensen it did bother her that he had obviously been following them. What reason could he possibly have? The answer to that question came almost too quickly: Chandler-Langtree. That company was the one constant that every one of the strange happenings seemed to revolve around. While she didn't know how, it must have something to do with Chandler-Langtree. She'd call Al tomorrow like she had planned. Maybe he'd invite her out to his house and they could talk. Right now, she felt like she really needed to talk with him.

Later that night, after everyone else had gone to bed, Mark knew that he wouldn't be able to sleep. With everything that had happened, his mind was just too keyed up. He took several papers from the box, including the letter which he had opened earlier, and went downstairs to the parlor. He settled into the chair, placed the stack of papers on the table beside it, then slid open the envelope to reread the letter from Blake Sorensen. After reading the letter, and staring off into space for a few minutes just contemplating what its contents meant, he placed it back into the envelope and picked up a stack of the other papers. He was completely fascinated by Blake Sorensen's grasp of theoretical physics, particularly as it applied to time travel. He was definitely ahead of everyone else living during his time period; a virtual Einstein to his contemporaries. He actually never knew that theories of time travel were that advanced during the late twentieth century. A lot of the theories and calculations that he read in these papers were advanced even for the twenty first century. And just reading through several of the pages, he had already found some flaws in his own calculations that could have proven disastrous if an actual person had attempted it. He was grateful for the contents of the box. They had obviously arrived just in time. While he hadn't gone through much of Blake Sorensen's work yet, he could already tell that it would move their research forward by months, if not years. Then there was the letter that he had found in the box. That letter was the most fascinating part, and to him was the undeniable proof that they were on the right track with their research. It did contain personal content, however, written specifically to him from Blake that was so unbelievable that he couldn't really figure how to tell anyone else about it. How could they possibly comprehend the scenario that the letter described? For now, he'd keep it to himself, simply content that it validated his research and his theories. Of course, he'd share the research that it provided with Dr. Langtree, but the contents of the letter were for his eyes only; at least for now.

CHAPTER 21
October 25, 2018
The Visit

Angela lay in bed listening to the birds singing outside her window. When she first woke up, she had looked around the room and discovered that Rebekah had already left. She looked at the clock and it was nine twenty-five already, so it wasn't really surprising that she was the only one in the room. Since everything had been happening, she had found it harder to get to sleep at night, so she was sleeping later in the mornings than she usually did.

She continued to lay there looking up at the ceiling as she thought about the events of the previous evening. How Blake Sorensen knew the number of her hotel room from Myrtle Beach still bothered her. Just the fact that she and Mark must have been followed during that trip made her slightly uneasy about what was happening. She didn't like being followed and she definitely wanted to find out who it was. She also hoped to find out if Al was really Blake Sorensen. She had decided to call him when she got up to see if she could go over and talk with him. While she knew that she wanted to talk, she hadn't fully decided the best way to bring everything up, but she did hope that a brisk bike ride over to the beach would help her figure it out. She wanted to find out if he was Blake Sorensen, but she also wanted to find out his thoughts on what she still thought of as her and Mark's time travel experience from last Tuesday.

As she sat up on the edge of the bed, she contemplated calling Al. She had only met him once, so she really didn't know him, but from the first meeting she did feel like she could trust him, and she was usually a good judge of character. Getting up from the bed, she walked over to the bathroom to comb through her hair, and then came back into the room to get dressed. Retrieving her purse off of the chair next to the window, she found the piece of paper that Al had given her and shoved it into the back pocket of her jeans before walking downstairs to see who was still around.

As she had thought when she first woke up, Mark had already left for the lighthouse, but most everyone else was still around as they were finishing up with a late breakfast. Taking a seat next to her father, she scooped some eggs, sausage, grits and gravy into her plate.

"I think I'll go out to the beach for a bike ride after breakfast." she remarked.

"Do you want some company?" asked Dan.

"No, I think I'd just like to clear my mind. A lot has been happening lately, and there's still a lot to sort through. Sometimes I like to take a bike ride just to listen to the surf, and think."

"Alright, but let me know if you change your mind. Scotty and I are probably going out to Bud's house a little later to meet with his friend to see if he can decrypt the radio signals. I'll have my phone with me."

"Good luck with that." she said. "I'll be interested to know if you're actually successful and can find out anything."

After arriving at the boardwalk, Angela reached into her pocket and pulled out the piece of paper with Al's phone number and turned it over and over between her fingers while she stared out at the surf breaking on the beach. Thinking of exactly what she'll say is harder than she originally thought. Even if Al really is Blake Sorensen, he might not want to admit to it. Pulling her phone out of her back pocket, she dialed the number printed on the paper.

"Hello, who is it?" came an older man's voice on the other end of the line.

"Hello? Al?"

"Yes, this is Al. Who's this?" he answered abruptly. From his tone, she was starting to wonder if it was a good idea to call him after all.

"It's Angela. Remember? We met at the boardwalk on Tuesday?"

"Yes, Angela! I remember now; how are you?" His voice now took on a much more pleasant demeanor after realizing who she was, and her apprehension began to melt away.

"I'm good. Listen … Al? Remember that you said to call you if I needed anything? Well … something's happened. Can I come out to your house? I need to talk."

"Yes, please. Come on over. Where are you?"

"I'm already at the boardwalk. I can be there in about five minutes."

"Alright, see you then. Just come in the gate from the beach."

As she hung up the phone and put it back in her pocket she stared out at the waves, wondering if this was a good idea after all. Al was pretty much a complete stranger and she was about to trust him with information that anyone else would never believe. Most actually would wonder about her sanity. But somehow, she knew that if anyone would understand, it would be Al. She stepped off the boardwalk and walked her bike through the loose sand before jumping on and riding out to his house. Leaning her bike against the gate, she opened it and stepped through into his backyard. She immediately saw him waiting for her on the balcony.

"Come on up! The stairs are over to your left."

As she walked up the wooden stairs to the balcony overlooking the ocean, she realized how nervous she really was about this meeting. A part of her just wanted to leave and go running down the beach, but another part had to find out what was happening, and Al might be the best chance to do that. As she walked across the wooden deck toward where he was standing over by the railing, she could picture Blake Sorensen standing there. Al was exactly how she had pictured Blake from the night before.

"It's good to see you again Angela. Can I offer you a drink?"

"That would be nice. Do you have bottled water?"

"I should be able to find one." he replied as he disappeared through the sliding glass doors that opened out onto the balcony. She followed him through the doors into the room, which was obviously his study. As he disappeared down the stairs at the far end of the room, she continued to stare out the window toward the beach. The view certainly beat the view from her apartment window back at the university. Studying the room, she walked over to his desk. There were several stacks of papers on the desk, one of which appeared that he had recently been looking through it. As she picked up the top page from the stack and began to read it, a startling realization flooded through her mind. She was looking at a page from the Chandler-Langtree journal! The same Chandler-Langtree journal that the Protectors had downloaded! At that moment, she suddenly realized exactly who Al was! She had been trying to figure out where she had met him before, since something about him had seemed familiar from the first time that they had met. Now she suddenly realized where that was. She remembered the night that they had met The Protectors. The voice on the phone, "Hello, who is it?", was the same one that she had heard just a few minutes ago when she had dialed Al! This would definitely explain where he got the page that she had just been perusing. Al was the Squirrel! No wonder he knew so much about Chandler-Langtree! She now also remembered another thing that he had said that night, "Give her whatever she wants. She might be able to help us." But how could she really help with anything? She didn't understand any of this! She's the one who needs help trying to fit all of the pieces of this puzzle together! A noise from across the room let her know that Al was back. She quickly put the page back on the desk, hoping that he hadn't noticed what she had been doing, while also hoping that she didn't look too guilty about doing it.

"Here's your water." he said, handing her the plastic water bottle.

"Thanks." she replied, definitely not knowing what to say now. She was rattled by what she had just realized and she hoped that it wasn't too obvious. Al did seem to have noticed how uncomfortable she had become just since he had been gone, however, picking up on the trepidation in her voice. He actually was wondering the reason. He motioned for her to join him back on the deck, so they both walked back outside and sat at one of the tables near the railing overlooking the ocean.

"So, you said on the phone that something's happened?" he inquired.

"Yes … last night. A man named Richard Sorensen, who's staying out at the bed and breakfast where we're staying, gave Mark a box that his dad Blake had left for him when he died three years ago."

She studied his face as she said this trying to observe if he showed any recognition of the names Richard or Blake Sorensen.

"Oh ... what was in the box?"

He seemed curious, but she still couldn't tell if he showed any recollection of the names. She continued, "It was some papers I think. Something that Blake Sorensen had been working on that he wanted Mark to have, possibly to continue his research. Blake was a Professor of Theoretical Physics at NC State."

When she mentioned that Blake was a Professor of Theoretical Physics, she thought that she saw increased curiosity on his face that could mean that he knew who Blake was, but she just couldn't be sure.

"Do you know what his reasearch was about?" inquired Al.

"No, Mark hasn't shared that information with me yet. I'm suspecting that it might have something to do with time travel, though."

"What makes you think that?"

"Because of the combination that the note that came with the box told Mark to use to open it. It was my room number from the Ocean Reef Resort where Mark and I stayed on the sixth of this month when we went to Myrtle Beach for a weekend getaway! Since Blake died three years ago, he couldn't possibly have known that room number!"

"Could it have just been a coincindence that it was your room number?"

"No, his note didn't actually give the number. It simply stated that the combination was my room number from North Myrtle Beach!"

"That would be difficult for him to know! Do you think that Blake was a time traveler and followed you to North Myrtle Beach?"

"I really don't know what to think, but how else would he have known my room number?" she asked.

At this, Al seemed to be pondering the question that she had just asked. There certainly wouldn't have been many ways for him to know that information. But it wasn't Blake that gave Mark the box, it was Richard. And Richard was alive today. He definately could have followed them and known the room number, then worked things out to be staying at the same bed and breakfast now!

"What are you thinking?" Angela asked after a couple of minutes.

He paused for a few more seconds before responding, "Blake could have been a time traveller, and while I do believe that time travel is certainly possible, could what is happening here have a simpler explanation? What if it wasn't Blake that actually wrote the note? What if Richard is misrepresenting what actually happened for some reason? It could have been Richard that followed you."

"But what reason would he have for trying to get Mark to think that it was his father who actually left the box if he's the one who did?"

"I don't know yet, but that could be a possibility, and it would be much more likely than the time travel explanation. We don't know who Richard really is, so it's hard to know his motives. I've learned that everything is not always as it seems, and that the real explanation is not always the one that you think it is. It's not always the one that even makes sense."

She was sure that he was right about that last statement. It seemed like lately nothing was making sense.

"So what should we do now?" she asked. "How should we proceed if we don't know what's going on?"

"We need to find out what's really going on. If Richard is the one behind this, then we need to find out why. If Blake actually did write the note, then we need to find out how. Do you think that you could find out more about what's in the box?" Al asked. "That would certainly help us to plan our next steps if we knew more. Right now we're just speculating about what might be in there."

"I don't know how much Mark will tell me about what's in it. He's really secretive about some of this stuff."

"But the box doesn't contain Chandler-Langtree information. He's not bound by any secrecy contract for anything that's in it."

"True. I can ask him and see what he'll tell me. Maybe we'll get something to go on."

This was a different direction than she had expected this conversation to take. She had come here hoping to find out if Al was really Blake Sorensen. Now, she wasn't even sure whether Blake Sorensen really was a time traveler after all. Al had put those doubts in her mind. What if it really was Richard that followed them to Myrtle Beach and wrote the note? If that was the case, though, they would need to discover Richard's motives. If he's trying to pass the box off as something that his father wanted Mark to have, then he must have a reason for doing it. And he must have a plan. It seemed that the key to all of this might be the contents of the box.

"There is something else." she said hesitantly.

"What?" he asked.

"I'm not sure quite how to ask this, because I'm not sure that you really want me to know."

With this statement, Al was getting curious, "Go on. Just ask what's on your mind. Remember, we're friends now."

"You're the Squirrel, aren't you?" she asked.

When she asked this, she could tell by the look on his face that he was, even before he replied.

"You've found me out!" he replied, sounding more amused than upset.

"Why didn't you tell me before?" she asked.

"Because to be effective in what we're doing, we need as few people as possible to know our identities. Even with people that we trust, we wait until they figure it out before we discuss it. Most never figure it out. It's actually better that way. While we're performing a needed service, the laws would interpret what we're doing as illegal. It's not that I didn't trust you, it's just that the fewer people that know my true identity, the less the chance of it even accidentally getting exposed."

His reasoning actually did make sense, and she felt that if she were in his place, then she'd look at the situation the same way that he did.

"So, are you actually one of the Protectors?"

"Yes, and no. I'm the one that formed the group, but the others do most of the actual work. I step in when I'm needed, more as an advisor than anything else. Now, however, I mostly work alone, conducting my own research and investigations."

"What are you trying to find out about Chandler-Langtree?"

"What makes you think that I'm investigating Chandler-Langtree?" Al asked.

"Because you said on the phone when we were with the Protectors that I might be able to help you when they were asking how to get into Chandler-Langtree's computer. I'm not sure what help I could possibly be though, since right now I'm as confused as anybody else."

"If you can find out anything about what's in Richard's box, then that could be a big help. But even if you can't find out much, you're close to Mark. You're in a position that nobody else is in to find out what's happening by just observing him, watching what he does and where he goes, what he talks about and what's going on around him. Look for any unusual behavior that's different from how he usually acts. Anybody else would attract attention, but he trusts you. You could be our best source of information. Just keep alert and observe what's going on around you."

"I know he trusts me, and I don't want to betray that trust, but I suppose you're right. I hadn't thought about being in the perfect place to find out what's going on." she said, starting to realize that she really could be a big help, and possibly protect Mark in the process.

"Don't think of it as betraying his trust. Think of it as trying to keep him safe. I don't want to alarm you, but if they are working on a way to travel through time, then that's not inherently safe. Unlike most of the TV shows and movies on the subject, where people travel through time as if it's as easy as boarding a train, actual time travel contains it's dangers. Just a small error in any calculation could make the difference between success and being stranded in the past with nobody even knowing where you are. And the margin of error is extremely small."

"Now I am worried." she replied.

"A certain amount of worry is good. It keeps us alert!" he remarked.

"I'm just not sure Mark is worried enough, though." she remarked. "He may not be as careful as he needs to be."

While it was a shock at the time, Angela was slowly getting used to the idea that Al was the Squirrel. In some ways, it actually made her even more at ease with him. It gave him a certain amount of credibility, since she knew how he got his information. And from the way that he was talking now, he almost seemed like an expert on time travel, almost like he had done it before! Her thoughts went back to earlier when she had thought that he might be Blake Sorensen. Maybe, she thought now, he really is. What better person to have the knowledge that the Squirrel has than a real time traveler! Her thoughts were going back and forth at this point, but she actually was still suspecting that he might really be Blake after all! If that were true, though, then why hadn't he said anything when she brought Blake's name up? This now focused her thoughts back to the other item that she wanted to discuss with him before being sidetracked by the realization that he was the Squirrel.

"There is something else as well." she continued.

He listened intently to her next statement.

"I think Mark and I actually have travelled back in time."

She studied his face to see his expression, but other than intense interest in what she had to say, she really couldn't tell much more.

"When?" he asked.

"It was this past Tuesday night. I had gone out to the lighthouse to pick up Mark and as we turned the car around, I noticed that something was different about the lighthouse. We got out and walked over to the lighthouse to see what was different. After looking around us, we realized that the tower they erected beside the lighthouse wasn't there any longer. That seemed strange, because where would it go? It had to be there! That's when Mark realized what might be happening, and we went back over to the Mobile Command Center and powered it back up. Mark had realized that the lighthouse was probably in a different time period, and he tried to figure out what time period it actually was in. The best that he could figure was that it was somewhere around 2010."

"So Mark didn't have the command center powered up when the lighthouse opened to another time?"

"No, we actually were getting ready to leave. Everything was already shut off for the evening, and like I mentioned before, we were in the car about to drive away."

"Interesting. " he said, with an inquisitive look.

He pondered this for a few minutes, trying to figure what could have created the right conditions for the field to open up. He knew that ripples contained their own source of power, but usually they had to be acted on by an external force to actually open up.

"Did anything feel different when you were out at the lighthouse?" he asked.

"Yes, it was a lot colder. That's something that we noticed right away."

"That's reasonable. The temperature could be drastically different in another time. But did you see or hear anyone else out there?"

"Not that I can remember. Why?"

"I don't want to alarm you, but it's entirely possible that the field could have been opened by someone in another time period. It's also possible that we're still learning how these things work. Maybe they really can open to another time by themselves. If you didn't see or hear anyone else, then maybe the explanation is the latter."

"So you do believe me then?"

"Yes, I believe you." he answered. "The way that you described it is exactly what I would expect to happen."

"Do you have any more information about Chandler-Langtree than the Protectors gave me?"

"No, unfortunately not yet. We may have to hack back into their system to see if we can find out more. Would you be up for that if I decide we need to?"

"Probably." she replied.

"If it opens up again though, be careful! Don't just go walking blindly into another time period. A ripple that opens by itself is not entirely stable. It can collapse at any time, leaving you stranded in that time period."

"What's a ripple?" she asked. She had encountered that terminology in the journal, but she wanted to hear Al's explanation of it.

"A ripple is the building block of the temporal field." he replied, "It's what opens up the field to another time period. A temporal field is not just sitting there stagnant, ready to open. It's constantly in motion like ripples in a lake extending outward from the center. It's our interaction with those moving ripples that enables us to travel to a different time period. Since ripples are self sustaining, though, they could possibly open by themselves to random time periods."

"I hadn't really thought of it that way. I had thought of it more as just a big pulsing donut."

"Those pulses that you see are the ripples." he went on to explain. "If you observe closely, you'll see that the pulses are actually moving from the center to the outside."

"While I'm starting to get used to all of this, I still wake up every morning thinking this is all a dream."

"I know; it's a lot to get used to. But remember, it's just science. Like I mentioned to you before; radio or television would have seemed impossible before radio waves were discovered. This is just an advanced branch of science that only seems impossible because we're only just scratching the surface of its potential."

Angela and Al talked for a little longer, and then she headed back down the beach on her bike. They had actually talked longer than she had thought, since it was already three thirty in the afternoon. She didn't think anyone would be concerned just yet, though. Her family was used to her taking long bike rides around the island. She pondered the conversation that she had just had with Al. His knowledge of time travel was amazing to her. He must have been studying Chandler-Langtree for a long time. And to find out that he was actually the Squirrel that the Protectors had talked to the night that they met was even more incredible! She hadn't really thought much about the Squirrel since that night. They had called him, he had given them the information that they needed to get into the computer system, and then they hung up. That had been the extent of his involvement. Yet now, after meeting the actual person and having a conversation with him, she realized that he was so much more than just a disembodied voice to talk to when you get stuck on something. He seemed to be the incontrovertible expert on ripples and time travel! And after their meeting she surely knew more than she had before. Somehow, his affirmations about time travel made all of the events of the past month actually seem possible, where in her mind they hadn't been before. She'd watch Mark more closely now as well. Al had confirmed what she had been suspecting all along, but wanted to deny; that what Mark was exploring was dangerous. While his revealing that information did worry her, she felt that she really did need to know, and surprisingly now felt that she could deal with it. After all, it's better to be aware of a danger than to blindly assume that it doesn't exist! That's what she thought Mark was doing. He was so intrigued by the possibilities that he wasn't choosing to even consider the dangers. Maybe part of it was that the movies they had watched always had a built in solution for anything. If something went wrong in the movies, they'd just twist a few nuts and bolts and everything would be fine again. Everything always turned out fine in the movies; the errant time traveler always got home. Somehow, she'd have to get better about making him aware of those dangers before it was too late.

CHAPTER 22

The Necklace

Mark came rushing through the front door of the bed and breakfast. He went into the parlor, but nobody was in there. He then went back to the kitchen, where Mrs. Nelson and Angela's grandma were finishing cleaning up from lunch.

"Why hello Mark!" remarked Dianne, surprised that he was home this early. It was just a little after three and usually he wasn't home until at least five or six. Sometimes it was even later than that, depending on what he was working on.

"Hello Mrs. Nelson. Is Angela here?"

"No, she went for a bike ride out on the beach earlier today and isn't back yet. I'm sure she'd have been here if she had known you were coming home early."

"I know, but it's just as well." He reached into his pocket and pulled out a small bag. Opening the bag, he revealed a small jewelry box.

"I just got this down at the jewelry store in town." he beamed happily. "It's for our six month anniversary!"

Smiling, both Dianne and her mother came closer to see what he had gotten her. The box contained a small silver heart with a diamond in the middle. It was beautiful the way that the diamond and the silver around it sparkled in the light.

"She'll love it!" both women said in unison. Dianne even gave Mark a huge hug. She could see how much her daughter loved Mark, and she had to admit that she hoped to have him in the family one day as well.

"It's a new charm for the necklace that I got her for her birthday.

You remember, the one that she wears a lot with the round charm engraved with an "A" and the other one with her birthstone?"

"Yes, I remember that one! She wears it most of the time." said Dianne.

"I know." he said. "Do you know if she was wearing it this morning?"

"I'm not sure." Dianne replied.

"Can you go up and check?" he asked. "If she didn't wear it this morning, I'd like to surprise her by adding the charm and giving it to her tomorrow night at dinner. I have reservations for us at Grant's Steak House at seven!"

Dianne walked up the stairs to go and check for the necklace.

"Grant's is a wonderful choice for dinner!" remarked Jan. "I remember when Wendell took me there for my birthday last year. It was the best dinner I'd ever had! And the atmosphere was so romantic as well. Did you request Renaldo to play for her?"

"Renaldo?" he asked.

"He's the violinist at Grant's. You can request him to come to your table and play any song that you want for her. That really is a nice touch. Wendell did that for me, and it made the evening extra special!"

"I'll call and request him then!" he said, smiling. "That would be a romantic touch. I'll get him to play her favorite song, 'Simply Love'. Thanks for suggesting that!"

After a few minutes, he heard Dianne coming back downstairs.

"You're in luck, Mark! It's here! Come to think of it, I think I remember her wearing the other one that you gave her this morning, the one with the gold starfish."

"Great!" he said, smiling as she handed him the necklace case. "Do you know if Grandpa Wendell has a couple of small jewelry pliers that I can use to put it on?"

"I'm sure that he does. I'll go out to his workshop and check." answered Jan. "Wendell's out with Dan and Scotty right now, but I know where he keeps all of his tools."

After she had left, Mark opened the box to reveal the necklace. He planned on adding the new charm, then wrapping it back up in its case and giving it to her tomorrow evening. He had decided on this as an anniversary present, since this had become her favorite necklace. He was really lucky that it was here today. On most days, she would be wearing it, so things were working out well for the surprise. He couldn't wait to see her face when she opened the case! The only problem that he could foresee right now was that Angela might want to wear the necklace tomorrow night. He'd asked her mom to suggest the pearl necklace for tomorrow night, so that hopefully she wouldn't notice that the case was missing.

"So, how'd you manage to get time off this afternoon?" Dianne asked after Jan had gone out to find the pliers.

"I just told Dr. Langtree what I was planning for tomorrow night, and he understood. It turns out that he has a girlfriend back in Wilmington. She works at the Institute as well. Her name's Melissa Greenwood and she's his personal assistant. They've been dating for about three weeks now, I think."

"That's nice. I never really thought of someone like Dr. Langtree falling in love." she remarked. "I always pictured those types being in love with their work. No time for a personal life."

"I did too, actually. It was kind of a surprise when he told me about it. Melissa's a nice lady, though. I can see them being good for each other. By the way, where's mom? I thought she'd be here with you."

"I think she went into town. I thought that she'd be back by now."

"I know mom when she starts shopping. She might not be back until late."

They heard the back door open and Jan came back in with the

pliers. Mark opened the case and removed the necklace, laying it down on the kitchen table. He removed the small heart from its box and opened the jump ring using the pliers. He placed the ring on the side next to the round charm on the opposite side from her birthstone, so that the round charm was in the middle. He then tightened the jump ring with the pliers and held the necklace up to the light to admire the charms. It looked exactly like he had hoped that it would!

As he picked up the necklace case to place the necklace back inside, the case slipped from his hand and dropped to the floor. As he reached down to pick it up, he noticed that the felt backing had separated from the case and he could see the edge of what looked like a small optical disk protruding out the side. He picked up the case and put it down on the table, then gently lifted the felt backing and pulled out the disk, looking it over carefully. It was about two and a half inches in diameter, completely blank with no writing on it at all.

"What's that?" Dianne asked inquisitively.

"I'm not sure. It looks like some sort of a computer disk, but I'm not sure why Angela would have it hidden in her necklace case. I'm not even sure why she would be carrying a disk anyway. I thought that she stored all of her work on a USB drive that she keeps on her keychain."

"She must have a reason for keeping it in there. You'd have to ask her, though." replied Dianne.

"I will." Mark replied. "Now, is there any wrapping paper around here, or do I need to run down to the store and get some?"

"I think there's some in the upstairs hall closet," replied Jan, "but I'm not sure what you'll find. It may be all Christmas and birthday paper."

Mark ran up the stairs to the hall closet and opened it to look for the paper. As Jan had thought, there were several rolls stored on the top shelf, but all of it was Christmas paper. He'd need to run out to the store after all. Before leaving, he placed the disk back under the felt backing, and then snapped it back in place before placing the necklace back into the case. He put the case in his pocket before leaving for the store.

After he left, Dianne looked at her mother with an inquisitive look, "I wonder why Angela would keep a computer disk in her necklace case?"

"Who knows." replied Jan. "It is an odd place to keep a computer disk, though. It seems like you'd only keep it there if you didn't want anyone to find it."

"That's what I was thinking too." said Dianne. "I wonder what's on it."

"I bet Mark will find out. She'll tell him." replied Jan.

On the way to the store, Mark was still wondering what was on the disk. While he'd wanted to take it and put it in a computer to see what was on it, he knew that he'd never do that. If Angela wants him to know what's on it, she'll tell him when he asks, but until then whatever is on it belongs to Angela. While he does accept that, it still doesn't help with his curiosity. An even bigger question to him than what's on the disk is why she hid it in the necklace case. For it to be hidden in such a way behind the felt backing seemed to indicate that she didn't want anyone to find it. He was definitely curious, but it would have to wait until he got the chance to ask her about it.

Upon entering the gift shop, Island Boutique Gifts, he immediately walked over to where they kept the general wrapping paper. The aisle had a lot to choose from in all colors and patterns. He decided for this occasion just to go with a simple pattern of small colored lines on a silver background. Since the necklace box was small, any large patterns wouldn't be apparent anyway. This one seemed just right for the occasion, simple and elegant.

As he turned to go back up front, his attention was drawn to a grey haired man studying greeting cards on the opposite side of the isle. He hadn't been there when Mark had first come in. Where had he seen him before? He was certain that he had seen the man, but exactly where he just wasn't sure. He must still have been watching the man as he walked by, because the man turned in his direction and spoke to him as he did.

"Special occasion?" the man asked him.

"Yes ... it is. It's my and my girlfriend's six month anniversary." he replied awkwardly. While he had been looking at the man out of the corner of his eye trying to figure out how he knew him, he hadn't expected him to actually speak to him. It caught him slightly off guard.

"Congratulations, then!" the man replied, "There's nothing quite like young love!"

He paused for a few seconds, then continued, "By the way, my name's Al. Pleased to make your acquaintance."

"Mark Duncan." Mark replied hesitantly, "Nice to meet you too." Actually, Mark wasn't used to encountering strangers that were quite this friendly. From past experience, he had found that they usually wanted something, like possibly a hand-out. But this stranger didn't exactly fit the usual homeless stereotype. He was too well dressed for one thing, and his hair was too well groomed.

"So, is today your anniversary?" Al inquired.

"No, it's tomorrow, but I'm shopping and wrapping up the gift today."

He actually surprised himself by actually retrieving the necklace box from his pocket and opening it to show Al.

"She must be a special lady!" Al remarked as he studied the sparkling necklace as it shimmered in the lights of the card display.

"She is. There's nobody else quite like her." Mark replied, smiling. "I actually gave her the necklace for her birthday earlier in the year, but I added the diamond heart for our anniversary."

"She's lucky to have such a romantic boyfriend." Al remarked, "What's her name?"

"Angela." Mark replied, smiling as he said it. It really was out of character for him to be carrying on a conversation of such a personal nature with a complete stranger, but Al seemed so easy to talk to. He had the kind of personality where you felt you had known him all your life.

"Angela." Al repeated, letting the name trail off. "Such a lovely name." He had actually known who she was even before he asked. He remembered seeing both of them together on the beach two days ago. He couldn't quite tell whether Mark recognized him from that encounter or not, but Mark was looking at him like he was trying to figure out where he had seen him before.

"Yes it is." Mark replied. "Do you live around here?"

"Yes, I have a house here on the island. How about you?"

"I'm actually going to school in Wilmington. I'm in my last semester before graduating next year. I've got an intern job and we're working down here on the island for a couple of weeks."

"Sounds like a pretty good internship, getting to work down here on the island. There are not a lot of businesses here, though, that would need interns. Where are you working?"

"I'm actually working for Chandler-Langtree in Wilmington. We're doing some work out at the lighthouse."

"Ah … that must be what the trailer that I've seen at the edge of the parking lot is. What kind of work are you doing out there?"

At this point, Mark was starting to get a little irritated at the interruption. And he didn't feel comfortable with all of the questions; especially since he couldn't really talk about what they were doing.

"I'd love to stay and chat," Mark replied abruptly, "but I need to get back and get this wrapped before Angela gets home. You understand, right?"

"Yes, of course. It's been a pleasure talking to you. Maybe we can do it again sometime."

As Mark turned and began walking down the aisle toward the cash registers at the front of the store, Al surprised him once more as he called after him, "Be careful Mark. Some things are not meant to be tampered with."

He looked back around at Al then continued toward the front of the store. That last comment unnerved him. Did Al really know what they were doing out at the island? And what had he meant by, "Some things are not meant to be tampered with?" It was almost as if he knew something about what they were actually doing here on the island after all.

As Dan, Scotty, and Wendell pulled into the driveway of the light blue beach house, they were met by Bud.

"Sorry you came all the way out here," he said to them, "but I just got a call from Al. He's not going to be able to make it today. You can all come on in though. I can let you listen to some of the recordings that I've made over the last couple of weeks. There doesn't seem to be much going on today, though."

As they all went in the side door next to the carport, Bud led them to a small room at the back of the house where he had his ham shack. There was a large window overlooking the beach next to the table where he had his radio equipment set up. They all sat down around the table where Bud had his laptop with the SDR dongle plugged into it. SDR was an acronym for Software Defined Radio, and it was what he had been using to record the seemingly encrypted transmissions. Bud opened a program and began to play a file. He was right, Dan thought, it did sound like an encrypted transmission. And for a digital transmission to be received that clearly, it had to be close by. He had to wonder if maybe it really did have something to do with Chandler-Langtree and what they were doing here on the island.

They all were disappointed that Al hadn't been able to make it. It would have been nice to see if he could decrypt the transmissions, but maybe he'd be able to come by soon, hopefully before they had to leave. They spent a couple more hours visiting with Bud out at his beach house before leaving to go back to the bed and breakfast.

"Give us a call if Al can come back out before we have to leave." Dan said. "We're all leaving Monday, so hopefully sometime over the weekend might be good."

"I'll check with him and see." Bud responded. "Hopefully we can work something out."

CHAPTER 23
October 26, 2018
Anniversary Dinner

Mark turned a few dials on the console in the Mobile Command Center while staring intently at the monitor in front of him. Dr. Langtree was in the woods around the lighthouse taking field measurements as the temporal field was brought into alignment. Mark could see him on one of the video monitors as he plugged a portable computer into the terminal at the base of the emitter in sector 4. Dr. Langtree keyed the mic on his radio.

"Go ahead and transmit the parameters for Emitter 4." he instructed.

Mark typed some instructions on his keyboard, then replied, "Parameters sent. How does it look?"

"Looking good, Mark. Those updates that you made to the matrix are getting us a lot closer."

Two nights ago when Richard had given him the box, Mark had stayed up most of the night studying the papers that Blake Sorensen had written. Like a good novel, he couldn't put them down. But the most important thing in his mind was that even that first night of reading Blake's research had helped him discover some major issues with some of his calculations. He had spent most of the day yesterday reprogramming the matrix to fit Blake's parameters and running simulations to validate the new numbers. Now today, he had loaded the new matrix as soon as he got to the command center and now both he and Dr. Langtree were testing and calibrating each of the emitters to be sure that the new information loaded correctly into each one. Dr. Langtee was going around to each of the emitters and verifying that the new parameters were loaded and that the emitters were tuned EXACTLY to the new matrix. If there was even the slightest variation, then he'd have to manually calibrate each emitter, and then retest. For what they were doing here, there was absolutely no room for error. What was shown on the displays in the command center had to be precisely what each emitter was putting out. The precision needed for time travel was incredible. There really was no such thing as "close enough" for what they were doing here.

After Dr. Langtree had finished all of the calibrations and everything looked good from the remote tests that Mark ran, it was time for what Dr. Langtree called an "active simulation". During the calibration that they had been doing during the morning, the emitters were only brought up to about ten percent power. This was enough to validate the resonance of the temporal field. Now for the active simulation, the emitters would slowly be brought up to about seventy percent, with field readings taken by Dr. Langtree at each five percent interval. They wouldn't go past seventy percent because that was enough to validate that the field was in alignment and the ripples were in resonance with the emitters. Anything past seventy percent and they would risk the field actually opening to another time period, and during the day with visitors at the lighthouse, that definitely wouldn't be the best thing to happen. That test would have to be reserved for evening, after the lighthouse had closed for the day.

But it would also have to be another evening, because Mark had plans for tonight. After a successful active simulation, Dr. Langtree suggested that Mark take the rest of the afternoon to get ready for his date tonight, which he eagerly obliged. It still wasn't early, it was almost four o'clock, but Mark felt that he could use the extra time to at least rest up for the evening. He'd had trouble concentrating on his work today anyway since he had been thinking about tonight. As interesting as the reality of time travel was, to him Angela was even more interesting, and tonight they had special plans. He thought that Dr. Langtree had noticed that he had been somewhat preoccupied today as well. Since he and Melissa had been dating, he was more in tune to the relationship between Mark and Angela and tried to accommodate them when he could. It was something that only couples in love would notice.

"You and Angela have a good time tonight." he said with a smile as Mark opened the door of the Mobile Command Center to leave for his date.

"Thanks." Mark said as he looked back at Dr. Langtree. While he had become more personable since he began dating Melissa, there was still something about him that seemed a mystery to Mark. There was a layer to his personality that he just couldn't seem to get through, and this seemed to prevent Mark from really getting to know him on a personal level. He supposed that Melissa had gotten farther than most people, though, since he had seen a change in Dr. Langtree lately. In time, maybe Dr. Langtree would open up more to him as well.

As Mark drove down Lighthouse Road, his mind was lost in thought about the evening. He could almost picture Angela now, sitting across from him at Grant's Steak House, their eyes lost in each other's gaze. He had meticulously planned the perfect evening, down to the smallest detail. He had called the restaurant to make sure that they had a bottle of Angela's favorite wine, and after her grandmother's suggestion had called and hired Renaldo to play for them at their table. He had planned an evening to remember.

Like most areas along the North Carolina coast, Green Island had it's share of small sandwich shops and diners. One of the most popular among both tourists and locals alike was the Sand Crab Diner. Around lunch and dinner time it was always crowded. People loved the food and the casual island atmosphere. For those who wanted to eat outside in the fresh air, there was a taco truck that parked across from Bud's General Store. It was right beside a small park with picnic tables, so that folks could order their tacos, then find a table in the park to eat them. Slightly farther from town, diners enjoyed the Mariner's Cove out at the Harbor Inn. It was slightly more upscale than the Sand Crab with more entree dishes and less sandwiches. But for fine dining by candlelight, the island only had one choice: Grant's Steak House. It was where birthdays, anniversaries, and other special occasions were celebrated. Owner Dave Grant prided himself on creating memories for his diners just like his father Evan did when he started the restaurant almost fifty years ago, and that's one of the things that has kept folks coming back. While he did advertise in many of the local coastal publications, he always thought that most of his business came from personal recommendations. So when Mark wanted a special evening for their six month anniversary, there was only one choice, and that was Grant's.

Rebekah had been in the kitchen styling Angela's hair since around three thirty. The previous night they had both been looking through some of Rebekah's magazines trying to decide on a "look" for Angela for the evening. After a couple of hours of looking through the magazines, Angela decided on one where she let the back of her hair hang down to around her waist, while the sides were pulled around and tied up in a twist. It didn't look that hard from the picture in the magazine, but it took Rebekah several tries to get just the look that they both wanted. While the finished product did look a little different than the magazine, Angela actually liked it. The rest of the preparation wouldn't take as long since her mom and Mrs. Duncan had taken her shopping last night at one of the local island boutiques to find a dress for the occasion. It came down to a difficult decision. There were four that Angela actually liked, but between the three women they finally decided on a lovely red one that came slightly below her knees. It had frills around the hem, neck and sleeves and Dianne thought that it would go just right with the pearls that Mark had given her along with her cream colored sweater. She originally was going to wear the charm necklace that Mark had given her for her birthday, but Dianne had convinced her that the pearls were more elegant for a candlelight dinner.

About half way through their hair styling adventure, they heard the front door of the bed and breakfast open. A few seconds later, Mark poked his head into the kitchen.

"Hi girls." he said.

"Mark! Go away! You're not supposed to see her yet!" cried Rebekah.

"I thought that was only for weddings." he answered with a grin. Still, he figured that he'd leave them alone for now. He heard his parents in the sitting room with the Nelson's and the Sorensen's, so he thought he'd drop in there and say hello.

"Ready for the big night?" asked Kate as Mark walked through the door. "Those girls have been in the kitchen for the last hour! If Angela doesn't look absolutely gorgeous tonight, it won't be for lack of trying!"

"Angela always looks gorgeous." he answered. "And I think I'm ready. I stopped and picked up my suit on the way home. I called the restaurant on the way home too, to make sure that they were able to get the wine and that they remembered to have the table that I selected ready. Seems like everything's set."

Mark took his suit up to his room, then came back down to visit with everyone for awhile before it was time to get ready for the evening.

"Have you had a chance to look through that box that Richard gave you Wednesday night?" asked Scotty.

"I've looked through some of the papers, but I haven't had a lot of time in only two days. Most of them appear to be journals of his work. Since he was a theoretical physicist as well, I guess he thought that maybe I'd find some of his work useful."

"Exactly what was he working on that he thought that you'd find useful?" Scotty continued.

This question caught Mark off guard and he really didn't know how to answer. If he was truthful, then he'd be giving away what he was working on with Dr. Langtree, and that would violate the secrecy agreement with Chandler-Langtree.

"I can't really say a lot about it, Dad. The work that I'm doing is pretty secretive. Sort of like national security type stuff."

He knew that last part was a stretch. It really had nothing to do with national security; but then he hadn't really said that it did, he'd just said that it was "sort of like" it. He guessed that could be construed into a true statement, if one had a lot of imagination. While Scotty wasn't completely satisfied with that answer, he did understand that there were some businesses where the employees couldn't really discuss their jobs, and apparently Chandler-Langtree was one of them. He'd mentioned to Mark when they had talked in Wilmington, before coming down to the island, that he had his concerns about them. He still wondered exactly what they wanted from Mark. He had explained to his son that companies don't just give all of those types of perks: offices, cars and salary to interns who are still technically in college just because they want to be nice. They want something in return for all of the benefits that they're giving away; nothing is free. Mark still didn't fully grasp what he was trying to say to him and just told him that he didn't have any reason to be concerned; that he was just like Angela, worried at every little thing. But Scotty knew Mark only too well. He knew that he had the tendency to take things at face value and not see what's underneath. Sometimes, Scotty felt that Mark could be too trusting.

"Have you thought about why he would want to give this stuff to you?" continued Scotty, referring to Blake. "And how did he even know you? You were just a freshman when he died. "

Mark actually did know how Blake knew him. It was all in the letter that he had found in the box. But he didn't want to say right now. Not just yet. He wondered if anyone would even believe him anyway, so he pretended not to know, at least for now.

"No, I haven't gotten that far yet. It's only been two days. I think I might have met him at a lecture, though, when he came to the school during the beginning of my freshman year as a visiting professor."

The last part wasn't true, but it seemed to satisfy Scotty, at least a little. The truth was he never remembered actually meeting Blake.

After visiting for a while down in the sitting room, it was time for Mark to go upstairs and get ready for his date. Angela and Rebekah had already gone upstairs about forty five minutes ago, but it took them longer to get ready than it did him. He laid his suit out on the bed, and then went in to shave and take a shower. After getting dressed, he gathered up his tie and jacket and walked downstairs. Angela wasn't there yet, but then he hadn't really expected her to be quite this soon. It was only six twenty, and he knew her well. She'd have to have everything just right. For her and her sister, getting ready for the date was half the fun. It was bonding time for the two girls. She'd be his for the rest of the evening, but right now it was her and Rebekah's time, and he knew that. He sat down in one of the chairs in the sitting room, quieter than usual, just anticipating Angela walking down the stairs.

It was around six thirty-five when Angela finally walked down the stairs and into the sitting room. Mark slowly stood, not able to take his eyes off of her. She looked absolutely stunning in her red dress and pearls. Since it was nearing the end of October and the evening was cool, she wore a cream colored cashmere sweater over her dress with shoes that matched the color of the sweater. To complete the ensemble, she carried a small clutch purse that matched the color of her sweater as well. Rebekah could be a hair stylist to the stars one day as well. Angela's hair was the most breathtaking that he had ever seen, with two jewel inlaid silver combs holding it in place on either side near the back of her head, and a twist formed where the hair had been pulled together and fastened with the combs. The rest was simply allowed to hang down to her waist, which definitely completed the look. He couldn't imagine a professional stylist doing any better. Mark was practically speechless.

"Wow! You look great!" he remarked, still not able to take his eyes off of her, but walking over to where she was standing and giving her a kiss.

"You do too." she said, as she looked deeply into his eyes.

Kate pulled her Smartphone out of her purse.

"Let's get some pictures!" she remarked. "We need to remember this night forever."

"Mom," Mark protested, "we're going to be late!"

"Just a couple of pictures." Kate said, as she directed them to stand over by the fireplace. This attention made them both feel like two high school kids going off to the prom, rather than two young adults celebrating an anniversary of being together. In a way, it was similar, but in another way it wasn't.

After the photos were finished, with both sets of parents participating in the photo shoot with their phones, Mark and Angela said their goodbyes and went out the front door and down the steps of the bed and breakfast with Mark holding his right arm at a right angle for Angela to hold on to. They seemed to be the perfect couple and so much in love.

As they drove down Main Street to Grant's Steak House, Angela laid her head on Mark's shoulder. This was what she had needed for a long time. And while she was definitely looking forward to the dinner, the main thing was that she got to spend the evening with the man that she loved.

It wasn't a long drive, about three minutes. Most of the time they simply walked into town from the bed and breakfast, but tonight wasn't most nights and with Angela wearing heels, walking down the street at night probably wouldn't be the best idea. Besides, at a place like Grant's, pulling up out front and walking into the restaurant while the valet parks your car is much more romantic. At around five till seven they pulled up at the front doors and the valet walked around the car and opened Angela's door, then held out his hand to help her out. Mark slipped the valet a five as they walked around the front of the car and into the restaurant.

The maître d', Evans, was waiting by the front door when they walked in, and he greeted them with a cheerful, "Good evening, welcome to Grant's Steak House."

"Mark Duncan," replied Mark, "I have a reservation for two at seven."

Evans consulted his tablet that he was carrying, then remarked, "Ah yes, Mr. Duncan and Ms. Nelson! We have your table ready. Please follow me."

They both followed him, hand in hand, as he led them to the table that Mark had picked out earlier, the one by the window overlooking the harbor. As they reached the table, Mark moved to one side and pulled Angela's chair out for her so that she could be seated first. After they were both seated, Evans recited the specials of the evening and informed them that Alexandre would be their server as he placed a menu in front of each of them. Alexandre walked up just as Evans was turning to leave, carrying a tray with two wine glasses, a loaf of rye bread, and a bottle of Hatteras Red Reserve. Angela smiled at Mark and reached over and squeezed his hands as she noticed that he had ordered a bottle of her favorite North Carolina wine for the evening.

"My name's Alexandre, I'll be your server for the evening." he said as he placed the bread in the center of the table, and then set a wine glass in front of each of them. He popped the cork on the wine bottle and proceeded to pour some in each glass, setting the bottle on the table when he was finished.

"Would you like time to look over the menu?" he asked.

"Yes, thank you." replied Mark.

After Alexandre left, they both picked up their menus from the table and began looking over the entrees. Everything on the menu looked good, but since both of them were in the mood for a steak, they each decided on their favorite. Mark picked the ten ounce t-bone and Angela chose an eight ounce sirloin. Both came with a salad and their choice of sides, and they decided on sautéed mushrooms as an appetizer as well. Once they had made their decisions, they closed the menus and placed them back down on the table as a signal to Alexandre that they were ready to order. Angela picked up her wine glass and took a sip.

"It's really beautiful here by the harbor." she remarked.

Mark looked out at the lights of the boats as they would come and go. The view really was spectacular.

"Yes it is." he said, then looking back over at her continued, "And it's even more wonderful being here with the most beautiful lady that I know."

At this she looked away blushing, but she still gave Mark a smile that said "There's nobody that I'd rather be here with either."

After Alexandre had come back over and taken their order, Mark pulled out a small wrapped box about nine inches long from his inside jacket pocket and placed it on the table in front of her.

"I got you a little something to say 'I love you'." he said, smiling at her.

"I have something for you, too, but it's back at the bed and breakfast. I don't have any pockets."

She smiled back at him as she gently picked up the box from the table and slid a fingernail under the tape on one side to separate the paper. As she separated the paper, she noticed that the box looked a lot like her necklace case. She peeled the rest of the paper off and carefully opened it. After seeing the contents, she looked up at Mark with a look that he couldn't quite place, and it wasn't exactly the look that he had expected. It was her necklace that he had given her for her birthday! But why was he giving it to her again? She had a puzzled look, until she noticed the small silver heart that hadn't been there before. The diamond in the center glistened in the lights of the restaurant.

"I wanted to give you my heart." Mark said.

"Thank you, it's lovely!" she said smiling. She looked down at the case, and it seemed that the felt backing was still in place. Maybe he hadn't seen the disk that she had hidden inside after all. She had been concerned when she first saw the case, since she had been keeping the disk in there to keep it safe and hidden. She still wasn't sure that she was ready to tell him everything just yet, but then she knew that it was a secret that she couldn't keep much longer.

"Will you put it on me?" she asked.

"Of course." he said getting up out of his chair and walking over behind her to unhook the clasp on her pearl necklace. She took the necklace out of the case and replaced the pearls inside it. As she pulled her hair up above her head to hold it out of the way, Mark wrapped the necklace around her neck and fastened the clasp. When he went back around and sat down across from her, he could see the diamond sparkling.

"You're the most beautiful girl in the world!" he said. She blushed again, smiling back at him.

She handed the box back to Mark for him to put back into his jacket pocket, and about that time Alexandre came back to the table with the mushrooms. As they were dipping the mushrooms into Grant's special sauce, they heard music coming from the back of the dining area. It seemed to be getting louder as it got closer. As Angela looked at him and smiled once again, he knew that she recognized the song, "Simply Love". It had become her favorite song. It was actually their song; it had been playing on the radio the night that they met. As the music got closer, they both saw the person playing it, a short Mexican man wearing a black suit with gold and purple trim. It was rhinestone studded and each one sparkled as he moved. He wore a wide brimmed sombrero that also was rhinestone studded and had gold and purple hat bands. He played the violin as he walked toward them, and then stopped at their table right beside Angela. She looked up at him and smiled. He finished "Simply Love", and then played several more songs as Alexandre delivered their main course. It was a really romantic touch to be serenaded as she ate. About three songs into his set, as Angela was listening to the words of the songs, she realized that he wasn't playing a random collection of songs; each song had been carefully selected to communicate exactly Mark's feelings for her. She had never felt more special and loved than she did right now. She reached across the table and took Mark's hand, gazing deeply into his eyes as Renaldo played.

After Renaldo finished playing for them, and they continued with their dinner, Mark noticed that the woman sitting at the table behind Angela seemed to be watching them. She looked to be in her late forties or early fifties, attractive with medium length brown hair styled into waves. He had seen her come in soon after they had been seated, and remembered wondering why such a lovely woman would be eating alone at a restaurant like this. He had actually expected a gentleman to show up at any time to join her, but none ever did.

After dinner, they both walked out front and Mark handed the valet his claim ticket. Within two minutes his car was pulling up out front. He walked around and held Angela's door for her, then came back around and slipped the valet another five before getting into the car and driving off.

As the car passed the bed and breakfast and continued down Henderson Road, Angela was wondering where they were going. What other surprises might Mark have in store tonight? She was at least relieved that Mark hadn't asked about the disk in the necklace case. It was hidden inside the felt backing, so maybe he hadn't actually seen it. That was her hope at least.

They drove out along Sea Spray Drive, and then Mark parked the car and went over and opened her door.

"How about a romantic walk along the beach?" he asked as he bent down to give her a kiss.

"That sounds lovely," she said, "but I'm wearing heels!"

"Not to worry." he replied as he retrieved a pair of new loafers out of the back floorboard.

"Mark, you think of everything!" she said smiling.

After changing into the loafers, they walked along the beach, hand in hand, reminiscing about when they first met and the times that they've had since then. The waves breaking along the beach set a relaxing mood as they strolled up the beach. With the breeze coming off the ocean along with the late October chill in the air, Angela's sweater and Mark's jacket weren't quite enough to keep them very warm. As he put his arm around her shoulders, he felt her shudder in the cool air. He immediately stopped, took off his jacket, and placed it over her shoulders.

"Thank you," she said quietly, "but won't you get cold?"

"I'll be fine." he said, "Just being here with you will keep me warm."

As they turned around and started back down the beach, they noticed someone else coming toward them. It was the first person that they'd seen out here tonight. As the person came closer, Mark could see that it was the woman from the restaurant. What a coincidence that she'd be out here tonight at the same time that they were!

"Hello." she said to them. "You're the couple from the restaurant!"

"Yes," replied Mark, "I'm Mark Duncan and this is my girlfriend Angela Nelson."

"Sally Bennett." the woman replied. "Nice to meet you both. I see you two are obviously in love. What's the occasion?"

"It's our six month anniversary of being together!" said Angela.

"Well congratulations, then." answered Sally.

Sally was obviously friendly, but Mark did have to wonder if she was actually following them. It seemed to be too much of a coincidence to see her at the restaurant and then out here at the beach, especially when she was the only other person that they'd seen out here tonight. They talked for a few more minutes, and then they parted ways as Sally continued on up the beach while Mark and Angela continued toward where they had parked their car.

As they walked, arm in arm back up the beach, continuing to talk as they went, Mark asked the question that she had been hoping to avoid; the question that she wasn't quite prepared to answer yet:

"I was wondering, why is there a computer disk in your necklace case?"

He hadn't really thought too much about it when he said it; he was simply making conversation, and he had remembered seeing it yesterday and making a note to ask her about it. With everything going on, it just hadn't come up until now. Her mannerism suddenly changed, however, and he could see that it must be a bigger deal than he had originally thought. He almost wished that he hadn't brought it up at all, at least not tonight. He hadn't wanted anything to spoil this night. She stopped and looked at him with the strangest look that he had ever seen. It was almost the look that he'd have expected if he'd just slapped her in the face.

"Disk?" she said, almost in a whisper. "You saw the disk?"

CHAPTER 24

The Confrontation

"I wasn't looking for anything." Mark said as his eyes met hers. He took both of her hands in his. "When I picked up the case to put the necklace back inside, I dropped it and the backing separated. When I bent down to pick it up, I saw the corner of the disk sticking out from the case. It seemed strange that a computer disk would be in there, and I was curious. That's all."

She was looking at him now with a look that he couldn't quite place, and he really wondered if he should just let it drop. She'd tell him about it when she was ready. It really wasn't that important.

"If it's personal and you don't want to tell me about it, that's alright. We can talk about something else. I didn't realize that you'd have this reaction, or I wouldn't have even brought it up. I wasn't trying to upset you."

"No, Mark, I should have told you about it before now. I just didn't quite know how. Let's go over to the benches on the boardwalk and sit down."

Her voice was quivering, and he could tell that it wasn't just from the cold. She was actually starting to scare him now. What could possibly be on the disk that would cause this reaction? As they both sat down next to each other on the bench overlooking the ocean, she didn't look at him at first. She just stared out at the ocean, wondering how to begin. As comfortable as he was when he was together with Angela, she was starting to make him feel uncomfortable now. Finally she turned to him and looked into his eyes, still holding his hand. He could feel her hand trembling. He'd never seen her like this before.

"Mark ... I'm sorry ... but I did it for you. I love you more than

I've ever loved anyone, and I was just worried."

Her voice trailed away as he wiped away a tear as it trickled down her cheek.

"I couldn't take a chance of losing you."

"You're not going to lose me. Nothing you could ever say or do could make me love you any less. Whatever it is, you can tell me."

"I hope you still feel that way after I tell you what I've done."

He smiled at her. "Don't be afraid, Angela. Nothing you could possibly do would drive us apart. Our love is strong enough to get us through anything."

Angela continued, "The disk contains information about a 'Project Vortex Elimination'. I don't fully understand it all, but according to the information on the disk, things were completely different before May 20, 2016. Dad had a different family and I wasn't even a part of that family. The strange part is that I have memories of things that happened before that date that are different than what's on the disk! Actually, I don't understand it at all, but there are pictures that just couldn't have been taken because those things never happened! It's all on the disk, but it just doesn't make any sense at all."

"Hold on a minute!" said Mark. "Slow down! You're losing me here! What do you mean things were completely different before May 20, 2016? How could your father have had a different family before then?"

"I think it's time travel!" she replied. "The journal entries on the disk indicate that things changed because of time travel! Dad originally owned the lighthouse, only it wasn't the lighthouse that we know today. It was run down and hadn't been lit in decades. Somehow that was because of the things that were different then. Apparently, Dad's company that he owned in the life before May 20 had built something called the Vortex Accelerator sometime in the future at the lighthouse. Two men who were part of a committee had travelled back in time to fix things so that the Vortex Accelerator was never built. The ability to travel through time and change events had gotten out of hand in their time and a small group called The Committee decided that the ability to travel through time shouldn't be an ability that anyone has because they will always abuse it. The two men worked with Dad to get him to sell the lighthouse so that his company wouldn't build the Accelerator and things would revert back to the way that they should have been."

"Wait a minute!" Mark interrupted. "Dr. Langtree and I are still working on time travel. We're close, but we haven't quite gotten there yet. How could it be time travel that affected the past?"

"Because time travel destroys the linear time line. It makes it really hard to tell what events came first because the future can get interwoven into the past. Maybe you and Dr. Langtree aren't the first to experiment with time travel and maybe someone in the future has already done it! Maybe they could have even travelled back to this time and changed things. In time travel you have to be really careful or things can really get messed up." she replied.

As she said this, it brought on a feeling of deja vu. He remembered several weeks ago having a conversation with Dr. Langtree about the interesting anomaly that he had discovered superimposed on the ripples. Dr. Langtree had actually suggested that it may be a power source in the future! Could that be true? Could someone else from the future have actually perfected time travel before? And could this thing called the Vortex Accelerator be the power source in the future that's powering the ripples?

"So does your dad remember any of this?" Mark asked, "About working with these men to sell the lighthouse and anything about his life before May 20, 2016?"

"No, his memories are like mine. We remember things with our current family even before May 20 and he doesn't remember anything different before then. That's one of the parts that I can't explain."

"Then how do you know any of the things on that disk are true?" he asked, actually starting to wonder why she had been so afraid to tell him any of this. It obviously sounded like a fictional story to him. He and Dr. Langtree were still working on time travel using the ripples, but they hadn't been successful yet. He felt that they were close, but not quite there. He didn't like to consider the possibility that someone else had already been successful, but he had to admit that given the nature of time travel that it was a definite possibility.

"Because Dad had a dream on the night of May 20, 2016. In the dream, he was at the lighthouse when a fog came up. He heard a woman in the fog calling his name. He called back to her and when she came out of the fog she came running over to him. Her name was Kate. It was your mother in the dream, but that was over two years before he met her."

"So you think that it's true because my mother was with your dad in a dream? Maybe it wasn't even her. Maybe it was someone who just looked a lot like her."

"No, also on the disk were pictures with names given on them. According to the information, Dad was married to your mom before May 20, 2016!"

This time it was Mark's turn to show a strange expression. "Where exactly did that disk come from?" he asked. "Where did you get it?"

"It came from Chandler-Langtree." she said hesitantly. "

As she spoke this last statement, she carefully studied Mark's face to see his expression. He was silent for close to half a minute with just a blank stare. Finally he asked, "How did you get a disk from Chandler-Langtree?"

Just as she had feared, as he spoke those words, she could tell a noticeable change in his tone and mood. It was close to an accusing tone, and it had hints of anger as well. This made it even harder to tell him what she had to tell him now. At the time, she had the best of intentions. She wouldn't have even been interested in the Chandler-Langtree Institute beyond the rumors that she'd heard around campus if Mark hadn't started working there and getting all of those perks! He was the reason that she had done it! She felt that she had to know what was going on to keep him safe! She didn't want to lose him, but now she feared that by her actions that might be exactly what would happen. She turned her head away from him and stared out at the ocean. He reached over and gently turned her head back to face him. As he looked into her eyes he could see that she was afraid.

"Angela, where did you get a disk from Chandler-Langtree?" he said, slightly more forcibly this time.

"I'm sorry! I should have told you this before now, but I did it for you! For us! I didn't know that we would find what we did!"

"Who are 'we'"? he asked, seeming to begin to lose patience with her now. "What did you do, and who else did you drag into this?"

Now she really was afraid to tell him, but things had gone too far. She didn't have a choice now.

"You remember my friend Janice?"

"Yes, I remember. What does she have to do with this?"

"Her boyfriend, Glen, is a cyber security expert. He knew some people that had experience accessing computer systems. We met one night and they were able to get into the Chandler-Langtree computer system and retrieved the information that's on that disk."

Again, she studied his expression as she said this last statement.

"Hackers?!" he remarked, "You used hackers to break into our computer system to spy on me?!"

Mark was really irritated now and was close to losing his temper, which he had never done with her in all the months that they had been dating.

"Not to spy on you! I needed to find out what they were doing. I wanted to make sure that you were safe!"

"You could have just asked me! I thought that we had an honest relationship; that we could talk things over without going behind each other's back and spying on them!"

"I did ask you! I asked you several times, but all you would ever tell me was that there was nothing to worry about!"

"That's because there isn't anything to worry about! You know I can't really talk about any of the details about what we're doing, and I've already told you too much already. I wish you could just accept the fact that there's nothing to worry about!"

"But there IS something to worry about!" she insisted. "There's a lot to worry about. I don't think Dr. Langtree's telling you everything."

"He tells me what I need to know to accomplish what we're doing. He'll tell me anything else that's important as well."

"No he won't! Not about Project Vortex Elimination! He'll consider that to be the reality before this one, a reality that doesn't concern you; but you need to know!"

"No! Dr. Langtree trusts me and I won't betray that trust! Apparently it's YOU that can't trust me anymore!"

As he said this, he got up and began walking back up the beach toward the car. Angela followed behind, trying her best to hold back tears.

"Mark, that's not fair! I DO trust you, I just thought that maybe you didn't realize what you were getting into!"

He continued to walk down the beach, not saying a word and not turning to look at her. When they arrived back at his car, he did still open her door for her, but the drive back to the bed and breakfast was completely silent. Neither of them really said anything. Angela did look over at him several times, but he never returned her looks. He just kept staring straight ahead at the road as they went.

Upon returning to the bed and breakfast, Mark stayed out on the front porch in one of the rocking chairs, while Angela went inside. He needed time to think; to really try to understand what Angela had just told him. He hadn't expected that from her at all. When he had asked about the disk, he really didn't expect it to contain stolen data from his company. He hadn't thought Angela would do something like that. He had known for quite awhile now that she was concerned about him working there, but he never imagined that she'd commit a crime because of it! What was she thinking?! Stealing information from a government contractor was probably a felony! Of course, he'd never say anything to anyone that would get her in trouble because of it. Still, it did bother him that maybe she wasn't as honest as he'd thought. Maybe he really didn't know her after all.

"How was the evening?" Dianne asked cheerfully as Angela walked through the front door and stood in the entrance to the sitting room. Her mood quickly changed as she looked into Angela's eyes; eyes that were red with tears.

"Is something wrong?" she continued as Angela just stood in the doorway with a blank stare, "Where's Mark?"

At that, Angela bolted up the stairs, choking back sobs as she went.

Dianne started to get up out of her chair and go after Angela, but Dan motioned for her to stay seated as he rose from his chair.

"Better let me go." he said in a worried tone.

He walked up the stairs and knocked on the closed door to her room.

"Angela? May I come in?"

There was no reply from inside the room, but after a few seconds the door slowly opened. It was dark in the room, apparently she hadn't turned on any lights. Even with no light, however, he could tell that she'd been crying.

"I think I've lost him." she said as they both walked over and sat on the bed.

"What happened?" Dan asked, concerned.

"Mark found the disk with the information on it that I hid in my necklace case. He asked about it tonight, so I had to tell him what was on it and where I got it. He's really upset with me right now. He thinks that he can't trust me anymore, since I wasn't honest with him from the start and we broke into the computer system and stole that information. I've been wanting to tell him for some time now, but I was afraid that what happened tonight would happen. I didn't want to lose him."

"I understand. You did the right thing by telling him tonight. He needed to know."

"But do you think that I did the right thing by breaking into the computer system? I'm beginning to wish that I'd never done that!"

"I think you did what you felt was best at the time. If it was the wrong thing to do, then at least it was for the right reason. You love Mark and just wanted to protect him. Nobody can fault you for that. Maybe working with a group of hackers to break into a top secret computer system is a bit extreme, but at the time you must have felt that it was justified."

"I did. At the time, I couldn't really think of anything else to do."

She sat silently for a couple of minutes, then quietly asked, "Do you think Mark will turn me in? I could go to prison for what we did!"

"I think I know Mark well enough to believe that you don't have anything to worry about there. He may be angry now, but I've seen the way that he looks at you. He'd never turn you in, no matter what you did."

At that she did finally give him a faint smile. "I hope you're right, Dad, but he's really mad."

"Do you want me to talk to him?" Dan asked.

"I don't know if it would do any good." she replied.

"Maybe not, but it's worth a try. I may be able to get through to him."

"Thanks Dad!" she said, reaching over and giving him a big hug, "I think Mark's on the front porch."

When Dan walked out onto the porch, Kate was there with Mark. She had been trying to find out from him what had happened, and was surprised to learn that Angela had actually told him about the information from Chandler-Langtree. Besides that, he really wasn't in very much of a talking mood.

"Can you give us a few minutes?" Dan asked Kate.

"Sure." she said as she got up to go back inside. "He knows." she whispered to Dan as she walked past him and opened the front door to go back inside.

"Angela told you what happened?" Mark asked as Dan sat down in the chair beside him.

"Yes, she told me." Dan replied, his gaze meeting Mark's.

"I guess you knew about the disk?" Mark asked.

"Not the disk specifically, but the information on it. She talked with me about it when we arrived in Wilmington last week. She needed someone to talk to because she didn't understand any of what she found out. It was something that she hadn't expected to find. She didn't know what it meant and was bothered by it, and even a little frightened."

"She shouldn't even have had that information! It's her own fault!"

"Yes, maybe it is, but she did it for the right reasons. She just wanted to protect you; to keep you safe."

"I know that, but she still should have talked to me about what was bothering her instead of going off and doing something stupid like breaking into a computer system! That just showed that she didn't trust me."

"If she didn't trust you, she wouldn't have said anything about it tonight. Did she not try to talk to you earlier? What did you tell her?"

"I told her to stop worrying. That there's nothing to worry about; I'm not in any danger. She should have just accepted that explanation."

"Even if that explanation isn't true?" Dan inquired, as he looked Mark in the eye now. His gaze made Mark feel uncomfortable.

"What do you mean?" asked Mark.

"It isn't exactly true that you're not in any danger, is it?"

Mark thought about the letter that was in the box that Richard Sorensen had given him. Reading it that first night was the first time that he had really stopped to consider the risks that he may be taking. The scenario that Blake depicted in that letter actually outlined a specific danger that he had to consider.

"I guess there is some risk in anything that we do, and potentially what we're doing here has more risk than most things. But Blake Sorensen's research helped a lot in finding some of the flaws in our original thinking. I think it's eliminated most of the risks."

"Are you sure about that? If you're attempting what I think you are, do you really think that even Blake discovered all of the risks that you may encounter? Couldn't there be things that even he missed? It seems to me that travelling into a different time period is inherently dangerous, especially while you're still working out all of the issues with it."

"But I haven't travelled into a different time period!" Mark protested.

"Not yet," Dan interjected, "but isn't that the plan? And when that day comes, there may be risks that even Blake never thought of."

"I suppose, but there's some risk in everything that we do!"

"Some yes, but not to the same level. Any time that you walk into another time period, you take the risk that the door will close unexpectedly and you'll be trapped in that time period, twenty, thirty, possibly even forty or a hundred years in our past with no way to get home. Am I correct?"

"Well, yes I suppose that could happen." Mark hesitantly replied as Dan's last statement forced him to really consider the warnings that Blake had given in his letter and made him wonder if Blake really had considered all of the potential hazards after all.

"So you weren't being completely honest with her either, when you told her there was no danger. So she went looking on her own to find out for herself. It wasn't that she didn't trust you, she just thought that maybe you didn't realize what you might be getting into. She thought that you might be too blinded by everything that was happening that you weren't thinking straight."

"Maybe I was leaving out some of the danger. Maybe I was even trying to convince myself that what we were doing really wasn't dangerous as well. But simply telling Angela that there's nothing to worry about so that she won't worry is quite a bit different than committing a crime to get information!"

"Yes, and I'm not condoning what she did. It was wrong. Even more, it was breaking the law. But sometimes Angela doesn't think of things quite that way. All she was thinking about was you, and how she didn't want to lose you. Maybe she went about things the wrong way, but like I said before, she did it for the right reasons. She loves you, Mark; more than anything. She didn't tell you what she did earlier because she was afraid of losing you, not because she didn't trust you. Don't let her lose you now."

Mark didn't say anything; he just sat staring across the street, simply thinking of what Dan had just said. When Angela first told him about the contents of the disk, and breaking into the Chandler-Langtree computer system, he felt betrayed. They had always had an honest relationship, and he felt like he couldn't trust her to be honest with him anymore. But Dan was right; had he been completely honest with her? Maybe if he had been, she wouldn't have felt the need to do what she did.

"I don't want to lose her." Mark finally replied as he looked back over at Dan.

"Then go and tell her." Dan said. "She's upstairs in her room."

Angela sat up on the edge of the bed as she heard someone coming up the stairs. She wondered who would appear in the doorway; Mark, if her dad had been successful in talking with him or her dad to tell her that Mark wouldn't see her. A glimmer of hope appeared in her eyes as she saw Mark stop in the entranceway to the room. She stood slowly and ran over to him wrapping her arms tightly around him.

"I'm sorry." he said. "Your dad and I talked and I understand now that you were just worried about me."

"That's the truth!" she said, "I really was just worried about you! I love you, Mark!"

"I love you too." he answered.

"So you're not mad that I broke into the computer system?"

"Yes, I'm still mad, but I understand now why you did it. Can I have a look at what's on the disk?"

"Yes, of course. Let me get it and my computer."

She grabbed the disk along with her laptop and they went over to the desk in the corner so that Angela could share with him everything that she'd found out. They were still looking at the information when the rest of her family came up around eleven thirty to go to bed, so they took the computer downstairs to the parlor to continue their investigation. He couldn't believe some of the information that she had found on the Chandler-Langtree computers, especially the part about Dr. Langtree and Dr. Chandler being from the future. Given that he still hadn't met Dr. Chandler yet, he had to wonder if maybe he had gone back to the future. Still, if Dr. Langtree was really from 2164, then why did he need Mark's help now? Shouldn't he already know what to do? And why wasn't he being completely honest with Mark about what they were doing? The problem was that he couldn't even ask Dr. Langtree about any of this for fear of getting Angela in trouble. He definitely wouldn't take a chance of doing that.

He also was intrigued by what happened on May 20, 2016. He didn't fully understand it all, but apparently neither he nor Angela were a part of that alternate reality. Before that date, his mom was actually married to Dan, and his father was married to someone named Belinda. His father and Belinda had a son named Greg and Dan and his mom had two children, Danny and Amy. He read about Dan's meeting with Dr. Chandler, and the plan to sell the lighthouse with the intent of changing the reality so that the Vortex Accelerator was never built. He didn't understand, however, what had gone wrong. If everything had worked the way it was supposed to, then why were the ripples still here? And he still had to wonder now what Dr. Langtree needed him for. What exactly was Dr. Langtree trying to do?

With all of the information that he had found out tonight, he wondered how he would ever be able to get any sleep! He also wondered how much of the information on the disk could be believed, but since it all came from Chandler-Langtree he supposed that all of it could be accurate. Hopefully they'd be able to find out more in the coming days. They both went back upstairs and gave each other a goodnight kiss before turning in for the night.

CHAPTER 25
October 27, 2018
Radio Transmissions

Al had come over to Bud's house around seven forty five in the morning. They planned to finally work on decrypting the radio transmissions that Bud had recorded. He had asked Al if he wanted him to call Scotty to see if he wanted to come back out and join them, but this time Al had suggested that just the two of them work on it. He pulled out the first one and played it for Al. It had been recorded several days earlier. In fact, Bud had a collection of recordings which didn't sound like anything at all except for garbled voices with a slightly metallic sound. He'd been recording them since he first discovered them, in hopes that they would eventually be able to be decrypted.

"That's what they sound like." said Bud. "What do we do now?"

"Well, let's try to put them through this filter."

He tapped a couple of keystrokes into the computer and then hit the play button. Nothing seemed to have changed. Al had brought a USB drive with him with several different decryption algorithms on it. The first one didn't seem to work, so he tried the second. The sounds were different than the first, actually seeming to be worse rather than better.

"Don't sound like its working." said Bud.

"Give it a minute. I haven't tried all of the filters yet. Sometimes it takes a while to figure these things out."

Al went through several more filters but none of them seemed to work.

"How do you know if you're getting closer?" asked Bud, "Some of the filters sound slightly different, but the words are still garbled. Shouldn't we start to be able to understand something?"

"Probably not. These are digital transmissions, so it's not like analog. We probably won't understand anything until we finally get the right conversion filter. When we do then we should be able to understand everything. Since none of these appear to be working, let's run it through this analysis program."

"What will that do?"

"Every digital transmission is like a computer string. Before the actual audio, it should have headers that describe the transmission. Embedded in the header should be the encryption key. It's probably a dual key system, though, so it would have to match with another key on the computer in order to decode the audio."

"But we don't have the other key on the computer, do we?"

"No, but that's where this program comes in. If we're lucky, it might be able to construct the second key from information in the header. Since these keys come in pairs, it should just be a variation on a known algorithm. Once it can construct one, it might be able to construct the other."

Al clicked a few buttons, and a different program came up on the display. He played the audio file again and different words and data scrolled down the screen. He analyzed what he was reading, and then pushed another button which generated a second encryption key. He played the audio again, but it was still garbled. This was definitely slow work. Bud was beginning to think that it was hopeless to try and decrypt the transmissions, but Al was at least a little more optimistic. He'd done things like this before and knew that at times it could be a little tedious, even if you were on the right track.

"I think that we're getting closer. I know it doesn't sound like much now, but there's still a lot that we haven't tried."

As it turned out, there were quite a few things that they hadn't tried. The digital algorithm proved to be more complex than Al had originally thought, so it was taking longer than he had expected.

Finally after another two and a half hours, they finally had success with decrypting an entire transmission.

Al tapped a few more keys on the computer keyboard and hit the play button. While the transmission still had that slightly metallic sound, all of the words were finally able to be understood, though to understand what they were talking about would require listening to more of the recordings.

"Turn up the level on the base emitter to about twenty one percent until it reaches the correct threshold to be able to control the field. Set the auxiliary temporal emitters to forty percent to achieve the maximum phase alignment."

After a few seconds of radio silence, another voice broke in, *"I'm getting more fluctuations in the subtemporal field alignment than expected. Looks like emitter seven might be out of phase. From the readings that I'm seeing, it looks to be about .0007432 millicores off of the standard correlation deviation. Can you run a phase variance test on emitters two, five and seven? Adjust seven's variance to less than .00025 microcores of the correlation between two and five."*

About three more minutes elapsed before another transmission replied, *"Looks like that's working. The subtemporal field is stabilizing."*

"What exactly are they talking about?!" remarked Bud as Al seemed to be listening intently to the transmissions. It sounded to him like they were getting close to their goal. If they could get the subtemporal field into alignment and keep the phase correlation stable through eighty percent power, then they might actually be able to open a doorway! Of course, he knew that Bud wouldn't understand any of this.

"They're just adjusting some of the weather instruments around the lighthouse." Al replied.

Bud looked at him with a puzzled look. Al looked back at him wondering why he was getting such a strange look.

Finally Bud continued, "You forget, I'm a ham radio operator and a member of the Coastal Storm Spotter group. I attend their monthly meetings and go to weather spotter training every two years. In all of my years of going to their meetings, and in all of the training that I've attended,

I've never heard of a subtemporal field. A millicore also isn't a weather measurement, so what are they really talking about? It has nothing to do with the weather, does it?"

Al rubbed his chin with his right hand, wondering how to continue this discussion. Bud was obviously too versed on the weather and weather terminology to be fooled by that explanation. He'd have to come up with something else, and do it quickly.

"You're correct; I suspect that they're not adjusting weather instruments."

"Then what made you say that they were?" inquired Bud. He knew that he had been told by Steve that they were doing weather experiments, but he wondered why Al would mention that as well, especially if it wasn't true.

"I ran into Mark's girlfriend last Tuesday walking on the beach. She said that Mark told her that they were doing weather experiments."

"It looks like that seems to be the official story, but you don't think that they're studying the weather, do you?" continued Bud.

"It's a little hard to explain." said Al hesitantly. He knew that he'd need to tell Bud what he thought at this point, he just wasn't sure how.

"I think it has to do with time travel." he finally replied.

"You're messing with me now." said Bud. "You have to be to come up with a story like that. What do you really think that they're talking about? What is it that you don't want to tell me?"

"No, really; think about it. They're talking about a subtemporal field. What does that sound like? You've heard of the word temporal before?"

"I think it means 'time'." Bud said hesitantly.

"Exactly! A subtemporal field is a time portal!"

"You're really serious!" remarked Bud, a surprised look on his face.

"Yes, I really believe that's what they're talking about."

"So you think Chandler-Langtree is attempting time travel? But that's not possible! That's science fiction! Why would you even think that? Surely there's another explanation that makes more sense."

"Another explanation might make more sense, but it probably wouldn't be the correct explanation."

"Alright, then, that may be what they're attempting; but you don't personally believe that it's possible, right?" Bud continued.

"Let's just say that I believe that there are things that may be possible that we just haven't discovered yet."

"Fair enough; I've got more recordings for us to listen to. Let's see what else we can find out."

Bud was actually starting to be a bit intrigued by all of this. If any of what Al was telling him was even close to what was really going on, then he certainly was starting to understand why they'd need encrypted transmissions. They spent the next several hours running the rest of the recordings that Bud had made through the decryption program, and then Al copied them to the USB drive so that he could analyze them later. When he finished copying them, they decided to listen to a few more that had been decrypted. Most of them seemed to be routine transmissions, simply sounding like they were adjusting some of their equipment, but there was one that really caught their attention:

"The readings are looking good here. We're up to fifty-two percent with no fluctuations. Everything looks stable, but I don't think we should go any higher right now. Why don't you come on back now?"

"I'm returning now. With these latest adjustments, do you think that we'll still be able to plan for Sunday night?"

"I think so. We'll discuss it more when you get back."

"When was this recording made?" asked Al.

"Let me check. It looks like last Wednesday the twenty fourth."

"That means that what they're planning is planned for tomorrow night!" exclaimed Al, "We have to work fast! Thanks for your help! I'll tell you more when I know more!"

Al gathered up his equipment, put the USB drive in a pocket in his computer bag, then hurried out the back door which opened onto the beach. He then walked the half mile along the beach to his house. He dialed Angela's number as he walked.

"Angela, this is Al. Can you come over? There's something urgent that we need to discuss."

"Alright, I'll be right there." replied Angela, wondering what could be so urgent.

As she hung up the phone, Mark asked, "You'll be right where?"

"I need to go over to a friend's house for a few minutes. I'll be back soon."

"Wait a minute! What friend?" Mark asked.

"He's just someone that I met the other day. I won't be long."

"I'm going with you!" Mark insisted.

"It might be better if you didn't. He might feel a little uncomfortable with you there."

"Why would I make him uncomfortable? Who is he anyway?"

At this point, she knew that Mark wouldn't be dissuaded. He had overheard her conversation, and with the tone of her voice had become concerned.

"Remember the man on the porch of that big house that we saw last Tuesday while riding our bikes along the beach?"

"Yes, I remember him. What about him?"

"After you left to go out to the lighthouse, I sat down on one of the benches along the boardwalk. While I was sitting there staring out at the ocean and thinking, he walked up behind me. His name's Al. We talked for a few minutes."

"What did you talk about?" Mark inquired.

"That's the really odd part." she replied, "We talked about time travel!"

"You discussed that we're working on time travel with a complete stranger?!" exclaimed Mark, starting to sound upset again.

"No!" she remarked, "That's the strangest part; he's the one that brought it up. I wasn't going to say anything."

"Why would he bring it up? Who is he exactly?"

"Remember the men that I told you about that helped me get the information from the Chandler-Langtree computer? He works with them. He's known as The Squirrel. I didn't find that out until two days ago, however, when I met with him at his house."

"Are you sure it's safe to meet with someone that you just met at his house? You don't need to be so trusting of everyone that you meet!"

"He's in his seventies! He's harmless, and I do trust him. There's actually another thing as well; I think that he might really be Blake Sorensen!"

"Why do you think that?"

"Because if Blake Sorensen really is a time traveler, then he could have come to this time period and followed us down to Myrtle Beach. That could be how he knew my room number!"

Mark studied her expression as she said this. She did seem to believe that it could be possible.

"Al is not Blake Sorensen." he replied after another minute.

"How can you be sure?" she asked, "It would make sense if he was."

"He's not." continued Mark, "I found something else in the box that Richard gave me that proves that. I'll show you later."

She really was curious now, but she had told Al that she'd be right there, so she did need to leave. After the conversation that she and Mark just had, he insisted on going with her, so she finally gave in. Hopefully Al wouldn't mind. He and Mark might actually have a lot to discuss.

As they got the bikes out of the shed and began to pedal down Henderson Road, both of them wondered what could be so urgent that Al needed to talk to Angela about. It didn't take them long to arrive at the beach, then after walking their bikes up the boardwalk stairs and out onto the beach, they continued the ride out to Al's house. As they leaned their bikes against the fence which surrounded the house and walked through the gate, Al was watching them from the deck above. He had seen them coming up the beach, and wondered why she would be bringing Mark. Surely she hadn't told him about their conversations, especially since he was part of Chandler-Langtree, but then why else would he be with her now?

"Hello Angela!" he said as she and Mark walked up the steps onto the deck. "And Mark; I didn't expect to see you!

Mark immediately recognized Al as the man from Island Boutique Gifts where he had gone to buy the wrapping paper for Angela's gift. He had a look of surprise that Angela picked up on immediately.

"Do you two know each other?" she asked.

"Sort of." Mark replied, "I met him two days ago at Island Boutique Gifts when I went to get the wrapping paper for your necklace. He was on the wrapping paper aisle, and we talked for a few minutes. I didn't realize that you already knew him, though."

"I'm sorry that I didn't tell you," Al replied, "but I just wanted to meet you, and maybe find out a little about what you knew. You didn't let on anything about what you were working on that day though, so I had to explore things from a different angle. That's when I found what I called you out here for. So, how much has she told you?"

"She's told me pretty much everything. We spent most of last night discussing it."

"He's seen the journal that we downloaded from Chandler-Langtree." she informed Al.

Mark could immediately tell that Angela was right about Al. He really did come across as someone that could be trusted, even though he had secretly tried to get information from him when they met in the gift shop. Still, someone in their seventies is not the type of person that you would think would know a lot about time travel. It seemed a bit out of character for him. Al was somewhat thrown off by Mark's arrival as well. He needed to tell Angela that something was happening tomorrow night, but wondered exactly how to do that with Mark around. It wouldn't be quite as easy to talk candidly. He finally decided to proceed as planned and possibly find out a little of what Mark knew as well. After all, Angela had said that Mark had seen the journal. And he'd definitely know what they had planned for tomorrow night. He just didn't know if Mark had told Angela about that.

"It has just come to my attention that something is being planned for tomorrow night out at the lighthouse." Al stated. He studied Mark's expression as he said this and immediately knew that he was correct. Mark couldn't hide his surprise at Al's last statement.

"How do you know there's something planned for tomorrow night?" Mark asked, his voice betraying his surprise.

"It is true, isn't it?" continued Al.

Mark was silent, staring out at the ocean, wondering how to reply. He didn't want to discuss tomorrow night with anyone, and he especially was hoping that Angela wouldn't find out.

"Mark, what's he talking about?" asked Angela hesitantly, a worried look coming across her face now. Mark remained silent, still staring out at the ocean. How could Al possibly know what was planned for tomorrow night? Only he and Dr. Langtree knew that!

"Mark! What's planned for tomorrow night?!" she said more insistently now. "Mark! Look at me! What's planned for tomorrow night?!"

Mark slowly turned to face her, still wondering how he would begin. He didn't feel exactly comfortable discussing what they were planning with Al listening, but then obviously Al already knew at least something about what they were doing anyway. After all, he's the one that called Angela over here to discuss it. Exactly how much Al knew was still a mystery to him, but Angela had said that he had discussed time travel with her, so he obviously knew more than either of them would suspect.

"We think that we have all of the coordinates in place for a live test." he said, studying her face as he said it.

"What's a live test?" Angela asked, slightly confused.

"I think he means they're going to try to open up a ripple," interjected Al, "a doorway to the past."

Mark was totally and completely surprised by Al's last statement. How could he possibly know about ripples?! That was Dr. Langtree's theory! Then he remembered what Angela had told him about Al; he was one of the ones that had helped her get into Chandler-Langtree's computer system! He probably had all of the information that she had!

She looked back at Mark, "Is that true? Are you going to try to travel into the past?"

He was silent for a couple more minutes, staring out at the ocean again.

"Yes," he said, looking down at the floor, "we're going to try."

"No!" Angela shot back at him, "You can't do that, it's too dangerous! When were you going to tell me about this?"

"Angela, listen to me! You've known that this was what we were doing ever since we first talked about it."

"I know, but when we talked about it before, you weren't going to do it tomorrow night!"

"I think we're finally ready, though. It's perfectly safe. The information that was in Blake Sorensen's box has helped us to reprogram the matrix; we've worked out all of the dangers."

"Are you sure about that?" asked Al, arching one eyebrow.

"What do you mean?"

"Are you sure that the information that you got from Blake Sorensen has eliminated ALL of the risks?"

"Yes, it's gotten us a lot closer."

"Closer, yes; but it hasn't eliminated ALL of the risks, has it?"

"I think it's eliminated all of the major ones."

"Really? What about that pattern that you found? The one that was superimposed along with the ripples?"

Again, this last statement caught him by surprise, but he did remember the information about the pattern being in the journal as well. Obviously that's how Al knew about it.

"Dr. Langtree said that it's nothing to worry about."

"And you believe him?" inquired Al, starting to wonder if Mark has really thought all of this through.

"Why would I not? If he thinks that it's nothing to worry about, then it probably isn't."

"Because I've analyzed that same data from what we were able to download from Chandler-Langtree, and if it's what I believe it is then you may have a lot to worry about! If I were you, I would try to convince Langtree to hold off on the live test until you can analyze that pattern more.

I think that it could open up unknown variables that could make what you're doing a lot more dangerous than you believe!"

Angela had read this part about the odd pattern in the journal as well, but since she didn't fully understand what it was talking about, had just dismissed it. Now it seemed to be a huge issue!

"Mark, if there's even the slightest unknown about this, then please don't go through with it!"

"Angela, listen to me! EVERYTHING about what we're doing here is unknown! We're the first ones to try it! Don't you think that Neil Armstrong's family was worried when he was going to be the first man to walk on the moon? It had never been done before, so there were a lot of questions. Anytime that you're the first one to attempt something, there are going to be risks, we just try and mitigate them the best that we can."

"Are you going to be the one to go?" she asked timidly.

"Yes."

She turned away from him, a small tear starting down her cheek. She didn't want to lose him, yet here he was determined to go through with this! In her mind now, after tomorrow night, she may never see him again!"

"I think Angela's right," Al continued, "the ripples shouldn't be opened up right now. I've been looking at the data since we downloaded it, and there's something not quite right that I just can't put my finger on yet. It's not just the unusual pattern in the ripples; it's more than that. Angela's dad and your mom have been having visions that I think may be generated by an alternate reality that is somehow being driven by the ripples. I haven't figured out exactly how that could be happening yet, but I do think that they're connected. Since that's something that shouldn't be happening, I believe that it opens up a huge risk. I'd talk to Dr. Langtree about holding off on the test until you can analyze that pattern some more."

"What do you mean 'visions'?" asked Angela, "They've only had one dream and that was over two years ago!"

"No," Al replied, "they've had more than that, some back in

Wilmington last weekend, and some since they've been on the island this week as well. And these have been when they were awake during the daytime!"

"But … Dad didn't say anything about those."

"He probably didn't know how, or didn't want to worry you."

Angela thought about this some more, and then she looked over at Al with a questioning look, "How did you know about those visions? Those weren't documented in the information that was downloaded from Chandler-Langtree!"

"I have other sources of information that I'd rather not discuss right now. But it is true; they have been having more dreams and visions, and while I believe that they are caused by the ripples, I still don't know exactly how or why."

This was the most mysterious that Al had been since she had known him. Before this, he had always seemed to be more forthcoming with his ideas. While she was curious about how he did find out about the visions, especially since her dad hadn't even told her about them, she was more concerned now about Mark."

"Mark, please, don't go through with it tomorrow night! I can't lose you!"

"I'll talk to Dr. Langtree and try to get him to hold off on the test until we can analyze things further. I agree with Al, if the ripples are what's causing my mom's and your dad's visions, and if it has anything to do with the odd pattern in the ripples, then we definitely need to know more!"

As they said their goodbye's to Al and walked down the stairs to the beach, Mark had more questions. How did Al get all of his information? While most of it probably did come from the journal entries that were downloaded from Chandler-Langtree, he did wonder what Al meant by 'I have other sources of information that I'd rather not discuss right now.' What could those other sources possibly be? And most people really wouldn't understand a lot of what the journal was talking about, either. Al, however, talked like an expert on the subject! While he didn't know what this meant, he did agree now that there were too many unknown factors for a live test to be done tomorrow night. More did need to be learned, or the same thing that happened before could happen again! Maybe the information from Blake Sorensen hadn't solved EVERY problem after all!

As Al watched Mark and Angela disappear down the beach, a worried look crossed his face. He had to wonder if maybe it was already too late. Sally opened the sliding glass door and walked out onto the balcony to join Al. She had been listening to the entire conversation through an open window.

"Mark will do the right thing." she said.

"I hope so," replied Al, "but just in case he can't convince Ryan to put off the test, we will need a backup plan."

CHAPTER 26

An Unexpected Change of Plans

"Why didn't you tell me that you've been having more visions since you arrived for Parent's Weekend?" Angela asked her father. "You only mentioned the one dream and that was over two years ago!"

When she and Mark had gotten back from their visit with Al, she had immediately asked to talk with her father in private. She wanted to know why he hadn't told her about the latest visions that he'd been having. This was information that she felt was important for her to know, and she wasn't sure why he had withheld it from her. Dan suggested that they walk into town and discuss it over a chocolate malt from Carl and Peter's Malt Shop. They usually liked to go there when they visited the island and had only been once this week. Now, sitting across the table from his eldest daughter, Dan had a look of total surprise.

"I wanted to tell you about the visions, I just didn't know how. Mostly it was because I didn't understand them myself, and still don't."

"When we talked the first time, it seems like that would have been the perfect time. That was when you told me about the dream from two years ago." Angela remarked.

"Yes, it would seem like that would've been the right time, but you have to understand, I had just had the first one a few hours before and was still a little shaken up about it actually. I didn't feel comfortable talking about it because I knew how it would sound, and I really didn't have any explanation. Remember, at that time I hadn't yet met Kate. I'd only seen her in my dream from two years ago and that first vision, so there was a lot that I couldn't explain."

"I understand. I probably would've felt the same way if it had happened to me; especially that soon after it happened."

"The thing that I don't understand though," said her father, "is how you found out about the visions. It's not that I was purposely trying to hide them, but Kate and I were the only ones that knew about them and I hadn't told anyone else. I doubt that she told anyone else either."

She had promised Al that she wouldn't mention their meeting with her father, but since she had already brought up the visions that he had told her about, she didn't see a way to avoid that now. She should have anticipated that her dad would want to know how she found out; she just hadn't thought that through earlier.

"Last Tuesday when Mark and I went for a morning bike ride, I met a man. His name's Al and he came up to me while I was sitting on the bench at the boardwalk after Mark had left for work. He lives in the big house along the beach with the deck that wraps around the house. It's not right on the beach, it sits a little ways back with a lot of trees around it, but there is a good view of the water from the deck. Anyway, he started asking a lot of questions about Mark, which made me a little uncomfortable, but the longer that we talked, the conversation turned to time travel. I was actually trying to avoid that topic, since I knew how it would sound, but he's the one that brought it up. He seemed to be trying to convince me how it could be possible. Earlier today, he called me and said that he had something important to talk with me about, so Mark and I went out to meet him. When we got there, he wanted to tell me that something was going to happen tomorrow night. We never found out how he knew that, but Mark actually admitted that they were planning to attempt to travel into the past tomorrow night. Al didn't think that was such a good idea, and in trying to warn Mark he mentioned your visions. When I told him that you'd only had the one dream two years ago, he informed me that you'd been having them recently as well and they were during the daytime now."

Now Dan was really curious. How could Al know about the dreams? How could anyone know about them? He thought that he and Kate were the only ones who knew. Then he remembered the night that he had met Kate for the first time.

"Remember last Saturday when we met Mark's parents for the first time and I told you that I had met Kate the night before? There was something else about that night that I think I may have forgotten to mention. There was an older man with grey hair in the lobby with us. I never talked to him, but he was watching us and probably listening to our conversation as well. We were startled when we got up and discovered that he was watching us through the window, so we had Patrick call the police. They looked around the hotel, but never found him. We found out that his name was Warren Evans, the CEO of Evans Microsystems. We saw him on several other occasions around campus, then here at the lighthouse as well, but we never figured out why he seemed to be following us. I wonder if Warren Evans and Al could be the same person?"

Angela listened intently to his story, "It sounds like he could be. Al has grey hair as well and is probably in his seventies."

"Do you think that he would agree to meet with me now? It sounds like he could answer a lot of questions about what's been happening here, especially if he really is Warren Evans."

"I can ask him and see." she replied.

"Fair enough." Dan replied, "And you don't have to mention that you told me about him, since you promised that you wouldn't. Just ask if he'd be willing to meet with me now."

"I'll call him later." she said.

Then she continued, "So Dad, tell me more about these visions. How many have you had?"

"I've had three so far. The first one was on the trip from Greenville to Wilmington. That one was a little scary because it was the first one and I was the one driving. It felt like it lasted for several minutes, but nobody in the van seemed to realize that anything had happened. The second one was when we were watching the movie at the lighthouse museum. The third one was when Kate and I went out to the lighthouse while everyone else was busy doing other things. Warren Evans actually followed us that time, but we lost him. In most of them, I'm out at the lighthouse when a dense fog comes up and I hear a woman's voice in the fog. The woman is Kate. She finally comes out and a cold rain starts. That's when the dream usually ends. The last one was different though. We went out to the lighthouse to look around, and then we seemed to be drawn into the vision. In that one, unlike the others, it was nighttime, even though it was the middle of the afternoon when we went out to the lighthouse. This one was longer than the others as well. Kate came out of the fog the same way that she's done in the others, but while we were standing there, instead of the cold rain immediately starting, we heard an SUV drive up. Two men got out and retrieved something from the back. They carried it over to where the lighthouse was, and then seemed to get into an argument about something. A few minutes later they came running back out toward their SUV as a bright white flash of light blinded us. It began to rain as a strong storm came up, and as we were running to take cover at the lighthouse we saw that it had changed. It was completely in ruins now, looking almost like it could topple any minute. We still went inside to try and get out of the storm, but in most places the roof was missing and the rain was pouring in. Suddenly, we ended up back in our van and drove back to the bed and breakfast. That was also when we noticed that Warren Evans was following us. We stopped and tried to turn around to find out where he would go, but we lost him."

"What do you think that the visions mean?" Angela asked.

"I don't really know. That's one of the things that I've been trying to figure out. I'm also trying to figure out what might be causing them, but so far I haven't come up with anything. The dream back in 2016 and the vision in the van on the way to Wilmington were both before I'd even met Kate, so that makes them even more unusual."

"Al's been doing a lot of research. Maybe he has some ideas about them, especially since he's the one that brought them up. I think it would be good for you to talk to him."

They finished up their malts and decided to head back to the bed and breakfast. When they walked through the front door, Mark was waiting for Angela in the parlor. He looked a little nervous, like he had something to say but didn't quite know how to say it.

"I have something to show you," he said to her as she walked in, "I've been trying to decide if I should show it to you or not, but I think it's too important not to let you know. Let's go sit out on the front porch."

As they sat down beside each other on the front porch swing, Mark handed her a small envelope with the words "Mark … Personal" written on the front.

"I'd rather that you just keep this between us for now." he said.

"What is this?" she asked.

"It's the proof that Al is not Blake Sorensen."

Angela withdrew the note from the envelope and unfolded it. It was hand written and addressed to Mark. Mark studied the expressions on her face as she read the letter. Several times she looked up at him with a questioning look of disbelief on her face. Finally, she looked up at him, not fully knowing what to say.

"Mark …" she began in a low, apprehensive voice, "What does this mean? Is this true?"

"Yes … This envelope was in the bottom of the box that Richard gave me. It's from his father."

"Then you ABSOLUTELY have to convince Dr. Langtree not to go through with the plan for tomorrow night!" she exclaimed after a couple of minutes of just trying to understand what she had just read.

"I've already said that I'll talk to him and try to get him to postpone the test." Mark replied.

"You have to do more than TRY! You HAVE to convince him to postpone it! According to this letter, the field collapses and you don't come back! I can't let you do this, Mark! I need you!"

"I'll try to convince him, but even if I can't, Blake's worked out all of the issues that caused the field to fail the first time. I've incorporated them into the setup matrix and all of the tests have worked flawlessly."

"But what if Blake missed something?! He had a lifetime to work on the theories, but he couldn't test them! What if there's something that he didn't consider?! And you've only had three days to study his information! What if YOU'VE missed something?!"

"I've been going over his calculations since I received the box. I've run them all through the simulator many times. I think it will work this time."

"But what if it doesn't?! The same thing could happen this time as well! The field could still fail and you could be trapped back in 1960 just like the first time! The field collapsed once, it could happen again! Please, don't risk losing what we have! I can't go on without you!"

"It won't happen again! I've fixed the issues that caused the failure the first time. The first time, I didn't have the benefit of Blake's notes. Now I've implemented his changes, and I've tested the results. Everything works much better and much more reliably. That greatly lessens the chances that something will go wrong."

"But something could still go wrong!" pleaded Angela. "Mark, please don't do this even if you can't get Dr. Langtree to agree!"

"Alright, I'll definitely get Dr. Langtree to move the test until we can run more simulations and further minimize the risk. I won't attempt it tomorrow night."

"Thank you!" she said, somewhat relieved as he pulled her close to him and gave her a kiss. She knew that there would still come a time when she'd have to deal with Mark walking into another time period, but at least it wouldn't be tomorrow, and that would be better. This was too much for her to deal with right now since everything was happening so fast. Before reading the letter, the thought had never even occurred to her that Mark actually could be Blake Sorensen. And now she realized that if that were true, then that meant that she had come close to losing him forever, and that was something that she couldn't bring herself to even consider. At least she had convinced him not to go through with it tomorrow night, and that was when the letter had said the field would collapse.

Mark felt guilty not being completely truthful with her. He'd assured her that he wouldn't go through with the test; that he wouldn't step through the gate into the past tomorrow night. The problem was that he didn't honestly know if he'd be able to keep that promise. He'd try to convince Dr. Langtree that more testing was necessary, but if he couldn't convince him then he may still have to go. He honestly didn't know if he'd be able to refuse to do it. If he had to attempt it, then hopefully everything would work like the simulations, but there was still a slight chance, even though it was small, that something could still go wrong.

Al had a serious look on his face as he stared at the computer monitor. Things had begun to move much more quickly than he had anticipated. He believed Mark when he said that he'd talk to Dr. Langtree about postponing the live test until they could study the anomaly in the ripples more, but he also knew Ryan Langtree, and there was a good chance that he'd continue the test despite any argument that Mark could give. He was focused on a single goal, and it might just be that nothing could dissuade him now. They needed to have everything in place just in case Mark wasn't successful.

"Do you think Mark will be able to persuade Ryan not to go through with the test?" Sally asked him.

"I hope so, but I just don't know. Sometimes Ryan's not one to listen to reason."

"Then we have to move now. We have to set up the temporal dissipater that I brought with me, and it has to be set up today."

"But we haven't run all of the diagnostics on it yet. It's not ready!"

"It'll have to be." she insisted, "We're out of time."

He knew that she was right. If they had any chance at all of accomplishing their task, it had to be done today.

"Do you think Ryan's told Steve to inform him of any deliveries so that he can personally approve them?" Sally asked.

"Possibly, but I doubt it. Ryan probably won't be thinking about anyone trying to interfere with the test. Let's load the temporal dissipater into the van and get it down to the lighthouse."

Al and Sally had been setting up the plan for weeks now; they had just thought that they had more time to get everything ready, but this latest news had forced them to move ahead with the plan now. At least they had the van ready. Al had borrowed one from his company, painted it black, and had a graphic artist paint a copy of the Chandler-Langtree logo on both sides. Now they opened the van's back doors and loaded the temporal dissipater. Al opened the garage door and Sally drove the van out. After closing the garage door, he got into the back of the van with the Dissipater so that he could finish programming it on the way out to the lighthouse. He hoped that since it was Saturday that Ryan wouldn't be out there, but they'd turn at the first road and go around to the back of the house just in case. By doing that, they'd only be visible from the Mobile Command Center for less than thirty seconds and unless Ryan was watching the cameras at that precise moment, he'd miss them.

As the lighthouse came into view from Lighthouse Road, they were both relieved that there were no cars or vans parked out by the Mobile Command Center. They drove around to the back door where all of the deliveries came in and Sally walked up to the door and knocked. Arlene, Steve's wife came to the door. She immediately noticed the black van parked next to the door, especially since she'd been seeing quite a few of them lately.

"Hello, I'm Barbara Mason from the Chandler-Langtree Institute. We have a delivery that we need to set up at the top of the lighthouse for our weather monitoring." said Sally. They had found that name in the materials that they had downloaded, so they decided to use it as an alias so that if anyone checked, Barbara Mason really would show up as employed by Chandler-Langtree.

To her relief, Arlene simply said, "Alright, you can bring it through here."

Since the lighthouse was still open for visitors, a small crowd gathered as they moved the Dissipater through the lobby and into the base of the lighthouse. It was about five feet long, but only a foot square with several openings along the length of it, and an access panel for programming. Several rods protruded out of the sides near one end. Luckily it was made from an alloy which was even lighter than aluminum, so they didn't have to be too concerned with the weight as they maneuvered it up the spiral staircase. The length of the dissipater made the process go fairly slow, however, but finally it was up at the top where it could be mounted inside the lantern room.

One of the visitors came up to Arlene after Al and Sally had taken the object into the lighthouse tower.

"What's that they're taking into the lighthouse?" he inquired.

"They're using the lighthouse for some weather experiments." she answered. "We get deliveries periodically, but that's definitely the largest one so far, next to the Doppler radar that they set up outside."

It took about twenty minutes to mount the temporal dissipater inside the lens right below the light, then Al armed it and they headed back downstairs.

"We're all finished." Al said to Arlene as he and Sally went out the back door. "Thanks for letting us put that in place."

As they drove away, both were relieved that the delivery and setup had gone so smoothly. Hopefully this part wouldn't be necessary; hopefully Mark would be able to convince Ryan to postpone the test. Still, they were glad to have the dissipater installed just in case he wasn't successful. Now they'd just have to hope that everything was set correctly and that it worked flawlessly. This is the part that still concerned them both. While they had double checked their work, they'd had to move quickly. If any of the calculations for the setup were off, the results could be catastrophic.

That night, Mark found that he had trouble getting to sleep. He lay awake just staring at the ceiling, going over and over the matrix setup and temporal calculations in his mind. He was also wondering what he would say to Dr. Langtree tomorrow to try to get him to postpone the live test. The more that he thought about it, he did wonder why Dr. Langtree wasn't more concerned about the odd pattern that he had found in the ripples. It was something that was definitely there and since he didn't know what it was, he hadn't included it in any of the calculations when he set up the matrix, and this concerned him. Since all of the calculations had to be so precise, any deviation could throw everything off. Suddenly, he realized that whatever the odd pattern was could definitely be what caused the field to collapse the first time and send him back to 1960, and if that was the cause then it was very likely to happen again! He knew now that he HAD to persuade Dr. Langtree not to go through with the live test.

CHAPTER 27
October 28, 2018
Temporal Changes

Sunday morning started out to be a bright sunny day. Angela had awakened early and called Al to see if he'd agree to meet with her father. To her surprise, he thought that was a good idea.

"Things are starting to move fast," he said, "so it's probably about time that Dan and I meet face to face. Can you both come over in about an hour?"

"I'll talk to Dad. I'm sure that we can."

As it turned out, Dan was more than ready to meet with Al, especially since he and Angela had discussed the possibility that he might be Warren Evans. It was eight thirty in the morning and Jan had cooked a big breakfast, so Angela and Dan decided to sit down and have some before going out to meet with Al. As they were scooping out their biscuits and sausage gravy along with some eggs and bacon, Mark came downstairs.

"Dad and I are going out to meet with Al at his house after breakfast." Angela told him, "Do you want to come with us?"

"I'd like to, but I can't. Dr. Langtree's expecting me out at the lighthouse at nine thirty. I'll just have some breakfast and then I'll have to leave."

As he said this, Angela was reminded of their conversation yesterday and a worried look crossed her face again.

"Remember what we talked about yesterday." she reminded him.

"Yes, I remember, but I do need to go out and talk with Dr. Langtree about it."

"I know, but once you talk to him, will you be coming home early?"

"I don't know, maybe. It depends on what else he wants to do." he replied.

"Alright then, but remember what you promised." she reminded him.

"I remember." he said, looking away so that he could change the conversation. He knew what she was saying, but like he was thinking last night, he really didn't know if he'd be able to change Dr. Langtree's mind about the live test. This was something that he couldn't tell Angela, though, and he hated himself for having to keep this from her. But what else could he do? Everything wasn't in his control. He worked for Dr. Langtree, and he had the final say.

As they got up from the breakfast table and went to get their coats, Mark headed out to the lighthouse while Angela and Dan went out to meet with Al. Dan had asked Kate to come with them, but since she had only told Scotty a small part about what was going on, she felt like it would be better if she stayed. She knew that if she went with them, then Scotty would want to go as well, and he wouldn't understand much about what they had to discuss, and would just have a lot of unnecessary questions. Dan promised to tell her all about it when they got back.

As they drove down Henderson Road toward Al's house, both of them were quieter than usual. Dan was lost in thought, wondering if Al really was Warren Evans, while Angela was worried about Mark. She was concerned with how things would go between him and Dr. Langtree this morning. While he had promised her that he would talk to Dr. Langtree about postponing the test, in the back of her mind she knew that Dr. Langtree might not agree and she just couldn't get this thought out of her head.

Turning into Al's driveway, they saw him sitting on the porch waiting for them. Dan knew immediately that it was Warren Evans. He had seen him enough times lurking in the shadows, just out of reach, watching them. Now, for whatever reason, Warren wasn't hiding in the shadows, but was ready to talk. Maybe now Dan would finally find out what's been going on, both back in Wilmington and here on the island.

"Welcome to my home." greeted Al. "I'm glad that we can finally meet."

"Warren Evans?" asked Dan.

"Yes, but please call me Al. My full name is Warren Albert Evans, but I prefer to go by Al. That's what all of my friends call me. Please, come inside."

The three of them walked into a spacious foyer with stairs off to the left and a sitting room straight ahead. Angela realized that she had never been in this part of the house. She had always approached from the beach and entered from the deck on the ocean side.

"Can I offer either of you a drink?" Al asked, playing the part of the proper host.

"No thanks." they both replied.

The three of them walked up the stairs and down the hallway to Al's study.

"Please, sit down." Al offered, knowing that Dan would have a lot of questions. The first one he had anticipated, knowing that he would have that same question if he were Dan.

"So, Al, it's nice to finally meet you." Dan remarked as he and Angela settled into the plush sofa, "but I do have a question. I know this may be an awkward way to start our meeting, but why have you been following me and Kate?"

"It's not an awkward question at all. If I were you it's what I'd want to know as well. I'm sorry for all the secrecy, but I wasn't ready to discuss things until now. I needed to find out more information first, and felt that getting it by simply following you and trying to listen to your conversations would be the best way."

"You mean information like finding out about my and Kate's visions?" Dan asked.

"That's part of it, but there's a lot more to the story."

"We'd like to hear more about it." Dan replied.

"I'll get to your visions in a minute, but first I need to let you know why all of this is happening. For the past several months, I've been researching the Chandler-Langtree Institute. I've been studying what they've been working on and have discovered that they've found a temporal field out at the lighthouse. Ryan Langtree has been studying ways to control the field in order to open a doorway to the past. Normally, this would require an enormous amount of energy, but he's discovered that the ripples in the temporal field generate their own energy. That energy just needs to be controlled and brought into alignment in order to open the door. From what I've been able to tell, with Mark's help Ryan is getting really close. He actually plans to attempt to open a doorway tonight."

"Mark's going to talk to him and get him to postpone that." Angela interjected.

"Hopefully he can." Al replied.

"He promised me that he would." she said. "I believe him!"

"I know he'll try, and I don't want to worry you, but Ryan Langtree can be a stubborn man. When he gets his mind made up about something it can be difficult to change."

Now Angela was concerned again. She knew Mark well enough to know that if he said that he'd try to change Dr. Langtree's mind, then he would, but now she was wondering if he actually could. Still, he had assured her that he wouldn't do it regardless of what Dr. Langtree said. She'd call Mark after their meeting with Al to see how things were going.

"Do you think that Dr. Langtree will be successful?" Dan asked. "Do you believe that time travel is actually possible?"

He studied Al's expression as he asked the question. After all, many times you can learn as much from a person's expression as you can from what they actually say.

"Actually I do." he replied, "That's why I've been so interested in what Chandler-Langtree is working on. I want to see for myself if they can actually accomplish it."

"What do you know about Project Vortex Elimination?" asked Dan, knowing that Al had read the same information that he had from the Chandler-Langtree papers.

Al studied Dan for a minute or so, just trying to think of how to begin. He somehow felt that Project Vortex Elimination was the reason for Dan's and Kate's visions, he just didn't know exactly how it all fit together yet.

"Tonight isn't the first time that time travel has been attempted at the lighthouse." Al began, "It's been attempted successfully many times before now. The Vortex Accelerator was the creation that made it possible and it was used many times to both travel to and alter the past, thus also affecting the future. I imagine that what you've read in the journal is true, that several folks from the future decided that man shouldn't have the ability to alter the past. It was too easy to abuse it, so they developed a plan, Project Vortex Elimination, to put the world back to the way that it would have been if the Vortex Accelerator had never been invented. Just like the journal says, you were probably a part of the original plan. The problem that I'm having with this, though, is that if the plan worked, and the Accelerator never existed, then why are the ripples here now? It's the ripples that I believe are the cause of the visions that you've been having. Your life before May 20, 2016 was with Kate, and the visions that you both are having are probably a remnant of that life."

"Hold on a minute!" Dan interjected, "I've read the term in the journal, but what is a ripple exactly?"

"It's what the temporal field is made up of." answered Angela. "Al explained them to me when he and I met earlier this week. It's the ripples that make time travel possible. They're what opens the door to another time period. Am I right, Al?"

"Very good!" Al remarked, "You may have almost as good of a grasp on this concept as Mark!"

"But how could the ripples contain a remnant of our lives before May 2016?" Dan asked, somewhat confused at this point, "If the Vortex Accelerator was really eliminated, then shouldn't that have eliminated all traces of our previous lives as well?"

"It should have, but somehow there must be some traces of your previous life still imbedded in the ripples. Unfortunately, I haven't figured out how this could happen. According to everything that I've read, when the Accelerator was eliminated, it should have taken all traces of your previous life with it."

"If it didn't, though, do you have any ideas why?"

"I have been studying the information from Chandler-Langtree since we downloaded it, and I do have a few theories. The first one is that the Vortex Accelerator actually was eliminated, but during the time that it was in operation, it created self-contained ripples that contain elements of your previous lives. The second is that the Vortex Accelerator never was actually eliminated, but still is controlling the ripples. Either way, my opinion is that the ripples are what's causing your and Kate's visions."

"Do you know why the visions are just starting back now though? It's been over two years since Kate and I had the first dream and we haven't had any since then. Now, we've had three separate visions, and these have been while we were awake during the day, not at night when we were sleeping!"

"I think it might be because of Ryan's recent experimentation with the ripples. Bringing them into alignment definitely causes them to get stronger. Also, I've detected that for whatever reason, the ripples might be getting stronger by themselves."

"That could've been what caused the field to open up the other night when both Mark and I walked into it, right?" asked Angela.

"Yes, that actually could have been the cause." replied Al. "Ripples seem to generate their own power, which means that they're not entirely under our control. They might be able to open up by themselves when the conditions are right."

"So if the Vortex Accelerator was never actually eliminated, then does that mean that something went wrong?" asked Dan.

"Maybe or maybe not. It's difficult to say when something goes wrong, or it's just a behavior that we haven't anticipated. All of this is a new science, so it really is hard to know what to expect."

"So what do we do now?" asked Dan.

"We watch what happens tonight. If Mark is successful at convincing Ryan to hold off on the live test, then at least we have more time to figure out what's really happening here. This would give us more time to find out how the ripples are interacting to cause these visions. If he's not successful, and they attempt the test, then we'll just have to wait and watch what happens."

"He'll be successful!" remarked Angela, "He has to be!"

"I hope you're right," replied Al, "but you have to face the fact that Ryan Langtree might not postpone the test, despite any of Mark's objections."

"But Mark doesn't have to listen to him. He has his own free will. If he thinks that it's too dangerous, then he can refuse to go through with it!" argued Angela.

"Yes, he definitely can refuse, but you know Mark; do you think he will?"

Angela did know Mark very well, and that's what worried her. She knew that he might not refuse, despite their conversation earlier. She knew that he wouldn't intentionally lie to her, but she also knew that Dr. Langtree seemed to have somewhat of a hold on him. Mark might go along with what he wanted to do despite his better judgment.

"I don't know." she finally said quietly, looking down at the floor as she said it.

"Thanks for agreeing to meet with me." Dan said as he shook Al's hand, "This sure has cleared up a lot in my mind, even though I still have a lot of questions. I'm still having a hard time really believing everything that's happening, but I'm trying."

"It's a lot to accept I realize, especially since what's happening here goes against everything that we've always known is impossible. Angela has my number if you need to get back in touch with me."

As Dan and Angela walked back to the van waiting in Al's driveway, they looked back and gave him a wave. Now Dan at least knew who Al was and why he was following them. Like him and Angela, he was trying to piece together everything that was happening as well. Still, he couldn't help but feel that there were things that Al wasn't telling them; things that he was holding back.

When they got back to the bed and breakfast and pulled into the parking area in the lane beside it, Kate immediately came out onto the porch to greet them. All she had been thinking about all morning was their meeting, and she was wondering what Dan might find out.

"Al is Warren Evans." he said as they climbed the steps to the porch.

Angela left her dad and Kate on the porch to discuss their meeting as she went inside to the parlor to call Mark. After their meeting with Al, this was as worried as she'd ever been and she just needed to hear his voice and find out what was happening out there. Al hadn't been particularly reassuring and this bothered her.

Dan and Kate walked over to the porch swing and sat down. He began to relate the story that he and Angela had been told by Al as to why he was following them.

"Al told us that the visions that we've been having are most likely caused by ripples, though even he wasn't sure exactly how or why that was happening."

"So are ripples actually glimpses into our alternate lives, the ones before May 2016?" she asked.

"In a way they are," Dan answered, "since according to Al, ripples actually open the doorways into the past. They're what the temporal field is made up of. Al thinks that somehow there are traces of our previous lives embedded in the ripples and that's what's causing our visions."

"Do you think we'll have any more visions?" she asked.

"I don't know, but it does seem likely, especially if Al's thoughts are correct. If he's right, then the ripples are getting stronger even without Dr. Langtree's experiments."

As Angela dialed Mark's number on her cell phone and heard his voice on the other end, she was relieved to hear that he sounded more upbeat than he had earlier.

"Hi," he answered, "it's good to hear from you. How did the meeting go?"

"It went pretty well. We found out that Al is the Warren Evans that's been following my dad and your mom. That's how he got most of the information on their dreams and visions that he told us about yesterday. He also thinks that the dreams are related to the ripples."

"That's what I would suspect as well." he told her. "And I've got more good news! Dr. Langtree has agreed to postpone the live test until we can study more about the strange pattern in the ripples! He agrees that we shouldn't rush into it if there's something that we don't understand that could affect the outcome."

At this news, Angela was overjoyed! It was like a great weight had been lifted off her shoulders and she could finally breathe again! She wouldn't have to worry about Mark not coming home tonight!"

"That's wonderful!" she replied excitedly, "I can't wait to see you tonight! Will you be coming home early?"

"Maybe, but Dr. Langtree still wants to run some more tests. We're going to see if we can isolate the pattern and possibly study it. Just isolating it should take the rest of the day, but I'll see you soon."

"I love you." she said.

"I love you too." he replied as they both hung up the phone.

After finishing her conversation with Mark, she ran outside to tell her dad the good news.

"Dr. Langtree agreed to postpone the live test!" she chimed happily.

While this did surprise him from everything that Al had told them earlier today about Dr. Langtree, still he was happy for her.

"That's great," he said, "let's go into town and get some lunch to celebrate! How about the Sand Crab Diner?"

"That sounds like a good idea." they all said.

"I'll call Scotty." remarked Kate. "He and Wendell went into town to go to the General Store to pick up a few things. Maybe they'll want to meet us there."

As they all walked down the front steps of the bed and breakfast and started down the street toward town, none of them stopped to look back. If they had they'd have noticed that the building looked slightly different than it had only moments before, and the sign above the front porch now read "Island Charm Bed and Breakfast".

Out at Al's house on Sea Spray Drive, he and Sally were sitting out on the deck overlooking the ocean sipping a cup of coffee. It was early afternoon, but still only a few people were walking along the beach. They were both concerned about what might happen if Ryan decided to go through with the test.

"Do you think the temporal dissipater that we put in the lighthouse tower will work if Ryan does decide to go through with the test?" she asked.

"I hope so." he replied. "I think I set up all of the parameters in the matrix correctly, but I'd still like to have had more time to test it out. At this point, we'll just have to wait and see."

Al got up and walked across the deck and went into his study. Sally followed as he walked over to his desk and picked up the remote to turn on the sixty inch TV which was located in his bookcase. They both sat down on the sofa in front of the large screen. He used the remote to change the channel to a live video of the lighthouse. Last week he had gone out and mounted a hidden camera at the edge of the woods facing the lighthouse. It wasn't in an area that usually got a lot of tourist traffic and was well enough away from the Mobile Command Center that he didn't think that it would be noticed. It was also small, only about an inch in diameter and mounted about eight feet up on the side of a tree. He had run the antenna up one of the tree branches so that he could get good reception out at his beach house. A small wire also ran from the camera down to the ground to a small lithium power pack which he had buried just below the ground in a waterproof case. He had gone out there this afternoon right after Angela and Dan had left and turned it on. With the power pack fully charged it should provide about two days worth of viewing. Now, the lighthouse was on the TV screen, lit brightly by the afternoon sun.

"At least we'll be able to watch from here to see what does happen." Al remarked.

"Hopefully the TV show won't get too exciting!" Sally remarked jokingly. "I could use a nice quiet evening."

"Me too." said Al, though from the way that his voice trailed off, it was obvious that he was deep in thought.

"What's bothering you?" Sally asked.

"It's still the dreams that Dan and Kate are having. They shouldn't be having those. They're from their previous reality which isn't connected to this one. I'm concerned that something is happening here that we're not thinking of."

"You're right. I can't think of any reason that they'd be having those either." she replied.

"But they are having them, and there is a reason that they're having them, and it concerns me that we can't think of that reason because it might be something really important here that we're missing."

Dan, Kate and Angela arrived at the Sand Crab Diner. Kate had called Scotty while they were on their way to the diner, but he and Wendell were still at the General Store visiting with Bud. He told her that they'd join them when they finished up there. Dianne was spending the day with her mom since they'd all be leaving to go back home tomorrow, so she wasn't with them. They halfway expected to run into them, since when those two get together a shopping trip frequently is the result. Still, they had gone somewhere in Jan's car, so they might have just decided to take a walk along the beach or maybe go out to the Harbor Inn to the Mariner's Cove restaurant.

As their server took them over to their usual table to be seated, Angela was looking around the diner more closely than she usually did.

"Dad, do you notice anything different?" she asked Dan.

"No, like what?"

"Well, like the counter as you come in for one thing. Wasn't it in the center three days ago? Now it's off to the right side and more tables are set up as you come in. I don't think that counter's moveable either, it looks like it's fixed to the floor. And the chairs seem different too. And what about the display window at the front? They never had a display window there before! There were always tables there!"

"I think you're just imagining it being different." replied Dan. "They wouldn't have had time to make those changes in only three days, especially since there's no evidence of construction."

"No I'm not! Look at this photo!" she replied showing him a picture on her Smartphone, "This is a selfie that I took last Thursday of me and Mark. We were sitting in that table over there and you can clearly see the front window behind us. There are tables there with no display in the window. "

He had to admit that there was no display window there, but there couldn't have been one built in only three days!

"Maybe you're turned around. Could that be the side window instead?"

"No Dad, think back to when we've been here this week! Have you ever seen a display window there?"

Dan was looking confused at this point. At Angela's insistence, he did start to look around more and there were subtle things that did seem different. Not only the counter and display window, but the tablecloths and pictures on the wall as well. Those were things that could have easily been changed overnight, though. He just couldn't be sure that it wasn't his mind playing tricks on him because she was putting those ideas into his head.

"I see what you're saying, it seems there are things that look different, and I do think the counter was in the center last week, but it's probably not as permanent as it looks. I bet it's not fastened down and they can slide it to where they need it. It might even have wheels underneath."

At this, Angela got out of her chair and walked up to where the person was standing behind the counter.

"I have a strange question." she asked the employee, "Can this counter be moved to wherever you want it, and was it in the center in front of the door last Thursday?"

The employee looked confused. "No, it's bolted to the floor so it can't be moved. It's been right here since I started working here three years ago."

"How about that display window? How long has it been there?"

"It's also been there since I started working here." he answered, looking confused, "We change the display every once in awhile depending on what's happening here on the island, but the window's been there for quite awhile."

"Thanks." she replied, walking back over to their table where everyone had been curiously watching her.

"See what I mean! The counter's been right there for three years, along with the display window! So how could the display window not be in my selfie from three days ago?!"

Dan had to admit that he was confused at this point. He knew what the restaurant looked like now, but he also knew what it looked like in Angela's photo from three days ago.

"I don't have a good answer for that one," Dan replied, "but I am wondering if it has something to do with the lighthouse. Remember our first day on the island when I thought the sign on the bed and breakfast was different?"

"But it wasn't." replied Angela, "We all walked back outside and it still said Baker Family Bed and Breakfast."

"I'm not exactly convinced of that." said Dan, "I know at the time that we all thought that I was just imagining it, since it couldn't have been different, but Kate saw the same thing that I did. I'm convinced that it really was different. The same thing that caused that could be happening here today."

Their server came over to take their order, with both Dan and Angela getting their usual. Kate went ahead and ordered for Scotty and Wendell since they had said they'd be here soon. After ordering, Kate, who had also been looking around the diner since Angela mentioned the differences also agreed with him.

"You know, Dan, I think you're right. There are subtle changes that are different than the other day when we were here. There are also other more striking differences as well. I don't remember the display window either. I don't know if any of it has to do with what's happening out at the lighthouse, but there are definitely things that have changed here."

"And remember, the person at the counter said that it has always been the way that it is now, even though I have a picture that proves otherwise." added Angela, "I think dad's right, it might have something to do with the experiments that they're doing out at the lighthouse."

She passed her phone around the table to let them all look at the picture. None of them actually had a better explanation for what they were seeing, yet they couldn't deny what they were seeing now.

"Nice picture of you and Mark." remarked Scotty as he and Wendell walked up after just getting back from the General Store.

"We took it here last Thursday." said Angela, "We were wondering why the background on the picture is different than the way that it looks here now."

"They probably redecorate sometimes." offered Wendell, "I wouldn't wonder about it too much. That is a good picture of you and Mark, though."

As Al and Sally sat out on the deck, looking out over the ocean, an uneasy feeling swept over them both. Sally shivered as a cool breeze swept in from the beach. There were clouds forming off in the distance, indicating a change in the weather.

"Looks like a storm might be coming in." remarked Al, this time referring not only to the weather. "I just wish that we'd had time to understand more."

CHAPTER 28

Temporal Collapse

Angela continued to pace the floor in the parlor, occasionally walking over to the window hoping to see Mark's car pulling into the parking area beside the bed and breakfast. It was already eight thirty, much past the time that she was expecting him to be home.

"Why don't you sit down and try to relax." Dan suggested. "At the rate that you're going you'll wear a path in the carpet."

"I can't relax until Mark get's home. He should've been home by now! If they called off the test, then what can they be doing out there so late?!"

"I don't know, but you know Dr. Langtree. They've been late before when they've been working on an issue." replied Dan.

"I know, but tonight's not the night to work late! Mark needs to be home at this hour!"

Dan knew what she was feeling, and he was starting to wonder as well if Dr. Langtree had actually postponed the test after all. He had expected Mark around six, and began to wonder what was keeping him as the time continued to get later and later. Still, he didn't want to let Angela see that he was also concerned. He needed to be there for her to comfort her, not to worry her more.

"He might already be on his way." Dan suggested. "Why don't you give him a call and find out. If he is, then you can go ahead and stop worrying."

"And if he's not?" she replied.

"Then you can keep worrying." Dan remarked in a half joking

tone.

She gave him a look that indicated that she wasn't amused at his attempt at humor. She knew what he was trying to do, and she really did appreciate his attempt to get her mind off of the situation, but she just wasn't in the mood for it tonight.

"Seriously though, if he's not, then you've at least gotten to talk with him and maybe find out when to expect him."

"You don't think they're going through with the live test after all do you? Mark told me that Dr. Langtree had agreed not to do it!" remarked Angela.

"It could be anything." Dan replied, trying not to worry her any more than he had to, "They could just be studying the pattern in the ripples trying to figure out where it's coming from. I wouldn't start worrying just yet."

"Too late," she answered, "I've already started worrying. I've been worrying all day. I think it started at the diner and became worse when Mark wasn't home at five! I know that I won't stop until I see Mark's car pull into his parking space. I think I'll call him and see if he's about ready to come home!"

"Good idea!" said Dan.

She pulled out her cell phone and dialed Mark's number. After a couple of rings, she heard his cheerful voice.

"Hi, Mark!" she said, "Are you on your way home yet?"

"Angela, it's nice to hear your voice. I'm not on my way yet, but hopefully it'll be soon. We're just running some tests on the ripples to see if we can isolate the strange pattern. I think we should be done within the hour."

"You're still not going to walk into the ripples tonight, right?"

"No, we're both here in the command center. Dr. Langtree is still fine with not doing that tonight."

When he said this, she was immeasurably relieved. That had been what she had been thinking about the most for the last hour. Now at least he confirmed that he was safe and that the plan hadn't changed.

"Alright, I'll see you in a little while. I love you."

"I love you too, Angela. I'll see you soon."

As she was hanging up the phone, Kate walked into the room. "What are you two doing?" she asked Dan and Angela, the tone of her voice indicating that she was also worried.

"We're just waiting on Mark." replied Angela. "I just got off the phone with him. He's still out at the lighthouse, but he said that he's just finishing up with some tests. He should be home soon."

"I'm glad to hear that!" Kate replied, her voice sounding more relieved now as well.

"Why don't we put on a movie!" suggested Dan. We'll get interested in what's going on in the movie and before we know it Mark will come walking through the door."

"That's a good idea!" remarked Dianne and Rebekah together, "We bought a new one the day before yesterday at the bookstore. We can watch that one!" continued Rebekah.

"I don't think I could get interested in a movie tonight, Dad." Angela said as she walked through the archway into the foyer, then out onto the front porch into the cool night air. Dan followed her out onto the porch, with both of them standing over by the railing. The crickets were chirping and the tree frogs were singing their nightly song as she looked up the street toward the direction of the lighthouse. "Even though I know Mark's safe for now, I still won't completely stop worrying until he gets home."

"So far everything looks good!" Sally remarked as she got up off of the sofa and went down the hall to the kitchen to get a drink. Al was over at his desk looking over some figures on his computer monitor. He still couldn't shake the uneasy feeling that he'd had all evening. He was missing something and he knew it, but as hard as he tried, he couldn't figure exactly what.

"What are all of those people doing out along the beach?" asked Sally as she came back into the room with two drinks and looked out the window. She set one drink on Al's desk for him, then popped open the other one for herself.

"What people?" asked Al, getting out of his chair and walking over to the door leading outside. He opened the door and walked out onto the deck to get a better look.

Sally was right, there were about 10 people with flashlights walking along the beach, the muffled sound of their voices drifting up to where he was. Unfortunately they were still too far away for him to be able to understand anything that they were saying. Sally joined him on the deck and walked over to the railing where he was standing.

"I wonder what they're doing. They seem to be looking for something." she remarked.

As they watched, one of the people from the group separated from the rest and came walking through the sand up to the house.

"Good evening!" said a familiar voice. It was Bud, flashlight in hand as he opened the gate and walked through it. "May I come up?"

"Sure, come on up!" Al invited.

"What's happening down at the beach?" Sally asked as he came up the stairs and walked out onto the deck.

"We're searching for the two girls that disappeared this afternoon; Amy Nelson and Veronica Norwood."

"Who?" Al asked, turning to face him now, a look of total surprise on his face.

"Amy Nelson and Veronica Norwood." repeated Bud, "They disappeared this afternoon out at the lighthouse."

"What are you talking about, Bud?" he asked.

At this point, Bud pulled out a piece of paper with two girls' pictures on it. Showing the page to Sally, he asked, "Have you seen these girls?"

"No, I don't think I have;" she replied, "Who are they?"

"It's Dan Nelson's daughter, Amy and her friend." answered Bud.

At this, Sally looked over at Al, a puzzled look on her face.

"What's he talking about Al?" she asked, "Dan doesn't have a daughter named Amy."

Looking back at Al, the look that she saw was what could best be described as a frightened look of surprise. His face had gone completely white.

"Al … Do you know what he's talking about?" she asked again.

"This can't be happening!" Al said, as he ran back inside leaving both Bud and Sally staring after him. He ran over to the TV monitor that was trained on the lighthouse. The camera was now looking through a hazy fog where he could barely make out the outline of the lighthouse, run down and falling apart, with scaffolding set up around the tower. The scene looked nothing like it had this afternoon when he went out there. Suddenly he knew what he had been missing! It had been there all along, he had just missed it, probably because he hadn't been thinking along that particular train of thought.

"Sally, get your coat! We have to get out to the lighthouse now!"

Sally grabbed her coat and followed Al as he raced down the stairs and out the front door, leaving Bud standing out on the deck wondering what was going on with Al.

"What's happening?" she asked as she opened the car door and got into the passenger side. Al backed the car out of the driveway and went racing down Sea Spray Drive toward the lighthouse.

"I know what's been causing Dan and Kate's visions!" he said, "It's been right in front of me the whole time! The unusual pattern that Mark found in the ripples is the pattern of their alternate reality, the one before May 20, 2016. Somehow that reality has gotten crossed with this one so that the ripples actually contain traces of both. I believe that the alternate reality is somehow overlaid on top of this one. When I set up the parameters in the temporal dissipater that we put at the top of the lighthouse I didn't account for that pattern, only the one for our current reality. Ryan must be going ahead with the live test anyway and the Dissipater is absorbing the ripples for this reality but not the alternate one. That means that the alternate reality is becoming the dominant reality and getting stronger! We can't let that happen or the resulting catastrophic temporal collapse could completely destroy the balance of the entire universe!"

Turning onto Lighthouse Road, they suddenly encountered a thick fog which made them have to slow down significantly.

"I hope we're not already too late!" Al remarked.

Back at the bed and breakfast, Angela was still pacing the floor in the foyer, becoming more and more concerned as each minute went by and Mark still hadn't shown up. He had said that he should be home within the hour, but an hour and a half had already gone by and he still wasn't home. The others had gone into the parlor and started the movie. She had gone in there a couple of times to try and watch some of it, but her mind was still focused on Mark. She finally decided to go back out onto the front porch and wait for him there. Dan decided to go out there with her to keep her company, since he felt that she probably needed him now. Suddenly she was startled by the sound of her phone ringing, sounding even louder in the quietness of the night. She quickly grabbed it out of her back pocket and hit the answer button before even looking at the display to see who it was.

"Mark?" she asked excitedly.

"Angela, this is Al! You and your dad need to get out to the lighthouse immediately! Bring Kate too if she's there!"

"What's this about?" she asked nervously. "Has something happened to Mark?"

"I'll tell you when you get here. I'm on my way out there now. Be careful when you get here, though; there's a thick fog that begins right after you turn onto Lighthouse Road."

As she hung up the phone, she was already headed for the door to get her jacket.

"Dad, that was Al! We need to go out to the lighthouse now! He sounded like something's wrong! I think something's happened to Mark!"

"I'm going with you." said Kate as she pulled on her jacket and headed out the door with them. Scotty joined them as well, though he didn't fully understand what was happening.

Al had been right about the fog. As soon as they turned onto Lighthouse Road it was so thick that they could barely see five feet in front of the car. Even though they wanted to go faster, it was pretty much impossible as thick as the fog had become. It seemed that the road was narrower and had become rougher as well.

As Al and Sally turned the corner and the lighthouse came into view they were both startled at the sight! While they had both seen it on the TV screen before they left, it was even more striking in person now as they saw it totally in ruins, with the scaffolding surrounding the tower. It was illuminated by several powerful floodlights that surrounded it outside the circular wall. They could barely make out the lights of the Mobile Command Center through the fog as it sat over next to the woods at the far end of the parking lot. Al drove over toward the direction of the command center lights, hoping that they weren't already too late. It had taken them a little over twenty minutes to get here from Al's house and the ripples had been keeping the doorway open for that entire time! They parked right behind Mark's car with Al jumping out and running over to the Mobile Command Center. He began beating his fists against the door.

"Ryan, open up! The realities are merged! You've opened a doorway not only to the past, but to an alternate reality as well! Shut off the emitters now before it's too late! The alternate reality is becoming the dominant one!"

Both he and Sally listened for any motion from inside, or any sound at all for that matter, but quietness was all that they heard.

"Ryan, I know you can hear me! We have to shut off the emitters now!"

After another few seconds with no sound from inside, Sally remarked, "I don't think he's going to come to the door."

"Stand back!" he instructed her as he pulled out a small eight inch long silver teardrop shaped object from a pouch on his belt. He held it near the door handle and a bright white flash of light blew the handle off the door. He threw the door open, as a startled Ryan Langtree swiveled around in his chair.

"What's going on here?!" he demanded as Al stepped into the command center.

"Shut off the emitters immediately, Ryan! You've opened up a doorway to an alternate reality instead of only going back in time and now that alternate reality is encroaching on this one!"

"What are you talking about?! Do I know you?"

"It's me, Ryan. It's Philip."

Ryan stared at him in disbelief, trying to figure out how this could be.

"You can't be Philip! Philip was killed in the storm out at the lighthouse two years ago!"

"No, not killed. The collapse of the field sent me back to 1977, but I'm very much alive. I can tell you all about it later, but right now we have to shut off the emitters! We have to shut the door to the alternate reality now!"

"It's probably already too late." replied Ryan, "I've been trying, but the ripples contain their own power source. Simply shutting off the emitters won't automatically close the door. I don't understand how this could have happened though; the ripples only go backward and forward in time, they can't cross realities!"

"Yes they can! The ripples had gotten crossed before you even powered up the emitters! They contain elements of both realities! It probably happened back in 2016 when we went out to the lighthouse that night to install the temporal dissipater to absorb the remaining resonant ripples after Dan tried to help us eliminate the Vortex Accelerator. We should have stuck with the plan, and none of this would be happening now! YOU should have stuck with the plan that we came here to do!"

"But we had the opportunity to start over! Now WE can be the ones with the ability to travel through time! WE can have it under OUR control!" objected Ryan.

"No, Ryan, if we do this, then it'll end up being abused, just like the first time. We have to end this now!"

"Do you know why the ripples opened the doorway to the previous reality instead of our current one?" inquired Ryan, "That reality shouldn't even be possible to open! Even if it is superimposed on top of this reality, this reality still would be the overriding one!"

"We installed a temporal dissipater in the lighthouse tower, but I didn't realize that the ripples contained patterns of the alternate reality as well. It's absorbing the ripples for this reality, and the alternate reality is getting stronger! That's why we have to shut off the emitters now!"

Ryan moved over to one of the keyboards and tapped a few keys. Immediately several gauges on the computer monitor began to decrease.

"I'm turning the emitters down to thirty percent. I've already been lowering the power on them a little at a time though. If we turn it off all at once, the field could collapse! Where did you get a temporal dissipater anyway? The one that we originally brought with us was destroyed that night two years ago!"

"Never mind that now. We need to concentrate on closing the doorway!"

As Dan and the others drove into the area surrounding the lighthouse they also were startled by the way that it looked. It looked like something from another world, which indeed it was, since it shouldn't even exist in this reality. As Dan slowed the van, Angela opened her door and jumped out.

"Angela, get back in here!" Dan shouted as he quickly brought the van to a stop.

"It's Mark!" she replied excitedly as she began running toward the direction where she thought she saw him, "He's at the edge of the fog next to the lighthouse!"

"How can you see anything through this fog?!" Dan said. "I don't see anyone! Get back in the van! You don't even know that it's him!"

Still, she continued running toward the direction where she thought she had seen Mark, obviously oblivious to everything else around her. She quickly disappeared into the fog as Dan opened his door and started to get out and go after her, but as he did this, suddenly he felt himself being drawn into another dream as the massive power of the ripples increased.

It was still night as he found himself in the center of the grey tube of fog again. He looked around at the lighthouse and it seemed to be back to normal now. He turned back toward the fog as he again heard a woman's voice drifting out from it.

"Kate!" he shouted, "Kate, I'm over here!"

"Dan! Where are you?!"

"Over here, Kate! Follow the sound of my voice!"

Within a few minutes, Dan saw a shadow coming through the fog. Within minutes, she was in his arms again.

"Why does this keep happening?!" she asked.

"I'm not sure, but this time the timing could have been a lot better!"

"How did we get here?" she inquired, "We were driving up to the Mobile Command Center just a second ago!"

They both looked over toward the command center. "Where is it?" they both asked in unison, as they wondered where the command center had gone. It obviously wasn't at the edge of the parking lot any longer.

The streetlights around the parking lot illuminated the night as their cones of light shone through the fog. As they heard a vehicle approaching and saw car lights through the fog they ran toward the edge of the wall and hid outside it just inside the fog. From this vantage point they had a good view of the approaching car and also of the lighthouse. As the car came into view and parked in one of the parking spaces nearest to the lighthouse, they noticed that it was actually an SUV.

"Is this scene familiar to you too?" asked Dan.

"This is starting to feel like the same dream that we had last Wednesday afternoon when we came out here!"

"I think it is! I believe that we're back to May 20, 2016, the night of the big storm! This time I want to get closer so that we can hear what they're saying." replied Dan.

As they continued to watch, two men got out of the SUV and went to the back and opened the hatch. They removed a long object which looked to be about five feet long and carried it to the front of the vehicle. One of the men went back to close the rear hatch then walked back to the front. The men picked up the object, one man on each end and began carrying it toward the lighthouse. As soon as they went behind one of the smaller buildings, Dan and Kate began to run toward that direction.

"Be careful, we don't want them to see us." whispered Kate.

"They won't. If it's like the first time, they'll come running out in a few minutes. They won't pay any attention to us. I just want to get close enough to hear what they're arguing about this time."

As they got closer, they could hear voices which were getting increasingly louder. They reached the small wooden building, and then slowly walked around the left side, staying against the wall of the building, until they could get a glimpse of the men standing in the clearing between the building and the lighthouse.

"That's Dr. Langtree." Dan whispered. "The other one must be Dr. Chandler."

"We'll need to set it up in the top of the lighthouse." said Dr. Chandler. "I'll use the beacon to disable the alarm system."

"Wait, think about it, Philip; do we really want to do this?" replied Dr. Langtree.

"Do what?"

"Destroy the ripples! We have a chance to start over! We can be the ones controlling the past and the future now!"

"No, Ryan. We were sent here to make sure that the Vortex Accelerator never existed, and the only way to do that is to continue what we came for. We have to set up the temporal dissipater to eliminate the last traces of the ripples. We can't use them for our own purposes."

"Why not?! It was the government in our time that misused time travel! We have the chance to get it right this time! Think of how much good we could do!"

As Dan and Kate listened, their voices gradually became louder and louder as their argument escalated.

"Ryan! Do you hear what you're saying?! If we don't destroy the ripples now, they'll end up in corrupt hands just like the first time. Nobody, not even us, can be trusted with the power to change the past, present and future!"

As Dr. Chandler tried to continue walking toward the base of the lighthouse, Dr. Langtree pulled the temporal dissipater out of his hands. The end that he had been carrying crashed to the ground with a loud thud.

Ryan quickly pulled open the side access panel and reversed the temporal phase pin before setting the dial on the side to full power. He then broke off the knob so that it couldn't be turned back down. Philip just stood there watching him, not fully realizing what he was doing until it was too late. The object began making a high pitched whistling sound as a blue glow emanated from between the tubes which composed the object. It was interacting with the ripples, but with the phase reversed it was overloading and the phase was getting critical. It was like a radio transmitter that was mismatched to the antenna. A thin mist began to form around the object, taking on an eerie blue glow as it was illuminated by the glow within the object.

"Ryan, why did you do that?!"

"I couldn't let you destroy the ripples! If we have the control, we'll get it right this time, you'll see!"

"But you've set it to overload the temporal matrix! We don't know what that will do!"

"I wouldn't stay around here to find out!" Ryan said as he began running as fast as he could toward the SUV.

Philip stayed with the dissipater and was attempting to reverse the phase of the conduit controlling the matrix, but it was getting too hot as it approached maximum temporal velocity. The mist around the object was getting thicker as well, which was greatly hindering his ability to see what he was doing. Finally, he realized that the device had gone past the point of no return and was reaching critical mass. He began running toward the SUV as well, but he had no sooner gotten to his feet and started running as fast as he could before he was surrounded by a bright white light as the temporal dissipater exploded, unleashing enough power to totally collapse the temporal field, imploding the ripples.

Dan and Kate turned away, since they knew what to expect from the time before, but were still blinded by the bright white light. As the temporal field collapsed, torrents of rain began to fall and almost continuous lightning followed! Circular lightning bolts arced from cloud to cloud, completely surrounding the lighthouse. As they started to run toward the direction of the lighthouse through the blinding rain, they noticed that it was in ruins again! Suddenly, a bright flash of lightning totally blinded them as it hit the top of the lighthouse tower, sending pieces of brick and stone flying through the air! Not able to see where they were going, they had to temporarily stop as they struggled to regain their composure from that last powerful blast.

CHAPTER 29

The Coming Storm

As their eyes adjusted, they discovered that they were back in the van again. The rain had stopped and the night was silent. As Dan noticed that his door was open, he suddenly remembered Angela. She had jumped out of the van and ran into the fog after Mark! He quickly got out of the van and ran around to the back, pausing as he stared into the fog looking for any sign of motion. Seeing none, he went back around to the driver's side, lifted the seat and pulled out the flashlight that he kept in the under seat storage. He then ran back around the van and started running as fast as he could toward the lighthouse.

"Wait! We're coming with you!" called Kate as she and Scotty got out and started after him.

"Angela!" Dan called as he shined the beam of the flashlight through the dense fog. He got no answer from her as he, Kate, and Scotty made their way toward the lighthouse. Even though his flashlight was a military grade high-brightness tactical light, it was still having trouble piercing the fog. As they approached the wall surrounding the lighthouse, however, the fog began to get thinner and the light was finally able to illuminate one of the walls of the house. It resembled something out of a horror movie as they viewed the lighthouse through the fog, illuminated by the flashlight's beam, with most of the roof missing and a large portion of each wall falling down. It was in ruins again, just like in their visions, only this time what they were seeing was real! Dan and Kate exchanged knowing glances as they both recognized this lighthouse. It looked exactly like it had in their visions, though neither of them could fully grasp why it was like this now. This wasn't a vision or a dream! This was reality; at least the reality that they had been pulled into.

"Where did Angela go?" asked Scotty, "And didn't she say she saw Mark? I don't see either of them out here!"

"I'm pretty sure that she went toward this direction," said Dan, "but I'm not sure where she would have gone from here."

"Mark would have probably gone over to check out the lighthouse." answered Scotty. "Let's go over toward that direction."

Kate agreed, so the three of them continued. As they walked through the gate and into the circular area inside the rock wall they stepped out of the fog and into an area that was completely clear! The fog wasn't just thinner; it was not here at all! Both Dan and Kate recalled a sense of déjà vu as they stopped and looked around. Both of them had been here before, yet neither of them had really ever been here. The dreams and visions that they had been having were suddenly merged into reality as they stood inside the grey tube that both had seen several times before. Scotty was also looking around wondering what was happening.

"I've never seen anything like this!" he remarked, "It's like there's some sort of invisible barrier keeping the fog out! Have you ever seen anything like this?"

As Scotty spoke these words, Dan suddenly realized what was happening. He had read about it in the journal from Chandler-Langtree that Angela had given him. Earlier he had been so focused on finding Angela that he hadn't really given much thought to the fog and the grey tube. But now as he looked around again, he realized that they were in a different time! The invisible barrier keeping the fog outside the wall was the invisible barrier of time! While he didn't know exactly what year it was, he instinctively knew that it was no longer 2018 inside the circular wall! Still, where exactly were they? Were they in the past or the future? He never remembered the lighthouse being this run down at any time during the history that he knew, so he wondered if maybe this could be the future.

As they continued walking toward the lighthouse, Dan called for Angela once more. Inside the wall where it was clear, his light was much more effective, but there still was no sign of either Angela or Mark. They walked up the steps of the lighthouse and pushed on the wooden door which immediately came crashing down just inside the room. As they entered the room, Dan shined the light all around, surveying the scene before him. Looking to the left, the staircase to the second floor was completely gone, a large hole in the floor marking the spot where it had once been. Paint and wallpaper was peeling off the walls, and several of the walls looked like they were about ready to fall down. Most of the ceiling was gone as well and the rafters were exposed. The whole place had a damp, musty smell.

"It looks like nobody's been here for decades!" Scotty said.

"I doubt they have." answered Dan. "Be careful, some of these floorboards don't look too sound, and there're plenty of holes in the floor as well."

"What happened to this place?!" asked Scotty. "It wasn't like this several days ago when we were out here! It looks like it's been abandoned for a century or more!"

Dan and Kate both looked at Scotty wondering what to tell him that would be believable to him. They'd either have to tell him something, or pretend that they didn't know why it was like this either. Dan finally decided to let him know what was happening. He'd either believe them or not, but at least they'd be honest with him.

"It probably has been abandoned for a century or more." said Dan.

"What do you mean?" asked Scotty with a puzzled look on his face, "We were just out here a few days ago! I remember the original lighthouse lens display was right over there in the center of the room."

"I mean Chandler-Langtree is experimenting with time travel. I don't know what time period we're in, but I'm pretty sure that this isn't 2018 anymore."

Both he and Kate looked at Scotty to see his reaction, but he just had a blank stare. He paused and looked around the room trying to process what Dan had just said.

"We can't be in another time period;" he finally said, "that's impossible."

"Look around you, Scotty." Kate said. "If you can think of another explanation, I'd like to hear it."

"Unfortunately I can't think of another explanation for this," he said, as he looked around the room, "but are you sure it's time travel?!"

"I'm not sure of anything," Dan replied, "but I've seen some compelling evidence to suggest that Chandler-Langtree is working on the ability to travel through time. Remember Mark's college major: Theoretical Physics. That would fit perfectly if that's what Chandler-Langtree is really attempting."

"I'll have to admit, that is what it seems like; it's just hard to believe that's what it really is. I'm not sure I'm ready to believe in the impossible just yet."

"I know what you mean." said Kate. "It took me awhile too."

"So you've known about this for some time?" Scotty asked. "Did Mark tell you?"

"No, I found out in other ways. It still took awhile to accept."

She didn't want to discuss the visions that she and Dan had been having with him just yet. She wasn't sure how he'd take that and she figured that he needed time just to think about the time travel explanation some more.

They continued walking through the foyer and across to a room along the side. Dan called for Angela once more but there was still no answer.

"I don't think they're in here." interjected Kate.

"No, I don't think they are either." answered Dan. "Let's go look out front and see if maybe they went around there."

They walked over to the front door and pushed it. It was a little hard to get open at first, since the hinges were quite a bit rusty, but finally it gave way and swung outward. They stopped on the porch and looked out over the front lawn. Because of the fog, they couldn't see as far as the water even though they could hear the waves as they gently broke onto the beach.

"Angela!" Dan called again, "Angela, where are you?"

Each time that he called her name and got no answer, he was starting to become more and more concerned. She had to be here; where else could she have gone? He began to think of where she and Mark might be.

"Maybe they've already gone back to the command center." Kate suggested.

"That could be;" answered Scotty, "they don't seem to be out here and Angela could have found him and they went back."

They decided to head back to the command center and see if Angela and Mark really had gone back there. As they walked into the fog again they all noticed how much colder it was in the fog than it had been around the lighthouse. It also appeared that the fog had gotten thicker as well, since the flashlight didn't seem to be penetrating as far into it as it had earlier.

"Are we going in the right direction?" asked Kate. "I can't see anything!"

"I think so," replied Dan, "but it's hard to be sure."

As they walked, they strained to make out the lights of the Mobile Command Center, but it was nowhere to be seen. The only light was the light of Dan's flashlight and the fog was so thick that it was basically just reflecting that light back to them.

"I think it's back the other direction." Scotty finally said.

"Why don't we try that way then," said Kate, "since we're not finding anything this way. Dan, what do you think?"

Dan agreed and they changed direction about ninety degrees to the right. While none of them could see very far ahead, they were trying to navigate by objects around them such as trees and bushes, but a lot of them looked a lot alike in the darkness and fog. They were almost on top of their van before they finally saw it, but at least stumbling across it confirmed that they were going in the right direction this time. They got back into the van and Dan cranked it up. The headlights were tunneling through the fog slightly better than his flashlight had been, but they still drove slowly as they continued around to the Mobile Command Center.

As Dan parked the van behind Mark's car, the three of them got out and hurried over to the open door, where Dr. Langtree was frantically trying to close the doorway to the alternate reality, still appearing to be having no luck. While the emitters were turned down to only twenty percent now, the other readings were showing that the temporal velocity in the ripples was increasing at a rapid rate.

"What's happening?" asked Dan as he surveyed the scene before him from the open door. "Are Angela and Mark here?"

"No, I haven't seen them. I thought Angela would be with you." said Al.

"She thought she saw Mark as we were driving up and got out to go after him. We've been looking around for her out at the lighthouse, but nobody seems to be there."

"I hope she's not out at the lighthouse. The ripples are pretty unstable right now." added Dr. Langtree. "I haven't been able to reach Mark either."

"Did he go out to the lighthouse?" asked Scotty.

"Yes," said Dr. Langtree, "he went out to take some readings a little while ago. He was supposed to come right back after taking the readings, but I haven't been able to reach him on the radio since he went out there."

"I'm going back out there to look for him, then!" said Scotty. "Dan, are you coming?"

"I'm not sure that it would be a good idea to go out there right now." Dan told him. "The fog's getting thicker and the conditions seem to be deteriorating."

"I know. That's why we need to find him! Remember, Angela's out there too!"

"I know, and I'm concerned about her too, but remember the fog as we were coming back? We couldn't see three feet in front of us. I'm not sure that we'd be any more effective now than we were a few minutes ago; we'd probably just get lost in the fog. I want to find her and Mark as much as anyone, and if I thought we'd be any more successful now I'd be out there looking, but I need to find out what's happening here first. Hopefully the fog will begin to lift soon, and then we can go back out and look for them. Al, what IS going on here?"

"Ryan's inadvertently opened the doorway into YOUR alternate reality, the one before May 20, 2016, and now it won't close. We've been trying to shut down the emitters, but that doesn't seem to be having any effect."

Scotty looked at Al with a puzzled look, trying to understand what he had just said.

"What does he mean 'YOUR alternate reality'?!" asked Scotty. "What really IS going on here? What's Mark working on? Is it more than just time travel?"

"Chandler-Langtree is experimenting with time travel," said Dan, "but there seems to be more than that going on here. I'm not sure exactly what is happening, but I seem to have lived a completely different life before May 20, 2016. I'm still trying to figure out what that means and how it fits into what is happening here. I'll need to fill you in later on the rest."

Ryan was frantically studying the display in front of him, then quickly turned to Al, "Philip, change the phase on emitters four, six, and nine! Maybe we can use that to destabilize the field!"

Dan looked over at Kate with a look of bewilderment, then he met Al's gaze. "Philip? Did he call you Philip?"

"Yes." Al replied as he went over and sat down in front of a computer terminal and began typing several commands, "My real name is Philip Oliver Chandler. Two years ago I tried to prevent the collapse of the temporal field which resulted in the merging of the two realities, but was unsuccessful in that attempt. The resulting collapse sent me back to the year 1977. I assumed the identity of a businessman named Warren Albert Evans who had died in a building collapse at a construction site about a month before I arrived. In the ensuing years, I founded Evans Microsystems. As CEO of that company, I provided a lot of the computers and lab equipment for the Chandler-Langtree Institute. This allowed me to monitor the company to keep up with their research. I only realized today that the resulting storm that occurred over two years ago on May 20 was not only a result of the temporal field collapse, but the severity was also driven by the collision of the two realities as they merged into one. Your and Kate's dreams were also probably a result of the instability of the ripples due to the fact that they were composed of two different realities."

As Philip explained this, Dan actually had a recollection of their talk on the boardwalk over two years ago as Philip told him their plan to eliminate the Vortex Accelerator. He suddenly remembered Amy as well and also saw himself comforting Kate out at the Harbor Inn after her disappearance. This was the first time that he had actually remembered Amy since all of this had started, and all of these memories were vivid, like they had really happened. Things that he had never remembered before were now coming back to him, and suddenly he remembered his and Kate's wedding! He could remember looking into her eyes as they said their vows, their first kiss as man and wife, then running down the aisle and out into a shower of rice.

"I just remembered our wedding." he remarked to Kate as he looked into her eyes.

"Me too." she said, looking back to where Scotty had been standing, expecting to have to explain what she and Dan had just said. Scotty, however, was nowhere to be seen. Had he gone back out into the fog?!

"You're remembering your wedding because your alternate reality is getting stronger," replied Ryan, "and this reality is getting weaker."

"The ripples are destabilizing!" Philip announced after he had changed the phase of the emitters.

"The alternate reality is still getting stronger, though!" replied Ryan.

"The temporal dissipater in the tower is siphoning off too much energy from this reality!" said Philip as he stepped away from the console and hurriedly went out the door into the fog.

Surveying the scene, there were visible ripples starting to form as the temporal field was destabilizing. Cracks and inconsistencies could be seen as he viewed the lighthouse. He had to think fast, and there was no time to analyze what the results of his decision would be. He only knew that right now the ripples which composed the alternate reality were much too strong, threatening to wipe out everything in this reality and destroy the continuity of the time matrix. He had to stop the temporal dissipater from eliminating this reality and he had to do it fast! He raised the silver teardrop object toward the lighthouse and a bright white light shot out from it striking the temporal dissipater in the lantern house. Immediately the entire lighthouse exploded in a blinding white flash which lit up the entire area as bright as daytime. The sudden destruction of the temporal dissipater acted like a dam burst as the ripples for this reality flooded back in, colliding with the ones for the alternate reality. The resulting energy created by the collision collapsed the temporal field and further destabilized the ripples. Clouds formed and lightning flashed as the ripples struggled to regain their equilibrium and restore the balance to the temporal field. The resulting thunder shook the ground as the heavens opened and a flood of rain washed over the area. Both Dan and Kate were glad that they were in the relative safety of the Mobile Command Center this time instead of in the center of the storm, but they still were worried about their children who were still out in the storm. Dan quickly closed the door to keep the heavy rain from flooding inside as Philip hurriedly came back inside. All of them stared in awe out the window toward the direction of the lighthouse. As the brightness of the white flash began to fade, they could see that the fog was still there and it was difficult to see the lighthouse through it despite the floodlights still shining in that direction. Kate hoped that Mark, Scotty, and Angela would be safe and would survive this storm.

"One thing that I still don't understand," said Kate "is why Dr. Langtree needed Mark. If he was trying to travel through time, didn't he already know what needed to be done since he'd done it before?"

"That's easy;" explained Philip, "Two years ago when the temporal dissipater overloaded and exploded, the resulting destabilization of the ripples created a completely different temporal signature. The fact that ripples for two separate realities were superimposed into one also complicated the equation. Things didn't work the way that they did before, so the matrix needed to be reinitialized. He knew the mechanics of time travel, but I was the mathematician that came up with most of the precise calculations to set up the matrix and make it all work. We each had our roles, and I was missing. Ryan had tried for two years to be able to control the ripples and open a doorway with no luck. He needed someone with a fresh approach that could take my place, so he went to Dr. Carson and asked if he could read some of the student's term papers. Most were rather disappointing, but he saw something in Mark's paper that made him realize that Mark's way of thinking about things might be just what he needed. That's when they took Mark to lunch and offered him the position so that he could help Ryan figure it out. The turning point in their research came when Mark was given Blake Sorensen's papers, which he had worked on his entire life. This helped them to discover the flaws in what they were doing so far and get a lot closer to success. They probably would have succeeded if they'd only realized that the ripples still contained the old reality as well as the new. Have I missed anything, Ryan?"

"If you had just gone along with my plan from the start, all of this could have been avoided." Ryan replied. "But you wouldn't even consider anything except for destroying the ripples! You wouldn't even talk about learning to control them! We could learn a lot from the past!"

"It's because I've seen where that leads. Things start out fine but then people are tempted to try things that shouldn't be attempted, like actually ALTERING the past. If it could have been limited to simply VIEWING the past, the way that we started out, then maybe things would have turned out different. You're actually right, we could learn a lot from the past, if we could just get over the temptation to CHANGE it."

Just then, they heard a loud pounding on the door. Opening the door, a cold and wet Mark stumbled inside as Dan quickly shut the door behind him as the wind was really picking up speed outside.

"What happened?" he asked, "What was that bright flash? And what is everyone doing here? Mom; why are you here?"

"Dr. Chandler called and told us that we needed to come out here." said Kate. "He had just figured out what was happening, and he had realized why the doorway opened to an alternate reality instead of another time period along this reality."

"Dr. Chandler?" asked Mark, "You've met him?"

Al walked over to where Mark was standing, "Nice to meet you again, Mark. I'm Philip Chandler."

"You're Dr. Chandler?!" he asked still trying to understand what was going on.

"Yes, I just needed to gather the information that I needed to discover what was really happening in order to eliminate the ripples. Since I knew that Ryan and I had a different agenda, I felt that it would be better to gather information secretly to be able to put all of the facts together and then take action. I actually cut it a lot closer than I would have liked."

"Did you see Angela and your father?" asked Kate, "They went looking for you."

"No, it was all that I could do to make it back here through the fog and blinding rain. I didn't see anyone else out there!"

"Did you not hear us out at the lighthouse a few minutes ago? We walked out there and called for you and Angela." said Kate.

"No, I didn't hear anyone else out there. I started running back here when the lighthouse exploded into that blinding white light! Luckily I was already almost to the gate. Why would Dad and Angela go looking for me in all of this fog, anyway?!"

Everyone in the trailer suddenly got quiet, simply glancing from one person to the next, and then all of them turned to look out at the lighthouse which looked normal now, with most of the wisps of fog beginning to get thinner. The steady rain was still coming down, but the lightning and thunder was diminishing. All of them were wondering about Angela and Scotty.

"Angela got out of the van before we got to the trailer." said Dan as a strong feeling of dread built up inside of him, "She thought that she saw you and got out to find you! I tried to stop her, but before I could, Kate and I were pulled into one of our visions. So you didn't see her?!"

"No, she never found me!" Mark replied, "She didn't go out to the lighthouse did she?!" he asked almost in a panic.

"I think that she might have." said Dan as he opened the door and stepped out into the cold rain which was actually beginning to get lighter now. As he walked around the trailer and stopped to look at the lighthouse, Mark joined him, both of them feeling helpless and alone.

Another flash of lightning signaled to everyone that the storm was not yet over. In fact, for Dan, Mark and Kate the storm was actually just beginning. As Kate joined them and they began walking out to the lighthouse, Philip and Sally came outside and watched them as they went.

"Do you think they'll find them?" asked Philip.

"I think they eventually will," replied Sally, "I just don't think it will be today."

"I hope so." Philip remarked as Dan, Kate and Mark disappeared inside the gate surrounding the lighthouse. The rain was getting lighter now as the ripples settled back into alignment. The worst of the temporal storm was over, but the days ahead would still be difficult. The sun would come out again, but lives would still be changed. All of them could only guess right now where the road ahead would lead.

AUTHOR COMMENTS

Foggy Point Light was originally intended to be a single book, with the complete story concluding there. When I finished it, however, and was deciding on my next project, I began to consider expanding the story into a trilogy. While the ending seemed to finalize the story and would have been a satisfying conclusion, what if there was more there than meets the eye? In Ripples, I decided to introduce new characters to take the events in a new direction while still keeping many of the old characters and continuing on with their story as well. While the ending of Foggy Point Light only scratched the surface of what was really happening on the island, Ripples delves deeper into the underlying mystery surrounding the lighthouse in a way that challenges the reader to consider the impossible in a way that attempts to make everything completely believable. Thanks for taking this journey back to Green Island and Foggy Point Light along with me. I hope you enjoyed it as much as I did when I was writing it. I look forward to continuing with the third and final volume in the series, Project Vortex, which will examine some of the ethical and moral issues from Ripples in more detail and finally resolve the mystery surrounding Green Island and Foggy Point Light.

- Jeff Burns

"… A ripple is the building block of the temporal field. It's what opens up the field to another time period. A temporal field is not just sitting there stagnant, ready to open. It's constantly in motion like ripples in a lake extending outward from the center. It's our interaction with those moving ripples that enables us to travel to a different time period …"

Albert

The Complete Foggy Point Light Trilogy Availability

Volume 1 - "Foggy Point Light" – Jan 2016

Volume 2 - "Ripples: Return to Foggy Point Light"–Dec 2017

Volume 3 - "Project Vortex" – Early 2019